By the same author

The Remnant
A novel published by Hodder Headline Ireland, Dublin

Second Son
A novel published by Hodder Headline Ireland, Dublin

The Joseph Coat and Other Patches
A collection of poems published by Gilbert Dalton, Dublin

Out Foreign and Back
A collection of poems published by Gilbert Dalton, Dublin

Strings and Things
A collection of poems for children published by Paulist Press, USA

Miracles and Me
A collection of poems for children published by Paulist Press, USA

Maura's Boy... A Cork Childhood
A memoir published by Mercier Press, Cork

The New Curate
A memoir published by Mercier Press, Cork

Life after Loss
A handbook on bereavement published by Mercier Press, Cork

Christy Kenneally is also a scriptwriter and presenter of the television
series *Heaven on Earth* and *The Lost Gods*.

Tears of God

CHRISTY KENNEALLY

HACHETTE
BOOKS
IRELAND

First published in 2009 by Hachette Books Ireland
First published in paperback in 2009 by Hachette Books Ireland
A division of Hachette UK Ltd.

1

A CIP catalogue record for this title is available from the British Library.

ISBN 978 0 340 96169 8

Typeset in Adobe Garamond.
Printed and bound in the UK by CPI Mackays, Chatham ME5 8TD

Hachette Book Ireland policy is to use papers that are natural, renewable and
recyclable products and made from wood grown in sustainable forests. The
logging and manufacturing processes are expected to conform to the
environmental regulations of the country of origin.

Hachette Books Ireland
8 Castlecourt Centre, Castleknock, Dublin 15, Ireland

www.hachette.ie

A division of Hachette UK
338 Euston Road, London NW1 3BH

To Linda, Stephen and Shane –
as always and for the same wonderful reasons.

Jerusalem

The Crusader Knight stood silhouetted against an inferno of candles so that the man who knelt before him had to squint against the glare. Behind his back, his hands tugged vainly at the cords that bound him and he grimaced as the blood dripped from his fingers. He had seen the witnesses arrive before the servants of the Knight had trussed him and flung him down.

This is a nightmare, he told himself frantically. I'll wake and—

The Knight's thunderous voice chased the words from his brain.

'We left our kingdom at the behest of Urban, the Bishop of Rome, and for the glory of God. We travelled over land and sea to the gates of Constantinople and there fought bloody battles for the ingrate Patriarch. When one of our number took his hand from the plough and sought to enrich himself at the expense of our sacred Crusade, I, Baldwin, pursued Tancred, the apostate, into Cilicia and plucked his conquests from his grasp by force of arms. We who were faithful had no thought for ourselves but only for our sacred mission. And so we came here and set our ladders against the city walls and slew every living creature that had dared to tread, breed and barter where Christ our Saviour had died and risen from the dead.'

The silhouette loomed larger as the Knight stepped closer.

'Oh, God,' the man whimpered. 'Oh, God.'

'And when my brother, Godfrey, leached of his ardour by those who stank of incense and putrid piety, refused the crown, by the will of Christ he sickened and died. Then did God call me to fulfil his command and my destiny. With the edge of this sword, I scraped the city clean of pagan vermin. By the strength of my arm I raised up the blessed buildings the pagan had thrown down.'

He stepped closer still, filling the captive's vision.

'My brother,' he rasped, 'my brother, may his woman's soul wail for ever in Hell. He played me for a fool. He sent messages to the Bishop of Rome informing him of a great treasure he had found, a treasure that ensured that the kingdom of Jerusalem would withstand its enemies for ever. That secret he took to his grave. I will have it,' he roared, and the great sword flashed upwards.

With shame, the captive felt his bowels loosen.

'I ask again,' the Knight shouted. 'Where will I find the Tears of God?'

The man before him made a great effort to gather his wits. 'Please, please, believe me,' he begged. 'I do not know.'

With a bellow of rage, the Knight swept the sword in a mighty arc. The man's head rolled across the paving stones, blood puddling at the Knight's feet. Exhausted, he lowered the tip of the blade to the floor and bowed over the cross-guard. His glacial blue eyes swept the assembly of stricken faces in the gloom.

'Do not fail me,' he whispered. 'Find the Tears of God.'

On trembling legs, the witnesses scurried from his presence. When the last had stumbled through the great door and the sound of their footsteps had faded, a servant approached. The Knight gestured contemptuously at the remains on the floor.

'Take this … thing,' he said, 'and throw it to the infidel.'

The Island, Ireland

Michael Flaherty gripped the handrail of the ferryboat until his fingernails dug half-moons in the polished timber. Moments before, when he had finally ventured from the tiny cabin, the sea had dazzled him. Now, eyes screwed shut, he steadied himself against the roll of the ship, the beat of the engines pulsing through him. Eventually the sound and smell of the water as it parted before the prow lulled him, and he began to relax.

He didn't know how long he'd been standing there, lost in the slow rise and fall, the wind ruffling his hair and cooling his skin, the gulls shrieking above.

When he opened his eyes again, the sea had turned to blood. The ache he had trained to hover just outside his consciousness returned to the bullet hole in his chest and began to pulse in time with the waves that slapped against the hull. Sweat bloomed from his pores, dragging a cold saltwater finger from throat to navel.

'Breathe, Michael,' Dr Eli Weissman's voice whispered in his head.

He conjured up a picture of the lanky, skull-capped Eli sitting on his bed as he had done every evening of Michael's convalescence in Rome's Santa Sabina Hospital.

'Breathe, Michael, it's allowed, special dispensation from the Pope.'

'For all priests, or just the shot ones?'

'Especially the Irish shot ones, the ones who need permission to feel their pain and think a bullet goes no deeper than the body. Breathe.'

Michael took a tentative breath and the ache lessened. He risked opening his eyes, and the air locked in his chest. The Island was etched against the red wound of the evening sky. Reluctantly, he fastened his eyes on the Devil's Finger. Even in the lurid half-light he could see the sea-stack standing apart from the Island, the moil of white water chewing at its base. And now another voice began to speak, a cold angry voice he recognised as coming from that detached, armoured part of himself. 'Do you see it, Flaherty?' it asked.

'I see it,' he replied.

'You remember Lar, don't you?'

'I remember.'

'Sure you do. The boy who sat behind you in the classroom, a hulking, big-boned lad who dreamed of boats and water. He could never sit still, could he? Always tacking in his desk from one cheek of his arse to the other, twisting his head, time after time, to the slash of sea at the bottom of the window.'

'I remember.'

'Do you remember, when you were here last, how he sailed in there in that big launch – in there, by the Devil's Finger, where other men, who thought they were his betters, wouldn't pole a currach? And why? To get back a little of what you stole from him with little twitches of annoyance when his fidgeting in school dragged you from your books, when you pared him down to invisibility, looking through him on the road, when you fathered a child with the only girl who might have filled the hole in his heart. He's down there now, eyeless and empty, because of you.'

He tried to close his eyes but the voice was relentless.

'See the cliffs beyond? Go on, look at them. Gabriel, your younger brother, flew from there because you were missing. You were busy running, Flaherty, first to the army, then to the Church, the action-man who missed the real action.'

A young man's panicked voice rose to override the other.

'Catch me, Michael,' it screamed, 'I'm falling.'

'I'm here, Gabriel,' Michael whispered. 'I'll catch you.'

'Too late for that,' the voice continued. 'Too late for Gabriel. Never found. Never put in the ground with your mother. Look a little farther along the cliff. Yes, there. Remember Father Mack, your mentor, your friend? Remember him hanging from your hand over the edge with the blood bubbling in his mouth? You let him go – just opened your hand and dropped him.'

'He begged me,' Michael murmured, his right hand reaching out over the handrail. 'He said, "If you ever loved me, Michael, let me go."'

'Love! Did you ever know what it was outside of books or the 'duty' love for your dead mother?'

'I loved her. I loved him.'

'It wasn't enough to save them. Look out on the water where your brother Liam slipped away from the upturned boat.'

Again, a plaintive voice rose. 'I'm cold, Michael, so cold.'

'You saw in your father's eyes that he was glad it wasn't you, the scholar, only poor drunken Liam. Can you deny it?'

'I can't deny it. I saw it.'

'Death and the stoic, Flaherty. There's a thesis in it somewhere. And what of murder?'

'Murder?'

'Yes, the American in the water. You surely remember him?'

'I didn't kill him.'

'But you would have, could have.'

'He would have killed Tess in the boat.'

'But he didn't. He had only half a face and one good arm when you put him in the water for others to kill. You watched the rise and fall of oars until the mess that remained floated off like a cursed currach. Murder, Flaherty. You shot a priest in Rome. He was deranged and you shot him. You asked for the gun and got it. Intent and execution. So now you're back. For what? Hasn't enough blood been shed? Do you think the woman might love you, the child might warm to you, cuckoo that you are, raiding a dead man's nest? You know who you are, what you are. You are the hero, the bearer of heartbreak, the sower of nightmare. You're no priest. You're not even a man.'

Michael Flaherty pressed his hands to his ears, bearing down on the voice inside his head. He was in a vast whirlpool, circling down, down, the screaming of the gulls muted by the thunder of the water. Stippled kelp wound round him – the clutch of drowned men's fingers.

'Michael, breathe.'

Eli's soft voice penetrated the nightmare, dragging him back to rationality. Automatically, he inflated his chest, welcoming the pain. Behind the locked shutters of his eyes, he saw Eli at the foot of the bed. Mercifully, the neon tubes in the ceiling had been turned off for the night, and only the faint wash of streetlight penetrated the room.

'We need to talk about your dreams, Michael.'

'Dream, Eli.'

'How very singular,' the doctor said mildly. 'It's the same dream, then,' he continued. 'You exhibit all the symptoms of a drowning man.'

'So, you qualified as a psychologist when, Dr Weissman?'

'No, but I—'

'You what? You have no right, Eli, you're a doctor.'

'I have the right as your friend.'

Michael exhaled, his face to the ceiling.

'People close to me tend to die, sooner or later,' he whispered.

'Everyone dies, Michael,' the doctor continued, relentlessly calm, 'everyone, neither sooner nor later. They just die when they do. I know.' He sat upright and angled his body so that his face was in profile. 'I'll tell you a story.'

'Now it's bedtime stories. Great therapy, Dr Freud.'

'You have other time apart from bedtime? Anyway, Jung was the dream-meister, not Freud.'

He paused.

'When I was young – younger – I had a dream. It was a waking dream. I was just qualified in medicine and wanted to be a hero like Schweitzer or Dr Tom Dooley. I volunteered to go to Israel and work as a doctor in a kibbutz in the Negev desert. Perhaps my dream also included sabras in khaki shirts – tight khaki shirts, *capisce*?'

Michael waved him on.

'I didn't know that everyone worked the fields, even the

summa cum laude doctor, newly graduated from Johns Hopkins University. So the doctor sweats in the fields or steams in the plastic hydroponic tunnels. In the evenings, he treats his own cuts and blisters, then attends to his patients. Sometimes, there were rockets falling in the kibbutz, presents from Syria, delivered by the Palestinians, but, mostly, it was work. I met a girl, a teacher. It was in a bomb shelter, during a mortar attack, and she got everyone to sing – even me. Later, we became friends. We liked to walk in the desert in the dark. She – Sharon – knew all the stars. Then, one night, they crossed the wire and took us.'

He paused for so long that Michael thought he would not continue.

'They put me in an empty water-tank under the ground. It was ten paces long and five wide. I didn't know where she was but I ... I could hear her. Sometimes, I kicked the walls and shouted but I could still hear her.'

A car grumbled by outside and the swinging beam gleamed bleakly on Eli's face.

'I would have done anything, given them anything, but I had nothing they wanted. Then it was over. They took me back to the wire. I walked across and two men went the other way. I was free. At the debriefing I told them everything. Yes, I would have signed confessions, made broadcasts, given them information about the kibbutz, anything. No one was angry, only sympathetic. "You must get on with your life," they said. I came back to Rome to be the dutiful son and nephew, the caring doctor. I like to walk in the air, mostly at night. One night I was coming across the Tiber on the Milvian Bridge and climbed up onto the parapet to gaze at the stars. I looked down at their reflection in the water for a very long time. The same stars were above and below, Michael, and I made a choice.'

Eli planed his cheeks with his palms.

'I asked for information from my colleagues on behalf of a patient. Doctors have a constitutional fear of psychology. For four years now, I've knocked on a door every Monday at one o'clock sharp. It's four flights to a small room at the top of the building. There are two chairs and a big window that shows only sky. Outside is Rome, all the normal things; inside just me and the therapist. She lets me sit, or lie, or pace. Always ten paces this way, five paces that. Every Monday for one hour only, I've been digging my way out. I tell you this not as a boast but as your friend and for your hope.'

He stood and walked to the window.

'We're men, Michael. What happens to a man-child? My ancestors, in Rome, would put one on the floor at birth. If the father picked him up, they would keep him. They didn't name a man-child until he was five years old. If he hadn't died by then, there was a good chance that he would live. From the time he could walk, he carried a weapon and all the dreams of glorious Rome. I think perhaps all cultures weigh their children with dreams. Too many dreams, too many ideals, too many heroes and so much glorious death. *Dulce et decorum est pro patria mori.*'

'It is "sweet and right" to die for one's country,' Michael translated quietly.

'And not just for one's country,' the doctor continued, 'the list is endless. We're taught to live for others. Those who live for others don't live. They just take longer to die. It's a slow suicide. I wouldn't want that for me or you.'

He faced the priest in the bed.

'I've mended your body, Michael Flaherty. Only *you* can save your soul.'

When he was gone, Michael Flaherty turned to the wall. When he spoke, his voice was clotted with tears.

'I needed the pain, Eli. I needed it, and you took it from me. Pain and anger were all I had. I was good at them. What have I now?'

'Michael?'

'No more,' he shouted, 'no more.'

'Michael, it's Tess.'

'Tess?'

'You were talkin' a bit loud like.'

He was standing at the rail of the ferryboat. The sea was calm and luminous with the last light that comes before true dark. Tess Duggan, the skipper, was holding his arm, her wind-lined face fissured with anxiety. He began to breathe again, in, out, in, out.

'Sorry, Tess. I...'

'Arrah, sorry me arse. There's too much sayin' sorry and not enough shoutin' if you ask me.'

'But the other passengers?'

'Only four of them,' she said. 'English,' she added disparagingly. 'Over to stay the night on the Island to soak up the Celtic twilight. They're huddled on the other side of the wheelhouse. I think the mad monk bit was more than they bargained for. Come away into the cabin – I'm taking a tea break.'

She didn't wait for an answer and Michael followed her obediently into the beer-and-leather smell of the small cabin. 'Here,' she said, shoving a huge white mug at him. 'Wrap yourself around that.'

Tess Duggan's rough affection moved him and he held the mug two-handed, letting the steam's damp warmth wreathe around his eyes. Tess swivelled in her seat until she could survey the deck through the window and keep a weather eye on her brother in the wheelhouse.

'You look like shit on a slate,' she said.

He bowed his head, sipped his tea and coughed. It came all the way up from his toes and a tiny wave slopped over the rim of the mug. Tess' face tightened.

'I see you're still taking tea with your whiskey, Tess,' he managed.

'And you're still the same smart-arse you always were,' she countered. She looked at him for a long time. 'I heard you had a bit of trouble beyond.'

God, he thought, we Irish are the masters and mistresses of understatement. Who but ourselves could sum up years of murder and mayhem as 'The Troubles'? He knew with certainty that Tess would say, 'Soft day,' when rain was blinding the window of the wheelhouse and 'Weather,' when mountains of water raged all the way from Newfoundland. It was their way – our way, he reminded himself. He also knew it was an invitation, and declined it. Instead, he shifted into the ritual word-dance.

'Aye, a bit.'

'Well, there'll be some glad to see you home,' she said, and got to her feet.

He felt the judder of pipes as she turned the tap and placed her mug on the metal draining board.

'And some that won't,' he replied.

'Aye, them too. Give me here that mug and I'll top it for you.' As he reached out, he took her hand and held it firmly. 'There's something I want you to do for me,' he said quietly.

'Anything at all, Michael,' she said. 'God knows, I owe you. That American Skald would have killed me if you hadn't ...'

'There's no owing between friends,' he said. 'I want you to watch the water for me, Tess.'

'The water?'

'Yes. If … when they come, they'll have to come by the water.'

'How will I know them, Michael? I mean … what will they look like?'

'Like anybody and nobody,' he replied cryptically, as if talking to himself.

'I'll do that, Michael.'

Instantly he was back to his usual bantering self, a version of himself he wore like some kind of armour.

'Any chance you'd be sailing on to Boston?' he added, taking refuge in the banter they had shared the last time he was home. When was that? he mused. A lifetime ago.

'Not today. I've crates of milk for Finnegan's bar and 'twould spoil.'

'Another day then.'

'Aye.'

The door groaned and slapped behind her, and he watched her move to the wheelhouse.

❧

Iarla Duggan kept his eyes on the sea when his sister came in and checked the chart.

'Jaysus, sis,' he said. 'Isn't that yer man?'

'He's Michael Flaherty,' she said brusquely, 'and you can save the Jaysus for praying.'

It had been on the tip of her tongue to answer, 'It's what's left of him.' She had been shocked by the ranting figure at the rail, the claws of his hands curled to the same white as his face. But she had been frightened by the favour he had asked of her. She remembered the bookish boy who was kind to small ones, who shadowed the Island priest and who rarely looked at the water. She wondered if his stay at home this time would be better than the last. Couldn't be much worse, she thought, and shook herself. Iarla was gazing at her, clearly hoping for some revelation about the priest.

'Iarla,' she said quietly, 'I'm going to tell you something.'

'What, sis?' he asked eagerly, leaning away from the wheel.

'It's about the pier,' she said, lowering her voice to a conspiratorial whisper.

'What about it?'

'If you don't shove this bloody boat into reverse, we'll be wearing it.'

'Jaysus.'

She burst out of the wheelhouse and swung the fenders just in time to buffer the boat against the dock. Iarla was watching her from the window, his face a picture of apprehension. There were times when she could happily have dumped him over the rail with the slops but he had reversed and swung her boat hip-on to the pier with instinctive skill. Her brother had salt water in his veins. He'd do. She tilted her head at him in a rare show of approval. He was smiling like a gaffed fish when she turned to coil the hawser.

Jerusalem

'Shit,' muttered Detective Ari Avram. 'Shit, shit and double shit.'

'Eh, Detective?' the dispatcher's voice enquired nervously on the radio.

'What?' he snapped.

'You want backup?'

'Backup? Yeah, I'll have two F14s, medium rare, with a rocket salad on the side and a troop-carrier dip.'

'What?'

'Forget it.'

'Where to?' his partner asked, gunning an engine that had never been manufactured for the car they were sitting in.

'The Aqsa mosque,' he grunted.

'Oh, yeah,' she said sarcastically, 'to the Aqsa mosque and then to the Dome of the Rock and, heck, let's go on to Mecca.'

'You're seriously pissing me off,' he snarled, hauling out the seatbelt and trying to jam it into the lock.

'Doesn't work,' she said blithely, 'never has,' and stabbed the accelerator.

'You know what the trouble is with F14 jet fighters?' he asked conversationally, as they went head to head with a truck.

'No,' she said, and twitched the steering wheel at the last possible moment to fishtail round the truck and spray an ultra-Orthodox Jewish male with dust. She twitched it again and they were barrelling between two buses. 'What is the problem with F14s?'

'F14s …' he began calmly, watching the bus on the left loom ever larger in his peripheral vision, '… F14s …' Swear to God, he thought, we're now firmly attached to the side of bus number two.

'You were saying?'

'I was saying, they take off at such a lick that they're out of Israeli air space before they can turn. Turn, for Chrissake, turn!'

She turned, taking a bright red swathe of paint from the side of the vehicle. 'Language,' she said reprovingly, easing back on the pedal so that they were merely hurtling.

'Who the hell taught you to drive?'

'What? You get taught?'

'Pull over.'

They stepped onto the pavement, moved instinctively to the shadow of a shop awning and stood facing each other. As they talked, they performed a slow side-shuffle, turning full circle as they scanned over each other's shoulder.

'What's the scene?'

'Aqsa mosque. Call to dispatch. Lots of hysteria, imprecations, insults and threats.'

'Upset, then?'

'Somewhat. Time to move. Me first, you follow.'

He walked away and she scoped the human and vehicular traffic for pedestrian or drive-by threat. Nothing. He stopped, she walked. Same drill.

'Coffee?'

'Cappuccino.'

Inside, always inside, with their backs to the wall, facing the door.

'So?'

'Me in, you watch?'

'What?'

'Confucius him say woman detective wearing pants in mosque as welcome as fart in space suit.'

'Big guy, hat, end of bar? Carrying.'

'Ours.'

'Oh.'

'Go.'

Detective Avram toed his way out of his shoes and padded into the Aqsa mosque, picking up a skull-cap in the porch. He walked full-circle around the man crouched alone on a mulberry carpet, the amateur historian in him distracted by the Carrara marble columns donated by Mussolini and the painted ceiling courtesy of King Farouk. He also recalled reading of a deranged young man who had started a fire here in 1969 which had wrecked the Dome and reduced the pulpit to ashes. That focused him and he hunkered down beside the man on the carpet, flipping open his identity card. 'I am the imam,' the man whispered through ashen lips. A tendril of spittle dangled from his mouth and he wiped it away with a trembling hand, which he raised and pointed. Avram walked to the pillar and stepped round it. The head was resting on the floor. No blood-puddle, he registered, dead before delivery. He retraced his steps.

'Tell me what to do.'

'You are a Jew?'

'Retired.'

'Please, just take it away from here. If any members of my community should see this …'

'Two things,' the detective interrupted. 'The first is I'll get it away from here. The second is that you give your word to keep this secret.'

'Our mosque has been desecrated and you—'

'Listen, Imam. Last month it was the synagogue in Mea Shearim. That's secret too. Just so you know it's not about you.'

'Who … who could do such a thing?'

'I don't know. Yet.'

The imam glanced at the shoeless feet and skull-cap.

'You are Detective Avram.'

'Yes.'

'We have heard of you, a man of no faith who is fair to all faiths.'

'Can you come to Police Headquarters tomorrow morning to make a statement?'

'Yes.'

Avram peeled off his jacket as he walked to the pillar, bundled the head in the jacket and took it outside. A man pushing a broom across the far pavement paused to lean on the handle. The two detectives put their heads together so that their profiles bordered the frame. Click. The high-powered camera purred once and returned to the sweeper's pocket.

'Bomb?'

'Head.'

'Another? Shit.'

'Language!'

The Island, Ireland

Fiona Flaherty watched the ferry pivot, almost on its axis, to nudge and snuggle at the pier. She nodded at Tess Duggan, who returned the gesture. No flies on Tess, she thought approvingly. Berth the boat first, meet and greet after.

She saw Tess wave to Iarla in the wheelhouse and smiled. God almighty, she reflected, teaching Iarla had been her greatest challenge in the schoolroom.

'Iarla, where's your homework?'

'I must have left it on the boat, Miss.'

'That'll have them laughing on the mainland.'

'True enough, Miss.'

Iarla had been terminally sunny, content in the knowledge that he had merely to survive school to join Tess on the boat. On dry land, he had an extra ankle and elbow, the classic unco-ordinated teenager. Her eyes tracked him now as he swung lightly from the wheelhouse door to join his sister, expertly looping a rope between thumb and elbow. Two flustered couples bumped their baggage down the gangplank and tottered along the pier.

'Shouldn't be allowed,' one of the ladies remarked crossly, to no one in particular.

At last the cabin door opened and Michael Flaherty took a tentative step from the dark.

The light crept up from his feet to his face, and Fiona's eyes registered and parsed the details. His shoes looked comfortable rather than clean, and his trousers were creased at the front as if cinched too tightly at the waist. The grey windcheater was puffed out and she wondered if he had gained weight, but then the wind eased and it collapsed to hang straight down from his shoulders. If he turned full circle it wouldn't move, she thought, and a sob bubbled up in her throat. Her brother had always had high cheekbones, buttressing dark, almost Hispanic eyes, but she was struck now by how the dark half-moons beneath them stained the pallor of his face. She swallowed the sob and struggled for control.

'Fi.'

Even the use of her pet name, she sensed, owed nothing to emotion. The Michael she had known possessed a deceptive physical stillness; deceptive because it masked a tightly wound energy. She had seen him move like a lithe animal across the littered floor of their brother Gabriel's vandalised bedroom; a lithe and lethal animal. She had heard how her brother had hunted the killer Skald and put him in the water for others to finish. Now his eyes reflected the loss of vigour so evident in his body; their vacancy frightened her.

'What does a brother have to do to get a hug around here?' he said, and smiled.

That's how people smile when they've been bereaved, she thought. People who are searching inside themselves for someone lost and are distracted by condolence. Michael, her champion throughout her motherless girlhood in a house of boys, felt insubstantial in her embrace.

'Wait here,' she said brusquely. 'I'll be back.' It took all her self-control not to add, 'And don't stir,' as if she was shepherding a little one.

'You and Schwarzenegger.' He lowered himself onto a bollard.

∞✕∞

'Tommy, where's the car?'

'Tommy the Yank', as he was known locally, shifted a toothpick expertly to the non-speaking corner of his mouth as his round face went through the agonisingly slow process of assimilating the question.

'Why, back out yonder, t'other side of the pier, ma'am.'

Thirty-five years in the Bronx and he comes back sounding like John Wayne, she marvelled. 'Too far,' she said briskly, 'bring it right up to the boat.'

Again, the toothpick did its slow, spiralling dance across his expensive American teeth.

'Can't rightly do that, ma'am,' he drawled. 'They got ordinances about vehicular traffic on this here—'

'Shift yer arse,' she snapped, and was pleased to see the toothpick fall from his slack mouth.

'I'm on it.'

Fiona turned abruptly and came face to face with Tess.

'You saw him, Tess?

'I saw him.'

'Jesus, he looks like—'

'Fiona.' Tess' voice brought her up as short as if the other woman had shaken her shoulders. 'Fiona,' she continued, more gently, 'get a hold of yourself, girl. Your brother's been hurt and—'

'I know that.'

'No, listen to me now. He's been hurt … inside. Do you follow?'

'Yes, but—'

'But nothing. Men come back from the sea without their fathers or brothers. I've seen it, you've seen it.'

Fiona nodded.

'Women go mad,' Tess continued. 'They cry and tear their hair. Then they calm down and make arrangements. Men don't do that because, well, they're men. Then, all that stuff …' She shook her head suddenly as if ridding her hair of water. 'It can go bad and eat at them. Do you follow?'

'I don't know what to do, Tess.'

Tess rested a rough hand on her shoulder.

'Don't be doing anything, Fiona,' she said quietly. 'Just take him home and give him time … And now brace yourself, girl,' she said smiling. 'Tommy the Yank's coming up behind you like a full moon in a fog.'

They sat side by side in the back seat of Tommy's Ford. 'Hadda be Ford,' Tommy told anyone in Finnegan's pub who bothered to listen. 'Best damn automobiles in the free world.'

'How's about them Japanese jobs, Tommy?' someone would ask mischievously.

'From the people who brought you Pearl Harbor,' was always his solemn reply. The locals would return to their drinks, content in the knowledge that the salt-spiced Island air would eat the car out from under Tommy.

Fiona made the introductions, emphasising, for Michael's benefit, that Tommy had arrived only a few months before.

'Real glad to meet you, Padre,' Tommy intoned, checking the rear-view mirror for non-existent traffic. 'You like a missionary?'

'What?'

'Nah, it's just, if you don't mind me sayin' so, you look kinda tuckered out, just like my aunt Mary – Sister Agnes that is. Thirty years out yonder in Africa. Maybe you bumped into her some time? No, well, I guess it's a big place.'

Michael was still enough of an Islander to recognise a man marooned between two cultures. Tommy had left the Island all those years ago for a country he didn't know and returned all those years later to an equally mysterious one. Constant chatter was his way of keeping that reality at bay. He sensed Fiona tensing beside him and nudged her gently with his knee, relieved when he felt her relax. He looked out at the darkening Island and his own ghostly reflection echoed back, streaked occasionally by the lights of homes of a people he hardly knew any more. Me and you, Tommy, he mused, two of a kind. He rested his forehead against the cool glass and allowed Tommy's slow drawl to lull him down to darkness.

Police Headquarters, Jerusalem

Inspector Samuel Bernstein plucked a memo from his pristine desk, read it, balled it and dropped it into the bin. Then, methodically, he did the same with all the others. 'Keep a clean desk,' the time-management expert had said. 'Read everything once only and file it.'

Two out of three ain't bad, Bernstein thought, and glared across the desk at the two whose actions had generated the memo-mountain.

'So far,' he huffed, 'we have a complaint, attached to a bill, from the bus company, a truck driver claiming compensation for post-traumatic stress, a coffee shop tab left outstanding and—'

'Mine was a cappuccino,' Goldberg interrupted.

'—and, a slew of complaints from various Muslim worshippers concerning a female officer wearing pants in the mosque forecourt.'

'Confucius is never wrong,' Avram remarked, with satisfaction.

The inspector pinched the bridge of his nose between thumb and forefinger, concentrating on regulating his breathing. The man at the stress course had recommended this exercise. Avram and Goldberg, he concluded, were the unlikeliest of partners. The ex-paratrooper and the ex-New York cop and daughter of a Manhattan gold merchant were a match made in Hell. But – and there was always a but, as the director of the management-skills course had insisted – they worked. Worked, he thought, so far outside the box, to a different drummer, from a vantage of five hundred feet – and all the other damn clichés he remembered from all the other numb-ass courses he had attended – that they seemed to inhabit a parallel universe. And the imam had turned up this morning to make a perfectly ordinary statement and commend one of Bernstein's detectives for his sensitivity. Signs and wonders, he thought.

'What do we have?' he asked.

'Two heads,' Avram responded promptly. 'The first appeared a month ago in the Mea Shearim district, bloodless and burned. Cue panic and accusations.'

'Accusations?'

'Yes.' Goldberg flipped a notebook. 'In short, the ultra-Orthodox Jews attributed the insult and sacrilege to the Christian sects, the Muslims, Orthodox and Liberal Jews and the Israeli government.'

The inspector pinched his nose again.

'And today's offering?'

'Bloodless and unburned head behind a pillar in the Aqsa mosque,' Avram recounted. 'The imam just wanted it out of there, but he was concerned about possible reactions from his community, should they find out.'

'Will they find out?

'No.'

A light blinked on the desk intercom. 'Dr Yanov's here from Pathology, sir.'

Bertha Yanov, 'Bertha the Bag Lady', as she was known to the police, tended always to have with her a plastic bag or two. In them she carried folders, documents and, sometimes, body parts. More than one police officer, attending an autopsy in Bertha's department, had regretted leaving his lunch bag lying around. Inspector Bernstein kissed her on both cheeks and fussed her into a chair. As far as he was concerned, she might be on the slippery side of sixty and sartorially eccentric, but, in the realm of the dead, Bertha the Bag Lady had no equal.

'Coffee, Bertha?'

She nodded.

'And me,' said Avram.

'Cappuccino,' added Goldberg.

Bernstein pressed the magic button and his secretary eventually materialised with a tray. 'Sorry, we have no pastries,' she mumbled.

'I brought something,' Bertha said, dipping into one of her bags. The others sighed with relief when she extracted a paper bag of biscuits.

'What's the story, Bertha?' Bernstein asked, fortifying himself with a mouthful of biscuit against what he knew would be a lengthy reply.

'Well,' she began, 'you all know about the Mea Shearim head, so to recap. We have a German national, male, forty-five years old, who lectures in medieval history at Tübingen. He was also widely published and something of a daytime-television darling. You know…' She flipped some crumbs from her chest and affected a gushing interview tone, 'And tell me, Doctor, is it true that the medieval tax-collectors of Laza in north-western Spain pursued the villagers with sticks and cowbells?'

'Did they?' Goldberg enquired from beneath a cappuccino moustache.

'Please, Detective.'

'Sorry.'

'Well, they did,' Bertha said. 'Anyway, our Teutonic media star takes a month's leave of absence from the university, flies to Tel Aviv and arrives in Jerusalem – the King David Hotel, to be exact. We have sightings of him in the Holy Places.' She crooked two fingers at either side of her shaggy head to mime quotation marks and her proletarian disdain for such superstition. 'Also at libraries, museums, archaeological sites et cetera, et cetera. Always the same question: "Where do I find the Tears of God?" Mean anything to anyone?'

They shook their heads.

'Me neither,' she said. 'I have all the curators, museum directors and archaeologists on the lookout for anyone else asking about the Tears of God.'

'Good work,' Bernstein murmured.

Bertha waved a biscuit dismissively. 'Computers, Samuel. They do have a limited usefulness.'

'Still, it's not the same as a carrier pigeon, is it?' Avram offered. 'Slow but endearing.'

'And you could read the message and eat the courier,' Goldberg added.

Bertha choked a little and coughed.

'You two,' she gasped.

'So far, so nothing, Bertha,' the inspector interjected.

'Oh, ye of little faith,' she shot back, and he relaxed in his chair.

'Lead on, Maestro,' he said magnanimously.

'When I had … motivated those people in my department who think the aim of a university education is to equip one to Google, we dug a little deeper and, as the Americans say, whaddya know?'

'What do you know, Bertha?' asked Goldberg.

'Patience, little one. Remember *festina lente*, hasten slowly. Which reminds me, have you found yourself a nice young man yet?'

'Bertha, please,' the inspector implored. 'Before I retire, I'd like to have the information.'

'Okay, okay,' she grumbled. 'We found our telegenic

lecturer leaves his university mid-term, flies first class to Tel Aviv and comes on to Jerusalem by taxi.'

'And you deduce what, Bertha?'

'Money. Only big money could tempt such a person to risk his job. Only big money makes him fly first class and pay a monumental taxi fare to Jerusalem. There are perfectly good bus services from Tel Aviv to Jerusalem.' She sniffed.

'Added to which, he stayed in the King David Hotel. Not cheap,' the inspector remarked.

'No?'

'No.'

'The King David was a pick-up point. CCTV footage shows him in the foyer drinking their ridiculously expensive coffee before he's met by a young man and escorted outside to a car. We're working on the stills but I don't hold out much hope. The young man was wearing the flowing robe and headdress of an Arab, expensive enough to get him into the King David and yet obscure his face.'

'And the car?'

'Stolen and recycled. Dead end.'

It was an unfortunate choice of phrase and seemed to throw a pall on the room.

'Any developments on the bo— I mean the head?' Goldberg asked.

'Yes.' Bertha brightened visibly. What had gone before was good police work but basic textbook stuff. Pathology for Bertha was giving a voice to the dead and, with her skills, she could make them sing.

'Well, we know the first head was burned before it was delivered,' the inspector said.

'Yes and no,' Bertha replied enigmatically, dipping into a

plastic bag for a file which she opened on her lap. Gravity tugged her spectacles to the tip of her nose.

'Yes, it was burned, but not on a fire. Why destroy it when you want to flaunt it? I must confess to a macabre little secret,' she said quietly, as she arranged a mess of papers into something resembling order. 'I have more than a passing interest in that period. I mean the physical damage they managed to inflict on the human bo—'

'Bertha!' the inspector barked.

'Well, anyway, I was intrigued by the damage, which was largely confined to the upper part of the cranium. A bit of old-fashioned abrasion revealed fibres that looked like human hair, but not under the microscope.' She tipped her spectacles back to the bridge of her nose and looked up. 'Feathers, my friends. Hans Koenig was tarred and feathered. His head wore a pitch-cap when it was removed from his shoulders with a two-handed broadsword. I won't bore you with the science but it'll stand up to scrutiny. Also, the Jerusalem Museum and its curator have been immensely helpful.'

'And the most recent head?' Goldberg prompted.

'Same sword, no pitch-cap. But we must retrace the second victim's steps and look for similarities. Peter Johnson, archaeologist at the British Museum in London, takes a leave of absence from a dig he was supervising outside Istanbul and flies to Tel Aviv. The rest you can guess. But his final resting place is a mosque. Not just any mosque but the second most sacred Muslim shrine in Jerusalem. Now, my young friends,' she said, looking at Avram and Goldberg, 'crank up your brains and hypothesise.'

Avram began, 'Two academics specialising in medieval times ... I'm guessing the Istanbul site was medieval?'

'Correct. Continue.'

'Okay, two scholars quit their posts mid-term and mid-dig, which would suggest an incentive, a significant one, that includes first-class travel along the way and a meeting with someone who spirits them whither we know not.'

Goldberg picked up the baton. 'They both trawl through places that record or contain documents or objects pertinent to their area of expertise.'

'Such language. You must write my next submission for funding,' Bertha said admiringly, and Goldberg blushed.

'Questions so far are,' said Avram, ticking them off on his fingers, 'who in Jerusalem has that kind of money? What are these Tears of God they're searching for? Let's accept it was something from the medieval period.'

'It's a safe guess,' Bertha agreed. 'Onward.'

'They both turn up headless, courtesy of the same weapon, a broadsword,' Goldberg said, 'and in religious shrines where they're likely to cause suspicion that other religions may have been involved.'

'Very good.'

'What kind of madman are we looking for, Bertha?' the inspector asked wearily.

Now it was her turn to tick off the answers on her fingers.

'Rich, and obsessed with the medieval period. This man needs experts to trawl for something he wants. When they don't find it, he tortures and kills them in a medieval fashion and uses their body parts to insult or incite. I think he must be a Christian, a Western European Christian. He has access to medieval weapons and instruments of torture and knows how to use them. Cutting off a head with a two-handed broadsword is not easy, so we must also accept that he has a powerful physique. And, finally, he has a servant or servants who are in on the deal.'

She looked suddenly tired. 'And he is here,' she said bleakly. 'And he will kill again and again.'

'A serial killer.' The inspector groaned.

'Yes, old friend,' she answered, 'a serial killer who will continue to kill until he finds what he's looking for, and even then …'

She let the unthinkable settle in their minds until she was ready to go on.

'He is someone who wishes to promote hatred between the different faiths in Jerusalem. I'll leave you copies of my report.' She sighed. 'If we turn up anything new, I'll inform you. I'm sorry, my dears,' she said, addressing the two detectives, 'I wish I could be more helpful.'

Bertha fussed with her plastic bags as the inspector held the door. 'Be careful,' she said, when she was ready to leave. 'You young people imagine you're immortal.'

The Island, Ireland

It took him a moment to orient himself and unclench his taut body. Beside him, Fiona seemed to have absorbed some of his tension, watching him from the corner of her eye, her hand squeezing his elbow. Tommy was still in full flow: 'Golly, when Auntie Mary, that's Sister Agnes, came back from the missions, she was, I dunno, like someone sucked dry. Kinda yella, ye know?'

There was an awkward pause while he parked the car at the end of the lane that led to the Flaherty house. He plucked the small bag from the boot, weighing it in his hand, nodding to himself, as if it confirmed some theory he had conceived about emaciated Irish missionaries.

'Savin' your presence, Padre,' he muttered, as he handed it to Michael. 'I guess I tend to shoot my mouth off.'

'What's the damage, Tommy?' Fi interposed briskly, rummaging in her shoulder bag.

The round-faced man in the too-bright jacket shifted his feet awkwardly.

'Aw, hell, sweetheart,' he said shyly, 'it's been a privilege having you folks.' He rolled back behind the wheel and flashed the headlights in farewell.

'That fella could talk for Ireland,' Fi said, as they leaned into the hill.

'He does, Fi,' Michael replied drily.

He held out his hand and his sister took it, as she had always done years before. 'Well, sis,' he said gruffly, 'what say you and me jest mosey on up thar to the old homestead and have us a cup of tea?'

'John Wayne never drank tea.'

'The hell he didn't. He drank gallons of it in *The Quiet Man.*'

They were still hand in hand and bantering when they arrived at the front door. Michael stood aside to let her pass through, then hunted for the red twinkle of Tommy's tail-lights and watched them weave towards the glow of the village until they disappeared. He was still standing there when his sister joined him in the spill of light from the cottage door. 'Is there something out there, Michael?' she asked.

'No, Fi. Nothing at all.' Not yet, he thought. Not yet.

Washington University
'Coprolalia!'

That was the word. James J. Ford, President of the University of Washington, sat back in his plush office chair and allowed himself a congratulatory swivel. Coprolalia, he had discovered, was an affliction that compelled sufferers to articulate whatever came into their minds. They couldn't help themselves, the article in the *New Scientist* claimed. Just had to say it, whatever the circumstances, and damn the consequences. Well, he concluded grimly, pressing a button on his desk, Professor John Hancock of this university had said it in the worst possible circumstances and would be apprised of the consequences. He would help it, by God, or feel the wrath of the board. A small man, Ford wondered if he should ratchet his chair up another inch or so in preparation for the encounter. Before he could decide, the door opened and his secretary, Marjorie, ushered Professor Hancock into his presence.

Ford's wife had once remarked, rather breathlessly, he'd thought, that the new professor of hydrology reminded her of someone called Jones. Indiana Jones, if his memory served him right. Hancock, he noticed, had the largest hands he had ever seen. The palm he offered to be shaken was cross-hatched with small white scars, like little white worms writhing under the black wiry hair that bushed from the man's shirt cuff. Ford withdrew his hand as quickly as possible and gestured for the younger man to sit. Even seated, Hancock still towered over his employer and Ford found himself looking up at a tanned, craggy face and the most disconcertingly direct stare. He cleared his throat nervously.

'Want a glass of water?' Hancock asked, nodding at the carafe on the desk.

'No, thank you,' Ford replied automatically, and was even more discomfited to realise that he was discomfited. Damnit to hell, he was the university president and this young whippersnapper had better ... He took a deep breath and began. 'Professor Hancock, I thought we might ...'

At that point he made the mistake of looking up and his train of thought was promptly derailed by the other's intense gaze. Images of snakes and mongooses, rabbits and headlights all flashed through his brain as his mouth worked valiantly to salvage the interview.

'Eh, that is ...'

'Let me help you out here, sir,' Hancock said, leaning forward to fill a glass with water from the carafe. 'I had some politicians come swanning into my department last Thursday.' He handed the glass to Ford, who grasped it and held it protectively in both hands.

'Those politicians,' Ford managed to splutter, 'were senators from Capitol Hill and—'

'Yep,' Hancock agreed, 'that's where they came from, all right, and that's where I sent them packing.'

'Good God, man, you can't do that.'

'Why not?'

Ford struggled for some measure of composure, wishing to Christ he'd lowered the damned chair so that he could feel terra firma under his feet.

'Professor Hancock,' he began gently, as if he was speaking to a child. A very large child, as it happened, whose gaze seemed to bore holes in his skull. He looked away and tried again.

'Professor Hancock, these ... politicians, if you will, are extremely influential people who sit on the Environmental Policy Group. As I'm sure you're aware, this group has a research budget of some two hundred million dollars. Now, I and members of the university board have spent months lobbying—'

'Sir.' Hancock held up a huge hand, like a traffic cop at an intersection. Ford came dutifully to a halt, his mouth still open.

'Sir, I know who they are and what their budget is. As for research, we've already done the damn research.' Hancock stood up and leaned those enormous hands, now fists, on the polished acreage of the president's desk.

'Do you know that for every day those jerks sit drinking bottled water in their ivory tower and playing political poker with their budget, New Yorkers will draw more than one and a half billion gallons of water from a system with more leaks than the halls these numbskulls inhabit?'

He plucked the glass from the president's nerveless fingers and held it up before him. 'One and a half billion gallons,' he said slowly. He dipped his finger into the water and raised it until a single drop formed on the tip.

'This is the water they actually need, just two gallons per person for drinking and cooking. Meanwhile,' he flicked his finger, and Ford watched the trajectory of the drop until it splashed on the Great Plains of his desk, 'every year, more than ten million people die of waterborne diseases. I told that jumped-up collection of jackasses, who presumed to disrupt the work of my department because they were too damned self-important to make an appointment, that we need responses not research. I told them the world is slowly dying of thirst and I told them where they could shove their two hundred million dollars.'

I'm going to die, Ford thought. I can't breathe and this red-faced, hairy giant is the last thing I shall ever see on this earth.

The phone buzzed. In a daze, he lifted the receiver. 'Yes,' he managed to wheeze. John Hancock held him in that mesmerising gaze as the few remaining cells in his brain tried to process what he was hearing. He watched as Ford slipped from the chair and used one trembling hand to steady himself against the desk. 'It's for you,' Ford whispered. 'The White House,' he added reverently.

Calmly, Hancock reached across and took the receiver from him.

'Hancock … Yes. I see. Tuesday at ten in the Oval Office with the president and the cabinet. I have a faculty meeting at nine, so let's say ten thirty … Yes, that's what I said. Thank you.'

He placed the receiver firmly in its cradle and the glass of water in Ford's hand. 'Better drink that while you can,' he said darkly, and let himself out.

Slowly, President James J. Ford became aware of his surroundings. He registered that his secretary, Marjorie, was standing just inside his office door wearing a peculiar expression.

'He took a call from the White House,' he said tonelessly.

'Yes, sir.'

'They wanted him for a ten o'clock meeting in the Oval Office with the president and the cabinet.'

'Yes, sir.'

'He said … he said he had a faculty meeting at nine and he'd come at ten thirty.'

'Yes, sir.'

John Ford felt light-headed. He knew he had just recounted a series of events as incredible and alien to him as crop circles and Roswell and … Try as he might, he couldn't complete the analogy. After a long moment, he asked, 'Who is Indiana Jones?'

For the first time since this surreal conversation had begun, Marjorie's peculiar look was replaced with something like her usual expression.

'Oh, you think so too,' she breathed.

The White House, Washington DC

The African-American sitting behind the desk in the Oval Office looked up and smiled. 'My fellow Americans,' he began, 'they said it was a fantasy but, as you can see for yourselves, it's a fact. They said, "Not in our lifetime," but, hey, it's come to pass in your days and you will recount to your children how the dream became a reality as they will to their children.'

He paused and looked at the man sitting quietly by the door, reading a book.

'Maybe "hey" is a bit too folksy? Whaddya think?'

'A smidgin,' the man replied, without taking his eyes from the page.

'Smidgin? What kinda damn-fool word is that? No, don't tell me. It's a pigeon that got run over by a truck. Maybe it's a …'

The other man pressed his free hand to his ear, flipping the book closed, one-handed, and slipping it into his jacket pocket.

'Code?' he enquired politely. 'Correct, proceed.' He stood up and walked to one side of the double doors.

'Incoming,' he said calmly. 'Ten seconds.'

Joshua Harley, special agent, White House security detail, made it from the desk to the door in three. It took a further six seconds for him to normalise his breathing and heart rate. At a nod from his partner, they swung the double doors inwards.

'Good morning, gentlemen.'

'Morning, Ms President.'

That particular title had been the subject of the first wager of the new presidency between the two agents who were serving their third commander-in-chief.

'It's gotta be Mrs President,' Joshua had declared.

'So whaddya call the Queen of England?' Harry Grant had countered. 'Mrs King?'

'The lady's married, Harry.'

'I gotta twenty saying it's Ms.'

Joshua had lost that one but now ventured a smile of triumph as the president strode around the desk to sit in the chair. Ellen Radford was wearing a classic black jacket and trousers over a plain white blouse. No jewellery. Joshua had bet on a formal outfit for her first meeting with 'The Coven'; the scarily intense men and woman who made up her inner circle.

'Everything in order, gentlemen?'

'Yes, Ms President,' they chorused dutifully.

As she gave her attention to the papers on her desk, Joshua remembered his first meeting with the new president. He had drawn the short straw, which meant he had had to give the security lecture. Mid-spiel, she had interrupted.

'You just might recall that I've lived here for a time?'

He nodded.

'I've been in and out of this office a thousand times, Special Agent, so maybe we can move on?'

Joshua Harley felt again that bad feeling in the pit of his

stomach as he rewound, from memory, the remainder of their conversation.

'I have a question for you, Special Agent,' she had said, raising her eyes from her papers and locking them on Harley. Remember, he had reminded himself, you are obliged, should the circumstance arise, to take a bullet for this woman. But not bullshit. That thought had straightened his spine and allowed him look into those pale, unblinking eyes.

'How do you and Special Agent Grant know when I'm coming to the Oval Office?' she had asked.

Even now, his feet shifted uncomfortably at the memory.

'We always know in advance, ma'am. We get a coded call from the agent at the turn of the hallway. Eh, it's like ten seconds.'

'Was it the same procedure when I ... before I was elected president?'

Ground, Joshua remembered thinking, if you ever gonna swallow me, now would be good.

'Yes, Ms President.'

Ellen Radford's eyes had set his free for a few moments and wandered over some internal landscape.

'You mentioned a code,' she had said absently. 'What was mine?'

'Codes can change every day, Ms President.'

Some of the old steel had crept back into her eyes and voice.

'You haven't answered my question.'

Damn you, Ground, Joshua had thought. "Chickenhawk', Ms President.'

'That explains a—'

She took a deep breath and squared her shoulders. 'That

makes a certain kind of sense,' she said. 'Thank you, Special Agent … Harley, isn't it?'

'Yes, Ms President. Joshua Harley.'

Her eyes swept around the room.

'We need another chair. Could one of you gentlemen oblige?'

'I'm on it,' Grant said quickly, and eased into the corridor.

She waited until the door had closed behind him.

'While we have a moment alone, Special Agent Joshua Harley …'

'Yes, Ms President.'

'During my husband's presidency, there was quite a lot of speculation in Washington that he was keeping this chair warm for me. I never needed any man to do that then and I sure as heck don't need it now. Understood?'

Harley nodded dumbly, trying to keep his eyes fastened on a point about four inches above her head.

'Thank you,' she said. 'That will be all.'

He felt drained and picked his steps carefully across the carpet in time to swing the doors open and allow Grant to manoeuvre a delicate chair to join the crescent of others before the desk. The president looked critically at it.

'That one's an heirloom,' she declared, 'goes all the way back to the Roosevelt era. If anything happened to it, Eleanor'd be haunting my dreams and I wouldn't want that.'

Grant looked appraisingly at the chair, then lowered his impressive bulk onto it. It creaked and shifted slightly, but held.

'QED,' the president remarked.

'*Quod erat demonstrandum* indeed, Ms President,' Grant concurred.

The president's left eyebrow arched to join the other.

38

She allowed herself a small smile as the door closed behind the two men. So, she thought, Special Agent Joshua Harley aspires to oust me, if only from my chair, and Special Agent Harry Grant quotes the Latin footnote at the end of every mathematical proof – 'that which was to be shown'. Unlike the book he had almost concealed in his jacket pocket, of course. Impressive. And would Mother have been impressed to see her daughter here? she wondered. No, she concluded, Mother would have expected it. 'Why not?' had been her mantra whenever she herself had expressed misgivings. She got up from her chair and walked to the window that framed the Washington Obelisk. In the early morning light, it looked like a cold stiletto shoved up through the heart of the city. She remembered reading that Eleanor Roosevelt had always said she found it 'deeply comforting'. Gives me the creeps, the woman at the window thought, like some damn inverted Sword of Damocles. Automatically, she rubbed her upper arms and repeated a mantra of her own – it had kept her focused and steady during the election, the delegate-selection conference and the blizzard of caucuses before. 'I have fought the good fight,' she whispered. 'I have run the race and won the prize.'

She smiled ruefully as her mother's voice echoed in her head. 'A prize is a gate, Ellen. It's something you go through to achieve something else, not an end in itself.'

Thank you, Mother. Yep, there was never a silver lining but Mother could produce a cloud.

Her mood improved when she thought of Special Agent Joshua Harley's butt, so lately vacating her chair. Yeah, *her* goddamn chair.

The door cracked open, interrupting her reverie, and she frowned until the grizzled head of Senator Henry Melly poked through the gap.

'You still pinchin' yourself?' he asked, in a Southern drawl drizzled with molasses.

'Yep. Cinderella's at the ball and midnight is still a world away.'

Her political mentor and confidant grinned wolfishly.

'The sheep and the goats await without,' he whispered.

'Which is which?'

'You the shepherd now, Ms President,' he said. 'Ah'm jest the dawg.'

'Go fetch, Henry,' she said, and sat up straight.

☙❦❧

Casper Benson III entered first, as she had known he would. Henry Melly had waxed moodily eloquent about him at their tête-à-tête before the meeting.

'Calls himself Benson the Third. I knew the first and second, honey, and it causes me to question the omniscience of the Almighty. Heck, He'd already struck out twice and now He comes up to bat, spits on His hands and takes another swing. Likes to say he comes from old money, which means inherited rather than earned.'

The old man had looked in his glass for inspiration before draining the bourbon. 'Think Hoover with his brains spliced to McCarthy's paranoia and you've got Benson the Third. Course, his staffers sure like funnin' bout him. Call him Benson the Turd when they a few beers south of sense, always lookin' darkly over their shoulders, makin' like someone might be listenin'. When it comes to Benson, there's always someone listenin'. You heah me, Ellen?'

'I hear you, Henry. And I'm his third turn at bat.'

'Yep. Been super-spook to President Day before you and your … and the previous president. Benson's got previous, as the ole cons like to say – Kuwait, Afghanistan, Iraq. Some say Gaza and Beirut as well. Word on the Hill was that he had some dealings south of the border, way south, if you get my drift. Same word has it that some disappointed general thought to up his profile and his offshore accounts by pokin' a covert operation in among the powder families, run by some deranged major and his psychopathic sidekick. So far so humdrum. Drug lords killin' drug lords don't matter lickety-spit to anyone in Washington. But …'

'There's always a but, isn't there, Henry?'

'Ain't that the truth, honey? Now, listen up. From here on in we're movin' beyond this kind of everyday fiction into fantasy. Someone way up the chain of command gets cold feet and sends a dawg to catch a dawg.'

'Lost you on the first dawg, Henry.'

'Okay, let's jest check the perimeter. This place checked reg'lar for bugs?'

'Oh, for God's sake, Henry—'

'Ellen!'

'Yes?'

'This is strictly need to know.'

'If I'm to inherit Benson and all his works and pomps, I need to know.'

'Yes, I guess you do. But, once you know, you know.'

'You're being gnomic again, Henry.'

He raised his index finger.

'If you know, you can never say you don't know.'

'Okay.'

'No, it's not okay, Ms President. It's bigger than okay. This is resignation, maybe indictment territory. This is Richard Milhous Oh-no-I-didn't-oh-yes-I-did, so-long-it's-bin-good-ta-know-ya.'

Before she could protest, he raised a second finger.

'And,' he continued, 'you can never tell anybody.'

'That's unnecessary, Senator,' she said stiffly.

'No, it ain't, for two reasons. A secret is something known by one person. If you tell someone and they tell someone and that someone tells someone else who tells someone linked to this whole caboodle—'

'Get to the goddamn point, Henry.'

'The goddamn point is that those people can't leave you breathing.'

Ellen Radford reared back in her chair and lifted her fringe away from her eyes. She shook her head and laughed harshly.

'Are you telling me …? I'm the President of the United States! You can't believe that someone would actually—'

'Wake up and smell the horseshit, Ms President,' he said. 'You find somethin' in your oath of office that grants you immunity or immortality? In your lifetime,' he continued grimly, 'one President of the United States got himself shot dead and one got seriously wounded. Add one wounded pope and a serious attempt on the new guy. Add any number of heads of state throughout the world, including that lady who was leader of the opposition in her own country and—'

'I get the point, Henry. No need to stab me with it.'

'Good. Now you gotta decide if you want to hear the rest of the story.'

Ellen Radford placed her palms on the table. It was a gesture he recognised and he nodded approvingly.

'Tell the story,' she said.

'All righty. Let's bring you up to speed. So far we've got an illegal military force, under a mad major and his clone, causing mayhem among the cartels.'

'Tell me it gets better, Henry.'

'No, ma'am – well, not a whole bunch, dependin' on your point of view. Someone in army high command got wind of the operation and—'

'Sent a dawg to catch a dawg, whatever that means,' she added, waving her hand at him to go on.

'It means they sent in another covert military unit.'

'Christ, how many of these are there?'

'These days? More'n you have fingers and toes to count with. Now hush up and pay heed. They sent this unit in to search and destroy – no bodies, tags, traces or scandal. No South American ambassador thumpin' the desk with his shoe at the UN.'

'That was the Soviet Union, Henry.'

'Same difference and don't tell yo grandpa how to suck eggs.'

'Did they kill them all?'

'Depends who you mean by "them". Ya see, the hunters became the hunted. Of the second unit only one boy came home alive. The first team got back to pay-offs and demob. They were killed in an air crash, except two.'

'The major and his sidekick.'

'On the money, honey. Now, the Lords of Darkness who planned this mess of pottage got a problem.'

'The survivor from the second unit.'

'Yep again. Let's cut to the chase. A US agent organised a sanction on the major.'

'Say "killed", Henry.'

'Okay, killed, with a little help from a submarine.'

'Naturally,' she said. 'And the psychopathic sidekick clone?'

'Also dead. And the general who ate his gun. And, to make a long story even longer, the Powers of Light decided to let the survivor run free.'

'They took a hell of a gamble. What would stop him finding his very own Woodward or Bernstein?'

'They had assurances. And …'

'And?'

'They staked him out like a tethered goat, to draw any leftover badasses from the undergrowth.'

'Hell of a deal for a hero. So you think Benson could have been pulling the strings on this puppet show?'

'I think it's highly unlikely that the head of the CIA wasn't aware of what was going down.'

'You're not at a Congressional hearing, Henry.'

'Not yet, Ellen, not yet.'

'Should I fire him?'

'Well, on the one hand—'

'Henry, if I'd needed a one-handed adviser I'd have hired one.'

'Touché. Then the answer is no. You don't have proof. Also, it's a mighty controversial move for a new president. Furthermore, you know what Johnson said about appointing Bobby Kennedy as attorney general. Better to have him inside the tent pissin' out …'

'Than outside the tent pissin' in.'

'You and I must live in the real world, Ellen. Camelot was

always an aspiration – knights in shining armour are kinda thin on the ground in Washington.'

'Since we're on a roll of clichés here, Henry, aren't you forgetting about those who lie down with dogs?'

'Lyin' down with dogs can save your life in a blizzard, Ms President. Remember that, and the fleas can be a small price to pay.'

'I'll remember.'

President Ellen Radford surfaced from her reverie to find the head of the CIA watching her carefully. He granted her the slightest inclination of his balding head. She ran her eyes over his razor-thin frame in the funereal black suit he seemed to wear all day, every day. It provided a sombre backdrop for the alabaster hands and face, topped with heavy-lidded black eyes under bushy brows. Black is the absence of colour, she reminded herself. It's nature's gift to panthers and other nocturnal hunters, most appropriate for the high priest of the CIA.

Her gaze shifted to Ephrem Isaacson from Treasury: mid-thirties, saturnine and smart, as only a Harvard summa cum laude in economics could be. Sharp enough to cut himself, his opponents hoped. Or sharp enough to cut through the mountain of gobbledegook the chiefs of the armed forces were already shovelling across her desk, demanding billions. The Middle East experts were still howling at her appointment of a Jew to such a powerful position in her cabinet.

'Let them bay at the moon. He'll see right through any flim-flam from Tel Aviv' had been Senator Henry Melly's advice.

'But what about Tehran and Riyadh?' she had countered.

'You got a counterweight,' her mentor had answered smugly, 'a yang to his yin.'

She switched her attention to Melly's yang. Laila Achmed cut a diminutive and graceful figure between the CIA and Treasury representatives. Lebanese by birth and liberal Muslim by conviction, she had been plucked by Ellen Radford from academia and appointed secretary of state. The president, trusting in the Southern senator's political nous, hoped the hyper-intelligent and articulate woman would balance her team and make some headway in the morass of the Middle East.

She watched the little dance of protocol as the newcomers hovered uncertainly until Casper Benson folded himself into the chair at the centre of the crescent. Immediately, he reversed his chair a few inches, siting it slightly to the rear of the others. Isaacson and Laila Achmed promptly took point positions on either side. Melly slumped in the chair marooned by Benson's rearward shift, but not before angling it so that Casper 'the Ghost' was side-on rather than behind him.

So, this is how the pieces fall, the president mused. The fractious siblings of the one God sit opposed while the Ghost who would be God hovers over all. And good ole Henry, she noted admiringly, much too canny to have the CIA breathing down his neck, breaks the line.

She placed her hands on the blotter. JFK, she remembered reading, had suffered from nervous hands and would hide their trembling under the podium when he came to speak in public. Pope Pius XII, the same author propounded, had had something of a hand fetish and liked to flap them around when speaking, as if he was conducting some angelic choir. Ellen Radford was the daughter of a devout Methodist who had habitually laid her palms and her cards on the table. Time to deal, she decided.

'The decisions arrived at in this room will affect our

country for better or for worse. We can decide only according to the facts before us and act according to our collective abilities.'

She paused to read their body language. Benson sat, cold and immobile, as if carved from stone. Isaacson already looked bored and Laila seemed mildly disappointed. Okay. So far so trite, she thought. Time for Chickenhawk to ruffle some feathers.

'The two important words are 'collective' and 'facts',' she resumed. 'If it hasn't already happened, you will most certainly be lobbied by powerful interests from outside and inside this administration. That's to be expected in a democracy. But a democracy is where the people elect someone to decide and act on their behalf. Senator Melly and I are the only elected people in this room. Our remit is to represent the collective. Those of you I have appointed, or inherited,' she angled her head in Benson's direction, 'may listen to any and all groups but will advise me only on the basis of what is best for the people of the United States. Should I sense, or hear, that anyone in this room is marching to any other drummer, I will confront you with it. Once. Once will be regarded as an indiscretion. Two strikes and you're out.'

She paused again to scan the group. Isaacson and Laila Achmed were now angled away from her into two different corners. Benson sat rigid in his chair, wearing the righteous expression of a dormitory monitor hearing the rules of the frat house read out to potentially unruly freshmen. Melly, she was pleased to see, was covertly scanning left and right.

'With regard to facts,' she continued, 'the millstones of God and Washington grind exceedingly fine. Too often, what arrives in this office has been processed of all the fibre of truth and flavoured to the perceived taste of the incumbent. From you, I expect the facts of any given situation, raw and rendered down to intelligible pieces. As President Jimmy Carter once wrote in a memo to his White House staff, "In future, all memos to the President are to be in English." If you can't say it simply, then you don't know it. Furthermore, I like to see things coming down the line rather than, *post factum*, trying to hold the line or shore it up. If you, or your people, screw up, you 'fess up. That being so, I'll go to bat for you to the best of my ability. Nobody gets fired just for getting it wrong. Thus endeth the lesson,' she said briskly. 'And now to business. I'd like each of you to give a thumbnail sketch of your departmental priorities so that everyone is up to speed on the overall picture. Over the next few days I'll meet with each of you individually. Ephrem, the floor is yours.'

For the next two hours, Ellen Radford listened attentively and took notes, interrupting occasionally to ask for clarification. At the end of each contribution, she fed back an outline of what had been presented, allowing the speaker to add to or amend her perceptions. The lines at the corners of her mouth deepened as domestic and international crises seemed to suck the oxygen from the room. Unsurprisingly, Benson spoke last and longest. He had switched from righteous-monitor to bored-professor mode, with all the linguistic and facial tics of someone who had done it all before and was no longer pushing for tenure. The president resisted the impulse to let her eyelids or her guard drop, and divided her note-taking under various headings to help her think laterally and stay awake. Only Henry Melly was excused the briefing exercise. As her political eyes and ears, he would assimilate and break it all down later into its political significance.

'Thank you, all,' she said finally, shuffling her notes into a folder on her desk and placing it carefully to the left of the blotter. A place for everything and for everything a place. Thank you, Mother, but not right now.

'I suggest we powder our noses and bring some coffee and pastries back.'

Their surprised expressions caused her to add, 'Perhaps I should have mentioned it before. I've decided to invite particular experts, from outside the usual circles, to give us brief updates on topics allied to our concerns. One per meeting, actually. They get to talk and we get to ask. That's it, folks.' She rose from her chair.

The others stood until she had passed through the double doors, then filed out in her wake. Senator Melly brought up the rear, close enough to the CIA chief to hear his remark to Laila Achmed: 'That was a particularly cogent précis, my dear.'

The diminutive Secretary of State turned to look up at Benson.

'I thought it would save you reading the full report delivered to your office three days ago,' she said sweetly. 'And it's Ms Secretary.'

Go on, lady, spook the spook, the senator thought happily, and wisely kept that admonition to himself.

The Church of the Holy Sepulchre, Jerusalem
The Father Guardian prayed for patience and ached for a drink. It had been a mistake to grant yet another audience to Brother Werner who could bore for Bavaria. Today's topic was the hundred and one things Werner had to say about the deficiencies of the Franciscans in general and Father Guardian

in particular. His superior asked himself why the man had ever joined the order founded by a medieval Umbrian jongleur who had given away all his money and clothes and danced naked to the glory of God. He tried to imagine Werner following in the ecstatic footsteps of the founder, which brought on a fit of coughing. Instead, he allowed his features to harden into an expression of sincere sympathy and let his mind wander. Today's fugue, he decided, would be dedicated to the unlikely vocation of himself, Tim Conway, currently known as the Father Guardian of the Church of the Holy Sepulchre.

Tim Conway was Bronx born and bred. He was the classic local boy made good, educated by the Jesuits at Fordham High, thanks to the updraught of a scholarship. They had tried to make the best of it when their star pupil declared an interest in the Franciscans.

'But you have a good mind, Timothy. You could go far in the Church.'

He had taken this to mean the Jesuits were the high-fliers in terms of intelligence and job opportunities. The Franciscans, by contrast, were strictly economy class.

Ma had been vaguely supportive.

'That's nice, sweetheart, if it's really what you want. But Father Xavier says you could go to the Jesuit College, ya know. He says you got ability.'

His father, Tom, a bus driver in Queens, had been typically trenchant. 'Ya wanna wear a brown skirt for the rest of your life? Think I've been slavin' all those years to put you with the Jesuits and you go fartin' off to the Franciscans? Know how much it costs to keep you in Jesuit school?'

'I've got a scholarship, Pa.'

'Yeah, the scholarship. Does it put clothes on yer back 'n'

food in yer belly and books in yer bag? My ass. I say if ya wanna be a sky-pilot, fly jets not props. Step up to the plate with the best and show 'em what a workin' man's son can do. This is America, son, land of opportunity, movers and shakers, ya know.'

That had been round one; a fast and furious flurry of punches. Round two was marginally more subtle.

'Okay, so if ya don't want to be a Jesuit, why the hell can't ya be a reg'lar priest here in New York? Your ma would like that.'

Roll with the punches, he'd told himself, he'll tire. And, sure enough, the old man came around to at least a level of tolerance. Not that he ever admitted that, oh, no – he was Irish, after all. Any change of mind would have to be camouflaged in a story. They were sitting on the stoop outside the little house they had bought before the high-rises moved in next door. 'Did I ever tell ya the story 'bout the Jesuits and the chicken farmer?'

'Many times, Pa.'

'You're not too big for a strappin', so mind your lip. Anyways, this chicken farmer gets a visit from two Jesuits. They like to hunt in pairs, ya know. So the farmer serves up two cocks for dinner and them Jesuits suck the meat right off the bone. Sure I haven't told ya this one?'

'Yes, Pa.'

'After dinner they go for a stroll outside and they see the rooster crowin' for all he's worth on a fence post. "That's a proud bird," one of the Jesuits says. And the farmer says, "Why wouldn't he be proud? He's got two sons in the Jesuits."'

Most of his memories of Pa were of a man disappearing early every morning and reappearing late each evening, his fingers still curled from the steering wheel. He couldn't recall him ever coming to a ball game or PTA meeting; that was strictly Ma territory. She had badgered Tom into a suit and tie for Tim's graduation at Fordham High, where he had sat folded in on himself shooting his eyes left and right as if he was checking side mirrors for cops or bikers. Never said, 'Way to go,' or 'Well done,' or any damn thing when his son came walking back from the dais with the gold medal. High fives were as alien to Tom Conway as Nazi salutes. Next day, Tim had been mooching around the house, book in hand, grazing from the refrigerator, when the old man had appeared unexpectedly in the kitchen.

'Come on,' he said. 'Takin' her back to the depot.'

Tim Conway had sat up front in the empty bus, mesmerised by the narrative flow of the normally taciturn man.

'White Plains. Ya see that old lady, pushin' the stroller? That's just what she is, a pusher. No baby in that buggy, boy. Don't sell to little ones, though, I give her that. Very religious woman. Bronx Parkway. Guy in the work boots outside the Shamrock Bar? Been in construction for twenty years. Married to the bottle. Every two years, like clockwork, gets sobered up and goes home to Ireland. Presents for everyone, tab at the local bar, hired car, the whole nine yards. Comes back to the buildin' and the bottle till the next time. Bronx Zoo. Big guy in the Knicks windcheater, by the gate? Bang-bang man for the Salvatore family. More years behind bars than half the goddamn animals inside.'

And so it went on all the way to the depot, a tour guide who stripped away the façade of a place Tim had thought he knew and revealed the acuity, humour and compassion of a man he had never known.

The depot locker room was a hubbub of men changing out of drab brown uniforms into uniform chinos and plaid shirts.

'Busy in Queens, Tom?'

'Madhouse – gets worse by the day.'

'This your boy? Guys, come on over here – we got a celebrity.'

Within seconds, Tim's shoulder was sore from congratulatory punches.

'Yer pa tells me ya done good, son, gold medal 'n' all, wow.'

'So what do sonny come lousy mean anyways?'

He was saved the embarrassment of explaining summa cum laude by a huge man with hams for hands.

'Yo, hoop-man. Six slam dunks in the final game, my man.'

What winded him totally was that these guys knew. They knew about every test, honours list and basketball tournament.

'Good boy ya got there, Tom. Respectful, ya know.'

'Takes after his ma.'

It was so typically Irish, Tim thought, the compliment for the son and the affection for his wife, deflected sideways. Sometimes he wished he'd been born Italian. Man, they were the Sumo wrestlers of familial affection. He remembered when his fellow students, Vito and Enrico, had come to the funeral and wrapped his startled father in huge hugs. Go on, he had thought, half angry, half envious. Give him the full frontal. He's Irish, he'll hate it. That was Ma's funeral. Ma, who had slipped away quietly in Bellevue Hospital while her husband and son had had a silent coffee together in the waiting room. The only damn break they'd taken in a thirty-six-hour vigil.

Pa had come upstate to his ordination. Afterwards they'd

sat together on a garden bench. The retired city bus driver sniffed the air suspiciously.

'What's the funny smell?'

'It's the fresh air, Pa.'

'Too damn fresh, if ya ask me.'

He cast a jaundiced eye over the neat rows of vegetables.

'So whaddya do when yer hungry? Come out here and dig up yer dinner?'

'Yes, Pa. And we got the salt, pepper and Tabasco planted right over there.'

He saw the old man's shoulders shake and realised he was laughing. For the first time, he felt a huge upswelling of love for the cranky old bastard and angled his face away to watch a blurry Brother Brendan hoeing, shin-deep in cabbages.

'Time I was goin'.'

'I'll walk with you to the bus stop.'

'Son, I've been findin' bus stops for forty years.'

'Pa.'

'What?

'It's getting cold, better button up. Here, let me,' he added, as his father's thick fingers struggled. Ma had performed this particular ritual every morning and evening as long as he could remember, as if she had been preparing a particularly cantankerous child for school.

'You okay for money? I gotta coupla dollars in—'

'Thanks, Pa, but we take a vow of poverty.'

'Yeah, you take it 'n' we keep it. Don't be stuck, okay?'

'Okay.'

He was walking alone from the gate along the path between the vegetable plots when Brother Brendan spoke from the cabbages.

'Me back's gone a bit stiff, Brother. Could I take yer arm far's the monastery?'

He made a crook of his elbow, feeling the wiry strength and warmth of the arm that latched through his, slowing his pace to accommodate the old man, who seemed to have damn-all wrong with his back.

'Big cabbages, Brother,' he said lamely.

'Aye, they're big, all right. Start out small enough, though, just a wee slip of a stem and a puley leaf or two. But ye put them in the ground and ye water them every day and ye do your damnedest to keep the whorin' crawlies and weeds away from them. The one thing ye can't do is stand over them too much – blocks the light, ye know. The little buggers need a bit of space and light. Then, they grow like friggers.'

All Tim could think of was the angelic expression on Francis of Assisi's face in the monastery pictures as he communed with nature. He tried to align it with the salty language of the old Franciscan friar beside him, and began to laugh. He laughed till it hurt, till the tears ran down his face. Brendan chuckled along with him, occasionally tugging his elbow good-naturedly. Tim Conway knew then how much he missed his father and why he loved the Franciscans.

Werner was still droning through his own personal Doomsday List. Luckily, Tim managed to come back to full consciousness just before the end of it.

'… and der roof she is falling in. De brudders use too much vater for the vashing, alvays vashing. And ve haf liddle money. No American pilgrims come much. Mebbe dey are afraid of de rockets and de bombs. Dey should be afraid dat dey go to Hell.'

God, but Tim Conway found it hard to love Werner. He

wanted to say, 'The Church of the Holy Sepulchre is a holy wreck. It's a collection of architectural afterthoughts, for God's sake, razed and redesigned so many times over fifteen hundred-odd years that it doesn't know its apse from its elbow. Maybe we shouldn't squeeze the pilgrims for dollars to fix the roof. Maybe we should let the whole caboodle collapse around our ears and if Christians want it back they'll put it back. As for the community having the temerity to shower twice a day, it sure beats the hell out of standing upwind of one another or burning more incense to mask the odour of sanctity. And, by the by, if Todd and Tammy from Tuscaloosa are reluctant to catch a rocket or car bomb to Paradise and would rather vacation with Aunt Mamie in Sarasota, well, hey, as the kids say, like, hello.' Instead, he concentrated on bringing his shoulders down from around his ears and retracting his chin.

'Brother Werner', he began calmly. 'I realise that your job as Quaestor is not an easy one. Collecting money for the Church of the Holy Sepulchre is a difficult and unrewardi—'

'Nix on that,' the sassy kid from the Bronx who still chafed inside Tim Conway interrupted. 'Word on the street is that old Werner here is on the take.'

With a supreme effort, Father Guardian silenced his street-wise alter ego.

'It is always difficult to ask for money, Brother Werner.'

'My ass.' The kid was back and on a roll. 'Sheesh, Werner is to donations what the medieval Dominican Tetzel was to indulgences. Roll up, roll up. As soon as the coin in the box rings, the soul from out of Purgatory springs. Heck, if Werner had been on Tetzel's beat, Martin Luther would have studded the damn door at Wittenberg.'

'Brother Werner,' the Guardian said desperately, 'with

regard to the condition of the church, perhaps we should trust in Divine Providence. And, yes, I will urge the community to reflect on whether or not we are being profligate in answering our own needs and neglectful of holy poverty. As for the fall-off in donations, we must pray for the success of the peace talks.'

He was straining to keep his face expressionless while ignoring the raucous internal voice that yelled, 'Awesome, Timmy baby. Man, can you talk the talk. Goes ta show what a few years in Rome can do to a Bronx boy.'

'Bah,' Werner growled, and turned on his heel.

'Oh, Brother Werner …'

'Vat?'

'Thank you for bringing me your concerns. You may go now.'

Whosoever yanketh the chain bringeth the bulldog closer, he thought, with unChristian relish, as the door slammed and Werner's sandals slapped a fast retreat.

With the ease of long practice, Tim Conway hooked his big toe under the handle of the filing cabinet beneath his desk. His eyes trawled the tabs and stopped on the last one. It was flagged 'Prayer: answer to'. Behind the file, the bottles winked sympathetically. Irish or Scotch?, he pondered. In deference to his vow of holy poverty, he reached for the Scotch.

'Father Guardian?'

Tim Conway turned his reaching beneath the desk into a sweeping gesture of welcome.

'Ah, Brother Juniper, come in, come in.'

The gangly American friar plodded in his open sandals to the chair recently vacated by Werner. Tim Conway took in the long head of unruly red hair, dimpled with a brown skull-cap,

and the six-foot-something collection of angles that consti-
tuted Brother Juniper, the latest addition to the community.
Booting up his memory, he scrolled mentally through his file.
How come a graduate of MIT, an engineer, with a side-order
master's in the history of the Crusades, winds up in the
Franciscans? he wondered. And how come this genius starts at
the bottom and goes down? Six appointments in the last ten
years did not betoken a healthy career trajectory. Sure enough,
his memory provided the euphemistic comments of Juniper's
former superiors. Phrases like 'needs new challenges' and 'a
ministry more appropriate to his undoubted talents' had led
Tim Conway to one clear conclusion. Brother Juniper, in the
eyes of a lengthening list of former superiors, was a pain in the
ecclesiastical butt.

First, Werner the dodgy accountant and now Juniper, the
nomad engineer. God hates me, he thought. He was not
looking forward to this interview with anything approaching
relish.

Damascus Street, Jerusalem
Moshe Baruch owned the fruit and vegetable stall on
Damascus Street – or maybe not, he thought, as he reflected
on the most recent statement of accounts from the bank. He
turned again to the ledger with its accusing columns of figures
and sighed. 'Even the great Blondin couldn't balance this
book,' he said aloud.

He did that more often these days – and had done ever
since Sara had died. Leaning back in his chair, he glanced
through the gap in the beaded curtain. Haran, the Arab boy,
was busying himself buffing apples with his shirtsleeve. Right

idea, wrong implement, Moshe thought. And maybe that was an apt enough description of Haran. It had been wrong from the beginning. Rabbi Eliezer had insisted it would make a difference.

'He's sitting in a tent all day every day, Moshe. No school, no job, nothing but the violent influence of older youths and men. He's an orphan cared for by his aunt.'

The rabbi could have played strings with the Philharmonic. Reluctantly, Moshe had taken the boy. Haran was just sixteen, but his face reflected burdens beyond his years. He was coiled, tight as a spring, for the first few weeks, seeing kindness as patronage, the simplest and most innocent of questions as a form of interrogation. Now he was picking up words and phrases in Hebrew and polishing the apples. And now he'd have to go because Moshe couldn't magic the bottom line to any other colour except red. Moshe had even gone to the Wall, walking across the plaza with his head covered to ask God for a small miracle. Even there, in the fifty-eight-foot-high shadow of the wall Herod had built to buttress his temple, he was distracted. His thoughts ranged to the Six Day War in 1967 when the Jews had liberated the Wall from Jordan. Six days to throw back their enemies … Short enough to impress the world, long enough to lose a son. He wrenched his mind back to the problem of his finances, praying that God might have an accountant in Heaven who could advise him. There must be at least one, he hoped.

He sighed and tilted himself back to view the stall. Mrs Ben Haim was peering at his produce with a critical eye. He knew she wouldn't look at Haran, or speak Hebrew to him. An ultra-Orthodox lady like Mrs Ben Haim would use Hebrew only for prayer. He watched her point at the items she wanted, then wait to have them bagged, weighed and deposited on the counter before she reached to put her purchases into her basket. She counted the money carefully and left it by the till. No looks, no words, no contact: the dialogue of the mutually invisible. He shivered. Ritual humiliation. He groaned. The oppressed practise the language of oppression.

'Mr Moshe, coffee?'

'No – yes. Bring two cups, Haran, please.'

Sometimes, he wished he had gone to America with his brothers. But he had lived in Jerusalem all his life and would die there. Careful, Moshe, he admonished himself. From your lips to the ears of God.

Church of the Holy Sepulchre, Jerusalem

'Why Juniper?'

'Why what?'

'Suddenly you're Jewish. Why the name, for God's sake?'

'The dean of studies found me … distracting. I asked a lot of questions.'

'Nobody ever said a Franciscan had to check in his brain when he signed on.'

'In theory, that's true. In practice, it's a crock. With due respect, Father Guardian.'

'Mine named me Felix, same reason, same crock. I'm Tim, by the way.'

'Bob.'

'Why don't I give you the tour, Bob?'

'Why not?'

'Better fasten your prejudices, Brother. When it comes to tours, I take after my old man.'

Damascus Street, Jerusalem

'And that's how it is. I'm sorry, Haran. I can give you one more week.'

'I–I am understanding, Mr Moshe. Thanking you for ...'

He reached for the correct word but it eluded him.

'Perhaps if things get better we can ...'

'*Inshallah*,' the boy said.

'Yes, God willing.'

The Church of the Holy Sepulchre, Jerusalem

They stood together outside the door of the Holy Sepulchre. 'Abandon hope, all ye who enter here,' Tim intoned softly, not wishing to give offence to the stream of pilgrims that parted around the two friars standing in the forecourt.

'Dante could have written that to idealistic pilgrims,' he went on. 'This is supposedly the holiest shrine in Christendom. Allegedly it contains the site of the Crucifixion and the tomb of Jesus. The guidebooks say it's shared by six different Christian sects. The word 'shared' is just bullshit. In fact, over the centuries, we've squabbled over the Holy Places like kids over a bag of candies, each wanting the whole hog and settling for a sulky compromise. Constantine, the first Christian emperor of the Roman Empire, wanted a church here more beautiful than any other. Tucked away inside is where, according to legend, his mother Helena conveniently found the three crosses from Calvary and a bunch of nails. If all the pieces of the true Cross in all the shrines in the world were brought together, Jesus would have been crucified on the Amazonian rainforest.' Stay with the programme, Tim, he rebuked himself. 'The seventh century rolls around and the Persians knock it all down. It gets up again. In the eleventh century, Hakim, the lunatic Caliph of Egypt, knocks it down again. It takes a standing count of maybe eight hundred years and then your boys arrive.'

'What? Oh, yes, the Crusaders.' Bob took up the story. 'About the middle of the twelfth century, the Crusaders raised pretty much what we're looking at now, give or take a few earthquakes and alterations. Then, in the eighteen hundreds, the Greek Orthodox Church came to prominence and wanted to rub out any traces of the Roman Catholic Church, so the cenotaphs of the two most famous Crusaders, Godfrey of Bouillon and his brother Baldwin the First, were vanished.'

'Were vanished, Bob?'

'Yeah, someone stole 'em.'

The Wall, Bethlehem

Haran had once travelled on a Jerusalem bus with Mr Moshe. They'd been going to a warehouse to inspect a fruit shipment from Haifa. He was mesmerised by the sights of the city sliding past the bus window. There were two schoolgirls sitting opposite, their legs tucked up under them on the seat.

'Mr Moshe, why sit so?'

'Oh, well … Eh, you see, there was a bomb on a bus,' Mr Moshe whispered nervously. 'And the children … lost their legs.'

Haran did not look out of the window after that. He kept his eyes fixed firmly on the front of the bus and his feet planted firmly on the floor to still their trembling.

There would be no bomb on this bus that was taking him to Bethlehem. It was packed tight with people like himself and wheezed like an old donkey every yard of the six-kilometre journey to the Wall. At the Wall, he was searched by a bored soldier wearing glasses like mirrors. He saw two reflections of himself stretched into an X shape, then kept his face expressionless as the rough hands patted around his body, even his private places.

He recognised the man at the street corner and sensed he was waiting for him. He felt afraid and his legs went weak. From the corners of widening eyes, he saw other men fan out on either side so that he and the man could speak privately.

'*As-salamu 'Alaykum*,' the man said. He had a voice made whispery by cigarettes.

'*Wa 'Alaykum as-salaam*,' he responded politely.

'Come, little brother,' the man said, flicking his cigarette to arc and fall like a star. 'Let me show you our divided kingdom.'

Church of the Holy Sepulchre, Jerusalem
'A kingdom divided,' Tim whispered, as they tiptoed around Armenian priests in their all-enveloping cowls and habits and flattened themselves against a partition to allow a Greek Orthodox procession to swing noisily by. Armenians, Syrians, Greek Orthodox, Copts, Abyssinians and, of course, ourselves, he thought. All competing for a share of the action, all hating each other for the love of God. They were standing in the spare Franciscan chapel, which rested on a cleft of hewn rock – allegedly the site of the Crucifixion of Jesus.

'This is where Jesus was crucified, Tim. Probably the only thing all Christians are agreed on, and we split it in two.'

The other half of the small room was a riot of hanging lamps, spiralling candlesticks and icons drowning in gold. Two women, tears streaming down their faces, bent to kiss the niche in the rock where the Cross was believed to have stood. They crossed themselves and left, still weeping.

'A house divided, Bob?'

'Yeah, a house divided cannot stand,' Bob responded sadly, completing the quote from the New Testament, adding, 'As true here and now as it was at Babel.'

The Wall, Bethlehem

Haran let his eye travel along the pointing finger. 'That side of Bethlehem,' the man said, 'is Christian. This side is Muslim.' He waved his arm in an expansive gesture. 'We claim half a small island in a Jewish ocean. Do you understand, little brother?'

'Yes.'

The man pointed at the Wall that coiled around them like a snake.

'You know the door?' Haran nodded. 'Only Jews have a key,' the man said, in his smoky voice. 'Jobs are out there, markets are out there. Sometimes they open the door. Sometimes they don't. They decide.'

He came closer to Haran and dropped his voice so that the boy had to strain to hear. 'Half of our people do not work. Every day less of our fruit and vegetables go to market. The Christians go to America. Where do we go, little brother? To Jordan, Egypt, Saudi Arabia?'

He spat on the ground at his feet and ground his spittle into the dust with his foot. 'Our Arab brethren are with us in spirit, little brother. What is spirit? Can you eat it? Can you drive it to market? Is it medicine for a sick child?' With a flick of his wrist he sparked a small flame from a metal lighter and brought it to the tip of a cigarette. He sucked the smoke greedily into his lungs. The cigarette flared white-hot, uplighting the angry mask of his face. He blew a long stream of smoke.

'If we have nowhere to go, then we must make a stand,' he said.

Mount of Olives, Jerusalem
They were trudging up the Mount of Olives.

'More of a hill, really,' Tim panted, 'or it would be more like a hill if I was twenty years younger.'

In the fading light, long finger-shadows elongated east from the headstones that bristled on either side of the path.

'Divisions even in death,' Tim croaked. 'The Jews get ring-side seats overlooking Jerusalem for the coming of the Angel or the Messiah, whichever turns up first. The Muslims look east, all the way to Mecca, and the Christians look only as far as Jerusalem for the Second Coming. The dead are buried by the living, brother, useful propaganda right to the end.'

Bethlehem
They were wading through a narrow street thronged with young men who were cupping cigarettes against the wind to make them last or arguing over coffee at small tables. Where the man walked, the crowd parted, eyes averted. Haran heard a flapping sound, such as startled birds make when a boy looses a slingshot. He saw row after row of posters rattling in the wind against the wall that held them. The sight and sound reminded him of stories about restless *jinnee*, the desert spirits that lure a man to madness so that he circles and dies in the sand. He shivered inside his thin shirt and

tried to look away. But he couldn't tear his eyes away from the portraits of young men with Kalashnikovs or pistols, or bulked out with padded jackets, bigger than the ones the soldiers wore.

'Martyrs,' the man whispered reverently, 'heroes who brought terror to the infidel. They live now in Paradise with Allah and in our memories.'

Convent Church of St Mary Magdalene, Mount of Olives
The two Franciscans stood before a massive metal gate. The building, jigsawed by the bars, took away the little breath Bob had had in reserve after their climb. 'Yeah,' Tim said, as if he'd read his mind, 'it's what they call a temporal anomaly. Ya know, like finding a Nike sports shoe in a tar-pit full of mammoths. Jerusalem is where the eccentricities of the religious world come to die and the Convent Church of St Mary Magdalene is right up there with the wackiest of them.'

Bob thought the six onion domes of the Russian building could have held their own with anything in Red Square. A small figure, luminous in white, materialised at the gate. 'Ah, Father Guardian,' she smiled, 'welcome.'

Bethlehem
They waited in the filth and stink outside a broken-backed tent until the flap was drawn aside. Inside, the charcoal brazier lit the face of the old man as he sank slowly to sit cross-legged on the plastic groundsheet. The man bent and kissed him on both cheeks.

'Haran would hear your story, Father,' he said, sitting on the earthen floor and beckoning the boy to join him.

The Convent Church of St Mary Magdalene, Mount of Olives.

She must be a hundred years old, Bob thought, when the nun was helped into the drawing room. Under the white wimple, her face was as creased as a navigator's map but her eyes were clear and alert. They focused on Tim Conway and softened. 'You honour us with your visit, Father Guardian,' she said, her voice freighted with years and with the bass tones of her mother country.

'You honour us, as always, with your welcome, Mother Natasha,' Tim answered softly, leaning to touch her hand.

Bob was surprised to see the obvious affection between the wiseass Guardian and the elderly nun.

Tim made the introductions and added, 'I'm sure Brother Juniper would like to hear you speak on the Crusades, Mother. I know it's a pet subject of yours and he has more than a passing interest.'

'Ah,' she said, shaking her head dismissively, 'Godfrey and Baldwin and all the other so-called heroes …'

'Now, Mother, you mustn't tax yourself.'

The nun – who had entered unnoticed – was in her mid-forties, Bob conjectured, but the skin on her face was flawless, like porcelain. She was as tall as he and carried herself with cool authority, which was not lost on the young novice sister who bowed hastily in her direction.

'Good evening, Sister Raisa,' Tim said quietly, and made the introductions. Her handshake was limp and lifeless.

Mother Natasha was unabashed. 'At my age, dear sister,' she said spiritedly, 'breathing is taxing. Let us talk now. The grave will be silent.'

She turned her attention to Bob.

'The Crusaders were the sweepings of European prisons led by its bastard princes.'

The novice tittered nervously and blanched at a cold stare from Sister Raisa.

'Surely you are mistaken, dear Mother,' she said, in a voice of sheathed steel. 'Baldwin and his brother were the hand of God sent to smash the infidel and give us back the Holy Places.'

Mother Natasha glared briefly at her.

'And when they had slaughtered Muslims, Jews and Christians, they washed their hands of blood and changed their bloodstained tunics before going to weep at the Holy Places. They were godless,' she continued, 'and the blood they shed has salted the earth we stand on and made it fertile for martyrdom. Who knows better than we Russians what the godless are capable of? Did they not shoot our beloved Tsar, the Tsarina and their children?'

'This is all old history,' Sister Raisa snapped. 'We should—'

'We should what?' the old nun demanded. 'Forget? We who lived through such times do not so easily forget. What is forgotten comes again and again to haunt new generations. Can we forget how our dear Duchess Elizabeth was thrown alive into a mineshaft and had dynamite flung after her?'

She rose unsteadily to her feet and walked to a wall crowded with sepia portraits. 'These are our martyrs,' she said wistfully. 'Even in the harshest times, there were true Christians who brought out our icons and the bodies of our martyrs for veneration. Elizabeth, our dear friend and patron, rests here with us because someone did not forget. Someone risked the Bolsheviks and Siberia and brought her body to Peking and from there to Jerusalem.'

'You are living in the past, Mother,' Sister Raisa said dismissively. 'Today our Church has freedoms like never before.'

'Oh, yes, the Patriarch drinks tea in the Kremlin and Putin takes communion in St Basil's,' Mother Natasha shot back. 'We Russians have learned to play politics, which was always what the Bolsheviks wanted. We barter the Gospels for power. Engels laughs and angels weep.'

Bob, who had followed her to the portrait wall, sensed her deep sadness and attempted to distract her.

'Mother,' he said quietly, 'I would appreciate your help. While I was researching the Crusaders in the Vatican Museum, I had access briefly to the secret archives. I found a reference that puzzled me. Did you ever hear of the Lacrimae Dei? I beg your pardon,' he added quickly, realising from her blank expression that Latin could have played no part in her education. 'In English, it could be translated as the Tears of God.'

Mother Natasha's face seemed to sag and she stumbled slightly. Quickly, he eased his hand under her elbow. Turning uncertainly to the others, he glimpsed the naked fury that flashed across Sister Raisa's face. It was gone just as quickly and her face resumed its smooth inscrutable sheen. For a moment, the room was charged with tension. Then Mother Natasha broke the spell.

'My friends,' she said, 'old bones will no longer be denied their rest. Perhaps the young brother will lend me his strong arm.'

She tugged the surprised Bob towards the door.

'Please, take tea,' she said, over her shoulder, 'and come again, dear Father Guardian. Remember you are *drougoi*, a friend.'

The dark corridor outside was patterned at intervals with pools of light from tasselled lamps. 'I'm sorry, Mother,' Bob began, but she squeezed his arm to silence him.

'My son,' she said quietly, 'whatever you found, you must lose again. Some things are best left lost. And you must not speak of su—'

'I really don't s—'

'Please,' she whispered fiercely, 'I beg of you.'

He felt her shaking and patted her hand awkwardly. 'Have no fear, Mother,' he reassured her.

She turned to look into his face. 'Fear has kept us alive,' she murmured. 'Too much blood, too many martyrs.' He watched her white ghostly shape fade into the gloom.

Bethlehem

A worm of fear coiled in Haran's stomach as the old man began to speak. 'I was a tailor,' he said simply. 'I had a stall in Jerusalem and people came, Jews, Christians and Muslims, to me before the soldiers and the Wall. Then everything changed. My sons asked why we could no longer work in Jerusalem. I had no answer. I asked our imam but he just shook his head.'

He sighed deeply as if the effort at speech exhausted him, then gathered himself to speak further.

'I had three sons,' he quavered. 'They tell me they are martyrs in Paradise with Allah. They say it is better to be dead than to live like this.' He waved a feeble hand at the squalor of the tent.

He turned tear-filled eyes in Haran's direction and was about to speak further when the man interrupted. 'Thank you, Father,' he said hastily, 'your sons will not be forgotten. Come, boy,' he added brusquely.

Outside the tent, Haran breathed in the smoke-laced air.

He looked at the darkening mound of Bethlehem and the long, deep wall.

'You have nowhere to go, little brother,' the man whispered. 'Will you stand?'

The Garden of Gethsemane, Jerusalem
'Father Guardian, I—'

'We're still on tour, Bob.'

'Sorry. Tim, I feel I should apologise …'

Tim raised a hand to silence him. They were walking through the Garden of Gethsemane, through the olive trees and the false dawn that was the lights of Jerusalem. 'Bob, listen up. Maybe I made a mistake, bringing you to the Mary Magdalene. Look, I'm sorry if you were embarrassed. Not your fault. Let's sit down for a minute.'

They sat on the ground in the lavender-scented garden. Beside them, Bob saw an old olive tree that twisted the darkness into such a grotesque shape that he thought it might have earned the garden its other name: the Garden of Agony. He was chiding himself for being fanciful when his companion continued softly:

'Some of these olive trees are old enough to have been there. Ya follow me?'

He nodded.

'One of our brothers makes rosaries from the dried olive stones. Peddles them to the tourists. Nothing so sacred here that it can't turn a buck. In Jerusalem, God and Mammon have arrived at a relationship that is to their mutual advantage. The money-changers are back in the temple, Bob, with all rights restored because the temple needs them. You saw what goes down in the Church of the Holy Sepulchre. I try not to call it our church for obvious reasons. We, and I mean we Christians of whatever stripe, divvied it up six ways and now we argue over who sings what, when and how loud. The Franciscans get a carpenter to fix a chair today, the Copts get a carpenter to fix the same chair tomorrow. The place is bristling with more 'Walk, Don't Walk' signs than an intersection on Fifth Avenue.' He sighed and shook his head. 'Only Gehenna's got an 'Access All Areas' badge.'

'Gehenna?'

'Gehenna's the Franciscan cat, Bob. You'll meet him when he decides to grant you an audience. According to Brother Solomon, who's been here since before his royal namesake, he was named for the ancient garbage tip outside the city walls. Grim place, by all accounts. Way back, it's where the pagan followers of Baal burned babies in sacrifice. Later, the Jews burned their garbage and the bodies of bandits and heretics. Gehenna became the template for the Christian Hell – bodies burning so that the souls could never enter Heaven without them, eternal damnation. And just to be sure the fire did the job, they added brimstone. Which has absolutely nothing to do with the Franciscan cat. He's called Gehenna because he's one helluva cat.' He chuckled at his own pun.

'The Mary Magdalene, Tim. What has …?'

'Sorry. I was coming to that, but I was taking the Irish scenic route, as usual. I wanted you to meet Mother Natasha. You know she remembers Rasputin? Sorry, Bob, that's a story for another time. Natasha's a kind of icon around here. She's old enough and weird enough and so far removed from the political power-plays that go down between the different Christian sects that she's acceptable to all of them. You could say she runs a kinda Russian salon for the religious movers and shakers in Jerusalem. Her parlour is a DMZ, a demilitarised zone where the Father Guardian of the Franciscans can sip strong Russian tea with the Greek Orthodox Patriarch or the Syrian hoojah or whomever. I'm sort of in cahoots with the old bird. She volunteered me for a mission. Our mission, according to Natasha, is to convert the Christian leaders of Jerusalem to Christianity, to put an end to the scandal we are now.'

'How's it going?'

'I drink a lot of tea, Bob.'

He got up slowly and brushed down his habit.

'Come on, it's getting chilly here.'

They entered Jerusalem by the Damascus Gate and Father Guardian led his confrere through a labyrinth of lanes.

'Isn't this the, eh, Muslim Quarter, Tim?' Bob whispered nervously, as a curtain twitched and steadied in a nearby window.

'Yeah, not to worry,' Father Guardian said cheerily. 'The Ottomans kicked all the Christian religious orders out of Jerusalem except the Franciscans. They thought we were harmless. That brown bib you're wearing grants a certain kind of diplomatic immunity around here.'

❧❧❧

'*As-salamu 'Alaykum*, Muhammad.'

'*Wa 'Alaykum as-salaam*, Father Guardian'.

The proprietor of the coffee shop chivvied them to a corner table near the stove and hurried away to the kitchen.

'What gives with Sister Raisa, Tim?'

'Thank you, Muhammad, *shokran*.' He waited until the man had placed their coffees before them and bowed himself out of earshot.

'Oh, Raisa's a piece of work, all right, an enigma wrapped in a mystery, et cetera, et cetera. Natasha is White Russian, old Church, Tsarist to the bone. She represents the Church that went underground or to the gulag. For her, the Convent Church of St Mary Magdalene is the Russian Orthodox Church in exile, waiting for the restoration.'

'But surely Sister Raisa's right? The Russian Orthodox Church is top of the heap again, ever since perestroika and glasnost and all that?'

'All that, as you so succinctly put it, cuts no ice with Natasha, as you've gathered. You may also have gathered that Raisa waltzes to a different dance tune. Wouldn't surprise me if she's KGB.'

'Did you say KGB?'

'Yeah, or whatever passes for it these days. This is Jerusalem, Bob. This is the new Balkans. The superpowers like to keep their grubby fingers on the pulse here. Speaking of intrigue, what's with this Tears of God malarkey?'

Bob took a long draught of coffee to ready himself.

'As I said to Mother Natasha, I came across a reference in the Vatican Library to 'Lacrimae Dei', the Tears of God. It was in Godfrey of Bouillon's correspondence with the Pope, but it was all nod-nod wink-wink stuff.'

'If I recall correctly, dear brother, you said it was in the secret archives. So, how did you get in there?'

'I was fixing something. I'm an engineer, remember?'

'Yeah, plumbers in the Watergate and Franciscans in the Vatican. Do me a favour.'

Bob held up a cautionary hand.

'Tim, we had a professor in MIT who had the yea or nay over all sorts of permissions. First day I asked him for permission to do something, he said, "Bob, if ya gotta ask, I gotta answer." Okay?'

'Okay, okay. Just don't go all da Vinci on me.'

'It's a deal. This reference really bugs me. I mean, is it some kind of relic or what?'

'Yeah, like Jerusalem really needs a new relic. Anyway, it seems to me that Raisa was none too pleased to hear it mentioned.'

'You saw that too?'

Bob recounted Mother Natasha's conversation in the corridor.

Tim replaced his coffee cup in the saucer.

'You really want to follow this one?'

'Yes, I don't suppose you have much use for an engineer right now.'

'Anything else you can tell me about this manuscript reference?'

'No. Well, maybe it's not important. You know how the monks who copied manuscripts sometimes liked to add gossip or comments in the margins?'

'Yeah, I remember reading about that kind of monastic graffiti. It ranged all the way from "Maranatha, Come Lord" to "Brother Anselm was sober today".'

They both laughed and Muhammad reappeared with the coffee pot.

'So what was in the margin?' Tim asked, draining his cup and raising his finger for the bill.

'Just one word: '*cave*'.'

'*Cave*'? As in the '*cave canem*' inscription on the tile in Pompeii?'

'Yep. It means beware.'

'It surely does,' Tim Conway mused. Eventually, he looked up and said, 'As my old man always said, if you gotta itch, you gotta scratch, okay?'

He pushed some money under the saucer and rose to go.

'Just one thing, Bob,' he said seriously. 'Mother Natasha doesn't spook easily, so, *cave*, okay?

'Okay.'

The Wall, Bethlehem

The boy had repeated the instructions in his head as a mantra to lessen his fear of suffocation. The boot of the car he was hidden in was totally dark and smelled of kerosene and rubber.

'A brother will open the trunk and release you in Jerusalem. Do not look at his face. Go to the corner of Rivlin and Ben Shatakh streets. Do not stand still – they will notice and question you. A woman will come with a covered shopping basket. Offer to carry it for her. She will leave you near Damascus Street. Go to the stall of Moshe Baruch. Place the basket inside the back door. Lock it behind you. It will be collected later and taken somewhere else.'

He had tried to hold his breath and silence his thudding heart when the car stopped at the gates. The soldier's step rang loudly on the concrete for a few moments and then, to his surprise, the car rolled forward again. It had all happened as the man had said it would. Now he placed the covered basket inside the back door of the stall and locked the door behind him. Then he stood totally still. How will they open the locked door? he wondered. He frowned and the world flashed white.

෨෬

Tim Conway dreamed he was riding in the bus with his father. The old man was giving a tour of the afterlife.

'Heaven, all the guys over there in the fancy wings. Yeah, the ones playin' chess and doin' the crossword. All Jesuits. Purgatory. Full of Franciscans, who never made the cut.

Hell, your stop, son.'

He woke suddenly, thinking a noise had disturbed his sleep, then he turned over.

෨෬

Brother Juniper dreamed of an old nun crying tears of blood. He woke, went back to sleep and she was there again.

෨෬

The man lit another cigarette and drew on it. He checked his watch, following the second hand as it raced the minute hand to twelve. It was a dead heat. He'd put a new poster in the gallery of martyrs tomorrow. He stubbed out the cigarette in the overflowing ashtray and slept. He dreamed of walking alone by the martyrs' posters, aware that their eyes followed his progress until he came to Haran's. The boy stared at him accusingly. He moved on and became aware of yet another poster neatly tacked to the wall. It was blank. As he looked, a face began to form, as if someone was surfacing from a great depth. As the features focused, he began to scream.

෨෬

Moshe Baruch thought the pounding was coming from inside his head. Dreamily, he regretted the bottle of wine he had taken, instead of the sleeping tablet, and the two trips he had already made to the bathroom during the night. The pounding continued until he flapped and shuffled into bathrobe and slippers and unlocked his front door.

'What's the—'

'Moshe Baruch?'

'Yes.'

'You are the proprietor of the fruit and vegetable stall in Damascus Street?'

'Yes I am, but …'

'Come with us, please.'

He was frogmarched to a jeep where the soldiers who held his arms bent his head considerately and shoved him into the back seat. The jeep shot forward and rocketed up the straight street built by Emperor Hadrian. In the pre-dawn light, he could pick out the stump of a pillar and the dull ochre patches of Roman brick on arches and gables. In this way, he insulated his mind against reality. His sense of smell alerted him to it though, even before he saw the washes of yellow light from the emergency vehicles, the slow-shuffling forensics people in their wraith-like overalls and the devastation that had been his stall. The soldiers sitting on either side of him jumped out of the jeep, leaving him feeling vulnerable. Presently, a stocky man dressed in sweater and jeans eased into the seat beside him. 'Mr Baruch,' he asked, 'is this your stall?'

'Was my stall,' Moshe responded flatly. 'What happened?'

The man affected not to hear him. He leaned to study something happening outside the window and Moshe caught a glimpse of a holster as the sweater rode up. Mossad, he thought. Secret police.

'There was an explosion here about thirty minutes ago, Mr Baruch,' the man said. 'What time did you close for business yesterday?'

'About five. Business was very slack. There was no—'

'Did you close the premises yourself?'

'Yes … no. The boy was sweeping and—'

'The boy?'

'Haran, he …'

'An Arab?'

'Yes.'

The Mossad agent tapped the driver's shoulder. 'Morgue,' he said.

Moshe's heart sank as they squealed away from the scene.

❧❧

'Is this the boy Haran who worked for you?'

The agent had folded the sheet down just far enough to expose the face. Moshe thought his heart would stop. He forced himself to look at the bloodied face and sightless eyes, locked wide in death as if surprised. Wisps of coiled hair clung to the blackened scalp. It was Haran. Instinctively, his eyes tracked down over the boy's slight form, outlined by the white sheet, and dropped to the top of the gurney where the sheet levelled. This is just half of him, his mind registered, and he swayed.

In the small, cluttered office, he gripped the plastic coffee cup in both hands.

'He lived in Bethlehem,' he said in a whisper. 'Rabbi Eliezer arranged …'

The agent looked up from the form he was filling in with quick strokes of a blue ballpoint pen.

'We know all that,' he said, in that terrible emotionless voice.

'What will happen now?' Moshe quavered, his breath eddying the steam from the coffee.

'It's being taken care of. Just a few more questions, sir.'

The Jewish Quarter, Jerusalem

Avram savoured his coffee, making it last. Over the rim of the glass, his eyes roved, reading the street. A group of Japanese tourists trotted by, bowed under the burden of expensive Nikons. He wondered idly why they would suffer the constriction of economy class, the plastic meals and the risk of deep vein thrombosis to see the world through a viewfinder. Why couldn't they just curl up on a futon and view the glories of Jerusalem on the flat-screen at home? The tour guide held a thin pole topped with a fluttering pennant. When she jerked it, her charges wheeled and tacked like a school of fish, forming an orderly conga or an attentive circle. He knew her. Her name was Leah, cabin crew on El Al until she had been tempted to reduce excess baggage by stashing little bottles in her flight bag. He thought it would have been a misdemeanour anywhere outside Israel. Tough break. The pole twitched again and the shuffling line moved on to reveal Mahmoud, the blind beggar, sitting cross-legged on the pavement, palm extended. Avram waited until the thin, vacant face rotated in his direction and one of the blind man's perfectly sighted eyes winked. Good. Mahmoud was a fake but he was Avram's fake, subsidised to scan for the unusual with the innocence only a blind man can muster. Finally, Avram focused on his apartment building, four storeys teetering precariously one atop another, yellow-washed plaster scabbing on the walls. He thought it gave shabby a bad name.

The coins spiralled on the table top before gravity brought them rattling down. The detective was already stepping briskly across the street in the shadow of an old Palestinian lady, one of the few who still wore tribal tattoos on her sun-pruned face. At the pavement, he bent to untie and retie his shoelace, taking an upside-down look at the coffee shop he had left, checking for signs of undue interest or a following stranger. Nothing. He straightened and stuck his key into the door.

☘☙

Goldberg threaded her way through the crowded Mahane Yehuda market, occasionally doubling back to recheck the produce of a stall she had just passed, prodding fruit and haggling over prices. She knew all the stall-holders and their helpers, and asked after grandparents and children as she smelled fish and counted money. Her banter was light-hearted, her mobile features showing amusement or concern as the situation demanded. If the merchants noticed that her eyes rarely engaged theirs but flitted constantly to left and right, they ascribed it to the fact that she was American and therefore eccentric. The last port of call was always the florist, a large, slow-moving woman whose Crusader-blue eyes and wavy sandy hair made her as exotic in Jerusalem as the orchid she was wrapping in cellophane. Goldberg placed her money near the till and left the orchid on the stall. It was worth it. A single orchid meant the house was safe.

☘☙

Avram mounted the stairs two at a time and paused on the first landing. The marital dissonance of Hannah and Jacob percolated through their apartment door. Satisfied, he climbed to the second floor. A brisk rap on the door brought the sound of shuffling slippers.

'Maimonides got it wrong,' the bearded old man said. 'The revealed word of God is not set in stone. Revelation does not end in the twelfth century but continues as long as Jews are alive.'

'Check Rabbi Joseph Albo in the fifteenth century,' Avram said, over his shoulder, as he craned his neck to check the stairwell. 'He says the law was full of contradictions and discrepancies, so how can the imperfect be unchangeable?'

The old man seemed to digest this for a moment.

'You are an apostate and a pain in the butt,' he said eventually. 'Oh, another book has come for you from South America.'

Avram smiled and nodded. He had started ordering from Amazon in the old man's name. It avoided a lot of controlled explosions. 'Collect it later,' he said.

Third floor. Fourteen-year-old Shimon lounged against the wall, feigning indifference. Avram took guilty comfort from the fact that Shimon had been cast out, yet again, to this one-boy diaspora by his frazzled mother. He resolved to give him a book next time. He hoped, their conversation would progress beyond the usual grunts and shrugs. He gave him a sympathetic smile and climbed on up.

Fourth floor. Home. He fished a credit card from his pocket and ran it between the door and the jamb. There was no resistance, apart from the lock and the deadbolt. The seals were intact. Avram stepped into the small hallway, folding his jacket.

'Detective Avram,' the young man said politely, 'please sit.' He indicated the deep armchair with his head. His eyes never wavered from the detective. Neither did the mouth of the silencer.

ജ്ഞ

Goldberg knocked three times, paused, and knocked again. She counted off ten seconds and turned the key. The woman confronting her in the hallway held the gun in the classic two-handed grip. She was six feet tall and broad enough to block Goldberg's view of the sitting room.

'Flower?' she said grimly.

'Orchid,' Goldberg answered.

'Okay,' Anna Lebowski said, and jammed the pistol into the elasticated waistband of her jeans.

Anna Lebowski was formidable, ex-army and a recovering alcoholic. Goldberg didn't analyse why the two states seemed to co-exist so often. She was happy that she had hired her. Lebowski's bass voice was modulated with a touch of tenderness when she turned to the young woman seated at the window.

'Miriam, come and kiss your sister.'

Miriam stood up slowly and Goldberg was amazed, as always, to look on the living image of herself. She kissed her twin, then held her at arms' length. 'Had a good day?' she asked.

'Yes,' Lebowski grunted, from the cupboard, as she hunted for her jacket.

'Nice lunch?'

'Some salad and fruit,' Lebowski supplied, 'water and a little coffee.'

Goldberg hated the enforced ventriloquism but Miriam

hadn't spoken since … She wrested her mind back to the present.

'Go anywhere interesting?'

'As far as the hallway.'

'That's progress.'

'Yeah, every day in every way, yadda-yadda,' Lebowski growled, not unkindly. She bent to kiss the silent sister on both cheeks before punching Goldberg affectionately on the upper arm.

'Gotta go,' she huffed. 'Meeting tonight.'

'Someone or others?' Goldberg asked mischievously.

'Others, worse luck.' Lebowski almost smiled and then she was gone.

Goldberg locked the door behind her and led her unresisting sister to a chair. She sat opposite and tried, as she always did, to find some spark of vitality in the vacant eyes.

⍟

Avram watched the man's eyes while his brain raced to register and process other details. About five ten, he thought, slender but wiry. Dangerous, even in repose. He noted the blue-black hair, cropped tightly, and the pallor of the fine features. Turkish or Egyptian, he thought. The cop section of his brain admired the man's choice of seating for the detective. The old armchair was soft enough to swallow someone, so sudden moves were not an option.

'Place your jacket at your feet,' the gunman said. 'Now take your gun from the shoulder holster between the thumb and forefinger of your left hand and place it on the jacket.'

Avram did as he was told and reached behind casually to

adjust a cushion. The man's eyes narrowed slightly and the silencer seemed to yawn. Slowly Avram sat upright, bringing his closed fists to rest on his knees. 'Tea or coffee?' he offered.

The man laughed but his eyes remained wary. 'Detective Avram, always the kidder.' He smiled. 'Now, is that a ploy to put me off-guard or a behavioural tic? Perhaps it's a psychological souvenir of a particular night in the Negev when Commander Avram of the paratroop regiment killed … I beg your pardon … when a prisoner died under interrogation. Yes? No? It doesn't matter. All of that is dead and buried in the past and only comes back in bad dreams. Isn't that so, Detective?'

'Could you just cut the shit and shoot?' Avram said mildly.

'Yes and yes,' the man replied equably, 'but not yet. I have some questions. It'll be a novel experience for you to answer questions, Detective.'

'Why would I answer? You're going to shoot me anyway.'

'Yes, I am, but it might make the difference between shooting you in the foot, knee, balls and stomach first, then in the head.'

Avram remained silent. The gunman leaned forward slightly, a new intensity in his eyes.

'Where will I find the Tears of God?' he asked.

Avram seemed to consider the question. 'Probably in some Christian shrine,' he offered, 'along with the foreskin of Jesus and the last gasp of St Joseph in a corked bottle.'

Fury rippled across the man's features. 'Wrong answer,' he said tightly, and the silencer lifted. Avram closed his eyes and opened his right fist.

☙❧

Goldberg rocked the heavy knife expertly along a carrot before using the blade to sweep the pile into a saucepan with all the ease of a Vegas croupier. At the stove, she scanned the line of Post-it notes Lebowski had stuck along the rim of the eye-level grill. Sometimes, the minder-cum-housekeeper had difficulty joining the dots, hence the notes. 'Miriam smiled today when I tripped over the carpet. Bitch!!!' 'Car backfired outside = 1 hour in closet.' 'I am sober now.' She fished in the cutlery drawer for a box of matches and, turning her eyes from the flare of the phosphorus, saw a note that had escaped the grill and now nestled behind a gas jet.

༺༻

Even protected by his closed eyelids, Avram saw the magnesium flash as a pink explosion. He was already capsizing the armchair, his ears registering two pops as the armchair took two direct hits. He rolled behind the heavy antique desk as another pop made the window explode into the street. The tiny flare, hidden in the cushions and activated when he had opened his fist, gave him ten seconds tops before the gunman got his vision back. He risked an eye around the corner of the desk but the room was empty. He calculated the distance between himself and his gun and figured it was approximately the distance to the moon. In the sudden silence, he worked on regulating his breathing, letting his ears trawl the apartment for telltale sounds. Nothing. The guy could be in the kitchen, bedroom or bathroom. He could be anywhere.

On all fours, he crabbed across the carpet to the refuge of the bookcase, rising to stand in its meagre protection. In slow motion, he slid flat-footed along it, careful not to brush against its haphazardly stored contents, and turned quickly into a tae kwon do crouch to check the space behind him. Some primitive instinct splayed his right hand before his face as the garrotte dropped over his head. Fuelled by the burning pain as the killing wire bit deeply into the heel of his hand he stamped his heel on the man's instep and swung his left elbow in a vicious arc, tumbling the assailant across the floor. Desperately, he lunged in pursuit, to be arrested by the sight of his own gun pointed at his chest.

'Good, but not good enough', the man wheezed. 'Rest in peace,' he added, and pulled the trigger.

There was a loud click followed by a thud and a second click as Avram's foot connected with the gunman's jaw and smashed his teeth together. Avram scooped the pistol from the floor and pressed it, none too gently, into the base of the dazed man's skull.

'Police regs,' he gasped. 'Always leave the first chamber empty. As you say, good, but not good enough.'

☙❧

Should she? Shouldn't she? Surely it was voyeuristic reading Lebowski's notes? In for a penny she decided and flipped the paper. 'Cooker fixed,' it read. The chill surged all the way from the soles of her feet and stilled her breathing. Instinctively, she stuck the burning match into her mouth and closed her lips. Her mother had hated that particular party trick, she remembered, and then she was grabbing her sister, slapping the locks open and hurtling through the front door. Miriam screamed.

৪০০৪

Avram checked the bindings and was pleased to see the man's hands had already turned a satisfying shade of purple. Cursorily, he checked the gag that pulled the face into a mad grimace. Good, he thought. He was holding one end of the bandage tightly in his teeth as he wrapped his sliced hand. He grinned around it when he thought of recounting this to Gol—

Savagely, he punched the buttons of the cellphone. 'Yes. Listen. Shut the fuck up and listen. Armed unit to Goldberg's place. Now. You got that? And send the collectors to my place … One … Alive? So far.'

He lifted the gun and placed the muzzle between two eyes that mocked him. Slowly, his finger turned to ivory on the trigger. With a huge effort, he wrenched himself away and stuck the weapon in his shoulder holster. 'Someone will come for you,' he growled, pulling on his jacket. 'Rest in peace,' he added, and was surprised by the fear that widened the eyes above the gag.

৪০০৪

It was the florist who waddled to the rescue, swinging her shawl over the girl's head and shoulders and clutching her to her ample bosom. Goldberg heard the whooping of sirens and helped bundle her sister under the florist's awning. Avram, she thought, and began to punch numbers into her cellphone.

৪০০৪

Avram entered the safe house a scant two minutes after Miriam and Goldberg had been served coffee by a paratrooper who balanced a tray in one hand and an Uzi in the other. Goldberg had gone to the kitchen for hot water to dilute the sludge in her cup. She stood inside the doorway and watched him drop to his knees before her stricken sister, wrapping her in his arms and crooning comforting noises into her hair.

'Avram, in here.'

He came slowly through the door, a dazed expression on his face.

'Goldberg?'

'The original of the species,' she quipped, stacking mugs on the draining board, setting them down firmly so they wouldn't rattle.

'And … ?'

'Twin sister. Five minutes younger. Does it show?'

She sensed him come up behind her and felt his palms burn through her shirt to her shoulders. Blurrily, she registered the rough bandage.

'Shaving your palms again?'

'Yep, full moon tonight,' he whispered, his breath making her ear itch.

'What did Santa bring you?

'Gun and garrotte. You?'

'Bomb,' she said, and threw up in the sink. His unbandaged palm moved to her forehead and stayed until she hitched a last dry heave and began to breathe through her mouth.

'I've made a mess of the dishes,' she said faintly.

'Paratroopers wash them that way all the time.'

He took a dishcloth, soaked it under the tap, then used it to wipe her face.

TEARS OF GOD

'I was frightened,' she whispered, raising her eyes to his for the first time.

'Snap,' he said.

'Detectives.'

Inspector Bernstein gestured at the kitchen chairs.

They sat either side of the table, their eyes fixed firmly on its surface. The inspector plucked a page from his pocket and sighed. 'Goldberg, bomb in the stove,' he said. 'No prints, no match with any previous, no records from the gas company. Your housekeeper, Lebowski?' Goldberg nodded. 'Installer showed ID that matched. Showed him into the kitchen. Left him for five minutes only, et cetera, et cetera. Very distraught but says to tell you she's very sorry and she's not drinking.' He raised an eyebrow quizzically and Goldberg gave him the ghost of a smile.

'About five ten with close-cropped brownish hair and a pale face,' Bernstein continued. 'Thought he might be—'

'Egyptian,' Avram stated flatly.

'Yes, or Turkish.'

'We can lean on my guy, Inspector. Maybe he c—'

'Avram.'

'What?'

'He's gone.'

'Gone?'

'Gag and binding neatly coiled. No gun or garrotte. Okay,' he exhaled, 'until we run those foxes to earth, you two are—'

'No,' they said simultaneously.

'Grounded,' he continued, as if they hadn't spoken. 'I have no intention of letting you out there as—'

'Stalking horses.'

'Tethered goats.'

He looked pleased to see a glimmer of their old sparkle. 'I was going to say targets.'

'Targets is what we are,' Avram said quietly.

'All day, every day,' Goldberg added.

Bernstein pinched the bridge of his nose. 'Your sister,' he said to Goldberg, 'we have a place in Haifa. Lebowski says she'll go with her.'

Goldberg pondered and nodded.

'Let's hear it, Avram,' Inspector Bernstein said.

'Five ten, brownish hair cut close. Pale features, guessed Egyptian. Trim and manicured. Accentless.' Avram spoke as if he was reading from an autocue set slightly to the right of Goldberg's head.

'Knew about the Negev incident and … dreams.'

Goldberg's head angled into his eyeline and he lifted his eyes out of range. 'Asked, "Where will I find the Tears of God?"'

'The Tears of God? Where did we hear that before?'

'Bertha,' Goldberg answered. 'She said the Mea Shearim and mosque victims had been asking about it at the digs and museums.'

Bernstein moved to a white message board mounted by the door. 'Let's join the dots,' he said, picking up a red marker pen.

'Expert one, big money, museums and digs, asks after Tears of God. No luck,' Avram said, as Bernstein wrote.

'Two, head tarred and feathered, lopped by Crusader sword and left in Mea Shearim,' Goldberg continued, 'ibid., ibid., all the way except for the millinery.'

Bernstein stared at her.

'Sorry, Inspector, I meant same deal all the way without the pitch-cap.'

'According to Bertha,' Bernstein murmured, while writing, 'we're looking for a rich Christian with a Crusader sword who will kill again. We don't know who the next victim will be but we've alerted the curators and archaeologists to notify us if someone comes asking about the Tears of God. Question: who is this millionaire Christian with a fetish for Crusader weapons of individual destruction?'

'And?' Goldberg offered.

'And?'

'And where will the next head appear?'

Bernstein crooked a finger, and the two detectives joined him at a tourist map of Jerusalem tacked to the wall beside the message board. 'Mea Shearim here,' he said, stabbing the map with a blunt forefinger.

'Mosque here,' Avram said, pointing to a box marked with a crescent.

'Church of the Holy Sepulchre?' Goldberg wondered, leaning between them.

'Possibly,' Bernstein granted. 'But it's not a Christian church. It's six Christian churches all rolled into one.' He rubbed the side of his nose, leaving a smudge of red ink on the bridge. 'Caleb's children have files on each of the superiors,' he said thoughtfully.

The detectives exchanged looks. Caleb was one of the spies Moses had sent ahead into the Promised Land. 'Caleb's children' was cop-speak for Mossad, the Israeli secret police.

'Will they share?' Avram asked.

Bernstein raised his hand palm upwards in a gesture that didn't need explaining.

'You two are on indefinite leave of absence. Understandable, under the circumstances. Find a place to stay. If you need anything, call me – only me. Understood?'

'Understood,' they chorused.

Police Headquarters, Jerusalem

Inspector Bernstein accepted the blindfold without protest. It wasn't personal, just Mossad. Setting up a meeting with its boss had involved brief telephone conversations with anonymous voices who asked lots of questions without the grace of greetings and hung up without farewells. Courtesy is the first casualty in time of war, he reminded himself.

'Peace, if it ever comes, will be an enormous shock to our collective psyche,' he had told Esther, his secretary. 'The first task of the new era will be to implement a nationwide crash course in small-talk and good manners.'

The message on his desk after lunch had been terse and typical: 'Basement, four p.m.'

How can a message be delivered to the heart of a so-called secure building? he wondered. He took it for granted that the CCTV tapes would be missing for the relevant period of time and that the three-monkeys rule would be de rigueur for the staff. It was all so Mossad: telegrammatic, to the point, and leaving just a faint scent of menace.

The inspector tensed slightly as two bodies sandwiched him in the back of the vehicle. Saloon car, he guessed, by the sound of the closing doors, probably with tinted windows. He relaxed and waited for the first left and right turns in the road so that he could sway innocently against his human bookends. The one on the right, he surmised, was about six two and running to fat. His weapon was in a loose shoulder holster. The other was lean and muscular, felt smaller than his partner. There was nothing for his ears to sift, apart from the engine noises and the muffled surround-sound of the city. When that tailed off, he knew they were outside Jerusalem. A change in the engine note suggested they were climbing. His nose checked the enclosed space and found nothing out of the ordinary. There was no distinctive tang of threat or fear, just the earthy smell of the big man and the faint scent of underarm deodorant from his partner. Bernstein leaned a little to his left, closed his eyes and slept.

The lack of motion woke him.

They led him firmly by the elbows across bare ground that crunched underfoot. He felt the cool touch of shadow on his face an instant before a large sweaty hand pushed his head forward. The smell was of compacted earth, and their footsteps were barely audible. He concluded they were in a tunnel.

When the blindfold was removed, he blinked a few times, adjusting his vision to the low, artificial glow of the circular room. He sensed a presence behind him but knew better than to turn around. She sat behind a gunmetal grey desk, her attention on a laptop computer. In the cold, unforgiving light, Bernstein registered the pinched features under the stubbled white hair. She had never had an ounce to spare but now she seemed even leaner, as if some tension tugged at her frame from within. He forced himself to relax. She prodded a key with a skeletal forefinger, and the light blinked out.

'Brother,' she said.

'Sister,' he replied.

'They tell me you run a tight ship,' she said.

He wondered if being underground stripped a human being of ... of whatever it was that kept them human. He sensed that whatever remained of his sister was trying to connect with him at some level, and her obvious effort hurt more than if she had ignored him.

'They tell me nothing about you.'

The corners of her mouth twitched briefly.

'Only as it should be.'

The conversation, which had stuttered briefly, died away.

'You asked to see me, Inspector?'

He felt impotent rage well inside him. He wanted to bang the bare table. He wanted to shake her frail shoulders and shout in her implacable face, 'They're dead, Elena. We should be weeping and kissing instead of sitting like strangers nibbling at the silence between us.' He did none of those things. Instead, he said calmly, 'Yes, Director. An assassination attempt was made on two of my detectives. It was a professional set-up, too sophisticated for the usual criminal elements or known terrorists.' He paused, and she read the unspoken question in his face.

'It wasn't us.'

'If it had been, would you tell me?'

'If it had been, you wouldn't be here. Is that all?'

'No. We think we have a serial killer, someone who wants to stir trouble between Christians, Jews and Muslims.'

Her lips twitched again.

'Someone needs to do that?'

'This someone has access to funds and top-class intelligence. He uses young men as assassins – Turks, maybe Egyptians. Leaves heads in strategic places. No one has that kind of … competence except Mossad. So, if not you, then who?'

'You're wasting my time, Inspector.' She leaned sideways to activate the computer.

'Don't turn your back on me, Elena.' At his use of her name she whirled to face him. 'We are the police, you are the secret service,' he pressed on. 'We are both in the service of our country. We should be working together.'

'We are at war, brother,' she said flintily. 'You,' she stabbed a forefinger in his direction, 'keep the traffic moving and deal with petty crime. You do not work with us except when we ask you to.'

They locked eyes across the table and Bernstein willed himself to relax. 'You haven't answered my question,' he said calmly.

'If we have information we think we should share with you, we will.'

'While you are pursuing that protocol, innocent people may die.'

'Fortunes of war, Inspector.'

'Is that what your husband and daughter were, Elena – fortunes of war?'

Micah, his brother-in-law, and Sonia, his niece, had stopped for coffee in the wrong place at the wrong time. His sister had buried what could be salvaged of them after the bomb. He watched her face tighten to a death-mask and braced himself for her rage. A single muscle spasmed in her cheek before she turned away to the computer.

'This interview is ended, Inspector,' she said.

'Thank you.'

'For what?'

'For answering my question.'

'I didn't.'

'Silence gives consent, Director.'

She studied him for what felt like a long time. 'You were always stubborn, brother,' she said finally.

'It runs in families, sister,' he said sadly, and gazed at her face until the blindfold erased her.

When the inspector had been escorted from the room, she

leaned back in her chair and massaged her temples with the tips of her fingers.

'Impressions?'

The thick-set man, sitting in the shadowed corner, clicked his pen and glanced at his notes.

'He knows.'

'How much?'

'Enough to know that we know.'

'What do we know of his detectives?'

'Avram and Goldberg? We know everything there is to know.'

'And?'

'They're good. Good enough to be us.'

'Would they?'

'No. No need to go into all the psychobabble. They don't fit the profiles – they're different and dogged. And … they're close.'

'Keep up the surveillance on them. Upgrade if necessary.'

'And if they strike it lucky?'

'Terminate.'

'Inspector Bernstein?'

She didn't answer. The Mossad agent clicked his pen awake and underlined a quote in his notes:

'Silence gives consent.'

The Arab District, Jerusalem

'Here?'

Goldberg killed the engine and craned her neck to look around the small courtyard. 'Here for the car,' Avram grunted, and swung out of the passenger seat. 'Follow at twenty yards,' he muttered, and disappeared into a maze of laneways. She counted off his footsteps and followed. High walls shadowed the alley, bisected by slanted sunlight. They walked on the dark side. She noticed bulbous domes peeping above the walls, flat roofs necklaced with lines of drooping washing, the occasional exclamation point of a television aerial, the full stop of a satellite dish. The punctuation of the Jerusalem skyline, she thought, and dropped her eyes to cover his back. He disappeared left and she dawdled at the window of a small shop, checking the reflected street for threat. Satisfied, she angled left to see him stub out a cigarette at the next junction and peel off right.

A young Arab man stepped from a shop doorway. 'Miss, maybe you like … ?' Something in her face seemed to suck the breath from his body. He stumbled back, tripping in the doorway and scrabbled awkwardly on hands and knees to distance himself.

'Another time,' she said huskily, and walked on, flexing the fingers of her right hand to ease the tingling.

'Third door down,' Avram whispered, as she passed. 'The key is under the flowerpot.'

'How very secure,' she quipped, without looking at him.

The courtyard gleamed with foot-polished stone. A small fountain, at the centre, stood in silent accusation, its neglected bowl emerald with algae. Vine-pots lined the side walls at regular intervals, the vines drooping beyond the lattice frames. The entrance to the building was through a covered veranda. She heard the muted sounds of the city, like surf washing rhythmically on some distant beach, and shivered. The door in the wall behind her opened and closed.

'Home, sweet home,' she said lightly, as he drew level. He didn't answer, and she wondered what she had said that was such a big deal.

'Kitchen,' he said unnecessarily, waving a hand at the tidy

room. Man-tidy, she noted. A place for everything and for everything a place. Soldier-tidy, she amended, and stole a glance at his face. He was wearing his locked-down expression, the one he affected at crime scenes while he stepped around blood and bodies, looking for clues.

He gestured, and she followed him along a short hallway. Square patches on the walls mourned absent pictures. 'Sitting room,' he said. Covered shapes brooded in the airless room and she quickened her step to stay close behind him on the stairs. He pushed a door open on the first floor. 'Your room.' He didn't look inside. She stepped into a small bedroom whose wallpaper was alive with flying birds. A single narrow bed gazed up at a high, whitewashed ceiling.

'Bedclothes and stuff in the wardrobe,' he said from outside. 'Bathroom down the landing. I'll get some provisions.' And he was gone. She sat on the edge of the bright blue mattress, tracking the sound of his descent, the click of his heels on the stone-flagged courtyard, the solid clunk of the outer door.

'Someone just left,' she murmured aloud. 'I wonder who it was.'

The water in the shower came slow and lukewarm from the tank on the roof and she lathered herself with the bar of scented soap she found nestling in a porcelain dish. Too scented to be his, she thought, and a green-tinged scenario took shape in her head. This is where he brings women, she mused, and worked the shampoo more vigorously through her hair than was strictly necessary. By the time she was dried and dressed, she was tasting the term 'love-nest' and longing to spit.

'Spit it out, Goldberg.'

'Love nest.'

'What?'

'God, deaf and dumb.'

Did you say love n—'

'Don't say it.'

'What?'

'Love-nest. Shit!'

'You think this place is—'

'Don't say it.'

'You know the problem with women?'

'They fart in phoneboxes?'

'Wha'? The problem with women is the same problem as the problem with the F14 jet-fighter.'

'What?'

'God! Deaf and delusional. The problem with women is that they have this extra chromosome thing that works like the turbo-charge on the F14. By the time they open their mouths to say something, they're way outside the range of reason.'

'Lucky you're Israeli, Avram. No one eats pigs here.'

'You thought this was my love—'

'Don't say it.'

'I think we've just had a circular argument. Goldberg, look at me. Read my lips.'

'Yes, Ari.'

'You are my partner – you know what that means?'

'Yes.'

'Say it.'

'It means … trust.'

'And trust is built on?'

'Truth.'

'Do you want the truth?'

'So now you're Jack Nicholson?'

'It's not me who's having trouble handling the truth, partner. This is—was my home.'

'Home?'

'And Away, 'on the range', as in 'there's no place like', et cetera. Home damnit.'

'Home as in *Home Alone*?'

'No. Yes.'

'You sure you're not Jewish?'

'I wasn't alone then, I am now.'

'Divorce?'

'No.'

'Oh.'

'Remember the Negev incident?'

'You didn't talk about it.'

'I'm talking about it now. I killed a guy under interrogation. His friends couldn't get me back. They took the only available option.'

'Your wife?'

'And daughter.'

'Sorry, Ari.'

'It's okay. Maybe I shouldn't have brought you here. I couldn't think of anywhere else.'

His cellphone rang.

'What? Yes, Inspector. No, it's okay. I'll let you in.'

He clicked it closed and nodded at Goldberg.

'Partners?'

'Partners.'

Inspector Bernstein stepped into the courtyard and froze.

'I thought he'd come here. Is that pistol loaded, Detective?'

'Much as she can hold, sir. My partner's just checking your tail. Eh, that is, to see if you have one, sir.'

'Okay, clear.'

'Sorry about that, Inspector.'

'Next time take the safety off.'

'Couldn't trust myself. It's been a trying day, sir.'

'Mossad says it isn't them.'

'Well that's okay then. I prefer to be strangled by the other side.'

'I asked them who it was. They didn't say.'

'They don't know?'

'No, Goldberg, they didn't say.'

'So, they know and won't tell, which means … what?'

'It means, partner, that it's in their interests somehow to have a serial killer on the loose and they want us gone.'

'Is that it, Inspector?'

'Yes and no.'

'Is ambiguity a guy thing?'

'Listen up, you two. Yes, they do know who it is and, no, they don't want the next attempt on you to succeed. But if we pursue this investigation, they'll protect their asset.'

'It has a ring to it.'

'Yeah, like target-rich environment …'

'Friendly fire.'

'Will you two stop that? I can't order you to go on with this. If you do, your only chance is to find him and take him down fast.'

'You wouldn't have his address?'

'I have a whole list of names and addresses from profiles.

Here, read it and eat it. Have you linked up with that priest in the Holy Sepulchre?'

'Not yet, sir.'

'Now would be good.'

The Oval Office, Washington DC

'You look younger than I expected, Professor.'

'So do you, Ms President.'

Touché, she thought. She liked the direct gaze and easy manner of the young professor. So many people seemed to dissolve into simpering sludge in the presence of the First Citizen. She also liked the way he didn't capture her hand, just shook it firmly and let it go. Inside the Oval Office, Ellen Radford gave a brief introduction to John Hancock and sat between Senator Melly and Laila. 'Oh, one more thing, Professor,' she said, raising her hand in apology, 'if you'd like to use audio-visual aids, we've got a whole roomful just down the hall.'

'No, thank you,' he said. 'Like most folk in the United States, you've seen all the pictures and it hasn't made a damn bit of difference.'

In her peripheral vision, she saw Laila's jaw sag and Melly smother a chuckle behind his hand. Her mother had always said, 'Never hunt tigers unless you're prepared to meet one.' I may have met my tiger. She nodded at him to proceed.

After the tedium of the earlier session, she hoped she wouldn't nod. Her husband, she remembered, had perfected the art of dozing while seeming wide awake. Most times, she recalled with irritation, if he really woke up, he would attack the speaker, as if his lapse in concentration had somehow been the other's fault. Remarkable how the traits you once thought funny and endearing don't stand the test of time. Deliberately, she opened the pad on her lap and clicked her pen.

John Hancock was rumoured to be a good speaker, the kind who attracted students from other disciplines to attend his lectures. Good doesn't hack it, she marvelled. This guy is incredible. Like all speakers at the top of their game, he could dance that fine line between passion and persuasion, moving only when necessary so that his verbal and body language were all of a piece. His eyes never roved as if he was strafing the audience but locked on one person and then another as if he was conversing with each individual. In just fifteen minutes he had sketched word pictures of environmental crises in various parts of the planet, coloured them with cameo stories, giving them punch with a few stark statistics. When he paused to drink some water, she murmured, 'God, he's good.'

She was pleased and amused when Laila added in a whisper, 'And not too hard on the eye.'

John Hancock placed the glass on the desk beside him and invited questions.

The president thought the pause that followed owed more to awe than to embarrassment, yet she was relieved when the senator stepped into the silence.

'Professor, I thank you for a most enlightening lecture. Heck, if I had you teachin' me in college I might have made somethin' of myself.'

Isaacson and Laila both smiled broadly. Benson clicked and pocketed his pen. 'Seems to me,' Melly continued, 'there's been some freak weather these past few years in China, parts of Europe and right here in the United States. Now, insurance folk like to call it an act of God. What say you, sir?'

'I say read the small print very carefully before you sign,'

John Hancock said, smiling. The senator smiled broadly as the others chuckled.

'I say God is often a convenient fall-guy for human error and neglect,' he continued. 'The kind of freak weather that cost China eight billion dollars in 2008 is set to become the norm.'

'So, are you saying we have the science to stop a snow-storm, Professor?' Benson asked acidly.

'No, sir – at least, not yet. But we do have the science to predict it in plenty of time so that thousands of Chinese are not stranded at airports and millions are not marooned without adequate provisions in towns and villages. And when I say we have the science to predict and therefore prepare for that kind of catastrophe, I mean we in the United States have it. So the real question is why we're not making it available to the Chinese and to the other developing nations.'

'And how would making it available be in the best interests of the United States, young man?' Benson's cold voice con-trasted with the genial atmosphere that had been established by the Southern senator, and the president saw Laila and Isaacson stiffen with embarrassment.

The professor took a few moments to mull over the question before replying.

'I can understand, sir, why an intelligence agency, in any country, would want to keep its military secrets, but the science we all need to survive shouldn't be the copyright of any country. Seems to me that's just a covert kind of genocide.'

Incensed, Benson flicked a page on his pad. 'Seems to me,' he mimicked, 'you have very definite views on foreign policy for someone who is not a member of Congress or the Senate or part of the administration. Someone who is ...' he made a great show of reading from his notes '… a recently appointed professor of hydrology at Washington University.'

'Well, that's true, sir.' Hancock shrugged. 'I'm not a politician or a member of the Administration. And, yes, I am newly appointed to my position, as are three other persons in this room.'

Oh, you devil, Ellen Radford thought admiringly. Go ahead and drop the other shoe.

'But even new professors of hydrology have been known to read the newspapers. Everything I've said so far has been in the public domain for quite some time. But I'll be happy to move on to some very definite views of my own. I figure that China and what was the USSR built real and ideological walls and fences around their countries, not to keep us out but to keep their own people in. It didn't work for the Soviets and it's not working in China. The walls and fences are gone. The populations in those countries see what we have and they want it. But the big question they and all the developing countries will ask is, how come you have medicines, treatments, cures, and we don't? How come you have desalination plants and we have dirty water? How come you know how to do all those things and you let us go thirsty, starve and die?'

'So you say if we don't share, they'll do what? Just come and take it from a military superpower?' Benson sneered.

'Let me ask you a question, sir,' Hancock countered. 'How many billions did we spend this year on our military super-power? Or, to put it another way, how much did it cost to keep our wall high enough? How many billions next year? One of the significant differences between the First and Second World Wars was the difference between horses and tanks. We galloped into the First and got our collective asses kicked. But we rolled into the Second, we flew into Korea and Vietnam and we rocketed into Iraq. Will we laser into the next one or neutron-bomb our way into the one after that? Look, it stands to reason that if we hoard in a famine the neighbours will come calling. But this is not about giving them our food and our water or building higher and higher forts around our resources. This is about giving them the science to conserve and grow their own.'

Isaacson asked, 'With regard to our own resources, Professor, are you confident we have enough to see us into the future?'

'Time for show-and-tell,' Hancock answered, plucking an unopened water bottle from Benson's hand. 'I see you're conserving, sir,' he quipped. 'This, ladies and gentlemen, is the world's water supply. If we looked down from an Apollo spacecraft, it would appear vast, covering over two-thirds of the Earth's surface. Yes, we can go maybe three weeks without food and just three days without water, but where's the problem? We've got oceans of the stuff. But what did Coleridge write in *The Rime of the Ancient Mariner*? "Water, water, everywhere, and all the boards did shrink. Water, water, everywhere …"?' He looked expectantly at his audience.

'"Nor any drop to drink."' The president completed the quotation.

'Poetic licence, Ms President,' Hancock said, picking up his glass, which still held a quarter-inch of liquid at the bottom. He held it up for the group. 'Only two per cent of the world's water is drinkable. The fancy name is potable. It comes from the Greek *potamos*. Next time you cross the Potomac river consider how … aspirational the name is. Try a cupful and you'd better have health insurance. Two per cent. The good news is that millions of inches of rain fall each year on North America. The bad news is that most of it runs off back to the sea, or evaporates, or is polluted. Also, it doesn't fall all over at the same volume. Some places are very wet, like the far side of the Rockies, others are very dry, like most of the Southern states and the Midwest. The Shah of Iran said he'd swap all the oil for water. Too late for him, too late for Iran. Civilisation thrived only where there was water. Egypt has one major river, the Nile. Take a map and draw a thin green line either side of the blue Nile line. That's Egyptian civilisation. The rest's a moonscape.'

'But they built the Aswan dam,' Laila objected.

'Yes, Ms Secretary, they did. And why? To create a huge reservoir. To generate massive amounts of electricity. To control the flooding downstream so that the farmers could up their yield. So far, so wonderful. The downside is that the fertile black mud that always washed into their fields isn't coming any more. Therefore the farmers must use more fertiliser for the same yield. The fertiliser washes into the river, blooms the algae and kills the fish. As you go downriver, you get more and more of it so that when you reach the sea you find the fishermen sitting at home because the sardines have gone belly up in the poisoned water.'

He walked to the globe at the corner of the desk and spun it like a roulette wheel, letting his finger glide over the curve of the world until he stopped the spin.

'Right here, the Aral Sea is dead. The Black Sea, here, is almost dead. The Yangtse river here in China hasn't reached the sea in years. Faraway hills are brown and dry.'

'As you say, Professor, they are far away,' Benson grunted.

'So let's bring it all back home,' Hancock suggested. 'There are so many housing developments, farms and industries sucking from our rivers that the mighty Colorado no longer makes it to the sea.'

'Professor?'

'Yes, Ms President.'

'Towns need water, industries need water, farms need water. That's a given. We can't just turn off the tap.'

'We have so many dams on our major rivers now, ma'am, that we can do just that. But I take your point.'

He walked to the president and placed Benson's full bottle in her hand. He put a clean tumbler in her other hand.

'Pour some water in the glass for industry, ma'am,' he urged, 'and some for agriculture. Thank you. Now, what's left is what we humans have to live on. To drink and cook, we need just two gallons a day.'

He laid his hand gently on the hand holding the bottle.

'Okay, now fill the swimming pool.' He rocked her hand, and water splashed into the glass. 'Wash the car, sprinkle the lawn, wash the dishes, use the washing machine.'

She looked up at him. 'It's all gone,' she said quietly.

'Yes, Ms President. I think we need to put it all back in the bottle and think differently.'

'It's not the usage, is it?' Isaacson offered. 'It's the wastage.'

'Yes,' Hancock said enthusiastically. 'We need to move agriculture from a "Let us spray" mentality to "Let us drip". I'm talking hydroponics, bringing drips of water to the plant and not a flood to the whole damn field. I'm talking recycling plants in every industry so that the same water goes round and round – heck, we've got the technology.'

'Sounds like a hell of an ask for farmers and factory owners,' Laila said doubtfully.

'We already have the research to show they'll get their money back in the short term, ma'am, so we can sell it under hard-nosed economics rather than some kind of fuzzy green environmentalism. Selfishness is one hell of a motivation. And when it comes to the developing countries, digging wells is fine and dandy but it means man, beast and plant are tied to that hole in the ground. How long before it must be dug deeper and deeper until they hit the bottom of the aquifer – the underground lake that's been sucked faster than it can fill and becomes a cave? Give them the know-how to build small dams to hold the run-off. Give them the science to punch holes in a hose so that the plant drinks and not the field and so that they don't have stagnant ponds breeding mosquitoes for malaria and the worms that cause bilharzia.'

'Seems like a sound argument for keeping our wall in place,' Benson said, and closed his pad with a snap.

'Or,' Hancock said evenly, 'taking bricks out of that wall to build something better.'

'Beating our swords into ploughshares,' Isaacson quoted.

'Otherwise, the next world war could be about water,' Hancock concluded.

'You can't say that,' Benson riposted.

'You're right, sir.' Hancock sighed. 'I was being optimistic. What the former Secretary General of the United Nations, Mr Boutros Boutros-Ghali, actually said was that the next war would be about water.'

They were spent and a pall seemed to settle over the room. Ellen Radford shook herself and sat upright. 'Why am I left holding the bottle?' she asked of no one in particular.

'Because you are the President of the United States,' Hancock said gravely.

The Island, Ireland

Michael Flaherty watched the water, allowing the rhythmic flow and ebb to loosen his taut body. Mentally, he registered the warmth of the rock he sat on, the steady breeze that blew through his laced fingers and the stubble on his face. He relaxed his mind, as if he was unclenching a tight fist. His breathing deepened and, for a brief and blessed moment, he set aside his masks and roles and simply was. As a boy, this rock- and wave-filled vista had been his place of refuge, a place of sensation rather than thought, where 'being sensible' found its truer, deeper meaning.

Abruptly, simultaneous twinges in the healed wounds of his chest and shoulder tugged his surroundings into tight focus. In the undulating water, beyond the breakers, a seal rose to contemplate him with fathomless eyes. He knew then that his instincts had not deserted him. The boy was somewhere behind him in the tumble of rocks. A familiar surge of guilt assailed him. The boy had haunted his comings and goings since his return to the Island, flickering sometimes at the edge of his vision, sometimes sensed round the next curve of the stone-hedged path or just beyond the horizon of the headland. The boy was his son, Liam, named for the brother who had drowned, the brother who called helplessly in his dreams. His entire frame shuddered as he took a deep breath. The seal submerged, leaving only a perfect ripple. Slowly, Michael stretched upright and turned. There was no sight or sound to betray the hidden boy. He was a presence that registered on a level deeper than sight or sound.

He pushed himself to trot along the path that wound up to the headland, moving on the balls of his feet, upper body canted forward as the US Marine Corp had taught him an age ago, welcoming the dull ache in his calf muscles and the pain in his upper body as he sucked salt air into his lungs. He knew that running, for some people, was a way of flushing adrenalin through their bodies to clean their systems and sharpen their focus. Only children ran without thinking, he thought regretfully, lost in the exhilaration of the closest experience humans ever have to flight. As he pounded the path, the effort pumped thoughts and images through his mind. There was Kate, the girl he had loved, lost, found again, and now avoided: he had no map to follow that might lead him to her and fear armoured him against intimacy.

I am the bearer of death, he thought, and instinctively pushed his body harder. A man cannot break bread with bloodied hands. He thought of his father and the image hovered just behind his sweat-stung eyes of the head cupped by huge pillows, like an empty gannet eggshell marooned on a dune. He saw his father's face, weathered as a sliver of timber salvaged from the sea. As the ground levelled, he straightened, settling into a mile-eating stride. His feet drummed the meter of the poems he had read each evening to his dying father, poems from his childhood he could recite from memory, poems of boys who mimicked owls or dangled under kites; lost boys all. Sometimes, his father returned briefly from his dreaming to smile.

Running flat out now, uncaring of the buckled path or the odd and angled stones truant from the walls, images of his sister Fiona flipped before him like those he had drawn on the pages of a schoolbook. He saw her tiptoeing around his brooding, busying herself to baffle the steady hum of his silence. There would, he knew, be a reckoning, but not yet. Not yet.

He stopped and laid a hand on a wall, letting his heart rattle down to a normal rhythm. He swivelled and clutched its stones with the other, bowing his forehead to the benediction of cool limestone. I have always been running, he told himself, running hard to stay ahead of myself. Time to stop, Michael Flaherty. Yes, but not yet, the scholar in him prompted, eliciting a nod for St Augustine. Not yet.

He stood upright and scanned the harbour. He knew his ancestors had trimmed their prayers with the heartfelt plea, 'From the Norsemen, O Lord, deliver us.' It hadn't saved them then. It wouldn't save him now. For now, he must stay wakeful, watchful and apart.

CIA Headquarters, Washington DC

Catherine De Lancy carried a silver tray to the desk and set it in the pool of light. She spooned two sugars into the coffee and ran the cream over the back of the spoon so that it spread evenly over the surface.

'Thank you, Catherine,' Benson murmured absently, as she resumed her seat, pen and pad at the ready. He lifted the bone-china cup delicately between thumb and forefinger and sipped, held the coffee in his mouth for a moment and inhaled before swallowing.

'Excellent, as always.'

'Thank you, Mr Director.'

He leaned back into shadow and regarded his secretary over the rim of his cup. What age was she? Sixty-five, the file in his head responded. Yeah, Catherine keeps the files updated, so let's say sixty-five and holding, as the old gag goes. But, as his sainted Maman would have remarked, with a Brahmin elevation of an eyebrow, she was 'well preserved'. He noted the handmade, low-heeled black shoes and the expensively tailored black suit. A white silk blouse peeped from her cuffs and rose at her throat, hiding the wattling of age and directing light to her cheekbones. She was a ringer for Katharine Hepburn, he thought, with the ruddy complexion and the watery-blue eyes, topped with a shock of salt-and-pepper hair. He knew the gaggle of interns and typists who twittered beyond the door called her 'The Black Widow' and lived in terror of her bite. To them she was as old as God and marginally more aloof. A lover of the classics, he liked to think of her as the Cerberus who guarded his gate; the Charon who ferried souls from the light to the dark he dwelt in.

Catherine had come with the furniture, as Maman liked to say of old family retainers, part of the package when he had claimed top spot at the agency. He remembered vividly his first day in the office and the first time he'd summoned her. Sure, he had boned-up on her file but the word made flesh was still a revelation. She was 'old family', he was pleased to note, one of the kind who pledged sons to the military and daughters to marriage – the politically incestuous form of marriage favoured by Washington blue-bloods. Catherine's 'young man', as she would say, hadn't returned from Vietnam.

Benson allowed himself a small, cruel smile. He flicked the cover of his mental file on one Grayson Anthony, effortlessly translating the military-speak within. In short, Grayson Anthony, missing in action, had been a lethal combination of arrogance and stupidity, regarded by his superiors as having I and Q but not together. What he had had in his favour were two military uncles who had amassed eight stars between them and enough political clout to finesse the reservations of the Westpoint Commissioning Board. But Catherine wasn't to know that. She wasn't to know either that his troop in Vietnam had exercised their democratic right and good sense by wasting him. 'Fragging' was the term, Benson recalled. During that particular conflict, it had given 'friendly fire' a whole new meaning. Catherine preferred to honour the mask of myth and Benson kept the reality locked in his brain and in the wall-safe.

He had contemplated replacing her with someone even vaguely computer literate, the kind of administration chick who lived on lettuce and consulted a Filofax before going to the bathroom. Hell, he had even convened the meeting and played at the concerned employer, mouthing about 'the demands of the job', her 'invaluable contribution to the agency', the 'gratitude of the country'. She had sat through it all, an expression of beatific serenity plastered across her face until he had added, 'You know the old saying, Catherine, the new broom sweeps clean.'

To which she had replied sweetly, 'But the old broom knows where the dirt is, Mr Director.' Game set and match to Catherine De Lancy.

Abruptly, he surfaced from his reverie.

'What's that?'

'Your meeting with the president and her cabinet, sir. I wondered if you'd like to record some observations.'

She was Boswell to his Johnson, he reflected smugly. Within these four soundproof and bug-free walls, he could lower his guard and vent his frustrations in a way he had never managed to do with his wives, women who had been lured by 'the greatest aphrodisiac of all', as Kissinger had put it. They had learned to their cost that power is not for sharing and had settled for the perks. Inevitably, they had tired of being trophies, cut a deal and disappeared. On all three occasions, he had felt only relief. Benson propped his elbows on the desk, resting his chin on steepled fingers. The desk lamp made a death's head of his face.

'How does one ascend to high office, Catherine?'

The survivor of three administrations, Catherine was accustomed to rhetorical questions and sat in silence.

'Ability? Merit? Perhaps. But to achieve the highest office one must be elected, one must go to the people. Pericles never intended democracy for all the people, certainly not for the great unwashed, but this is America. So the politicians go to the people and the people say, "Lower taxes, cut the price of gas, increase benefits." And the politicians, particularly those afflicted with blind ambition and an insatiable desire for power, say, "Yeah, verily, it shall be so. And, as guarantee thereof, take ye part of my soul." And when some half-assed raghead zealot blows the fuel pipe, behold, the cars stop in the streets, the sprinklers grow silent on the lawns, the air-conditioning units cool not, and great is the tumult among the people. Then do the politicians come to us and say, "We must wage war. They have weapons of mass destruction. Find them." We give them satellite photographs, which the good general, right record, right colour, displays in the UN for all to see, and proclaims, "Here they are." But the UN produces its inspector of such things who says, "No, not so." And the general is shamed and the journalists rejoice and jokes proliferate concerning explosive cigars, beard-remover and the Bay of Pigs. Then the politicians come to us and say, "The Egyptians smite the Israelites" and we arm both sides. They say, "The powder blows from south to north," and we give helicopter gunships to the juntas and Stinger missiles to the rebels. Our masters rail at Iran, accusing it of arming terrorists, and at the Saudis for funding al-Qaeda, and it goes on and on.'

He barked a bitter laugh.

'Our client list and supply manifest go way back to Sandinistas and Noriega and right up to Saddam. Now that the Reds have discovered oil, money and BMWs, and are selling everything from army greatcoats to nuclear missiles, we have the most powerful standing military force on the face of the Earth. Who can stand against us? No one. No one is that stupid. We have become the bear in the anthill, capable of doing enormous damage if the ants would only clump together so that we can trample them. But they don't. They sting, nip and bite us from every angle. We lost Vietnam to guerrillas, Catherine. The best-equipped army in the world was brought down by small groups of peasants in black pyjamas who hadn't read the military manual, who didn't know that they should stand and fight like men, goddamnit. No, they put one punji-stick on the path for one grunt's foot, or one booby trap in the bush to kill four, or one grenade in a restaurant … You get the picture. The standing-army days are over. Now we fight terror with terror. Not just "an eye for an eye", we go for the brains and balls as well. We take terror and crank it up a notch to horror. The Israelites tied burning brands to the tails of desert foxes and set them running among their enemies. We do what the Saracens did when they couldn't match the armour of the Crusaders. We poison their wells. Like the Romans at Carthage, we raze their city and sow salt on the site. We learn from our enemies past and present. We answer fire with fire. Like the Cosa Nostra, if you kill my son, then I kill yours, his grandmother and the dog.' He exhaled loudly.

'Fresh coffee, sir?'

'No, thank you.'

He placed his cup firmly in the saucer.

'The new administration will appease our enemies,' he said flatly. 'Oh, Catherine, how we Americans long to be liked. We give them Marshall Plans, food aid and more money than they can count, and are amazed when they bite the hand that feeds them. We wanted to be the international sheriff, Gary Cooper on a white horse, peddling peace to the hostiles, backed up with two shiny Colts and a Winchester rifle. The Injuns didn't read the script. They wouldn't lie down and now they want their land back. They want an apology and some gaming licences so they can build casinos where the buffalo roamed. It's time to cry havoc, to change the fucking paradigm. I remember a gag that was popular when I was in college. Guys had it on posters in the frat house.'

He loomed into the light and intoned with mock solemnity,

'"Yeah, though I should walk in the valley of death, I shall fear no evil, for I am the meanest son-of-a-bitch in the valley." The new administration will move to appease,' he repeated, 'to ameliorate, confer, negotiate and the whole damn thesaurus of words that spell 'spineless' to the enemy. They will have us move our deckchairs companionably closer, hold hands and sing 'Abide With Me' as we disappear beneath the waves. They must be … distracted. I wonder what we'd find if we peeled away the hard-ass façade of Laila Achmed. Is there some family skeleton rattling away under that serene exterior? Maybe some relative in the Lebanon once walked on the wild side.'

The secretary's pen danced over the pad. She knew the drill. Benson's musings were a firewall – no instructions given, no records available in the event of a blowback. She would phrase the feelers to agents on the fringes in such a way that they would know what to look for without knowing who was looking. If the shit ever did hit the fan, heads would roll but the hydra in this office would survive.

'Same for Isaacson,' Benson continued. 'One wonders about Zionist influences. Let's not forget our dear friend, the oleaginous eminence from below the Mason–Dixon Line. Nobody rises so high without stepping on bodies along the way. As for Ms President …'

He trapped the 'Ms' between clenched teeth so that it buzzed like an angry wasp. 'Her Achilles heel is her husband. Remind me, which undeserving part of the world is currently blessed with his presence?'

'Nigeria, sir. He's offering himself as a consultant to the government.'

'Ah, yes, of course. And his predilections?'

'Generously catered for. I've downloaded the photographs to your computer. We also have the facility to provide real-time footage, if you wish.'

Had there been the trace of a taunt in Catherine's tone? he wondered. Her face betrayed nothing. He knew, to the cent, how much his secretary had paid a plastic surgeon to create that degree of inscrutability. Not for the first time, he speculated on what thoughts flickered, what emotions moved, behind that mask. An image flowered in his brain of Paul Newman as the chain-gang con in *Cool Hand Luke*, snatching the reflective sunglasses from the sadistic warden's face. He must have smiled. Catherine's lips stretched to reflect it. It was a thing she did, he realised, adopted the body language, vocabulary and tone of whoever spoke to her. 'Mirroring', the psychologists called it. Catherine was a chameleon, constantly shifting colour to blend with the background until you believed you were talking to yourself.

Benson leaned back in the chair and swivelled into profile. His secretary had long ago learned to interpret the mannerism. He was effectively tuning out his surroundings, focusing on some interior screen onto which he could project scenarios and possible outcomes. She knew she could clear away the tray and he wouldn't notice. Hell, she could whip out a feather boa and drape herself seductively across his desk and it wouldn't raise a flicker. Catherine sat, the pad in her lap, the pen held loosely, waiting.

Like a dreamer, Casper the Ghost grimaced and sighed, muttered and motioned as he gathered the strands of his thoughts and wove them into possibilities. Suddenly he was still and she raised her pen. His voice was still whispery from reflection but gained strength as he spoke.

'Advise the minders that Caliban will be going to Jerusalem.'

While her pen automatically coded the message, she wondered how the president's husband would react to the idea of leaving a potentially lucrative love nest in Nigeria, and parked that thought for later.

'Our friend, the Prince, is still on ice?'

'Yes, Cardinal Thomas is in a convent in Rome. Our ambassador to the Holy See negotiated with the Italian justice minister, as you suggested. The new arrangement is acceptable to both sides. The Vatican avoids the embarrassment of having a prince of the Church in prison and the minister is relieved that the Church will shoulder the expense and inconvenience of monitoring their errant cardinal. The media lockdown is watertight.'

'Cardinal Thomas failed me, Catherine. We gave him every assistance in his attempt to secure the Throne of Peter, and he blew it. I should let him stew in his megalomania, but "The stone rejected by the builder may become the cornerstone."'

'Sir?'

'We can use him,' he said flatly. 'If psychopaths were ineligible for service, this agency would be seriously under-staffed. Anyway, every knight should have his bishop,' he added enigmatically.

'Will there be anything else, sir?'

'No, thank you, Catherine. I have some calls to make.'

She placed the pad on his desk and began to tidy the tray as he twirled the dial of the wall safe and locked the pad inside.

'Good night, Mr Director.'

'Yes, I think it will be.'

Lagos, Nigeria

Jack Holland, former President of the United States and husband of the present incumbent of the White House, dreamed he was being targeted by a giant mosquito. He knew it was only a matter of time before it matched its flight plan to the thermals of warm air rising from his sleeping body and spiralled down to suck him dry. In his dream, he opened his mouth to scream.

'Mr Holland, Mr Holland, wake up, sir.'

He opened his eyes and stared into the face of Jed Armstrong, his fresh-faced young minder from the agency.

'What the hell you want?' he croaked, still shaken by the aftershock of a dream he couldn't recall.

'Eh, sir?' Armstrong motioned with his hand to the other

side of the bed and Holland swung his head to follow the gesture. The African woman widened her eyes playfully and giggled.

'Oh, Christ,' he mumbled thickly, 'get her out of here.'

He slumped at the edge of the bed, head pressed between his palms, until the door finally closed behind the giggling girl and Armstrong returned.

'So who was she?' he grunted.

'A gift from the general, sir.'

'Which one?'

'The one with responsibility for the appropriation of ordinance, I believe.'

Holland rubbed the stubble on his cheeks, pulling his eyelids down to expose rheumy red eyeballs. 'They teach you that kind of gobbledegook in spook school, kid?'

'Absolutely, sir. Along with Yoruba, Hebrew, Russian and a few more languages.'

Holland absorbed this.

'I had an adviser from the State Department one time who spoke seven languages fluently. Didn't make a damn bit of sense in any one of them.'

The young man looked a little nonplussed and Holland drew breath, satisfied.

'I presume you had other reasons for wakin' me besides informin' me of your linguistic abilities.'

'Yes, sir.'

'Well, they can wait until I've freshened up.'

He padded barefoot to the bathroom, clicked the door closed behind him and fumbled for the light switch. Reluctantly, he raised his eyes to the mirror. The man reflected there looked ten years older than he was. His dishevelled hair, spiked with sweat, cruelly exposed wide expanses of scalp denuded of cover. The patrician face was mottled, the eyes slitted behind engorged lids. With a sense of inevitability, he lowered his gaze to his pendulous breasts and swollen stomach.

'Hail to the Chief,' he said, raising his hand to his head in a mock salute. He emerged thirty minutes later, showered, shaved and fragrant with cologne, to pull on a white open-neck shirt and linen suit.

'Run it by me again, Jed,' he said briskly.

'Your … companion last night was a gift from the general with responsibility for buying weapons, sir.'

'Bribe?'

'Most definitely, sir.'

'Wonder how I'd list that on a tax audit, Jed. Think it comes under or over the threshold imposed on gifts?'

'That's a purely hypothetical question, sir,' Armstrong answered automatically, and regretted it immediately.

Jack Holland's face became stony for a few seconds and then relaxed.

'Of course,' he said easily. 'Questions of tax arise only when the gifts are made to the Head of State. A former president doesn't qualify, even if he is the First Man.'

'The agency really appreciates your efforts on behalf of commercial links between the United States and the government of Nigeria, sir.'

Holland laughed humourlessly.

'Oh, I bet it does. What do I get for last night's contribution, Jed? Silver Star? Or maybe a Purple Heart? Was she clean?'

'Yes, sir.'

'Nix on the Purple Heart then.'

His mind wandered and he looked around vacantly at the plush apartment. 'Bird in a gilded cage,' he muttered.

'Sir?'

'Nothing. Why did you call me, Jed?'

'Message came through for you, sir.'

'From the president?'

God, he hated the eagerness in his voice and the inevitability of the reply.

'No, sir.'

He'd known she wouldn't call, that it'd all been over even before she declared her candidacy. Heck, she'd had her reasons. He'd given her sufficient and then some. But she was political to her marrow, just like him, and they'd struck a deal. She would run for the White House and he would keep his fly zipped and hustle the caucuses on her behalf. If … when she grasped the golden ring, because he'd never doubted she would, all debts, obligations, commitments, the whole fucking three-ring circus, were cancelled. He could write his book, donate his papers, hawk his voice on the international lecture circuit, do whatever he damn well pleased, once he'd agreed not to write, do or say anything that might besmirch the presidency.

Besmirched. That was the word she had used five minutes after the back-slapping had stopped and before the champagne had gone flat – they'd been standing in a White House broom closet for privacy, with two nervous and heavily armed security agents outside the door, so close to him that he could see the fleck of amber in one of her amazingly blue eyes and smell her hairspray. Besmirched. Well, the publishers weren't forming a queue, and the invitations to lecture weren't clogging up the mailbox. Slowly, he began to discover why ex-astronauts found it hard to cope with walking on the earth after they'd looked down on it from the moon. And hard on the heels of that particular epiphany, Casper Benson had called. Talk about bolt from the blue, pigs will fly and all the other tired phrases that attempt to capture the unlikely. He'd agreed to meet out of a mixture of curiosity and ennui.

Casper the Ghost had this agency fishing lodge, tucked away upstate on some lake or other. The Ghost didn't hunt or fish. He sat in the boat while Jack Holland twitched an artificial fly over the placid water. Didn't catch a damn thing. Didn't much matter, on that expedition: he was the fish. He knew it and, with a sick feeling of self-disgust, knew that he'd rise to the bait. Any bait. Even Benson's.

'Can I speak plainly, Mr President?'

'Wouldn't like you to break the habit of a lifetime on my account, Mr Director Benson the Third. What say you we drop the titles, okay? You call me Jack, I call you Casper. Not for any other reason than for convenience – we never did see eye to eye, did we, Casper?'

'No, we did not.'

Benson had sat there in his funeral-parlour suit, his shiny black brogues planted in the half-inch of dirty water that formed a miniature tsunami every time the boat moved. 'I never liked you,' he said evenly. 'Never thought you had it in you to be great. Oh, you had energy and charm. You could work the room, I'll give you that. But, you didn't have what it takes to be the president of the United States.'

Even now, the brutality of Benson's summary hurt. It shouldn't have. The world and his mother knew Benson didn't 'do' people. 'Making nice' was something like a chamois glove he pulled over his metal fist only when his cold brain deemed it opportune. Holland had felt like laughing. Then he'd felt like raging at the smug spectre sitting in the boat and punching him on the nose to see if real blood ran in those icy veins. He'd done neither. Deep down, in the pit of his roiling gut, he'd known that Benson was right. For form's sake, he'd argued the point.

'You tellin' me that the peanut farmer and the cowboy had what it takes?'

'No, I'm not. They were deeply flawed in their own unique ways.'

'What about her?'

Benson looked out over the water without seeing it while Holland dreaded the answer to his question.

'She has … the potential.'

'What the fu—!'

'You asked,' Benson interrupted coldly. 'If you're not man enough to hear the answer, say so.'

Reluctantly, Holland nodded.

'She has the potential,' Benson continued. 'But … she hasn't been tried. Cuba was Kennedy's trial and he stepped up to the plate. I grant him that. Sure, he was pimped all the way to the Oval Office by old Joe. Too many promises made to too many people he couldn't or wouldn't deliver. It killed him. Reagan had the Iron Curtain. When we … when it was suggested to him that a Pole in the Vatican could be a lever, he listened. Ellen hasn't been tried,' he repeated. 'Sometimes the trial is inevitable and sometimes … it has to be arranged.'

'What the hell are you sayin', Benson?'

'You know what I'm saying, Jack. You were there. You know how it works, the things we did on your watch to keep America safe.'

'I was never told.'

'Oh, don't give me that shit. This is me you're talking to, not some fucking Woodward or Bernstein or a peacenik senator at a hearing. You never wanted the details, Jack, but you knew.'

'There's nothing on the record.'

'Of course there isn't,' Benson hissed. 'Who kept the record? We did. Who kept you out of the loop, out of the fucking nooses of a record that could come full circle and hang you out to dry? We did. But you knew, Jack. You didn't ask but you sure as hell knew. And that's how it should be. There needs to be, and there has always been, an arm of the state that operates independently of the head of state. That arm is us, Jack.'

'You know what you're saying? You know, if I was to tell—'

'You didn't tell anyone then, Jack. You're hardly likely to tell them now. They might have believed you then. Now …'

He raised his right hand and let it fall limply in his lap.

'Silence gives consent, Jack. It's a maxim of the law. It didn't save Göring and the other Nazis at Nuremberg. It wouldn't save you now.'

'What do you want with me, Benson?'

'I want to give you a second chance. I want to give you a chance to make up for the things you didn't do, for the president you never were when you thought the office was all about you.'

'And – pray, tell – what's that?'

'I want you to help me help Ellen.'

'She doesn't want my help.'

'I know that. I know all about it.'

'I bet you do.'

'Don't go sulky on me, Jack. I don't prize petulance. I know all there is to know about when, where and with whom. It's my job. I want you to help me help her. The trial is coming, one way or another. Between now and then, I want you to do as I ask. There are people you should meet. Your present status will give you the perfect entrée.'

'As the president's husband,' Holland said bitterly.

'Yes. Take it from me, Jack, Nancy picked up more valuable intel than Ron ever did. People in power let down their guard with a consort. They like the idea of being on first-name terms with the president's partner. They think it might give them access and influence. In a private capacity, you can go places and talk to people you couldn't when you were president.'

'And you'd be my pimp, Benson?'

'Yes, if that's the only way you can understand it.'

'You know,' Jack Holland had said, leaning the rod against the gunwale, 'some people in the Administration think you walk on water. Why don't I test that theory? I could claim it was a tragic accident.'

'There are two reasons why you wouldn't do that. The first is the reason you're not catching any fish. They get nervous when there are divers in the water. The tragic accident wouldn't be mine. And the second reason is, I'm the only show in town, with the only offer on the table.'

Benson looked towards the speedboat that had crept up on their blind side.

'And there's a third reason.'

He waited until he had stepped into the speedboat before he said, 'I think you still care for her. You'll call me, Jack.'

It hadn't been a question.

It had taken him just one week to realise what it meant to be forgotten but not gone. He had called Benson, and now here he was, wining, dining and whoring for his country. He hadn't lost his smarts entirely. His political nose soon picked up the stench of corruption that went all the way to the top table in this country. He knew why the general was so eager to have 'ordinance', just as he knew that his stated reason, 'To protect our borders from incursion and so facilitate the flow of oil to our friends', was a crock. The guns wouldn't be pointed out but in, at the growing band of political protesters.

'The call was from Benson, right?'

'Yes, sir. The director would like you to call him back, when you have a free moment.'

'Jeez, I feel a free moment coming on right now,' Holland said acidly, and plucked the phone from its cradle.

'This line secure?'

'Absolutely, sir.'

'That will be all, Mr Armstrong,' Holland said, with some of his old hauteur.

The young man stood perplexed for a moment, then left, the door banging behind him.

'You can see a shark as a pet, son,' Holland murmured, as he punched the numbers from memory, 'but the shark always sees you as food.'

For the next twenty minutes, he detailed meetings, impressions and information without recourse to notes.

Benson maintained his silence until Holland had concluded.

'With regard to the general,' he said, 'should we deal?'

Holland thought for a long moment.

'Depends what we want,' he answered carefully. 'If we want the future goodwill of the people here and to avoid the opprobrium of those members of the international community who have no strategic interest in this country and its oil resources, then we shouldn't. If, on the other hand …'

He allowed the pause to lengthen.

'Oh, well done, Jack,' Benson purred. 'Now, let's set the bar a little higher. I want you to go and stay with an old friend of ours in Jerusalem. I would value your views on the political situation there. Armstrong has made the arrangements.'

The phone clicked dead and Holland dropped it back into its cradle. He went to the bathroom and began to wash his hands. He didn't look at himself in the mirror.

Moscow, Russia

Olga longed to lower her feet into a basin of hot water. It had been a tiring day. At first light, she and the American researcher had lumbered out of Moscow on Vassily's temperamental bus to the Monastery of St Sergius. Happily, most of the early morning traffic had been inching the other way under a leaden sky. They had passed through the suburbs, where huge gouges in the earth promised even more Western-style landscaped villas and condominiums for the 'new rich'. They would stand in sharp contrast to the towering cement apartment blocks from the Communist era, but that was the New Russia. Glasnost and perestroika had wrought no economic miracle for those whose washing waved dispiritedly from the sagging balconies. 'Different circus, same monkeys,' she had murmured to her companion.

Olga wasn't usually so openly critical in the presence of foreigners. It wasn't easy, even now, to shrug off the condi-tioning of caution that had been honed to a fine art in the days when it was accepted that one family in every apartment block reported to the KGB. Sitting now in the busy foyer of the Best Western Hotel, trying to distance her mind from her sore feet and simultaneously catch the eye of a waitress, she had to admit that the American woman had been easy to work with. Unlike many of her ilk from the American media world Olga had chaperoned, Mary Brown listened intently and didn't indulge in critical comparisons. She had to admit this had been 'an easy gig', as Western media people liked to say. Even Vassily, the lazy fat-assed driver, had been almost courteous during the hour-long drive to the monastery and had waited until the American had left the bus before kicking off his shoes and switching on his damn game shows on the overhead screen. Bastard could 'make nice' when it suited him, she mused. She knew he would revert to type when the film crew arrived, but that was a bridge to be crossed in the future. The present challenge was to snag the attention of a waitress; no easy task in a tourist industry that had yet to discover the weird and wonderful world of customer service. At last, one of the gaggle of serving women made the mistake of lowering her gaze below the agreed focal point, approximately two feet above the customers' heads.

'A cappuccino for me and hot water for the lady.'

'Hot water?'

'Yes, the lady doesn't drink tea or coffee.'

'It isn't possible. It's tea or coffee.'

'Then tea, please.'

Olga smiled apologetically at the American but didn't offer to explain. It was a Russian solution to a Russian problem. The menu didn't include hot water as an option; therefore it was impossible. By capitulating and ordering tea, she had ensured the hot water would arrive in a mug with a teabag nestling in the saucer. The American researcher would have her hot water and the Russian obsession with ticking only the available boxes would be sated. Olga sighed.

'Tired?'

Mary Brown's grey eyes didn't miss much. Olga liked the fact that the American dressed for the weather and the work, neither flagrantly up nor condescendingly down. Today she wore calf-length boots to battle the snow-slush on the streets and corduroy pants topped with a woollen shirt, sweater and waterproof jacket to allow for cold and rain. She had been relieved to note the jacket didn't carry some vulgar American logo. Savvy lady. Some people around here had long memories. 'A little tired,' she answered, spooning sugar into her cappuccino, already savouring the cinnamon-scented steam and the warmth that seeped into her fingers.

'I think St Sergius will fit the bill,' Mary Brown continued, in her slow American voice. 'We can get some good establishing shots from the public car park across the valley. Those onion domes will be at their best at about seven thirty in the morning. Kinda quiet time for traffic as well, so no busy, noisy stuff in the foreground. Added to which, the monastery has all the icons we could ever want, the monks seem okay about a film crew invading for a few days and the local town has a McDonald's.' They both laughed.

Olga didn't think it politic to mention the five hundred dollars demanded upfront by the 'blackskirts', as she irreverently called the religious community. She had translated the demand into a suggested contribution to the upkeep of the monastery and Mary Brown hadn't demurred. She had displayed an incredible capacity for patience as she toured the paths within its walls, noting monuments, angles, icons and all the little details that would ease the execution of the filming, slated to take place six weeks hence. She hadn't seemed to mind the endless explanations to successive monks, who jealously guarded their own particular shrine or iconostasis and took every opportunity to point out the ravages age and decay had inflicted on their treasures and the expense of maintaining them. She had borne it all with quiet grace, even when that cranky old zealot, Brother Ivan, had dragged her into his musty sanctuary to show her something special. Olga had been hissed away and had attempted to save face by saying she was going to organise a group rate at Reception for the crew. In fact, she had gone to the sanctuary of the little café by the main gate and tried to get the smell of incense out of her nose.

She knew she would enjoy working with Mary Brown. What was the phrase in English? Ah, yes, with Mary Brown, what you saw was what you got. She'd already been given five hundred dollars for her day's work, free and clear, after lardass Vassily and all the other expenses had been taken into account. There would, she knew, be a 'consideration' from the hotel when the crew eventually booked in. All in all, a good day's work, now that Moscow had slipped from frontline news worldwide. Tanks in the streets and rumours of coups had brought film crews flooding in from all over the world. And with them, rich pickings for those, like Olga, who could translate '*nyet*' to '*da*' with large dollar denominations to the apparatchiks and smaller, crumpled 'considerations' to lesser minions. Olga flexed her cramped toes and sipped her expensive cappuccino.

❧❧❧

The American researcher, Mary Brown, let her grey eyes rove over the interpreter. She noted the slush-darkened, imitation leather boots and the drab brown woollen coat. Around her throat, Olga had tied a bright red scarf. It looked incongruous against the dullness of everything else she wore but maybe it explained the rouged cheeks and the purple tint in her hair. The 'Fixer' was not young but neither was she as old as her eyes. Mary Brown had read the file before coming to Moscow. She knew that the Russian was forty-five and a graduate of Moscow University in modern English and Russian literature. For recreation, she read Ian Rankin and Sergei Lukyanenko with equal fervour. A student fling had led to a daughter and marriage to the plastic surgeon Vladimir Ivanov Petrovich, who had honed his scalpel skills on the maimed faces of casualties from the Chechnya conflict, then amassed a fortune erasing the ravages of age from the faces of the oligarchs and their wives. Vladimir's long-term career plan hadn't allowed for Olga and the daughter, Ludmilla, currently studying medicine at Moscow University. She had been presented with the choice of a one-off cash settlement or risking a lot of money in the Byzantine labyrinth of the Moscow law courts. She took the money; he ran. Mistake number two was putting it all in the pension fund embezzled by the minister for pensions. Only in Russia, the American thought. Olga needed dollars to keep the show on the road. She was perfect. Quietly, Mary Brown reached into her bag and slid the sealed white envelope across the table. 'I want to give you a deposit, Olga, to secure your services when we come to film. Will a thousand dollars do it?'

She saw the colour leach from the older woman's face – the rouge looked feverish now. She waved away her stammered protestations. 'You've been very effective and efficient, Olga.'

It was the truth. Fluent in Russian herself, Mary Brown had listened carefully to all the conversations Olga had had with the bus driver and the monks. Occasionally, she had adjusted the translation to the American's sensitivities, particularly when Vassily had said he thought all American movie people were supposed to be beautiful. It hadn't fazed her. She accepted she had what Americans called 'homely features'. In her profession, it was an asset to look unmemorable, to have the kind of face that could be moulded to look like someone else. Unmemorable and unremarkable, just like the pseudonym 'Mary Brown'. Olga had never lied or cheated. Maybe she had pushed the boat out a little when she had slipped off to the monastery café, but even that had suited. The pistol and silencer Brother Ivan had passed across the table under the flat, disapproving stares of his icons were exactly what she needed.

Mary Brown's cellphone chirruped and she excused herself to take the call, pacing the carpet near the reception desk.

'Uncle, how good to hear you. How's everything in the office?'

'Tip-top, Mary dear,' Benson replied breezily. 'Everything's going according to plan. Cousin Caliban will be going to Jerusalem to assist with the Crusader material. I'd like you to join him there. You know what he's like on details. Maybe you could route through Rome and run the rule on a valuable icon they have in storage. Our agent there will give you all the details. I'll be in touch.'

The line went dead and she rejoined Olga.

'Everything okay?'

'Oh, yeah, everything's fine, thank you. Look, Olga, it's been a long day. Why don't you go on home? We can sort out the finer details by email. About the morning: I'll take a cab to the airport, so you just have a lie-in.'

'You are sure?'

'I am sure.'

Mary Brown allowed the Russian woman to peck her on both cheeks and watched through the revolving door as she waved goodbye from the pavement and disappeared.

For the next two hours Mary Brown sat before the mirror in her room and transformed herself into someone else. At midnight, she pulled the black curly wig over her short, mousy hair and focused on who she was to become. Almost immediately, her garishly painted lips slackened, her eyes, now black behind the contact lenses, became knowing and leery. The woman who walked away from the mirror was, in every respect, the antithesis of the scholarly researcher Mary Brown. One hour later, she was a perfect match for the woman who let herself out of the apartment building within a short walk of the hotel.

The American knew all about Anna Makarova – right back to the St Petersburg orphanage and up to the payment she had made to the local militia the week before in appreciation of their blindness. The woman who walked away from the apartment building was a certified disease-free prostitute in good standing with the local militia and about to go on the game. Standing under a shop awning, taking advantage of the shelter and shadow, Mary Brown watched her likeness totter away on impossibly high heels and waited. After ten minutes, Anna would arrive at the nearest subway station. She would watch the mosaics of heroic factory workers and farmhands slide by as the train left the station and ignore the sniffed disapproval of old women in headscarves and the ogling of beery young men. Within sight of St Basil's and Lenin's tomb in Red Square, she would ply her trade, taking her clients to a seedy hotel in a side street. She had a busy and profitable night, thanks to a group of Armenian businessmen who chose to loiter in the shadow of the Kremlin rather than linger in their Spartan hotel rooms. Early the following morning, she would recross the square, wishing long life to the brides who had come to have photographs taken and leave their bouquets at the tomb of the Unknown Soldier. Finally, she would have coffee and a croissant at a café in Gum, the famous shopping mall once reserved for the Politburo and their families, so that she could bat her false eyelashes at the young waiters who earned less in a week than she had the night before.

Fifteen minutes after Anna Makarova's departure, Mary Brown swore loudly in fluent Russian as she jiggled her key in the front door of the block. Inside, she took the stairs, clattering her heels noisily, occasionally muttering about the permanently busted elevator and the illegitimacy of the building superintendent. She stopped outside the door of 42A on the third floor and knocked.

'Who is it?'

'It's Anna, Irina dear. Can you spare a spoon of coffee?'

The glass eye in the door winked as the occupant viewed the woman at the door. The investigative journalist Irina Blok shot the bolt and opened the door. She wore grey slacks and a baggy knitted sweater. Her feet were bare. On the way to the door, she had stuck a thumb in her book to keep her place and her eyes, behind the thick spectacles, were preoccupied as if she was trying to remember what she had been reading. A small black hole appeared over her right eyebrow and she slumped to the floor. Mary Brown pocketed the silenced gun and checked the body for signs of life. Satisfied, she closed the door behind her and left the building. Just a block from her hotel, she lofted the gun into a building site. Standard procedures on search patterns ensured that it would be found at approximately three p.m. the following day, four hours after the discovery of the slain journalist Irina Blok.

Anna Makarova, the prostitute, would be questioned and fingerprinted before being ejected from the police station, thanks to her alibi and the verbal abuse she directed at the officers.

Following an anonymous telephone call, the more independent newspapers would splash the assassination story across the front pages of their early editions. They would link the journalist's death to the investigations she was currently undertaking into corruption at the highest level of government. They would claim that reliable sources had informed them that the murder weapon was of the type used by the secret police and could be traced directly to an officer in the Lubyanka. These headlines and the attached copy would be reproduced, albeit not on the front pages, of the broadsheet newspapers throughout Europe. The assassination and the investigative work of Irina Blok would be part of the news broadcast on Sky Television and CNN. The Committee to Protect Journalists would send a letter of protest to the Russian government, and the CIA would record the death of the journalist as a successful operation executed to remind the Kremlin that the Cold War had changed, not ended.

⁂

Olga would sleep late and set about preparing her daughter's lunchbox. She would not ask about her daughter's weekly visit to her father the night before because she had promised not to. Closing the plastic lid of the lunchbox with more force than was necessary, she would conclude that there are times when it is better not to know.

෨෭ඡ

Sitting in the business-class section of the British Airways early morning flight from Moscow to Rome, Mary Brown took a final look at the new name in her new passport before tucking it carefully into her carry-on bag. Now she wondered briefly why she was being sent to Baldwin the gun-runner and why the president's husband would also be a guest of the mad Crusader. As a veteran CIA agent, she knew better than to reason why. She was content to do what she was directed to do. Casper Benson had given her the chance to be someone other than herself when he had organised her release from the institution and recruited her to the Agency. He had made the past disappear. Tonight she would be in Rome. Que sera, she thought, before falling into a dreamless sleep.

CIA Headquarters, Washington DC
The director of the CIA sipped from a cut-crystal tumbler of neat single-malt Glenfiddich whisky and reached for the phone.

'Greetings, Sir Knight.'

'You humour me, Benson,' the booming voice responded from the squawk-box on the desk.

'Indeed I do, Baldwin, for now. I believe some of your plans have gone … awry.'

'A temporary setback, I assure you. Those who failed me will be punished. Those who oppose me will die.'

'To adapt a quotation from Oscar Wilde, Baldwin, to fail once might be regarded as a mistake, to fail twice sounds like carelessness. Added to which, our South American operation didn't go according to plan, did it?'

'The fault for that doesn't lie here, Benson,' Baldwin said harshly. 'I provided your angels of death in South America with the best weaponry available. It was superior to those carried by the angels of light sent to pursue them. Check the casualty list.'

Why do the insane prefer to speak in the language of the Bible? Benson wondered.

'You were well paid.'

'No more than was my due,' the voice responded. 'When the Western powers wished to divide the drug lords and set them against each other, so that the lucrative powder revenues could accrue to themselves, they called Baldwin. When they wished to guarantee the flow of Iraqi oil while decrying Saddam among the nations, they called Baldwin. When they desired to bring the squabbling children of Abraham to the peace table, it was Baldwin who supplied tanks to the Israelis and Stinger missiles to the Palestinians. Need I continue?'

Baldwin might be mad, but he was not stupid, Benson conceded.

'Spare me the sales pitch,' he said. 'Let's just say we're aware of the reciprocity that exists. It's to our mutual advantage, so long as it works.'

He allowed a silence so that Baldwin could chew on the implications of the addendum. Sometimes it was more effective to rattle a sabre than draw it. He resumed speaking, in a more conciliatory, almost playful, tone. 'Riddle me this, Sir Knight. How did the Crusaders ensure the loyalty of their allies?'

'Why would we have doubted the loyalty of allies?' Baldwin sounded intrigued, almost sane.

'Oh, come, Sir Knight,' Benson said teasingly. 'Urban of Rome could have waited until your masts dipped below the horizon, then excommunicated your entire force. It would have cast you adrift from every Christian court in Europe. The Patriarch of Constantinople could have blessed you with incense on your departure from his gates, then informed your enemies of your strengths. God knows, you gave him reason aplenty to play you false.'

Baldwin laughed harshly.

'God knows we did. It's a worthy question, but the answer is a simple one. We insisted on some tokens of their good faith. You understand, Benson?'

Oh, he understood all right. Tokens translated into hostages. A dilatory pope or vengeful patriarch might think twice about hostile action when significant personages from their own court or family travelled with the enemy.

'I'm sending you tokens of our good faith, Baldwin.'

There was a single beat of silence before the voice came back.

'Who?'

Despite his misgivings, Benson had to admire Baldwin's grasp of the game. He had been sharp on the pick-up, asking 'who' not 'what'. It was time to go for the big play.

'I'm sending you Ademar.'

The silence from the other end was so total that Benson imagined he could hear the hum of the electric atoms that ferried their voices across the ether.

Finally Baldwin answered, and Benson felt relief that his response was one of incredulity rather than anger.

'Ademar? The bishop Pope Urban gave us when we set forth for Jerusalem? He's been dead nigh on a thousand years, Benson.'

Benson never ceased to wonder at the fine line that

Baldwin walked between fantasy and reality. The true master works wonders with the tools provided, he reminded himself.

'I'm sending you a new Ademar as a sign of our faith and favour. This Ademar,' he pressed on, 'is the prince who might have been pope – our pope. The one we hoped would rally Christendom in the final battle against the infidel and plant the Cross for ever in Jerusalem.'

'But this Ademar failed. You failed,' the knight said slyly. 'Your master plans were brought low at the very steps to the throne by a mere priest, some meddlesome cleric.'

Unconsciously, Benson swayed in his chair as if letting the barb go by.

'Yes,' he allowed, 'your sources are impeccable as always. You already know, then, that this priest survived our little soirée in South America?'

'Yes. I also know he still lives and wonder why. Have you grown soft, Brother Benson? There was a time when—'

'It was expedient. Have no fear. I have plans for him.'

'Why would I fear?' Baldwin said silkily. 'You are the author of his misfortunes. Why would he come looking for me?'

Benson gripped the tumbler tightly until he felt the bevelled edges dig into his skin. He took a deep, shuddering breath and let the rage sigh from his body.

'You're right, Baldwin, he's my concern.'

There was more than a hint of warning in Benson's capitulation but Baldwin had smelled blood in the water and it made him bold.

'This Ademar you offer me was cast out, Benson.'

'Yes, he was, but no further than we can trawl.'

'What would I do with such a one?' Baldwin asked doubtfully.

'Do what you always do, Sir Knight,' Benson grated. 'Use and lose.' Again, he struggled for calm. 'I … I will let you know how the prince may serve our plans.'

'And the priest?'

The bastard just couldn't let it go, Benson mused.

'Where the honey is there will the bees be also.'

'He'll come to the prince?' Baldwin made no effort to soften his scepticism.

'He must.'

'And the price?'

Benson laughed aloud. It felt good to be back on familiar ground.

'Ah, Baldwin,' he said, 'under that shiny breastplate beats the heart of a true merchant. Not for you the dreams of Raymond or the ideals of Godfrey.'

'Benson, I—'

'Think, man,' Benson urged, overriding him. 'Think prize not price. The prize is what you have laboured for all these years. Think Jerusalem, its walls tumbled to dust and a Saviour come at last. You have laid siege to the citadel long enough. It's time to take it. I have the key. Do you want it?'

'Yes,' the voice breathed in reply. 'But there is something else.'

'Something else?'

'I want the Tears of God.'

'The Te—'

'It was denied me by my brother, Godfrey,' Baldwin babbled on. 'He conspired with the Bishop of Rome to keep it from me.'

Benson felt like screaming. He had just offered the mad bastard the fulfilment of all his dreams and he wanted something else? The Tears of God! He opened his mouth to laugh and thought better of it. It was like … what? Like offering a devout Christian the Holy Grail, the cup Jesus had drunk from at the Last Supper, and the fucker asks for the saucer. Again, hysterical laughter bubbled up from his gut and threatened to undo him. He made a supreme effort to ignore the madness and focus on the goal.

'Let me work on that,' he said soothingly. 'Now, listen up, Sir Knight, and receive the keys of your kingdom.'

Leonardo da Vinci Airport, Rome
Jane Wilson, a.k.a. Mary Brown, passed through Passport Control without meriting a glance from the uniformed official. This was partly owing to her rumpled clothes and forgettable face. It was also because of the aura of abstraction she projected. For the same reason, commuters could and did crowd around her on the train to Rome without feeling even the slightest inclination to engage her in conversation. Termini station was a constantly moving weave of arriving and departing passengers, and she threaded her way through the throng and the gauntlet of foreign nationals selling umbrellas. The young man who latched on to Jane Wilson dropped his price from four to one euro as the exit approached. Despite his ever more urgent pleadings, she stared straight ahead as if he didn't exist. He wheeled away in pursuit of another customer, already erasing the vague image of the young woman from his mind. Outside, her mantle of invisibility seemed to develop a fault.

'The signorina is American, perhaps from Pittsburgh, Pennsylvania?'

'Where there's a pawnshop on the corner,' she replied

automatically, while scanning him with her grey eyes. She figured him about twenty-seven going on nineteen. His sparse, blond-tinted hair straggled onto his shoulders at the back. The thin face seemed wary behind a rash of stubble and his jacket bore the logo that suggested a sex act to those who had spelling problems. Baggy, creased jeans belled at the hems over tattered sneakers. A hand-rolled cigarette hung dispiritedly from the corner of his mouth and he plucked it out left-handed to make small red arcs as he gestured.

'My name is Eugenio,' he offered.

She ignored him, slowly scanning left and right for signs of undue interest from passers-by. Eugenio was a cut-out, a local who made occasional money meeting someone at the station for the agency. His cover was that he was an art student who moonlighted as a tour guide. He could meet foreigners in any part of Rome without attracting attention. His belief was that he worked for an American cultural exchange organisation as an occasional meeter and greeter.

'Welcome to my Rome,' he said grandly, as he swept open the taxi door. 'I was born here.'

Yeah, and you've been waiting for me ever since, she thought, refusing to shift over in the back seat so that he had to climb in the front.

'*Dove?*' The driver stabbed the meter to flare into digital numbers. She knew he was disgruntled at the single bag she had on her lap. If she had agreed to put it in the boot he could have charged a supplement.

'Via Genovese, Trastevere, *per favore.*'

'*Si, si,*' he said.

Eugenio slipped into his tourist spiel as they swung into traffic.

'This, coming up on the left, is Santa Maria Maggiore. Remarkable ceilings,' he added lamely, as they swung into the grand avenue, lined on either side with shops and apartment buildings.

'Julius Caesar,' he pointed out unnecessarily, as the unmistakable bronze statue of the emperor glided by, locked in a permanent Fascist salute.

As they rounded the Forum, she observed that his patter needed work:

'Where Marcus Antonius make a speech for Shakespeare.'

It went downhill from there as he devolved from the trite to the obvious. She knew the driver was taking the scenic route and sat content, only occasionally tuning in to Eugenio.

'Isla la Tiberna, on your left,' he cried excitedly, as they nosed across the Ponte Sisto. 'Ponte Sisto builded by Pope Pius Six for Roman people.'

'By taxing prostitutes,' she answered, and relished the shocked silence that ensued in the front.

'You have been in Rome before?' Eugenio ventured.

'No.'

After the bridge, a labyrinth of narrow streets squeezed them into the narrower via Genovese. She took the keys to the apartment and climbed out of the taxi. Latin to the last, Eugenio couldn't resist a final sally. He stuck his head out of the window. 'Perhaps I will you see again?'

Jane Wilson paused, allowing the dark place inside her to open before she turned and walked back. She cocked her fist like a pistol and tapped him lightly above the right eyebrow with her extended index finger. 'You must pray that you don't, Eugenio,' she murmured, in flawless Italian. He jerked back so fast, he banged his head on the door frame.

The apartment was a high-ceilinged rectangular room with a box-like bathroom projecting at one end, supporting an open-loft sleeping area. The walls were washed yellow, the pictures suitably abstract and anonymous. She spent an hour pacing the space and memorising the details before pouring a half-glass of white wine from the bottle in the refrigerator and taking it to the tiny balcony. The campanile of Santa Cecilia de Trastevere loomed over the tumble of tiled roofs that filled her view. Below the balcony, a small courtyard stood guard on an aged motorcycle. One hour later, the intercom buzzed twice.

'Manicure or pedicure?' the voice crackled.

'No, come in,' she replied, and pressed the button to release the lock on the front door. She recognised the password as an old gag from a Marx Brothers movie and wondered briefly who the film buff in the Rome Office might be. As the footsteps swelled in the concrete stairway, she angled the metal reading lamp so that the doorway was brightly lit, easing herself into the shadows behind.

'It's open,' she called, in response to the single knock. Two men stepped uncertainly into the glare.

'What's with the third degree?' the larger of the two asked, keeping his arms straight down at his sides and his hands in plain view. 'You know me, Jane,' he added, allowing just a trace of impatience to inflect his voice.

'Yeah, Charlie, you I know. Who's your shadow?'

'Name's Eddie,' the big man grunted. 'He's our wheels.' Eddie kept schtum, blinking a greeting from behind Charlie's shoulder.

Groucho and Harpo, she thought.

'Sit at the table, boys.'

She waited until they were seated before switching off the light.

'A girl can't be too careful, Charlie. Drink?'

'Whaddya got?'

'White wine.'

'That it?'

'Yep.'

'Virgin's piss,' Charlie growled. 'Okay.'

She passed the bottle and kept her hand extended, palm up.

'You got it?'

Charlie reached slowly inside his jacket and produced a folded sheet of paper. She spread it on the table.

'The way I see it,' Eddie began, and froze as her eyes swivelled up to lock with his.

'Walks and talks,' she murmured.

'Eddie's a good driver,' Charlie added quickly. She nodded and returned her gaze to the plan, becoming engrossed to the extent that she seemed unaware of the two men who were sipping nervously from the wine glasses.

After what seemed to them a very long time, she straightened. 'Okay boys,' she said, 'this is how it goes down.'

Via Selci, Rome

Those residents of the quiet street near the Colosseum who noticed the Water Department van pull up outside at first light made immediate resolutions to buy bottled water on the way home from work and rushed to use the showers.

Inside it, Charlie eased himself from the passenger seat into the rear.

'Charlie.'

'Yeah?'

'What's with this dame?'

Charlie zipped the blue boiler suit all the way to the top. 'You like your job, Eddie?'

'Yeah, sure. It's—'

'Yeah,' the big man cut in, 'it's a peach, ain't it? They fly us in. We do the job. They fly us out. We get paid, tax free. As I say, Eddie, it's a peach. Don't start bitin' on the stone. Get my drift?'

'Yeah, yeah, it's just that she—'

'Eddie, Earth calling Eddie.'

'What?'

'Word to the wise, my friend. I've done a few gigs with her before. She don't do small-talk, nights out with the crew, all that wrap-party shit when the job's done.'

'Yeah, but she don't have to be such a fuckin' ball-breaker.'

Charlie fixed his peaked cap in place.

'This is your first gig with her, right?'

'Right.'

Charlie seemed to weigh his words before he spoke.

'Last time, we had this young guy up in Florence. Thought he was Fangio behind the wheel, but the kid could drive – could he ever. Only, he figured he had a V8 engine in his pants. Couldn't zip his lip, always braggin' and hittin' on her.'

Charlie checked his appearance in the full-length mirror fastened to the wall of the van.

'And?' Eddie prompted.

'There ain't no 'and', Eddie. She's number one. The agency can always get another driver.'

Via La Spezia, Rome

Sister Eileen consulted her shiny new watch and smiled. 'Waterproof to a depth of thirty metres,' the tag had assured her. She was certain the irony was lost on her brother Frank, who had presented it with a flourish to mark her retirement. Lodwar, her home of forty years in Kenya's Turkana desert, hadn't been a place for watches, she concluded, as she closed the door of the convent behind her with guilty relief. In the oven that had been her mission, sweat tended to rot leather straps and condense in metal bracelets to burn red weals on the wrist. A watch hadn't yet been made, waterproof or not, that could resist the fine sand that sifted through the zips of bags and left dusty tank-tracks on the clothes. There was a cultural reason also. The local people, nomadic herdsmen for the most part, saw no profit in slicing the day into measurable segments. You got up with the sun and it put you right back down again about noon. You got up some time later and worked until the sun dropped below the horizon.

'Turkana time is elastic,' John Foley had assured her, at their first meeting. 'Even tomorrow is too exact a concept around here.'

She remembered digesting that particular nugget of wisdom, surprised that the bishop who had delivered it had been flat on his back at the time with a wrench in his hand. Before she could argue, he had slid back under the lorry. Welcome to Lodwar. New times, new challenges, she reminded herself, as the articulated bus wheezed to a stop before her. Forty years earlier, she had left her native Ireland for an alien world. Now the wheel had come full circle and here she was, four decades later, back in a world that was equally alien. Never too old to learn, she thought, remembering her interview with the superior general.

'Forty years is a long time, Sister. It may take a while to adjust.'

By way of contrast, the young American sister who had responsibility for the retirement programme didn't do euphemisms. 'Eileen, honey, you've been the hotshot doctor for a zillion years, mistress of all you surveyed. Sure you thought about retirement, same as people think about dying. Usually they think of other people dying. Then the letter arrives and it's all over. We could and maybe should argue the merits of letting you die over there as against the slow euthanasia of spinning what's left of your wheels over here, but that's for another day. Fact is, you're here and you want to be there. So far, so normal. It's called grieving, Eileen, and it's all about learning to let go of where and who you were before you can have any kind of meaningful life here.'

'Bullshit.'

It was a word favoured by her brash and beautiful niece in Boston and she admired the economy of it.

Sister Susan hadn't raised a carefully plucked eyebrow.

'Way to go, Eileen.' She laughed. 'Don't swallow the placebos of "It's all for the best," or the unholy blackmail that "It's God's will." Wrestle with it, girl.'

So she had asked to spend her holiday year in Rome. Why Rome? Why not? She could have said Madrid or Prague or any other place – they were as foreign to her as Ireland had become. Anyway, all she wanted to do was read and think. There had never been enough time before and the original candlelight and eventual light from a generator hadn't been conducive in Kenya to intensive reading. And, yes, she wanted to think. She had always been a doer. The missions did that to you, she knew. The needs were so great and the resources so pathetically meagre it had always seemed an indulgence to take time out to think. Maybe she'd sit in on a few lectures at the university, attend an opera in Caracalla. Rome was a city of opportunities and contradictions.

She looked up as the bus negotiated the busy intersection at Santa Croce in Gerusalemme. Even at this hour a straggle of pilgrims climbed the steps to the door of the great church. Inside, they would follow the arrows to the shrine containing the relics of the True Cross. She had done the tour herself and had had to work hard on moderating her scepticism. Despite her firm resolutions, the word immediately conjured a picture of Sister Teresa.

Sister Teresa was one of the four Italian Franciscan sisters with whom she shared the convent on the via La Spezia. All four had spent their entire religious lives in Rome and, Eileen thought, it showed. She couldn't quite put her finger on it but it might have had something to do with the way they dressed and moved and greeted each other – as if they were within earshot of the Almighty. This gave a kind of liturgical formality to even the most casual encounters that was light years away from the rough and ready bonhomie one usually found on the missions. Added to which, she thought, the sisters seemed to have an unhealthy fascination with the machinations of church politics. Try as she might, she couldn't suspend her prejudices when Sister Teresa loomed large in the crosshairs of her critical faculties, as she had that morning after Mass.

The good Sister had declared herself 'indisposed'. Again! Sister Teresa, she thought admiringly, had raised psycho-somatic illness to an art form – which she tended to exhibit regularly. This morning it had manifested itself as a 'tension headache'. Sister Eileen snorted dismissively and the man beside her shifted away fractionally, raising his newspaper like a protective talisman. In Lodwar, they had experienced malaria, dengue fever, sunstroke and snakebite. She couldn't, after a fast trawl through forty years, remember a single presentation or diagnosis of 'tension headache'. Grudgingly, she had admitted it might be due to Sister's work at the prison and offered to do locum. The gapped teeth of the Colosseum appeared over the driver's shoulder, reminding her that her stop was coming up. Sister Teresa had been grateful if reticent.

'This particular ... eh, personage is being accommodated at this address, Sister. He is a man more sinned against than sinning. It might be better if you confined yourself to listening.'

Okay, she thought, as she gathered her bag. So this noble soul, this personage no less, had been transferred from prison to a convent. Curiouser and curiouser. God's ways are obviously not our ways, she thought, and double-checked the shortest way to the Convent of Santa Lucia on the via Selci.

Via Selci, Rome
Sister Eileen turned into the via Selci, still checking the directions scribbled on a scrap of paper. She was aware of the van parked at the kerb and the big man in the peaked cap and boiler suit bending over the manhole cover. Stepping sideways to pass him on the inside of the narrow pavement, she saw the side door of the van slide open. For a frozen moment, she looked into the eyes of a young nun, surprised in the act of fixing her veil. Then a hand clamped over Sister Eileen's mouth and she felt a stinging sensation in her neck, then nothing.

Charlie placed the nun gently on the floor of the van and turned her into the recovery position, pulling a blue blanket up to her chin. He nodded, and Jane Wilson stepped to the pavement. She was, in every respect, a religious sister, from the blue veil that hung to her shoulders to the navy skirt that swung modestly at her shins. She encountered no one on the short walk to the Convent of Santa Lucia. Had she done so, it was unlikely they would have remembered any detail of her appearance. She was just another nun in Rome, ubiquitous and therefore invisible. Confidently she climbed the steps to the front door. To her right, above the metal grille and the electric bell, she read the legend printed on a piece of card: '*Ho sete*' – 'I thirst.' She pressed the bell.

'*Buon giorno.*'

From the eyes at the grille, she guessed the sister was Filipina.

'*Buon giorno,*' she replied, in a voice she had practised in the van until Eddie had fidgeted himself into her awareness and earned a look. Her voice would betray no hint of accent, no key to her personality.

'You wish to have a relic, Sister?' the Filipina enquired politely.

Jane Wilson knew that the Santa Lucia enjoyed a special relationship with the vicariate office that dispensed licences for relics. She could select a relic of any of a thousand saints and martyrs and have it free of charge. There would, of course, be an 'administration fee'.

'No, Sister, thank you. My name is Sister Eileen. I have come in place of Sister Teresa who is unwell.'

'Again!' the Filipina blurted, and the eyes behind the grille widened in mortification. 'Please come to the side door,' she said breathlessly, and the grille closed.

Inside, Jane Wilson made her way to a lofty whitewashed parlour with another grille set in the wall.

'He will be with you presently,' the grille whispered, and Jane Wilson was alone. She turned a complete slow circle, imprinting the room and its sparse furnishings on her memory. She noted the faded framed prints of various saints and martyrs, holding the instruments of their torture. In pride of place hung a lurid painting of Santa Lucia, presenting her severed breasts on a salver. Jane Wilson resolved to refuse any offer of coffee.

A door creaked and a man entered. He stood at more than six feet tall but still managed to appear diminished. He wore the open-necked white shirt and black slacks favoured by off-duty priests. His African-American features were dusted with silver stubble. Cold black eyes scanned her dismissively before he spoke.

'You know what this place is? This is a Wal-Mart for relics, Sister.' He played with the syllables in a grotesque parody of Hannibal Lecter. 'Tell me what you want.'

She didn't doubt she was in the presence of someone with the most tenuous grip on reality and kept her eyes cast down demurely. Her silence seemed to irk him into sarcasm.

'How's about a feather from an archangel's wing? They tell me it's a hot item in the American angel industry. Buy one, get one free. Maybe your budget doesn't stretch that far.' He shook his head in fake disappointment. 'Can I interest you in a thread from the Virgin's veil, a thong from the sandal of St Francis? Come on, lady,' he cried in a barker's voice, 'the store is now open for the credulous and cretinous. Everything must go.'

He looked at her, expectantly.

'No? Okay, this is my final offer.'

She saw a muscle dance under his right eye and watched him gather his energy for one last manic pitch.

'I got here a two-thousand-year-old olive pit from the Garden of Gethsemane, I have a rush from the basket of Moses, a cup hewn from the horn of the ram Abraham substituted for Isaac! Make me a fucking offer!' he shouted.

She waited a beat until his breathing had become more controlled and he had wiped the spittle from his chin with a trembling hand.

'I offer you revenge,' she said calmly.

He risked a sideways glance and she fancied she could hear the tumblers whir in his brain as he tried to unlock the import of that single word 'revenge'. 'Revenge,' he said warily. 'The Afghans say it's a dish best served cold.'

'The Turks say the one who would set out to find revenge must first dig two graves.' She looked around the room, then let her eyes lock with his.

'In your case, that would be one. Sit down, Cardinal Thomas.'

He moved slowly to the Formica-topped table and lowered himself into a chair. 'Revenge,' he whispered, and gave a terrible, humourless laugh that shuddered soundlessly from his body without diminishing the agony in his eyes. 'Who the hell are you?' he asked, when the spasm had passed.

'A messenger.'

'From the Holy Ghost.'

'Just the Ghost.'

His face sagged with shock.

'I'm not forgotten, then?'

'No, Eminence. You're neither forgotten nor forgiven. The Ghost invested in you, and you … missed a payment.'

He nodded, his face set in bitter resignation.

'Have you come to collect?'

'Not yet. It depends.'

'Depends on what?'

Was that a whisper of hope in his voice? She let the silence stretch to screaming point, not because she had been instructed to torture but because she could.

'I make you an offer. You say yea or nay.'

'If I say nay?'

'Then I grant you the indulgence of a swift and painless release from your Purgatory. Yea means you get one more swing on the carousel, one more grab at the brass ring – insert your own cliché in the space available.'

Cardinal Thomas took a deep breath and some of the old charisma seemed to seep back into his face.

'The answer is yes,' he said firmly. Then, looking around as if for the last time at the cold room he sat in, he added, 'What have I got to lose?'

'Everything,' she replied, and shot him.

❧❧❧

Sister Emmanuel knew she should be concentrating on the words of the psalm sung by the young and old voices around her in the oratory. She tried to focus but her ears kept straining, questing in the silences between the phrases.

'"I shall look up to the mountains from where shall come my help,"' her sisters sang.

'Help' seemed to echo in the distance.

'"My help is in the name of the Lord, who made Heaven and Earth."'

'Help' resounded again, stronger than before.

'Help!'

When she slammed the grille open, she saw the visiting

sister kneeling on the parlour floor, cradling the cardinal's head in her lap. The unlikely pietà took her breath away and she disappeared from the grille. Her place was taken by a much older face. Mother Cecilia had lived through the Nazi occupation of her native city. She remembered screams in the night and bombs sifting plaster from the ceilings of the cellars they'd hidden in. 'Is he dead?' she asked calmly.

'I ... I don't think so,' the young nun quavered. 'I've called the ambulance and the police,' she rushed on. 'I don't know if that was the right thing to do. His eyes just rolled back and he – he ...'

'Calm yourself, Sister. He is in the hands of God. You did right to call for medical help.'

Mother Cecilia wasn't sure how the Vatican authorities would respond to the police being called but that was not of consequence now. The ringing doorbell interrupted her reflection and the young nun looked to her for guidance.

'Let them in, Sister, and please accompany the patient to the hospital. Should he revive, no one is to speak to him until a member of the Vatican Secretariat is present. Do you understand?'

'Yes, Mother.'

Mother Cecilia watched approvingly as the nun admitted the two paramedics. She was relieved to see that the girl seemed to have regained her composure as she chivvied the two men to place the cardinal carefully on the stretcher. It seemed only a matter of minutes before they had fastened straps across his body and removed him. The young sister waved distractedly from the doorway and followed. Mother Cecilia hoped she would not be too upset. Young people today were so cosseted from the harsh realities of life. In her day ...

She resolved to pray for her, after a small glass of grappa to steady her heart.

⊱⋆⊰

Jane Wilson plucked the dart from the cardinal's neck and pressed her fingers to the pulse point.

'He'll live,' she grunted. 'Drive, Eddie, keep it under the speed limit and don't run lights.'

'Yeah, yeah,' he grumbled, revving the engine.

'What about the nun?' Charlie asked.

'Surplus to requirements,' she answered, peeling the veil from her head. 'Dump her.' Gently the big man lifted the nun, still draped in her blue blanket, and hurried to the convent door. Placing her on the top step, he pressed the bell firmly and returned to the van. Eddie released the handbrake before the door had slid closed.

'Hey, Charlie,' Jane Wilson said slyly, 'funny time for trick or treat. Hope you're not going soft on me.'

'"The Lord giveth and the Lord taketh away,"' he answered calmly.

⊱⋆⊰

Sister Emmanuel crossed herself automatically when the bell sounded. She reminded herself to walk at a measured pace: the enclosed order of Santa Lucia did not run, ever. The six-inch rectangular grille, her only vista on the world, revealed an empty street. Puzzled, she craned her neck to look left and right. On impulse, she stretched up on her toes and immediately saw the body lying on the steps.

'Jesus Christ,' she exclaimed, before her training kicked in and she walked on spongy legs to seek the Reverend Mother's counsel.

§

Jane Wilson saw Eddie angle his overhead mirror as she exchanged the blue religious habit for a starched white nurse's uniform and veil. Later, she thought. Eddie jockeyed the van out of the Roman suburbs and on to the highway that would carry them all the way up the spine of Italy into the hills of Umbria. She flipped her cellphone and pushed the numbers.

'*Pronto*,' a voice crackled in response.

'Release the decoys and alert the Guardian Angel,' she murmured.

§

Almost simultaneously, three identical blue vans, similar to the one they rode in, hit the streets of Rome. One moved directly to Termini station, where it parked on a double yellow line. The driver quickly lost himself in the busy concourse. Fifteen minutes later, the traffic policeman was leaning on the bonnet writing a ticket when he noticed a cable extruding from a small hole bored in the base of the passenger window. Cautiously, he bent his tall frame to follow its passage, oblivious to the damp seeping into his trousers as he knelt to look under the van.

'Oh, Holy Virgin,' he breathed.

It was a full three minutes before he had controlled his

breathing and begun to whistle frantically, waving his arms to divert passers-by. Traffic quickly snarled to a halt, blocking the main access road to the station. Above the cacophony of competing horns, the officer heard the rising whoop of sirens and redoubled his efforts to clear a passage for the bomb squad.

છૐ

The second blue van was already travelling to the seaport at Ostia. It drove onto the ferry for Corsica, which departed the terminal two minutes before the port went into lock-down. The driver sat in a dockside café, sipping an espresso, as the ferry cleared the harbour.

છૐ

The third van parked in Area 4D at Leonardo da Vinci airport. The driver made his way to the terminal building and enquired at the information booth about the possibility of chartering an air- ambulance. He was given the relevant details by an official, who made a note of the query for the next shift and left almost immediately. It would be some hours before the small incendiary device in the back of the van was triggered by a timer and a few more before the information official would be roused from the bed of her lover to answer questions. Meanwhile, her husband would sit patiently in the police car, waiting to ask some questions of his own.

છૐ

At the sign for Tarquinia, Eddie nudged them out of the traffic and up the ramp. They wove into small country roads before rocking up an unpaved road through a gauntlet of poplars. Beside the stone farmhouse, the double doors of the barn yawned invitingly and the van disappeared inside. Minutes later, a Croce Verde ambulance emerged from the double doors at the other end and eased itself onto the highway. Eddie wiped his hands on his thighs, glanced in the rear-view mirror and froze.

'We got trouble,' he said.

Almost nonchalantly, Charlie unclipped a sawn-off, pump-action shotgun from under the dash and began to thumb cartridges into the breech. Jane Wilson ghosted sideways and glanced into the wing mirror. She saw a motorcycle carabiniere coming up fast, whittling away at the traffic between them until he slotted in right on their tail. He blinked his hazards twice.

'Oh, shit,' Eddie gasped, and leaned on the accelerator.

'Ease up, Eddie,' she snapped.

The driver didn't seem to hear her until she grasped the steering wheel with her left hand while showing him just enough of the knife she held below his right eye. 'He's ours, Eddie,' she grated. 'He's Guardian Angel, our cover all the way to Umbria. Okay, okay, now ease up on the pedal. Yeah, good. You got the wheel back, Eddie?' Slowly, she withdrew her hands as he regained control. His shoulders quivered and his sweating face glowed pasty-white.

'I'm okay,' he grunted. 'Just threw me, ya know, cop coming up like that. I had no idea. Why didn't nobody tell me?'

'Eddie, it's okay, okay, breathe,' she soothed. 'You're the driver and you've got this rig under control.'

'I got it,' he said testily. 'Just back up and give me some space here.'

She moved away and relaxed. In her peripheral vision, she could see Charlie watching her.

Police Headquarters, Capitoline Hill, Rome

Detective Giuseppe Fermi sat in the operations room of the Capitoline police headquarters and counted his blessings. Top of the list, he placed his wife of many years. Cybele had married the angular and mildly eccentric young man with a passion for archaeology and continued to love the angular and very eccentric old man whose passion had been diluted into a hobby and who made his living as a policeman. Fermi had a lifelong weakness for cowboy movies and American jokes; old American jokes, his friends said. It had been a smart move to marry a lady with no memory for jokes, he reflected. That way, she could enjoy the same old gag over and over. The joke that tickled his mind at the moment was the one about the Brooklyn stallholder who gets hit by a car as he's crossing the street. People rush up to him and ask, 'You doin' OK?' And he says, 'I make a livin'.' Fermi laughed aloud but it was a laugh tinged with regret. That's what you do, Giuseppe, he told himself, you make a living. He shook the thought away and added his two children to the blessings list. They were both adults and long gone from the family nest, but your children are always your children, right? Right, he agreed.

The detective looked around the empty room and sighed. His colleagues, Carlo and Antonio, were missing and would manage to stay missing so long as he was around. Consider it a blessing, his good angel prompted. Consider it your fault, the one with the tail countered. You're both right, he admitted, and they disappeared. If compromise had been an option for angels, the Fall would never have happened. His thoughts wound back from heavenly messengers to the nub of the problem.

He had brought his broken dreams of being an archaeologist to Cybele, all those years before, railing at the economic circumstances that had precluded university and the realisation of his goal. He remembered how she'd held him until he'd run to silence and said, 'Giuseppe, you gave your brother and sisters the chance you never got. You gave the same to your children. Those were choices – and good choices, no?'

'Yes.'

'Now you're a policeman and you still have a choice.'

'What choice?'

'To be the best policeman you can be. I didn't marry an archaeologist, I married you, and I don't want you wasting your life wishing you were anyone or anything else.'

Even now his eyes fogged at the memory. And Giuseppe Fermi had resolved to put his passion for excavation into investigation. And that was what had him, as the Americans said, in deep shit, between a rock and a hard place, in the toilet. As toilets went, this one wasn't so bad, he thought. He could stroll around the corner and have an espresso in the shadow of the Arch of Titus. In another part of the building, he could nod admiringly at the head of Constantine, the emperor who had elevated Christianity from the Catacombs, or marvel at Romulus and Remus sucking from the she-wolf. He congratulated himself on knowing that Constantine had probably remained a sun-worshipper and the she-wolf was actually Etruscan from the fifth century while the twin founders of Rome were probably positioned beneath her teats in the fifteenth century.

The Rome of antiquity had been like that, he thought fondly. Romans had always been the cultural magpies of the Mediterranean, snatching up a shiny piece of Etruscan art or an attractive Greek god to add lustre to their own heroic myth. His favourite piece stood in Exhibition Space 3 to the extreme right of the main entrance to the Palazzo dei Conservatori. The Spinario was a bronze sculpture from the first century, before the Christian era, of a boy trying to remove a thorn from the sole of his bare foot. Fermi would have traded all the Bernini cupolas and Buonorotti ceilings for that utterly focused boy, frozen in time. In some ways, it symbolised what his commissioner referred to as his 'problem'.

'Your problem, Fermi, is you don't see the bigger picture. You focus on the particular and you don't let go.'

It was the truth. He had encountered the phenomenon of the assassination of liberal Roman Catholic theologians and his focus had been narrowed to agonising clarity by the murder of his priest-brother, Francisco. Giuseppe Fermi had not let go. He had followed the trail of blood to the walls of the Vatican and beyond. Because he had never paused to consider 'the bigger picture', he had played his part in preserving the life of a pope, eliminating the psychopath who had been the instrument manipulated to murder, and arresting the man he held ultimately responsible.

'You arrested a cardinal, a prince of the Church, a man tipped to be pope,' the commissioner had shouted, his voice rising operatically at the end of each phrase. 'Are you mad?' he had crescendoed.

'No,' Fermi had replied, with the calm that was oxygen to the flames of the furious. 'I am not mad. I am a policeman.'

He smiled now at the quixotic nature of his stance. Policemen did not tilt a lance against the Lateran Treaty of 1929, which had created the Vatican state and granted those inside the walls immunity from the laws of the republic. Nor did they, even if Mussolini had salivated at the possibility, arrest potential popes like J. Arthur Thomas, the American cardinal. Inevitably, the status quo had shaken off these seismic happenings and reasserted the proper order. An official fire-blanket dropped over the fourth estate, ensuring the silence of the media and the ignorance of the masses – the apparatchiks on both sides knew the value of containing the blaze. There had followed a political gavotte, danced with exquisite protocol, behind closed doors, by the black suits of the Justice Department and the black skirts of the Vatican. The result was the classic Roman solution to a Roman problem. The cardinal would be released from Italian custody and detained at a Vatican property. There followed a brief flurry of mutual congratulations and pledges of mutual co-operation and then the file was closed. Naturally, those august personages who had been obliged to clean out this particular section of the Augean stables needed someone to dump on. The system is never at fault, only a constituent part of it, and he, Giuseppe Fermi, had been the only candidate for the role of scapegoat.

'What's the worst they can do? Fire me?' he had asked Cybele.

And she, with the ancient blood of Roman senators running in her veins, had known there were fates worse than firing. And so it proved. They couldn't risk firing him. After all, the signori and signore of the fourth estate, particularly those of a leftist persuasion, might have battened on his story. Why create a martyr when you can just make a man disappear? He had been excommunicated. It was the ultimate punishment for one who held views that differed from those of the Establishment. It gave Fermi a new appreciation of Galileo's punishment and his eventual denial of his discoveries. Detective Fermi would come to the office every day but not to work. And that was why he was sitting at his empty desk in the empty operations room when the phone rang.

'*Pronto?*'

Fermi went from incredulity to indignation to calm, methodical policeman in ten seconds.

'Tell the officers at the scene to secure the convent. No one is to cross the line without my say-so. Repeat, no one.'

He depressed the cradle with his finger and dialled again.

'Operations room, Capitoline headquarters. Code Cicero. Run a check on all hospitals for the admission of an African-American male. Alert security at Ciampino, Leonardo da Vinci and the Ostia seaport. Subject possibly accompanied by Caucasian female and two Caucasian males travelling in a blue van.'

He paused, drumming his fingers on the desk.

'Sir?' the receiver prompted.

'I'm still here, just thinking. Yes, request traffic officers to check for a blue van on the northbound highway. Read that back to me, please. Excellent. I am now going to the crime scene.' He rattled off his cellphone number.

'What? Oh, yes, sorry, it's Detective Fermi, Giuseppe Fermi.'

One of the trainee detectives, the 'bambini', as the old hands dubbed them, reversed from an evidence room as Fermi loped along the corridor. In one smooth movement, he plucked the plastic cup from the man's hand and whirled him towards the back stairs.

'Name?'

'Fausto Rizzari, sir.'

'Previous experience?'

'Guardia di Finanza.'

Good, he thought, propelling Fausto down the shadowed stairwell. Someone from the finance police was likely to be painstaking and concerned with detail. Added to which, in a country where tax evasion was seen as a patriotic duty, Fausto Rizzari would make people nervous. Excellent. He sipped the espresso before pushing on the fire-door.

'Sir, the fire doors are alarmed.'

'Yes, it should keep them distracted for a while.'

He scanned the array of vehicles in the courtyard.

'Can you drive, Fausto?'

Convent of Santa Lucia, Rome

Officer Cornelia Scipio regretted her decision to become a police officer, she did that most days as she circled the Colosseum, rescuing tourists from snarling traffic, hustling 'gladiators', rogue guides, umbrella salesmen and the 'dippers', who specialised in relieving tourists of their bags and purses. She had dreamed of becoming a detective, a dream fuelled by the cop-soaps she was addicted to and the antipathy of her mother.

'Nice girls don't wear trousers, Cornelia.'

Maybe she should have listened to Mamma, she thought, as she stretched the yellow tape across the façade of the Santa Lucia. Oh, Mamma, she prayed fervently as the black limousine with the Vatican plates eased to the kerb. Giancarlo, her lazy-bastard partner, had already disappeared 'to take statements', more likely an espresso and cigarette. As the black skirts stepped from the rear of the limousine, she pulled her cap firmly over an unruly head of auburn curls, tugged the jacket of her uniform and tried to stand taller than her five foot nothing. She knew she and Giancarlo had been plucked from Colosseum duty and directed to the Santa Lucia because a hysterical phone call from a convent hadn't merited the presence of someone more senior. Until, of course, she had managed to unravel the facts, interview the mystery sister found on the doorstep and call through to base. The two priests loomed larger and larger.

☙❦☙

It ranked up there with some of the most exhilarating moments of his life. Strapped into the police car and holding the strap for good measure, Detective Fermi discovered that the prematurely balding young policeman with the round, innocent face and unfashionable spectacles was to driving what Caravaggio was to painting. Working from a palette of light and shade, his mastery of his medium moved Fermi to the pit of his stomach and frequently below that point where parts of his anatomy seemed to rise of their own volition, seeking protection in the face of clear and present danger. Fausto alternated between a feather-light touch on the wheel, which shaded them in and out of seemingly solid traffic, to a foot-to-the-floor, palm-glued-to-the-horn intensity that startled lower mortals to find refuge on the kerb. The scream-ing straight run on the via del Circo Massimo was a valediction to pure velocity, the circuit of the Colosseum a

master class in the art of the controlled glide as he angled the
wheel with a nonchalant left hand and pressed the pedal with
his right foot, raising his considerable rump from the seat like
a yachtsman in a gale. It took a full five seconds for the
detective to clear the blur from his eyes after their squealing
stop at the convent of Santa Lucia. He staggered from the
police car on tingling feet at the precise moment when the
Vatican apparatchiks sandwiched the tiny female police officer
between their black-clad bodies.

'Fill your hands, you sons of bitches,' Fermi murmured and
strode into battle.

'Who are you?' the younger of the two priests demanded,
with a flick of the head such as one might give when irritated
by a flying insect.

'I know who I am, Monsignor,' the detective answered
calmly, 'and why I am here and by what authority. The
question to be resolved therefore is who you are and by what
authority you trespass on a crime scene. Of course, there is the
more immediate question of why you are physically intimi-
dating a female police officer in the course of her duties.'

Two mouths sagged open and shut while two sets of feet
retreated two paces in perfect synchronicity. Before they could
recover, he angled his body to exclude them and spoke to the
officer.

'Your name, please?'

'C–Cornelia Scipio, sir.'

Giuseppe Fermi noted the errant curls now swinging over
blue eyes set in a strained and beautiful face. The support
structure, he allowed, although bulked out by the regulation
jacket and ballasted with gun and radio, was trim and feminine.
He extended his hand and shook hers warmly.

'Good work, Officer Scipio. I am Detective Fermi. My assistant is Fangio – I beg your pardon, Fausto Rizzari. Will you accompany me inside, please?'

Cornelia Scipio was thunderstruck. So this was the fabled Fermi. Even the slack-witted Giancarlo called him 'a real policeman'. Before she could untangle her tongue, a clerical voice interposed, 'The Santa Lucia is Vatican property, Detective.'

Fermi seemed to give this serious consideration for a few moments, then inclined his head and moved a few paces away from the police officer. Reluctantly, the priests followed.

'You are correct, Monsignor,' he said, quietly enough to cause both men to lean closer. 'According to the Lateran Treaty, this convent does come under the jurisdiction of the Vatican state. As such, it has been the … refuge – shall we say? – of a certain church notable, who has been abducted, and the depository for a Catholic sister who has happily regained consciousness inside. The … revelation of either of these facts would prove embarrassing to the Vatican, which had a duty to contain the former and protect the latter. Perhaps it is in all our interests if the police are allowed to investigate these happenings before the Church is forced to confirm or deny them.'

He locked eyes with the larger of the two.

'You wouldn't dare,' the priest grated. 'Unless, of course, you have tired of being a detective and wish to spend what remains of your career writing parking tickets in Lazio.'

Again, Fermi allowed a short silence. 'Monsignor,' he replied, even more quietly, 'my name is Giuseppe Fermi. I am not unknown to your employers as the detective who arrested the person whose abduction brings us together.'

He saw them stiffen and pressed his advantage:

'If you do not wish to spend what remains of your career

ministering in a mountain village in Umbria, you will not detain me. As for parking tickets, your limousine is on a double yellow line. Move it, please.'

He knew John Wayne would have been more succinct, Gary Cooper more laconic, but he felt pretty damn good all the same. The synchronised clerics swivelled as one and left him.

'Now, Officer Scipio,' he said, 'Let's sort out the Santa Lucia.'

⚜

If Mother Cecilia had a weakness, apart from the occasional grappa, it was for mature, handsome men with courtly manners. Throughout the interview, she nudged the plate of plain biscuits in the detective's direction and refilled his cup from the battered cafetière.

'Reverend Mother,' he began, 'I am conscious of the great shock you and the community have suffered. To have the silence and serenity of this house of prayer violated in such a manner   is …' He shook his head as if lost for words.

'It pains me that, in the pursuit of my duty, I might be adding to your burden.'

'Oh, no, Inspector,' she breathed, promoting him and wishing she had served better biscuits all at the same time. For thirty cathartic minutes, she told this perfect gentleman all that had transpired, adding the grace-notes of her own observations on J. Arthur Thomas, Vatican subterfuge and the major player in what she termed 'a farrago'. It was a word she had long admired and had very few opportunities to use. She felt she could speak freely to this wonderful man, and did. Later, two very irate monsignori would accuse her of 'gross imprudence'. She herself would describe it to her confessor as an 'indiscretion', for which she had no real purpose of amendment. Fermi thanked her profusely and, before leaving the room to interview the sister found on the doorstep, gave her his most respectful bow.

ಬಿಂಬ

'You look like Lana Turner when she's been rescued from the snow by Max von Sydow,' Fermi said from the doorway.

'And you look nothing like Hercule Poirot,' Sister Eileen replied calmly, 'but you have 'policeman' stamped on your forehead.' She was propped up with cushions in a wing-back chair, a blanket hanging from her lap to the floor.

'I came around some time ago,' she said irritably. 'I haven't any side-effects but they insist on treating me like an invalid.'

'Perhaps we should wait for a doctor's opinion.'

'I am a doctor.'

'And, if I may say so, exhibiting all the symptoms of a doctor who finds herself a patient.'

She laughed, and the impatience disappeared from her face.

'I'm Eileen,' she said, and held out her hand.

He resisted the impulse to kiss it: Sister Eileen, he thought, was not a kissing person. She was Irish, of course. Had to be with that colouring and accent, and everyone knew the Irish were the Italians of the North Atlantic – passionate by inclination and repressed by climate.

'I am Giuseppe. May I sit, Eileen?'

'Please.' She gestured him to a stool and admired the way he perched there without awkwardness. Briefly, he sketched the arrival of a Sister Eileen at the door of the convent and the events leading up to the arrival of yet another Sister Eileen, wrapped in a blanket and lying unconscious on the top step. 'Any little thing you remember now might be of great help,' he concluded.

'There's an old joke at h—, in Ireland,' she corrected herself. 'It's about a tourist who asks a local for directions and the local says, "If I were you, I wouldn't start from here at all."'

Fermi smiled, and nodded at her to continue.

'I say that,' Sister Eileen said, 'because I shouldn't be here at all. I'm a retired missionary staying at the Franciscan convent. One of the sisters was indisposed this morning and asked me if I'd do her visitation for her. She usually sees prisoners and, to be frank, she wasn't too clear about the person I was to visit here.'

'Did she tell you anything about him?'

'No, not really. She did say he was an important person and that I should be suitably humble when I met him.'

'Would that be a strain, Sister?'

'"Important" can have a different definition in the desert, Detective. Superiors and Church dignitaries weren't often included under it.'

'Please continue.'

'When I walked into via Selci, I thought the man in the blue boiler suit was somebody from the Water Department because he was inspecting a manhole cover. I didn't think of it before but he had a peaked cap, you know, like they sell all over the place, with 'Roma' written on them.'

'Did it have 'Roma' written on it?'

'No, it had 'Penn'.'

'Facial features?'

'No, sorry. When the door of the van opened, I had a glimpse of another man, much smaller than the man in the boilersuit. I think he may have opened the door a fraction too early.'

'Why do you think that?'

'Because she looked at him.'

'She?'

'Yes. There was a young woman dressed as a nun and she was fixing her veil when the door opened. She looked at him as if she was furious. Then she looked at me.'

'You say she was dressed as a nun. You don't believe she was one?'

Sister Eileen tugged the blanket a little higher before she answered.

'No. At least, I hope not. I'm not a fanciful person, Detective. I've been a missionary doctor for a very long time and … well, let's just say I've seen a lot of frightening things, but I've never seen anyone look at someone in the way she looked at him.'

'And how did she look at you, Eileen?'

Again, she tugged the blanket.

'I met a lion once. That's a real conversation stopper, isn't it?' She laughed, and Fermi smiled encouragement. 'They came in after the cattle sometimes and I was walking outside the compound. We just stood and looked at each other. Then it disappeared. Maybe it had already eaten or just didn't fancy chewing bone and gristle. But it looked at me. You know how when you look in someone's eyes you see something? You can usually see surprise or recognition or interest or … something. There was nothing, Detective. I was nothing. I'm sorry if that sounds foolish but I think that woman would have killed me if it had suited her.'

'Thank you, you've been very helpful. If there's anything I can do …?'

'Actually, there is. Could you get me out of here? They've been very kind but I think they'd be relieved to see the back of me.'

'Of course, where would you like to go?'

He saw her hesitation and was unsurprised at her reply.

'I don't really want to return to the convent in the via La Spezia. Not tonight, anyway. Let's just say I don't have a good feeling about the place. Maybe I could find a small hotel somewhere, just for tonight.'

'I'll be back for you in five minutes,' he promised.

The Northern Highway, Italy

The sea revealed less and less of itself, like a stripper in reverse, Charlie thought, until it was completely covered with green and the green began to undulate. The countryside they drove through was folded in on itself. The occasional single hill with the obligatory village on top was replaced with higher hills standing shoulder to shoulder, as if keeping strangers on the outside. Charlie knew this was Umbria, where the sky rested on the hilltops and you could see rain coming from a long way off. In his peripheral vision, Eddie held the wheel, reeling in the miles of highway with the glazed boredom of a spinning fisherman. Jane Wilson sat in the back, occasionally checking the man on the stretcher, sometimes appearing in the gap between the front seats, staring at the road. Charlie watched the tic under Eddie's right eye begin to pulse and beat out the Morse Code of his tension. He wanted to say something – anything – to disrupt the charged silence. He knew it wouldn't make a damn bit of difference and joined the others in watching the highway.

J. Arthur Thomas was floating up to the light. So this is

death, he thought. The light dimmed slowly and resolved itself into a concave metal roof. His sense of smell registered gasoline with a thin overlay of human sweat. A woman's face hovered between him and the roof. 'You shot me,' he whispered, in a clotted voice.

'Not really,' she replied, loosening the restraining straps so he could sit up. 'If I'd really shot you, we wouldn't be having this conversation.'

'Are they searching for me?'

'Yeah, but they're kinda hampered by the fact that we have decoys running to delay them. We also have a Guardian Angel to see us through any roadblocks.'

She tilted sideways so he could see the head of the motorcyclist through the rear window.

'Also,' she continued, 'they're hampered by the fact that they really don't want you found.'

'Do the police know that?'

'If they don't, they will. They'll grumble and roll over.'

I know one who won't, he thought, and shifted his eyes to the rear window, focusing beyond the motorcycle cop on the road that connected him with Rome.

⁂

'Turn off at the next exit and follow the signs to the picnic area.'

Eddie jerked the wheel and watched in his wing mirror as the cop came behind in their slipstream. He followed the signs and when he looked again the mirror was empty. The van eased into a space, nosing against a small lawn that fronted onto a wood. A brown Volvo faced in the opposite direction at the other end of the car park, near the washrooms.

'Charlie, give me a hand to get this stretcher stashed away. Eddie, you get first turn at the washroom. You,' she said, pointing at Thomas, 'outside and stretch your legs.' Thomas threw her a mock salute and left the van, walking gingerly. Eddie looked like he might argue but thought better of it. Charlie watched him swagger off in the direction of the washroom.

'So, this is where we say goodbye,' he said softly.

'Yeah, I take the package on from here.'

'That's not what I meant.'

'Cool it, Charlie. You're not on the manifest.'

'Neither is Eddie.'

'Ask not for whom the bell tolls, Charlie. Okay?'

'Okay.'

'So, what's next for you?'

'I'm thinking of retiring. Got some kids somewhere. Might be nice to … ya know. Depends.'

'Depends on what?'

'On whether I'll be seeing you again.'

'Not unless you decide to write your memoirs, Charlie.' A gun appeared in her right hand. He knew she must have taken it from the waistband at the back but he hadn't seen her reach behind.

'You know how it goes,' she said, and the gun disappeared again as she slipped out through the sliding door.

'Yeah, that I do,' Charlie murmured bleakly, watching her flit between the trees towards the washroom. Now you see her, now you don't. Now you see her, now you don't. The mantra pounded in his head until she had gone into the brick-built structure. 'Now you see her,' he whispered. He strained his ears and heard nothing. Not even the squawk of the crow that launched itself suddenly from a pine behind the washroom.

'Now you don't,' Charlie whispered, watching the black bird circle once and glide away.

⊰⊱

Cardinal Thomas had never shaved in a woman's presence. He rummaged in the washbag she tossed him until she flicked her head in annoyance and went outside. The men's section consisted of six stalls, three urinals and two basins. Although the floor was sticky underfoot, and a paper dam blocked the outflow from the urinals, the place reeked of industrial-strength disinfectant. Carefully, he patted himself dry, stowed the razor in his bag and took one last look in the freckled mirror. His eyes strayed to the reflection of the stalls stretching away behind him, drawn there by some asymmetry that snagged his attention. He let his gaze run down the line until it rebounded from a closed door. Cautiously, he paced towards it, pulling against the suction of the filthy floor and the very real instinct that tried to restrain him. Slowly, he raised his hand to push the door open.

'It's occupied.'

He could feel a scream welling in his throat and gagged it back.

'I – I just saw the closed door and won—'

'It's occupied,' she repeated, in that toneless voice.

He stumbled past her into the car park, sucking huge gulps of pine-scented air and dabbing at the sweat in his eyebrows. As he approached the van, he saw Charlie sitting motionless in the driver's seat. His heart began to trip in his chest and his breath came in gasps as he walked to the open window.

'Charlie?' he croaked.

179

The man turned his head slowly. 'Sorry, fella,' he said easily, 'you got the wrong guy.'

He turned on the ignition and reversed the van so that Thomas had to step sideways. As the tail-lights winked on the corner, he sensed her come up behind him.

'Charlie's gone,' he said.

'Charlie who?' she answered.

She popped the trunk of the Volvo and tossed him a bag.

'Get changed.'

Thomas stood uncertainly, the bag clutched to his chest. His eyes wavered reluctantly in the direction of the washroom.

'Do it in the damn car,' she snapped.

When he stepped out of the Volvo, he was dressed in the fatigues of the US Airforce. Her uniform mirrored his, with the addition of wrap-around reflective aviator glasses.

'Lord, this takes me back.' He laughed nervously.

'You were Marines, Eminence,' she said, lacing a boot hoisted on the trunk.

'Just how much do you know about me?'

'All I need to know. How much do you know about me?'

'Hell, I don't even know your name.'

She stepped closer to him so that he could see his double image mirrored in her sunglasses.

'Make sure you keep it that way, okay?'

'Okay.'

'Okay, Lieutenant. From here on out I'm Flight Lieutenant Donna Bloom and you're Flight Assistant Harry Andrews. I get to call you Harry, you call me Lieutenant.'

'How come you outrank me?'

'Nobody notices the help, Harry.'

She slid into the back seat of the Volvo.

'The help drives, Harry, okay?'

'Okay.'

'Okay, *Lieutenant.*

So, where are we going – Lieutenant?'

'Israel.'

Airport, Florence

She flashed her papers and they were escorted immediately to a military truck that carried them to the secluded section of the airfield, reserved for the Italian Air Force. The truck halted to the rear of a matt-black Hercules that squatted ready for takeoff. 'Mind you get all the bags, Harry,' she flung over her shoulder, as she mounted the ramp into the belly of the plane.

'Yes, Lieutenant,' he said, through gritted teeth, and followed.

'Better tie yourself down,' she offered. 'These babies buck when they're empty.'

'Why no checks and balances at the airport?' he murmured, as the aircraft shook itself and began to roll.

'As far as the locals are concerned,' she said, cinching her harness, 'this is a rendition flight. See no evil, et cetera.'

The Hercules barrelled down the runway and clawed its way upwards to chew a hole in the clouds. She waited until the floor canted back to level, at cruising altitude, and Harry Andrews was snoring softly, before she made the call.

Convent of Santa Lucia, Rome

Fermi found Fausto with Cornelia Scipio, sipping tea under a picture that represented everything he hated about a certain type of religious art. They both stood as he entered. 'Please sit,' he said, pulling up a chair to join them. 'Our time is short,' he said briskly, 'so I'll be direct. Officer Scipio, you're a credit to the police force. In other circumstances, it would be a pleasure to work with you again.'

'Thank you, Detective Fermi.' She blushed. 'It was—'

'Listen carefully, Cornelia, and please do exactly as I say. When they question you, you must say I argued with the monsignori and you felt embarrassed by my rudeness, even though you didn't hear what was said.'

'But I didn't hear what was said,' she protested.

'Yes, but you must say so,' he said firmly. 'You obeyed my instructions because I was a senior officer and commanded you. This is a political matter. I don't want you involved. Do you understand?'

'Yes,' she said, crestfallen. 'Yes, I understand.'

He turned to the young policeman. 'Fausto, the same goes for you. I demanded you drive me here and that's it. We didn't speak in the car. I didn't tell you my name. Take the car back to the Capitoline. Remember, you don't know who I spoke to or where I've gone. Understood?'

Fausto's face seemed to sag. 'I would be honoured to work with you again, sir,' he said quietly.

'And I with you, but you know how it is.'

After they'd left, he opened his cellphone.

'*Pronto?*'

'Cybele, I would like to bring a nun home for dinner.'

There was a momentary pause on the line before the voice he loved above all others, even his revered Tebaldi, responded.

'And how would you like her cooked, my love?'

The Fermi Apartment, Rome
'Welcome to our home, Sister. I am Cybele Fermi.'

Sister Eileen stood awkwardly in the doorway until Cybele took her in her arms and pecked her on both cheeks. 'Let me show you to your room while Giuseppe prepares the coffee.'

'You have him well trained,' Eileen ventured, as they walked out of his earshot.

'Pavlov had it easy,' Cybele answered, and they both laughed. 'This is – was – my daughter Terentina's room, the tidier version.'

The bedroom was airy and speckled with sunlight sieved through lace curtains belling inward at the open window. Silver stars glinted from the pale blue ceiling and the walls were almost completely obscured by posters of famous paintings. Eileen recognised Raphael's *Transfiguration* and his bored cherubs leaning out of a poster above the headboard. When she remarked on the riot of colour, Cybele laughed ruefully.

'You should have seen it when she was in her teens,' she said. 'All day long she was listening to this person Leonard Cohen, all night long looking up at Bosch and Munch. Very scary.'

'She's an artist?'

'An art restorer who could never restore her room.'

'It must have been wonderful to grow up surrounded by such beauty.'

Cybele sat on the edge of the bed and patted the place beside her. For a moment, Eileen was transported back more than forty years to her family home in the West of Ireland. She remembered how her mother would make that exact gesture and say, 'Sit down there, Eileen, and tell me.' She sat.

'You must miss your daughter.'

'Oh, yes, and my son Giacomo also. He's a historian, very neat. When Terentina was little she didn't sleep very well. Sometimes I wake and think I hear her, or maybe I see a ribbon in the market and … When she moved to her apartment, I thought, Now I'll have time to do all the things I wished to do when I had children to care for. I'll go for coffee with friends or to exhibitions or for lunch with Giuseppe.' She sighed. 'My friends are like me, so always the talk comes round to our children. Exhibitions are not so wonderful when you have no little one to enjoy them with. And Giuseppe! I think it's different for men. Perhaps they like it better when the children are grown-up and they can meet them for coffee somewhere and argue about art or history. Sometimes I see him become distracted when he walks into the kitchen or the dining room, as if he's expecting to see someone who isn't there. And for me? I miss the feel of them so much my arms ache. Even the smell of them. Sometimes, when Giuseppe is away, I lie on their beds.' She took a deep breath to steady herself. 'Lunch with Giuseppe is … He's a policeman.'

She raised her hand in a gesture that might have meant exasperation or acceptance.

'I suspect he's a very successful policeman.'

'You're kind, Sister.'

'Call me Eileen, please.'

'Thank you, Eileen. When I brought Giuseppe home for the first time, my grandmother said, "Cybele, if you marry this man, you'll never be rich. If you don't marry him, you'll be a poor fool." My husband is a good policeman, but he'll never be successful.' She paused, and nodded once, as if validating her grandmother's opinion or her own choice of husband.

'And you, Eileen? My husband tells me you've been a missionary doctor for some time. Do you miss it?'

For more than forty years Eileen Cassidy had been a missionary and a doctor. She had enjoyed something akin to icon status within her religious order. She was held up to young aspirants as the strong, capable woman who had brought modern medicine to a most desolate place in Africa. Icons, she reflected ruefully sometimes, were two-dimensional paintings suggesting a third dimension above and beyond themselves. It had been a succinct summary of her role and a recurring question for her about herself. But, then, missionary doctors weren't expected to have a self. The work was everything and she had long ago anaesthetised that irksome question by giving everything to the work and then some more. And now, all that, all of what she had been and done, was over. There was no longer the enormous need of others to distract her from her own needs. And this woman, sitting beside her on the bed under a star-studded ceiling, was waiting for her answer. Eileen had always been cerebral by nature. She was surprised therefore to find her voice coming from some deep untapped place inside. 'I miss it.'

It was a simple sentence, just three words; three of the most difficult words she had managed to string together in four decades. They just popped out of her mouth like a cork from a genie's jar and she knew, with a mixture of fear and exhilaration, that they could never be put back.

'I miss it. I went out there as a young woman full of fervour and idealism. I went for many reasons. I wanted to do something for God, give something back. The people needed a doctor and I was going to do wonderful things. It was all very innocent. We were told it was better not to get too attached to the people. But how can you be with people and not become attached? And when you do, you can't just stop.'

She paused and tried to breathe deeply into her belly.

'And then it did stop. I miss the smell of smoke from the cooking fires in the morning and the way the children would take my hand and just hold it on the way somewhere as if I was the child. I miss the slow graciousness. Even when they were very ill, they would greet me and ask after my health.' She laughed self-deprecatingly. 'And, yes, of course I miss being in charge and doing, always doing, flying around in that old wreck of a jeep. Now I feel like I have my foot pressed flat on the accelerator but the jeep is up on blocks. When the letter came from my superiors, I was shocked. Isn't that remarkable? I'd known for forty years that this was going to happen – well, I knew it in my head.' She placed her hand flat on her stomach. 'Down here, it was … difficult. That morning, I went to the clinic in Lodwar and told the staff I was leaving. Cybele, people here, in the Western world, hug and kiss you and tell you how wonderful retirement will be. Africans absorb. It's the only word I can think of. The nurses and others just nodded politely and got on with their work. I can't remember a single thing I did that day but later, in the evening, I was staring at some paperwork when a deputation arrived. They said, "Sister, you will not go away. You will stay and sit with the elders."'

She began to cry. Cybele eased an arm around her and held her gently. When the storm of tears had passed, she led her by the elbow to the bathroom. She soaked a facecloth under the cold tap and gently dabbed Eileen's face, then dried it with a soft towel.

'I think, big important missionary doctor, you're beginning to find yourself,' she said. 'Now, come and help me rescue the kitchen from my husband.'

Fermi refilled the kettle to make fresh coffee when he heard the sound of approaching voices. Later, he would tell Cybele about the call from the commissioner and the call he had subsequently made to Mal, his detective friend in New York. Recalling that conversation, he smiled. He had made courteous enquiries about Mal's wife, Hanny, and Rosa, the Hispanic policewoman who had been with Mal in Rome during the Remnant affair. He had hoped the wily officer would intuit from his tone that this wasn't a social call and he hadn't been disappointed.

'Yes, old friend, Cybele is well, and the children, thank you for asking, although we are a little unhappy. Someone opened the cage today and the bird flew away. The cleaning lady says she knows nothing. It seems her cousin was helping out in place of her today and we think the cousin is responsible.'

Mal's voice was wary when he replied. 'It'll hardly fly to New York, Giuseppe.'

'No, no, not that far. I hope you and those you love will be safe and well. Ciao, Mal.'

He had every confidence that the New York detective would winnow the truth from the conversation while the chaff kept the listeners occupied. The truth, as he knew it and as he had coded it for Mal, was that Cardinal J. Arthur Thomas had been sprung from house arrest by a female CIA operative. The cardinal was unlikely to return to the United States but might very well arrange for someone to go to an island off the West of Ireland. Michael Flaherty lived on that island; the same Michael Flaherty who had been instrumental in foiling the cardinal's ambitions. He hoped Mal would warn the young man, who was like a son to him, that someone was coming. He knew in his gut that he was not being fanciful. Giuseppe Fermi was a man who had read Plutarch's *Fall of the Roman Republic* for pleasure. There wasn't much he didn't know about the thwarted dreams of would-be emperors and their passion for revenge.

CIA Director's Residence, Washington DC
The trilling telephone found Benson awake. Unhurriedly, he draped the purple bookmark between the pages of *The Lost Gospel of the Earth* by Tom Hayden. 'Know your enemy,' he had replied to the query of a neoconservative politician who had queried his reading material. Finally, he pressed the phone to his ear.

'Ademar returns,' the voice said.

Benson heard the heavy bass rumble of aircraft engines in the background. 'Flights of angels hie thee,' he replied, and broke the connection. The tall window overlooked the sleeping garden and he stood inside the heavy drapes, letting his night vision adjust. From the bushes, near the high wall, a tiny red meteor spun upwards and succumbed to gravity. He made a mental note to reassign that particular member of his Praetorian Guard of special agents to narcotics duty in one of the more lively projects on the rim of the city and retired to his desk.

Sitting deep in the antique studded-leather swivel chair, he added pieces to the jigsaw in his head, shifting and shuffling events, locations and personnel, until the picture formed. 'Peace,' he whispered, 'the charm's wound up.' For a man of literary leanings, he harboured an unusual enthusiasm for well-worn aphorisms and clichés. After all, he mused, the old and well-worn have stood the test of time; the new wasn't always better. Clicking his Mont Blanc, he listed clichés appropriate to the task. He regarded himself as an equal-opportunities cliché-meister and listed popular sayings with scriptural utterances and quotes from Shakespeare. And so, 'What goes around comes around', 'You shall reap what you sow,' and 'We but teach bloody instruction, which, being taught, returns to plague the inventor' flowed from his pen. The irony involved was not lost on him but he trusted implicitly in the firewalls he had painstakingly erected in the event that his actions and their consequences ever 'came home to roost', he added. He checked his Breitling watch and settled more comfortably, content to sip from a tumbler of Benedictine. Who says Americans don't do irony? he thought and waited.

The Shadwell Theatre, Dulwich, England

Eric Jones stared up at the headlights and bowed. Fanning out on either side of him, the cast followed his lead, more or less together. The leading man stepped forward to milk a final burst of applause and the curtain fell. Eric didn't envy him his seven seconds of individual acclaim. He knew it would be six seconds next time and then five. The toothy young fellow with the bouffant hair and tin ear was a television reject, destined to spiral down through provincial rep to the oblivion that was the home of the truly talentless. There would follow the twittering and air-kissing and hyperbolic compliments that came with RSVP attached by fragile egos. He'd have none of it.

Abruptly, he strode into the wings and down a musty corridor to the dressing room. Seated before a mirror flanked by two bulbs, he began to excavate his face with cream and tissues. The other cast members gave him a wide berth. Mr Jones, the younger ones believed, had trained with Stanislavsky and liked to surface slowly from his character. Mr Jones, the older thesps knew from bitter experience, was a catty, self-absorbed, twenty-four-carat bastard who would employ all his dark arts to upstage and wrong-foot a colleague at every opportunity. He was competent, they allowed, never late, drunk or lecherous. He had an eidetic memory and had once prompted a frozen colleague through an entire scene by feeding him paraphrases of his forgotten lines. And he was never 'resting'. God, how they hated him for that. Directors always seemed to find a part for the ageing pseudo-aristo with the languid air and limp wrist.

In their lust for limelight, they had been blinded to Eric's greatest asset as an actor, an asset that was now being revealed in the mirror lit by two forty-watt bulbs: his face. In an industry that devoured somebodies and excreted nobodies, Eric had the perfect facial features to be anybody. His face was a blank canvas on which any one of a thousand characters could be drawn. Similarly, his body possessed the requisite number of limbs attached to a torso neither men nor women would find attractive. Which all added up to him being the ideal foil, the supporting actor, the member of the cast who elicited faint praise and absolutely no lasting memory in the minds of critics or audiences. Benson had noted his talent and, after a diligent trawl through the shadier side of what passed for Eric's private life, had offered him the chance to play many parts for many handsome fees.

Eric did not do after-show 'drinkies' and he departed the theatre, passing through the knot of needy people at the stage door. He despised them as parasites who sought to feed their fantasies with the autographs of the spirits who, far from 'melting into air, into thin air', were rushing to get a drink before the pub closed or to release a babysitter. Eric was equally invisible at home in the apartment building he shared with ten other tenants who referred to him as 'the bloke upstairs'. He was upstairs when the phone rang.

'"Let thy speech be short,"' he quoted into the receiver, '"comprehending much in a few words."' His diction was crystal clear and the phrases flowed from his lips on a cushion of diaphragmatic breath.

'The damn play is over, Eric.'

'Oh, no, Benson. On the contrary, "All the world's a stage and—"'

'Eric!'

'Sorry.'

'You did good work on our little media problem.'

'Why, thank you. The lady journalist seemed hell-bent on publishing the indiscretions of your first secretary at the embassy until her own extramarital indiscretions appeared in the tabloid newspapers. Hoisted with her own petard, one might say.'

'The usual remuneration will be transferred to Zürich.'

'Thank you, dear boy, but something tells me you haven't postponed sleep, "the death of each day's life", to tell me that.'

'Isn't it bad luck to quote *Macbeth*?'

'Only if one is onstage performing *Hamlet*, Benson.'

'Touché. I'm casting a part I think would suit you, Eric.'

Benson outlined it. He added, 'You must scotch the snake, not kill it.'

'What? The Scottish play yet again. You really are a one-play man, aren't you, Benson?'

'No ad-libbing, Eric. Remember to stick to the script.'

'Oh, tut-tut, Benson. The leading male rarely dies, at least not until the end of the play. The supporting cast, however, enjoys no such dramatic immunity.'

'You'd better remember that, Eric.'

Eric Jones dropped the receiver into the cradle as if it were suddenly too hot to handle. He strode to the bookshelves and hauled an atlas to the floor. His finger travelled west from the UK to the West of Ireland coastline, paused, then moved a tiny space further. The bell of the town-hall clock caught his ear as it chimed midnight.

'"I go, the bell invites me,"' he quoted. '"Hear it not, Michael Flaherty, for it is a knell that summons thee to Heaven or to Hell."'

The Flaherty Home, the Island, Ireland

Michael Flaherty took a last long look and closed the door on the dark. The sudden warmth of the kitchen washed over him and he laid his forehead against the rough grain of the timber. Rest, his body urged him, just for a minute. He resisted the temptation and shook himself like a dog. 'I must stay alert,' he murmured. 'It could be now; it could be anytime.'

When he turned, he saw his sister staring at him with those fathomless green eyes. He remembered assuring her, long ago, 'It's only the dark, Fi. Everything out there is just as it was during the day. But everything needs the dark to rest, even the sea. I'll read my book here until you go to sleep.'

'Is it still there?'

'What?'

'The sea – you've been checking on it every fifteen minutes.'

Fiona nodded at the kitchen table. 'Sit down, Michael,' she said. 'It's time we had a talk. I've unplugged the telephone, so we won't be interrupted.'

'There's nothing to talk about, Fi,' he said tiredly.

'Sit down.'

He sat.

'Maybe you're right,' she said evenly, hooking a chair from the table and sitting opposite. 'Maybe you're right. Maybe a ghost is nothing – nothing real, anyway. That's what you've become, Michael.'

'A ghost?'

'Yes. I went to meet my brother at the boat and a ghost stepped on to the pier, this shadow-man who comes and goes at all hours of the day and night to watch the sea.'

'Ah, for God's sake, Fi.'

'This skittery, jittery excuse for a man who jumps when the door bangs or the kettle whistles and everybody has to look the other way and pretend it's grand and sure didn't he have an accident beyond in Rome, poor man.'

Her voice had been rising steadily and she reined it back with an effort.

'You didn't have an accident in Rome, Michael. Whatever happened to you there followed you here under my roof and I have a right to know what that is.'

'I had an accident, Fi. There's no mys—'

'Look at me, brother.'

Reluctantly, he raised his gaze from the table.

'I teach ten-year-old children,' she said evenly. 'I'm a living lie-detector.'

'It's the tru—'

'No, it is not the fucking truth!' she spat, standing abruptly to lean across the table. 'I'm not your baby sister to be minded whenever there's trouble. I stepped out from your shadow the day you left and I'm damned if I'm going to hide there now. So don't you dare patronise me.'

She sat down again and blew her fringe out of her eyes, exasperated.

'I'm sorry, Fi.'

'Ah, shit on sorry,' she snapped. 'Now tell me.'

He told her. Although she had armoured herself against all sorts of awful revelations, she felt as if she had been punched in the stomach. He saw the colour leach from her face so that her freckles seemed to float above her skin.

'You were shot,' she said, in a faraway voice, when he had finished.

'Yes, but I'm fine now.'

'Ah,' she said sarcastically, 'you're fine now, are you? Isn't it as well you never decided to become a doctor? If you're so damned fine, why do you go around like a fella with ants in his pants?'

He contemplated fobbing her off but his stomach soured at the thought.

'You remember I mentioned a cardinal, the one I exposed in Rome? He warned me, Fi. He said if ever I crossed hi—'

'No.'

'No what?'

'No, that's not it, not all of it anyway. I know you, brother. You wouldn't be afraid of that, even though you should be. There's something else, isn't there?'

He raised his head and her breath stopped at the haunted look in his eyes.

'He knows about Kate and Liam.'

She stretched her hand across the table and gripped his tightly.

'Oh, Jesus, Michael,' she gasped. 'Oh, Jesus. Does Kate know about this?'

He looked puzzled. 'No ... no, I didn't want to frighten her. I thought maybe ... maybe they'll only come for me.'

'Oh, brother,' she said, in amazement, 'aren't you the total eejit?'

'What?'

'Tell me, Michael, who scrambled your brains? Was it the Church that twisted your head off and shoved it up your backside? Let me be sure I have the right of this. It's okay if they come and kill you, is it? Okay for whom? Would that, I don't know, make up for something? Would it be some kind of heroic restitution for Liam and Gabriel and Father Mack?'

'I did not kill them,' he whispered fiercely.

'You protest too much, big brother. I accept you didn't kill them, but *you* don't, do you?'

'I don't know, Fi.'

She was heartstruck by the agony in his face but she kept her counsel.

'I think sometimes ... if I'd held on to Liam a little longer ...'

'"If" is such a waste of a word, Michael. It's the whip we use to beat ourselves because we're glad and guilty that 'twas them and not us. You're haunting yourself into a hole in the ground and you want to offer yourself up as a sacrifice to some mad bastard's revenge. And for what? You'll be just as dead as all the others. Dear God, Michael, is that how cheaply you hold your life?'

'It's not just me, Fi, it's Kate and Liam as—'

Her raised hand halted him. She leaned across the table and rapped him lightly on the forehead.

'Come out of there, brother,' she said firmly. 'Let's deal with the real world. Kate and Liam were doing okay before you washed up on the Island. She ran the medical side of things here better than any doctor. And she brought up a gifted son, despite that thing who married her. Kate might want you, Michael, but she doesn't need you. None of us do. I know that's hard to hear, and it isn't easy for me to say, but it's the truth.'

She ran her fingers soothingly down the side of his face and continued gently, 'You were always the good boy, Michael, always doing the right thing. You read your books and studied hard, and that pleased Daddy and Father Mack. You minded them, Michael, the child became father to the man. But what happened to you? What did you do with your grief and your anger at Mammy's death and Daddy going away inside himself? Our brother Liam was a drunk, Michael. I think he wanted to be a hero like you but he hadn't … hadn't what you had. So he drank. Oh, he could be funny and lovable but he had a sickness of the soul and it drowned him. And Gabriel? Gabriel tried to be you, the good boy who did the right thing. He stayed arsing around here humouring Daddy when he should have taken up the job they offered him at that university in America. And when he found out what was going on here with the American major using the Island as part of his drug business, he couldn't let it go. He stood up to them – imagine, Gabriel who could never fight his way out of a wet paper bag. They pushed him off the cliff.'

Her voice cracked and she swallowed hard.

'Fi?'

'I'm not finished,' she said, with spirit. 'You say you're concerned for Kate and Liam, and I know you are. But step outside yourself for a minute and imagine what it's like for her. You came back and you were further away than ever. Yes, I know you have your reasons, but she has a right to hear them. She's a human being who can make her own decisions about how to protect herself and her son. She doesn't need a hero, someone so busy protecting everyone else that they neglect themselves.'

The silence stretched between them, allowing the ordinary small sounds of the house to return.

'What about you, Fi?' he asked. 'What did you do?'

For a moment she stiffened. Then she said simply, 'Me? I'm a woman, Michael. We seem to have missed out on the hero gene. I – I got on with it. I grieved for Mammy. I still do, a bit. And I grieve for Daddy. He's not dead but he's been gone a long time. I'm a good teacher and I run a good school, and there's a widower beyond in Galway with two small children who thinks I'm not half bad.'

'Isn't he the lucky one, Fi?'

'Isn't he just.'

'Fi, I just wa—'

'No.' She sat back in her chair. 'Please don't say anything – not now anyway. I'm afraid you'll try to explain it all away or try to be funny and I couldn't bear that. I've had it up to here with heroes,' she said sadly. 'I want my brother back.'

Fiona Flaherty stood up from the table and walked into their father's room.

৪০০৪

Michael Flaherty sat alone at the table. He noticed that the flash of the lighthouse made the curtains glow at regular intervals. In the corner of the kitchen, the stove ticked as the peat fire settled into ash. Somewhere a dog barked and he raised his head. Another answered, then both fell silent. His brain raced, conjuring all the old images from his nightmares. He let them flicker inside his closed eyelids until the spool ran out and he could open his eyes to the normality of the kitchen. Old voices rose up and clamoured for his attention, so he breathed deeply into his belly until they tired and stilled. Finally, he rose from the table and lifted the latch, letting himself out into the night. The path wound away to the right and climbed up to a small cottage. A light burned in the window as a guide to islanders in need of the nurse. He didn't know what he was going to say to her and it didn't matter. Fi had spoken the truth. Others, like Eli, the doctor in Rome, and Raphael, who had given him refuge in a monastery, had offered similar truths and been rebuffed. He knew he had lived inside his head, locking up his heart, taking refuge in a role from what was real. He felt lighter as he walked the path as if, somehow, the force of gravity hadn't the same pull on him as before. He looked only at the light in her window, never once checking left or right.

The Nurse's House, the Island
When she opened the door, she had a book in her hand.

'Still reading Keats, Kate?'

'No – too much about kisses and blisses for my taste.'

'Father Mack always claimed Keats had flint and iron in him.'

'Maybe he wasn't talking about Keats, Michael. Come inside, we're letting the heat out of the house.'

'Is Liam about?'

'He's below in the bed since eight. He'll be away early in the morning to friends. I heard his book hit the floor an hour ago so he must be asleep. Will you have tea?'

The drumming of water into the kettle allowed him a space to look at her. Her raven hair shone in the light and, when she shoved it back behind her ear, he thought he saw gleams of silver at her temple. That hair and her sallow skin made her look more Iberian than Irish. 'Not all the sailors from the Armada drowned off our shores,' Father Mack had opined more than once. When she turned from the sink, her eyes were the dark pools he remembered. She noticed his gaze and a smile gleamed in their depths and surfaced slowly.

'Did no one ever tell you it's not polite to stare?'

'I suppose they must have,' he replied, without dropping his eyes. 'I don't remember.'

Kate poured the tea in silence and sat opposite, gazing at him appraisingly. 'God in Heaven, Michael Flaherty,' she said, 'I've had patients on their last legs who've looked better than you.' She sat back, as if she was waiting for some witty reply, and when none was forthcoming, she leaned forward again, resting her forearms on the table. 'I have a question for you,' she said. 'I ask this question day in, day out. It's an occupational hazard. Usually the people I ask answer by telling me what they're not. They say something like "I'm not too bad." Even the ones at death's door say, "I'm fine, Nurse." You know what we're like.'

He nodded.

'I'll ask you once and you'll have one chance to answer. If it's any of the answers I've mentioned or a variation of them, we'll have the tea, talk about the weather and you'll be on your way. Okay?'

'Okay.'

'So, how are you, Michael?'

He woke once during the night to the sound of rain pounding on the roof. Immediately he thought of the Island men trawling for their livelihood in small boats on the Atlantic and wished them a silent Godspeed. Once an Islander, he thought, and smiled in the dark.

They had talked … He had talked while the dark flooded the sky above the little house and stars flowered slowly into constellations. The words had fought him, at first, then had come gushing in a tumbling torrent, carrying all the feelings he had dammed inside. As a crescent moon scythed palely across the window, he had wept for the dead, those whose lives he had cherished and those whose lives he had taken. He had mourned also for himself, for the boy who had shelved his grief and the young man who had run from it. Sometimes, when he lapsed into silence, she reminded him gently of his gifts, of the pleasure his father, the Master, had taken in his son's insight. She spoke calmly, almost meditatively, of Father Mack, his mentor, and of the love he had borne the bookish boy and of how he had saved him from the gunman on the clifftop. Even when she spoke of Father Mack begging Michael in his agony to open the hand that held him and give him to the sea, she walked the fine line between judgement and consolation. Gradually she erected a scaffolding of deeper truths and realities around the horrors he had endured on the Island and in Rome. When he slumped, exhausted, she moved around the table to stand behind him, stroking the back of his head as his mother had done when he was a boy. Gently, very gently, she introduced a lighter, warmer thread into his dark memories.

'D'you remember your father quoting Wordsworth in our classroom? Lord, the innocence of the man. Come on, scholar,' she teased, gripping his shoulders and putting her cheek beside his own, 'what lines did he always quote?'

He was still for a moment. Then, in a raw whisper, he said, '"A violet by a mossy stone, half-hidden from the eye,/Fair as a star, when only one is shining in the sky."'

'Yes, and do you remember the day he asked what the last line meant and you said—'

'I said, it means that, when it's dark, a single star can be the most wonderful sight in the world.'

'Yes, you did,' she whispered, 'and you looked at me and I thought I'd float out of the desk. We went for walks on the headland and you told me the story of *The Great Gatsby* and I didn't hear a word you said. And then …'

She faltered, and put her lips close to his ear. 'And then I took you by the hand and asked if you'd walk off the edge of the world with me.'

'We went to the cave,' he said, matching her tone.

'The same cave you went to when Liam's body was brought ashore from the sea. You were drenched and all over the place. I was afraid you'd die of exposure.'

'I didn't care if I did.'

'I did. I took the sleeping bag from home – I can still hear my mother screeching after me – and I got you into the bag and climbed in with you because you were blue and the teeth were rattling in your head. And …'

They were silent and he was certain the world had stopped wheeling. She turned her head so he could see her eyes. They were luminous with fear and longing.

'Will you walk off the edge of the world with me, Michael Flaherty?' she said.

He had felt breathless at the sight of her beauty. Tentative and trembling, he had stretched his fingers to touch her, terrified she might shatter and disappear. She placed her palms on his shoulders, tilting her head back to look at him with huge, hazy eyes.

'I will not let you die,' she whispered. Carefully, he lowered his head and kissed her, feeling a rare and blessed peace exorcise his demons as they came together in the dark.

He lay now beside her and listened to the rain.

'What are you thinking?' she whispered.

'Who could think?' he said, and reached for her.

⋙⋘

'You'd better go down home,' she said, as she cleared the breakfast table. 'Fi will be anxious.'

'No, I don't think anxious is the right word,' Michael said, shifting his plate to the sink. "Smug' might do it and you could add 'insufferably', if you've a mind to.'

He put his arms around her from behind, holding her against him, resting his chin in her hair.

'We … we still have a long way to go, Michael,' she said.

'*Tosach maith*,' he whispered.

'*Leath na hoibre*,' she said, completing the proverb. '"A good start is half the work." I'll be along after you,' she added. 'The Master's my first call today.'

⋙⋘

After he'd left, she stacked the dishes to drain and took a last look round the kitchen. It felt suddenly empty, but the light from the window seemed more brilliant than before and every ordinary object somehow lustrous. Lord, where had that word come from? It must be catching. She swept her medical bag from the table and checked herself in the mirror. Yes, she thought approvingly, she was as the nurse should be: formal and professional in her navy suit and white blouse. She had one small reservation. The silly smile would definitely have to go, she resolved, as she opened the door to a glorious morning.

ജ

Eric Jones didn't do nature. He fully supported Graham Greene's preference for 'the sweet security of streets'. If there had to be a beautiful sunrise, he thought peevishly, let it be projected on a cyclorama. He liked fresh air but he liked it warm. The whole rustic scene was best painted on flats with none of the inconveniences associated with the real thing. The particular 'real thing' he had in mind just then was the gorse bush pressing painfully into his back. He was surprised to see the man leave the house and stroll jauntily down the path. According to the brief, Michael Flaherty wasn't supposed to have a walk-off part in this particular act. He shrugged and regretted it instantly as the gorse asserted itself. The woman would be next to leave and he'd have the stage to himself. As if on cue, the door opened and the nurse locked it behind her, then took the path to the Flaherty house.

'On with the motley,' he murmured, and rose from hiding.

The Pier, the Island
Iarla was in his element. Tess had finally done the unthinkable and taken a day ashore, muttering something about getting Shay

Brennan to caulk the boat. Exulting at being skipper for the day, he had spent hours checking and rechecking the fuel gauges, coiling ropes into neater and still neater whorls and taking regular trips to stand at the prow and gaze thoughtfully at the water beyond the pier. He would have been aghast if someone had suggested that this had anything to do with Celia Murphy, who was dawdling on the pier and certainly late for school.

At the mainland, a straggle of tourists stepped carefully up the gangplank, too nervous to appreciate his cheery greeting. Smiling broadly, he had clicked their tickets, oblivious to the man wearing a dun raincoat, buttoned to the top, and a plastic hat that wrapped his ears and tied under his chin. Iarla's gaze swept over the invisible man and snagged on the leggy teenager in the thigh boots and tight T-shirt. He tore his gaze away to drag the gangplank aboard and shout, 'That's it! All abreast!' Then he coloured to the roots of his hair and scurried for the wheelhouse.

Tess was pacing the pier as he swung the boat abeam the mooring. She caught the thrown rope and tied it fast as the passengers trooped off. When the way was clear she came onto the deck, casting glances at the coils and cleats.

'Hi, sis.'

'Seems to be intact,' she muttered.

'All shipshape and in order, Skipper.' He laughed, and saluted grandly.

'Tell me about the passengers, Iarla,' she said, filling the kettle in the galley.

'Ah, the usual truck,' he said airily, fishing two mugs from the press. 'Sure there's not many now, this time of year.'

'Anyone interesting?'

'Interesting?'

'Ah, for the love of God, Iarla, is there an echo in the cabin or what? Interesting – you know, different, like.'

'Well, there were the usual Yanks, with the plastic jackets and the tweed caps. Oh, and a girl from Boston. Her mother was from Galway. Went out to Boston in the eighties and married a fella from Cavan.'

Tess nodded sagely.

'Well, you certainly didn't notice her, did you?'

'Ah, sis.'

'Anyone else?'

'No … yes, arrah, I hardly noticed him at all.'

'What did you notice about this fella, Iarla?'

Something in her tone stilled his fidgeting. 'Well, eh, he had a big raincoat and a kinda floppy plastic hat. I could hardly see him inside it.'

'Go on.'

'For God's sake, sis.'

'Iarla, what else?'

'He had them rubber shoes on his shoes, ye know, like Tommy the Yank used to wear when it rained till people started laughin' at him.'

'Galoshes,' she said automatically.

'Yeah, them. I was thinkin', Chri— cripes, I mean 'twas a fine day and all, just a puff comin' from the south. I was thinkin' I hope we don't get the weather he's expectin'.'

Tess had always had an instinct for danger and trusted it. How else could you live off the sea? she'd argue, against the sceptical. Islanders must be able to smell the wind, or the wave might drown them. They must feel the sea through their feet and know when to cut the nets. She felt it now, a deep-down ache that wouldn't ease without action.

'Iarla, listen to me now. Run to the Master's house and tell Michael Flaherty I sent you. Tell him they've come.'

The Flaherty House, the Island

The telephone was ringing as he opened the door. 'I plugged the damn thing in only two minutes ago,' Fiona said. He saw her eyes move to focus over his shoulder.

'What is it, Fi?'

'It's Iarla,' she said, 'Tess' brother. There's something wrong.'

The telephone rang insistently as she stepped outside. Reflexively, Michael snatched the receiver from its cradle. 'Mal? What is it?'

As he listened, he placed his free hand against the wall for support.

'Giuseppe's certain?'

'Michael!'

He waved his hand at the interruption. 'Listen, Mal, I—'

'Michael,' his sister repeated, 'Iarla has a message from Tess.'

The healed wounds in his chest and shoulder ached as he twisted to look at Iarla.

'Tess said to tell you they've come,' the young man gasped.

Michael Flaherty dropped the receiver and ran. It swung like a pendulum from its cable. 'Michael – Michael?' a faraway voice called anxiously.

✣

She'd forgotten something. It nagged at her with every step she took on the path until she surrendered to it and stopped to lean against the dry-stone wall. Instinctively, her hand quested over the limestone until her finger found the tiny bowl of a fossilised shell. Michael would know what this is, she thought, distracted. She smiled – he'd probably know when it had been buried on the seabed and how it had come to ornament an Island wall. Ah, for God's sake, woman, she chided herself, you've forgotten something. What is it? Yes, Tom Brady's tobacco, a small present she had picked up for the seventy-four-year-old pipe-smoker. It would shorten his life but he always seemed somehow undressed without his briar. Anyway, life was the day that was in it, as the Islanders said. Who knew that better than herself? She turned back to the house.

❧❦

Eric Jones smoothed the paper on the kitchen table and began to write. His copperplate script was a matter of pride to him, now only slightly diluted by the cheap ballpoint he was obliged to use. 'Everything is traceable, Eric,' the spook instructor had cautioned, in that execrable American accent. It was also a matter of pride to him that he had never been 'thrown' on stage, not once. Even when flats or colleagues collapsed, Eric Jones could be counted on to improvise, make it all seem like part of the play and save the day. He heard the lift of the latch and had his gun and voice rock-steady as the woman opened the door. The shock on her face was classic. She was 'a natural', he conceded. But of course she was, he corrected himself: she hadn't been expecting him. So the dialogue ran in the brain of the strange duality that was Eric Jones.

'Who are you? Wha—'

'Pray, do come in, madam,' he said, with calm authority.

She took an awkward stumbling step inside the door. All naturalness flown now, he noted sadly, in the face of this reality.

'Kindly close the door.'

She backed and lifted the latch without looking, pressing herself to the closed door as if for comfort. 'Who …'

'A mere messenger, madam, who thought to leave his message and be gone, like a thief in the night. Your entrance is unfortunate. I am so dreadfully sorry but you are not in the script.'

Michael Flaherty hit the door at full tilt and drove it from the hinges. He was aware of Kate tumbling to his left as he controlled his fall to roll and lash outwards and upwards with his right foot. The gun barked once before the flipped table smacked the man onto his back. Michael was on him instantly, scrabbling for the hand that held the gun. A second shot sprayed plaster from the ceiling. His right hand grasped the man's wrist in a bone-crushing grip while his left hand sought and found his throat. The muzzle of the gun pressed into his opponent's cheekbone.

'Who sent you?' Michael gasped. Suddenly, the other man's body went limp, and when he opened his eyes, Michael saw a lack of expression in them that he had never seen before except in predatory animals. He relaxed his death-grip on the man's throat and waited as breath wheezed into his starved lungs. 'Who sent you?' he asked again, increasing the pressure on the hand still holding the gun so that the muzzle gouged deeper. He saw the lips quiver and strain to form words.

'Hamlet's father,' the man croaked, and a flash of contempt gleamed briefly in his eyes. 'And so, good night.' He pulled the trigger.

Michael felt the concussion of the gunshot like a physical blow. It robbed him of his hearing and set bells ringing inside his head. Staggering upright, he was horrified to find he couldn't see. Above the clamour in his skull, he heard Kate screaming his name. 'I'm not hurt, Kate,' he assured her, unaware that he was shouting. He felt her hands on his face, furiously scrubbing at his eyes until she came into focus. Her hands were smeared with blood. 'Are *you* hurt?' She placed a bloody finger against his lips and shook her head before hugging him fiercely. The din in his head was settling to a dull whine and he heard her say, 'I love you.'

'Kate, Michael!'

He looked over her shoulder and saw his sister standing in the door, spectral with shock. Behind her, Iarla tottered into view and threw up on the path. 'We're fine,' Michael said. 'Let's get outside.'

Kate clung to his side until they reached the small garden and slumped on the grass. She stared at the wild daisies, nodding to whatever secrets the wind whispered from the sea. Her eyes travelled on and up to the jigsaw stone wall that guarded her patch from the world. Sunlight sieved through the gaps between the stones and she felt overcome by a sense of fragility.

'They'll come again, won't they?' she said dully.

'Yes,' he sighed, 'they will.'

'Michael, what are we g—?'

'Listen to me, Kate,' he said urgently. 'You too, Fi.' His sister settled on her hunkers beside him. 'I must go inside for a few minutes,' he said. Kate tightened her grip on his arm. 'I must, Kate,' he insisted, and she released him. 'He – he might have something on him that will help us.' He turned her chin gently with bloodied fingers until her eyes locked with his.

'Did he say anything to you, Kate?' he asked. 'Anything at all that you can remember?'

She turned her face away and squinted at the sun. He saw the tracks of fresh tears through the blood on her cheek.

'He said he was a messenger,' she said.

He nodded and left them. Iarla slumped beside the women, his ashen face a mask of incomprehension.

The kitchen was a charnel house. Blood had sprayed across one wall in a scarlet fan and dribbled down to join viscous puddles on the flagstone floor. The body lay crumpled beneath the window, like a discarded puppet. Michael stepped carefully around it, every step revealing the devastation the bullet had caused. Half of the face was gone and a flap of scalp hung down over one ear. The remaining eye had the same flat expression he remembered seeing in it live and he shuddered. He widened his search until he found it. The corner of the sheet of paper angled from under the upturned table. Gingerly, he held it between thumb and forefinger and tugged. His eyes followed the ornate loops of the letters as his brain struggled to absorb and decode their message.

'It is necessary for one man to die for the people.

Next year in Jerusalem.'

A single drop of blood marked the bottom right-hand corner like a scarlet seal.

As he stepped outside, he waved to Fiona and inclined his head.

'Iarla,' she said, 'would you go on down to the house and sit with the Master until we get back?'

Iarla looked marginally less wan and hugely relieved to be excused from the nightmare.

Michael joined Fiona and Kate on the grass. He took the sheet of paper he had concealed behind his back and read the message to them.

'What does it mean?' his sister asked.

'The first sentence is a quote from the scriptures,' Michael answered. 'It means if I give myself up, they won't bother anyone else. The second, "Next year in Jerusalem", is a toast made by Jews living in the diaspora. The diaspora is anywhere in the world that is not Jerusalem.'

'Jerusalem?' Kate asked.

'Yes. That's where I have to go.'

Kate opened her mouth as if to object, then closed it again.

'We don't have much time,' he continued, 'and we need to plan. If we call the police, I'll have to stay and get tied up in the investigation or leave and be flagged as a fugitive to police all over the world.'

'Alternatively,' Fiona said calmly, 'we could get rid of the body and put things back to rights so no one would be the wiser.'

Michael looked at her, surprised, and she lifted her head defiantly. 'He's just another of that breed of bastards who murdered Gabriel,' she said, 'and he would have killed the pair of you as well.'

'Are you sure you can do this?' he asked.

'We can do it,' Kate replied, nodding at Fiona.

'It might be safer for you and Liam to go away until I – until this is over,' he said to Kate.

'I could send Liam to the cousins in Donegal,' she said slowly. 'They'll let no harm come to him. I won't be leaving.'

'But, Kate!'

'But nothing, Michael. This is my place. They'll not drive me out to hunt me like a frightened hare. If they want me, then this is where they'll have to come.'

'What about Iarla?' Michael asked Fiona.

'Tess'll sort him,' she said confidently. 'Anyway, we'll need Tess to get you off the Island. What is it, Michael?' she asked, seeing the expression on his face.

'I left Mal hanging on the phone,' he said. 'He'll be anxious.' He took off, running down the path.

'Anxious,' Kate repeated slowly. 'Did he say anxious?'

'Yes, he did,' Fiona replied.

'D'you think your brother has a tendency to understate things, Fi?' Kate asked, with the ghost of a smile.

'Maybe he has,' Fiona said mischievously, 'but I'm sure you'll put that to rights, as well.'

⊗⊙⊗

'Mal, Mal, could you calm down for a minute? … Yes, we're fine, okay? Now listen. We had a visitor. He had an accident, like the one our reverend friend had in St Peter's Square … You had a call from who? What exactly did Giuseppe say, Mal?' He listened for a long time before continuing. 'I think our visitor might be related to the cousins,' he said carefully. 'When I asked him who sent him, he said, "Hamlet's father" … Yeah, that Hamlet … I'm not sure. Hamlet's father isn't really in the play but he does make an appearance. He's a ghost, Mal. I don't know what it means either but it could be a code or something. Can you run it by some friends? … Okay … No, I can't tell you that but I'll be in touch. Hey, give Hanny a big hug for me, willya, and tell her I hope her brother has his trip of a lifetime? … Yes, that's what I said … You too, Mal.'

He replaced the receiver and took a deep breath. Unconsciously he rubbed his face and looked at his hand. He'd have to take a long shower and put his clothes in the stove.

'C'mon, Mal,' he whispered, 'I need your help here, old man.'

The O'Donnell Apartment, New York
As soon as he'd hung up, Mal replayed the telephone conversation with Hanny. 'Yes, Hanny,' he said, as he paced the tiny kitchen. 'Could you crank up your hearin' aid? I told you already, they're fine.'

'That's not what your face says.'

'Hanny, if we were judged by our faces, you'd be on Death Row. He said the guy who came for him was shot.'

'Was shot? What the hell does that mean, Mal? Shot by who?'

'Whom, Hanny.'

'Exactly.'

'Michael didn't say, so let's move on here. He figures the guy was CIA, agent or stringer, he doesn't know. And, yes, before you ask, it's a reasonable assumption after what Giuseppe says happened in Rome.'

'Go on.'

'Okay, now this is where it all starts to go hazy. Michael said he asked the guy who'd sent him and he said, "Hamlet's father."'

'Hamlet, like in Shakespeare?'

'Yeah. Then Michael says he wasn't really in the play.'

'Who?'

'Hamlet's father! For cryin' out loud, Hanny, who got your brains?'

'My mother asked the same damn question when I brought you home.'

'Okay, okay, keep your wig on. Michael says Hamlet's father isn't really in the play cos he's a ghost. I'm to run the rule over that one.'

'Anything else?'

'Yeah, yeah, "Give Hanny a big hug for me." Consider yourself hugged. Oh, one other thing, what's this about your brother and the trip of a lifetime?'

'Michael said that?'

'No, it's something I always wanted to know.'

'C'mon, Mal, you remember the time Luke was here on vacation?'

'How could I forget?'

'That's low, even for you. Remember how he was always talking about going to Lourdes and stuff?'

'Sure. Look, don't get me wrong, I mean, Luke's a nice enough guy, but even you gotta admit he's kinda hot on religion.'

'That's not such a bad thing, Mal, especially these days.'

'Aw come on. When it comes to religion, Luke's a few nails short of a crucifixion.'

'That's blasphemy, Mal.'

'I know, I tried to talk him out of it.'

'Very funny.'

'While you're laughin', Hanny, try thinkin', did your brother, Luke, the Grand Inquisitor from Ballina, County Mayo, ever say something about the trip of a lifetime?'

'Sure. He said the Holy Land was the trip of a lifetime.'

'You mean Israel?'

'Don't get political, Mal. Now, Mastermind, I got a question. What are you gonna do about all this?'

'Me, I'm retired, Hanny. Remember?'

※

'Zach? How ya doin'? It's Mal.'

'Mal, good to hear ya, fella. How's retirement?'

'I rust where I rest, Zach. Otherwise it's okay. I got a favour to ask.'

'For you, Mal, anything.'

'It's about some cousins, Zach, I—'

'Mal?'

'Yeah.'

'Call you back soonest, okay?'

※

'Mal.'

'Hiya, Zach. Thanks for calling back. Sorry to catch you at a bad time. You okay to talk right now?'

'Yeah, but not for long. Helluva queue outside the booth.'

'Booth? Oh, right. Sorry if I put you on the spot there.'

'Nah, but you know what it's like around here these days.

They got more taps than sinks, Mal, new-fangled James Bond stuff that gets all excited if you mention a certain kind of word.'

'Like cousins.'

'Especially cousins.'

'Zach, I gotta ask you this. Who's Ghost or the Ghost?'

'I'm one year shy of retirement, Mal.'

'Sorry. Take it we never had this conversation.'

'No need to be sorry, old buddy, just careful. We go back a long way, huh? Different world for all of us now. You remember when we started out? Heck, a rookie could run all the way with a case so long as he kept the desk sarge in the loop. Nowadays it's gotta come all the way from the top.'

'Thanks, Zach. I owe you one.'

'One!'

Cardinal Wall's Office, New York

Cardinal John Wall squared his feet, swung the putter and watched the ball glide across the coat of arms on the carpet to rebound from the rim of the cup … again. 'Damn,' he said.

The telephone saved his soul from further blemish.

'What?'

'Eminence, this is Michael Flaherty. You told me once to call on you if I was ever in trouble. I'm in trouble.'

The cardinal leaned his rear against the desk.

'Would this Michael Flaherty have a pain-in-the-butt detective friend called—'

'Mal O'Donnell.'

'Who has a lippy Hispanic sidekick called—'

'Rosa Torres.'

'What can I do for you, Michael?'

The Vatican Gardens, Rome

Pope John XXIV was distracted. He had scheduled this hour to sit in the gardens and read his breviary but the prayer book every Roman Catholic priest was obliged to study daily lay unopened on the stone bench beside him. His secretary had informed him, over breakfast, that there had been no new developments in the matter of the escaped or abducted Cardinal Thomas. In his desire to protect the Church, the former Vatican Secretary of State had agreed to a compromise acceptable to the Italian justice ministry and the Vatican. Deep down, the Pope accepted that he hadn't addressed the core issue and now it had come back to haunt him. Cardinal Thomas had masterminded the Remnant, a group of right-wing Catholic religious, who had murdered liberal Catholic theologians as part of a plot to assassinate the Pope and put Thomas on the Throne of St Peter. The thought of the errant cardinal loose in the world soured his stomach.

The call from New York hadn't improved his mood. Cardinal Wall had informed him of the threat to Michael Flaherty, the Irish priest who had been instrumental in bringing J. Arthur Thomas to justice.

'I'll do all I can, Eminence. Your call brings to mind another young man from the North American continent. Are you familiar with a young Jesuit called McFadden? It seems he's been upsetting some of your brother bishops.'

'Yeah, well, someone should. I heard the guy give a lecture in Columbia. He's smart, articulate and extremely critical of Mother Church.'

'I think your colleagues would like me to censure him.'

'I bet they would. Some of these good ole boys would also like you to reinstate the Inquisition and call for a Crusade.'

'What would you counsel, Eminence?'

'You know I'm from Irish stock, Your Holiness, so a story is inevitable. I'll make it brief. I had a Sister of Mercy here on my turf who was a consecrated pain in the – I think the modern phrase is that I found her challenging. She was a gifted theologian, highly articulate and a woman – every church-man's nightmare. When the complaints rolled in, I'd have her in for censure. I'd shut the office door, yell for a while and then we'd share a bottle of whiskey and talk. The Church was satisfied, a gifted girl got to use her talents and I was proud of myself.'

'You had every reason to be proud. Even Solomon might have envied such a solution.'

'Hear me out, Holiness. I thought I was doing the right thing keeping everyone onside. But I was acting like a political ward boss, not like a bishop. She needed a champion and I didn't stand up for her.'

'You speak of her in the past tense, John.'

'Her name was Kathleen O'Reilly, Holiness. She was murdered by the Remnant.'

'I'm sorry, John. If you didn't feel regret, you wouldn't be the man you are and I wouldn't think as highly of you.'

Immediately after the call, he'd given his secretary instructions for the papal nuncio in Ireland.

'Why Israel?' he'd murmured, standing at the window to look out on the square, wrapped in the protective embrace of Bernini's colonnade where, at this early hour, the pigeons still outnumbered the pilgrims.

'Why Israel?' he'd repeated, as his eye fell upon the obelisk taken into exile almost two thousand years before from Egypt. According to the legend, St Peter, the first pope, had been martyred *iuxta obeliscum*, close to the obelisk. So much blood, the Pope thought, so much blood.

'Israel, Holiness? Do you want me to give some instructions to our representative there?'

'No, Stefan. I will make other arrangements.'

He would not pronounce '*ecce homo*', behold the man. Michael Flaherty would arrive in Israel with every advantage the Pope could give him.

Now, sitting on the stone bench, framed by the Casina of Pius IV, the Pope checked his watch. His brief respite in the garden was about to be brought to an end by a Jesuit. The singularity of the word appealed to the linguist in him. The Society of Jesus, in his experience, comprised individuals of such diversity as to give the lie to the collective 'Jesuits'. If the Franciscans could be termed pious and the Dominicans fervent, angular was the only adjective that came close to describing an order that, he often suspected, had been created by God to preserve the Pope from complacency. He was aware of the debt the Church owed these 'shock troops' of the Counter-Reformation and he admired their formidable intellectual power but, individually and collectively, they were a two-edged sword. They could protect the Church from her ideological enemies and as quickly turn their blade against abuses within. Increasingly, in recent times, more and more of them had opted out of comfortable teaching posts in upmarket schools and into the barriadas and favelas of South America. Instead of recreating their church of origin, as many missionaries had been tempted to do, the Jesuits had championed the rights of the poor against repressive and neglectful governments. Hans Richter, the theologian who had become Pope, couldn't argue with that. But the Pope, who had been Hans Richter the theologian, knew only too well the political consequences for the Universal Church. The Jesuit now entering the garden epitomised the angularity of his order.

ჯიჯ

Father Shane McFadden, SJ, stood at more than six feet, and every inch of him appeared to operate according to a separate contract. The Canadian priest had a high forehead receding into a thatch of salt and pepper hair, wild enough to attract nesting birds. The eldest son of a Newfoundland fisherman, he employed the rolling gait of his ancestors and rode the path through the Vatican gardens as if he was tacking in a force-ten gale. When he finally dropped anchor in the Pontiff's presence, he seemed to sway gently at his moorings. The Pope knew, from an extensive file, that behind the yellowing Roman collar, frayed cuffs and trousers that hung a good inch shy of his shoes, Shane McFadden was a man of exceptional intellectual ability. The youngest ever doctoral graduate at the Gregorian University, he had displayed an omnivorous appetite for theology, history and anthropology. His professors had groomed and recommended him for academic advancement only to be surprised and disappointed when he had opted for a three-year stint at a Jesuit mission station near Cusco in Peru. According to the same file, he had experienced some kind of road-to-Damascus conversion there and committed himself to the study of eco-theology, an area frowned on by the official Church and absent from seminary curriculi. Eccentricity, they opined philosophically, was to Jesuits what poverty was to Franciscans. Shane McFadden might have ploughed a singular if fruitful furrow in his church career if he hadn't published. Even this might have passed undetected by the Roman radar. Catholic scholars published regularly but most were protected by a degree of political savvy or by the impenetrability of their prose. Somehow, Shane McFadden had retained a quixotic innocence while writing in accessible English. The ungainly Jesuit was now the best-read cleric on the North American continent and already touted as the champion of 'green' theology worldwide.

The Roman Curia had arrowed towards him like piranha to blood in the water.

An official and exquisitely worded letter 'invited' him to 'discuss' his views with the examining body in Rome. He had done so in such a robust and provocative manner that the presiding prelate had suffered a mild heart attack and two of the inquisitorial monsignori had requested leave of absence, citing nervous exhaustion. Time was when they could simply have silenced him and consigned the troublesome priest to pastoral obscurity. The controversial Jesuit theologian Teilhard de Chardin, the Pope remembered ruefully, had been referred to offhandedly by his Jesuit superiors as 'one of *our* priests'. Under threat of sanction from Rome, de Chardin had become 'one of our priests'. On this particular front, it would be all too easy to win a battle and lose a war. The other reason for reticence was that the priest was published and popular. Ironically, publicity had become the new protection. Most Roman Catholics of a certain age would remember television pictures of a finger-wagging pope looming over a kneeling cleric on a South American runway. Few, if any, would recall the priest's theological or political stance that had given rise to his humiliation. Faced with a potentially damaging PR incident, the Vatican watchdogs resorted to doing what their lay equivalents had done for centuries with a thorny problem: they kicked it upstairs.

There was an awkward moment as the Pope rose and offered his hand. The Jesuit seemed nonplussed by the gesture and, after a slight hesitation, took and shook it. The Pope sat and patted the bench beside him.

'Will you join me, Father?' he asked.

Shane McFadden of the Society of Jesus seemed to wonder if he was being asked to agree with the theologically conservative pope or to join him on the bench. He chose the latter option and sat.

'I've read your book,' the Pope said abruptly. German-born, he was more comfortable with direct speech. 'You don't, as the Americans say, pull your punches.'

'Newfies, people from Newfoundland, tend to say as they see, Holy Father.'

'In theological discourse, that's not always prudent, Father.'

'In the history of theological discourse, it led to one very memorable crucifixion and countless burnings, Holy Father.'

'You wouldn't be the first priest seduced by martyrdom.'

'You wouldn't be the first pope seduced by politics.'

The German Richter had often despaired of what he'd called 'bureaucratic obliquity', the verbal feinting indulged in by Church officials. He relished the cut and thrust of intellectual argument and had always encouraged his students to give as good as they got. If this young man wanted to throw down a gauntlet, well, he might just pick it up and slap him with it, he thought.

'This eco-theology is very new, Father. Would you agree that people can be tempted to follow the new simply because it is new?'

'You've asked two questions, Holy Father. You presumed the answer to the first by phrasing it as a question. Let's split them. Is eco-theology new? Hardly! Eco-theology has been around a long time in cultures more ancient than our own. The Celts of Middle Europe and the native peoples of the Americas and Australia were well advanced in eco-theology before we brought them the benefits of Bibles, muskets and measles. In our own religious tradition, it goes all the way back to our Jewish ancestors, to the prophets Isaiah and Joel in particular. Fast forward and you'll find it articulated by the Christian mystics like Hildegard of Bingen and Francis of Assisi. Nearer to our own day, your predecessor criticised the domination of the environment. So, no, it's not new. Are people more tempted to the new for its own sake? Yes, I guess some of them are, but I think most people look to the new when the old has been tried and found wanting.'

The young man stood abruptly and walked off a few paces before turning back.

'My old man's a fisherman. For twenty years he fished a particular bank because that was where the fish were. When they moved, we had a few hungry seasons before he followed them.'

'And you, Father, a fisher of men, as the Lord said apostles should be, would encourage the faithful to fish elsewhere?'

'Isn't that what Jesus did? But he wasn't asking everybody to do that; he was challenging the men who would run the new Church to do it and he was doing it from outside the boat. Let's look at the story. Peter, James and John fished all night and caught nothing. Then a carpenter comes along and suggests they fish the other side of the boat. What I'd give to have been a fly on the gunwale of that boat. But they take a chance, they risk the new and, well, I guess you know the rest of that story.'

'Yes, I do, 'the Pope replied thoughtfully. 'And their nets were in danger of bursting, so they called for help to the other boats. But surely they had a right to fish because Genesis, the first book of the Bible, says they had dominion over all living things. Is Genesis wrong?'

'No. We know what Genesis is. It's a creation myth, a story told to get across the truth that God made everything. We also know it wasn't the first creation story by a long shot. A much older creation story from the Tigris-Euphrates valley beat them to it.'

'The Gilgamesh epic.'

'Yes. So, the people we now call Iraqis had a similar creation story before our Jewish ancestors went to print. Americans sure love to hear that, I can tell you. And, no, I'm not saying Genesis is wrong, but it's skewed. Who wrote it? Reactionaries! What do you do when the cultures all around you believe the tree's a god, the rock and river are gods? You swing the other way totally. So now God's not down here any more, He's way up there. Out of it. Elvis has left the building.'

'I beg your pardon?'

'Sorry. It's just an expression. Let's stick with the pro-gramme. According to Genesis, God creates the world in six days. On that sixth and final day he creates humans – us. That doesn't mean we're tops, just last. Now let's run the evolution tape. Evolution tells us everything was alive and kicking and evolving for millions of years after the Big Bang. Everything except us. We sneaked in at the eleventh hour. Back to Genesis! According to Genesis, we sixth-day Johnny-come-latelies inherit the whole kit and caboodle. We get to be lords and masters and have dominion over everything, all Creation. And, with some honourable exceptions, we've been taking everything the planet had to give and putting nothing back as if there was no tomorrow, because tomorrow never comes, right? Well, it has come. And now, shock and awe! We've been digging the ground out from under our feet for generations and we're surprised to find ourselves in a hole. We're not the lords of Creation. We're not even the stewards of Creation.'

'What are we?'

'We're kin to all Creation, Holy Father, nothing more, nothing less.'

He looked spent.

'Please, walk with me,' the Pope invited.

They strolled along the path in companionable silence towards the top of the Vatican Hill, passing the statue of St Peter. Presently they arrived at the Fontana dell' Aquilae.

'I've read about this,' McFadden said enthusiastically. 'It's called the Eagle Fountain because Paul the Fifth was a Borghese pope and the eagle was the heraldic symbol of his family.'

'You found this information in the Vatican Library?'

'No. I'm sure I could have done but I just Googled the Vatican gardens.'

He noted incomprehension on the Pope's face.

'You know, with a computer. You just get on the internet and check it out.'

'I'm afraid I'm still back there with Gutenberg and the printing press.'

'Yeah, well, let's not knock Gutenberg. The printing press was Martin Luther's internet.'

'Does this Google say why the fountain was built?'

'Oh, yes. Paul V restored one of Trajan's aqueducts to bring more water in from Lake Bracciano. They called the new supply Aqua Paola and built the fountain in his honour.'

'So at least one pope can be credited with environmental awareness.' The Pope smiled.

'Touché.' The young Jesuit laughed. 'I'm prepared to concede there were others but some of them didn't really have much choice.'

'What do you mean?'

'From September 1870 to February 1929 the popes were prisoners here. When the new Republic of Italy took away their temporal powers, this is pretty much all they had for fifty-nine years. Did you know that Leo XIII came here twice a day? By all accounts, he was a helluva gardener, planted olive trees and vines. Oh, and he had this thing about stretching nets between the trees to catch small birds so that he could release them. Why do you think he did that?'

'Perhaps he felt one prisoner in the garden was sufficient.'

The Pope and the priest walked on until they came to the wood that covers four and a half acres of the Vatican gardens.

'You know what this is?' McFadden asked, lowering his voice as if they had entered a holy place.

'It's a wood.'

'Yes, but it's a lot more. This wood is the lungs of the Vatican, Holy Father. Let me show you.'

The Jesuit positioned the Pope close to the bole of a leafy holm oak.

'Okay. Now if you would just breathe, Holy Father.'

'You mean continue to breathe.'

McFadden placed himself on the other side of the tree where he could see the Pope's face.

'When you breathe out, you exhale carbon dioxide. The tree inhales that carbon dioxide and breathes out oxygen. So, while you're breathing the tree, the tree is breathing you. It's the most respectful greeting and blessing practised by some very ancient cultures – the Maori still do it when they rub noses.'

The Pope stepped closer to the tree and laid his palm against its bark.

'You know there are those within the Church who oppose your views. The word 'pagan' is mentioned.'

'The Romans called the country people *pagani*, Holy Father. It's just a word the elite use to elevate them from the ordinary. And we get 'heathen' from your own language. It means 'hidden things'. I think the duty of a theologian is to bring hidden things into the light.'

'They will also quote St Paul against you where he says that people who are attached to the natural world are fools.'

'Paul thought the end of the world was coming up fast, Holy Father. He wanted all eyes fixed on Heaven. When the world didn't end, the Church just took up his baton. The emphasis continued to be on up there. At best, down here was a distraction; at worst, a source of sin. The long and the short of it was that we were only passing through. You and I were both in seminary. The rooms were usually fairly okay but the corridors, stairs and landings were cr— shabby. Places for passing through don't get cared for. We have to make the point that the world and everything in it is sacred and needs to be cared for. Martin Luther King talked about "the appalling silence of good people". I know he was talking about segregation, not the environment. But who was he talking to? The 'good people' he was accusing were the leaders of the churches.'

The Pope plucked McFadden's book from the pocket of his white soutane.

'Is this your *J'accuse*, Father McFadden?'

'Yes, it is.'

'And do you include the Pope in your accusation?'

'I do.'

'Then I'd better read your book again.'

'Promise me one thing.'

'If I can.'

'Promise me you won't read it in the garden. There's something … skewed about sitting in a garden reading a book on the presence of God in nature.'

'Does that prohibition also apply to the breviary?'

'Especially to the breviary! What sort of pope goes to a garden to read his prayer book?'

Over the young man's shoulder, the Pope could see his secretary approaching the wood.

'I'm afraid I must say goodbye,' he said. 'Thank you for our discussion.'

'That's it?'

'Pardon?'

'I mean … I thought you …'

'Oh, you thought I might order you to stop writing and lecturing.'

'Well, yes, but maybe with some mild torture and temporary excommunication thrown in.'

The Pope's secretary heaved a warning sigh.

'It's Tuesday,' the Pope said. 'We don't do torture on Tuesdays.'

They shook hands and Shane McFadden swung away down the path. The secretary stepped into the shade of the trees and handed the Pope a document from the examining body. It recommended the censure of one Shane McFadden, SJ. The Pope scribbled 'no action' in the margin and handed it back. He had failed to act courageously once before and now a young priest's life hung in the balance. In whatever way he could, he would protect the young Jesuit.

'The envoy from the Patriarch of Constantinople is waiting for you in the library, Holiness.'

The Pope looked admiringly at the leaves and at the dappled light around his feet. He wanted to stand there and feel the breeze and smell the trees.

'What should I tell him, Holiness?'

'Tell him that Elvis has left the building.'

'Pardon?'

'It's just an expression, Stefan.' He smiled, holding his secretary's elbow as they stepped out of the wood. 'Did you know,' he asked, 'that a tree inhales the carbon dioxide we exhale and turns it into oxygen for us?'

'Yes, Holiness.'

'Do you believe that God is in this garden, Stefan?'

The Pope tried not to smile as his secretary stole a furtive glance back at the wood before replying.

'But ... God is everywhere, Holiness.'

'You're quite right, Stefan,' the Pope said, squeezing his elbow reassuringly. 'I have always believed that. I've never really thought of it until today. What building is that behind the Casina?'

'It houses the Pontifical Academy of Sciences, Holiness. They meet every quarter and submit a report.'

'To whom?'

'Eh ... to you, Holiness.'

'Do I read it?'

'Your Holiness signs it.'

'Are you sure you're not a Jesuit, Stefan? Could you make an appointment with the director, please? And now let us turn our thoughts to the envoy from our brother patriarch in Constantinople.'

'Istanbul, Holiness.'

'It's best not to let him hear you say that, Stefan. Our Byzantine brothers have long memories. Speaking of which, am I scheduled to apologise for the excommunication of Constantinople by Leo the Great, Bishop of Rome?'

'No, Holiness.'

'Well, that's a relief.'

'You did that at your first meeting.'

'I see. Well, only another half-millennium of wrongs remain to be righted and we can give our attention to the twenty-first century. We seem to spend so much time patching the past, Stefan.'

The Island, Ireland

Michael Flaherty stood at the end of the pier and looked out over the fog-shrouded water. Piers, railway stations and airports, he reflected, were places rife with contradictions. This was where the hopeful and heartbroken had stepped off the Island for America and opportunity. This was where they returned for holidays, calloused by their absence and experience, trying to restrain their deeper emotions under the mask of nostalgia. The dark mass of the Island pulled at his back. He longed to turn and reclaim his place, his family, his lover and child, all the people and places brought into sharp focus by the summons he had received and the death of the messenger. The words scrolled through his memory: 'It is necessary for one man to die for the people.' He sucked in the moist, salty air and let it out in a long sigh. 'Maybe they'll settle for me,' he murmured.

The pebble glanced off his shoulder and rattled on the pier. 'Liam,' he said, without turning. He heard the boy emerge from wherever he'd been hiding. 'I want to talk to you, Liam,' he said, and waited. God, he's grown, he thought, as the boy edged around to face him. Even in the fading light, he could see that the raven hair and sallow skin were Kate's bequest to her son. The tuft, standing up from the crown of his head, was his. Tiny pearls of moisture glinted there, seeded by the fog, and he resisted the urge to put his hand on the boy's head. Liam regarded him warily.

'I want to tell you … I'm sorry.'

The boy stiffened and averted his eyes.

'I came back,' Michael pressed on urgently, 'hoping that Kate, your mother, and you and I could make a life together. But,' he nodded over the boy's head, 'things out there followed me here. And they'll keep coming back if I don't put an end to it.'

'How will you do that?'

'I don't know.'

'Will you come back?'

'I want to, more than—'

'Michael!' Tess called, from the deck of the ferry. 'It's time for off.'

He turned away and loosed a rope from a bollard, tossing it to the deck. When he turned back, the boy had gone. 'I love you, Liam, my son,' he whispered.

They were well clear of the harbour and fog-blind to both Island and mainland when Tess soothed the engines to idle and left the wheelhouse. Together, they lifted the weighted canvas sack over the railings, consigning the gunman to the sea.

'God, I hate to pollute the water,' Tess grunted, as the bundle vanished beneath the waves.

He stood beside her in the wheelhouse as she shoved the boat into gear and swung her nose for the mainland.

'I'm sorry Iarla had to be involved, Tess,' he said quietly.

'Couldn't be helped,' she answered tightly, then shrugged and softened her tone. 'I'm just glad he got there on time. Iarla is an Islander, Michael,' she added. 'He'll get on with it.'

Islanders, he knew, didn't say goodbye, but he hugged her sideways when their boat bumped the berth.

The cleric sitting in the driver's seat of the black Mercedes turned the ignition when the back door closed. He made no attempt at conversation and didn't look in the rear-view mirror all the way to Dublin airport. Michael found a bag on the back seat and exchanged his clothes for the contents. When he emerged on the Departures ramp, he was Monsignor Michael Flaherty, thanks to the black clerical suit with the red bar beneath the collar and the documents he had found in the side pocket of the bag. The letter folded in his new passport requested all governments to facilitate the passage across their borders of Monsignor Michael Flaherty, papal envoy to Israel. It was signed by Pope John XXIV and carried a scarlet wax seal beneath the signature, indented by the ring of the Fisherman. He thought it looked like a drop of blood.

The O'Donnell Apartment, New York

'The ghost who walks.' Hanny snorted when she opened the apartment door.

'Really nice to see you too, Hanny,' Cardinal Wall replied.

She wrestled him out of his overcoat and fussed him into the kitchen.

'You remember Congressman Fox, Eminence,' Mal said, gesturing at the young man rising to greet the cardinal. The two men shook hands.

'Good to see you young fella,' the cardinal said warmly.

'Although not under these circumstances,' Fox replied.

'You'll be off so, Hanny,' Mal said cheerfully.

'Subtle as a swinging brick,' Hanny muttered, as she shrugged into her coat. 'When you hotshots are finished fixing the world. maybe you can help Mal fix the tap in the bathroom. I'll be down in Raymond's,' she flung over her shoulder, and slammed the door.

'How is Raymond?' the cardinal asked Mal.

'You took a big chance passin' his door. The Cisco Kid may have hung up his holster but his regard for Catholic clergy took a little dent when that crazy guy came callin'.' The three men knew that Raymond, in apartment 3E, had saved Hanny's life from a knife-wielding priest sent by the Remnant to distract Mal from pursuing one of their number in Rome.

'You fellas come by cab?' Mal enquired, holding up a bottle of Midleton, the rare Irish whiskey.

'I took the train,' the cardinal answered.

'I have a driver waiting outside,' Fox added.

'Gee, I guess I shoulda gone into politics.' The cardinal smiled.

'You did,' Mal said cryptically, and began to pour. 'Hanny's brother brought this little gift,' he said. 'Mean old bastard got two weeks' free board on the strength of it. Well, absent friends,' he toasted, and they clinked glasses.

'I've been telling Congressman Fox all I know, Eminence, to bring him up to speed. Maybe you'd like to fill him in from your end.'

'I called the Pope,' the cardinal began, and paused while the congressman choked on his drink. 'You wanna take it easy with that stuff, kid,' he offered kindly. 'Pope says there's nothing new. He's organised Michael's papers for Israel.'

'Isn't that sending him into danger?' Fox asked.

'Yes,' Mal said slowly, 'but the lad doesn't have a choice. They don't have a witness-protection programme on the Island,' he added drily. 'Anyway, Thomas – or whoever is pullin' his strings – won't give up.'

'You're sure there's someone else in the equation?' Fox pressed.

Mal stared into his glass as if he might divine what was hidden before replying. 'Thomas was lifted, Congressman. Sure, the Santa Lucia wasn't a lock-down institution but this wasn't the work of amateurs. This was planned and executed by people with resources and connections. They had to spring him and hide him. The Italian police haven't had a sniff. So, someone took Thomas and sent that bozo to the Island with a message for Michael. Ex-bozo,' he corrected himself, 'and good riddance. The only clue we have from that event is Ghost. My usually reliable and unusually nervous source says Ghost is someone at the top of the spook hierarchy.'

'Casper Benson?' the congressman spluttered.

'You really should take water with that, son,' the cardinal interjected.

'No – no, thanks, Eminence.' The young man sucked in a deep breath and blew it out slowly.

'Casper Benson,' he began, 'is the original ghost in the Washington machine. He's seen, maybe, three presidents come and go and, I guess, the only thing the three would ever agree on is you don't cross Benson. Runs the CIA like a personal fiefdom. Rumour on the Hill has it that he's had a finger in all sorts of clandestine pies over the years but nothing ever comes back to haunt him. Compared to Benson, Teflon is like Superglue.'

He sipped, and the silence lengthened. Somewhere in the neighbourhood a siren whooped once and settled into a rising wail that filled the apartment with sound and splattered the kitchen curtains with vivid blue until it faded away into the night.

'Well,' the cardinal said slowly, 'now that we've all peeped over our shoulders, what can we do for Michael Flaherty?'

'I could go out there and—'

'Mal!'

'What the hell would stop me? I could—'

'Mal, for cryin' out loud.'

'Well, I'm damned if I'm going to let Michael walk in there like a sheep to the slaughter so that some twisted cardinal can have his revenge. Sorry.'

'No need to be. But if it makes you feel any better, I accept your apology on behalf of the College of Cardinals. Now, listen up, Rambo. If Michael is in the firing line, he sure doesn't need to be covering your ancient ass at the same time. No, don't take umbrage, old friend. He doesn't need you or anyone else to go in there. He needs us to get him out, preferably all in one piece. So, let's pool our resources here, okay?'

'Okay.'

'All righty,' the cardinal continued. 'So far I'm way ahead of the game. Apart from calling the Pope, I called a guy I know in Jerusalem, the boss man in the Church of the Holy Sepulchre. He's a Franciscan, but no one's perfect. He'll be waiting for Michael at the airport. At least that will give Michael a base and, if I know Tim Conway, a lot more besides.'

'How well do you know this Tim Conway guy?' Mal asked sceptically.

'Knew him since he was a kid in the Bronx. His old man drove buses in Queens. Kid was smart as a whip so I – we – finagled a scholarship for him with the Jesuits. Blew them away, I can tell ya. And then he does a runner and joins the Franciscans. I don't think the Society of Jesus ever forgave me for that one. Tim's bright, Mal, and he's right at the heart of things in Jerusalem. He's got my number, so we'll know what's happening. Now, let's be hearing from you, Mal.'

'I have a hunch that this goes way beyond the whole Cardinal Thomas and the Remnant thing. Sure, some of his crazies are still on the loose but my information is that they're a spent force.'

Cardinal Wall nodded. After the attempt on the previous pope's life, the Catholic Church had pursued the Remnant with all the rigour of Church law. Those who had been discovered were defrocked or, where evidence of actual crime could be produced, handed over to the civil authorities for justice. To his shame, his secretary had been one of them.

'Anyway,' Mal continued, 'I don't think they have the juice to spring Thomas. Why would they bring him to Jerusalem? No, it doesn't pan out. This was a professional job. Fermi thinks it was masterminded by a special agent of some sort, and I trust his judgement. The question is, who has that kind of clout? Who has those kinds of resources in Italy to take him or in Israel to keep him? I can't believe they want Michael in Israel just to – to kill him.'

'We have,' Fox said softly.

'Who do you mean?'

'I mean the United States.'

He raised a hand to silence them and continued, 'What I'm going to say can never be even hinted at outside of here, okay?'

'That cuts both ways, Congressman,' the cardinal said evenly. 'I presumed when I told you about the Pope's involvement, I wouldn't be hearing it back from the whisper-circuit in Washington.'

'You did, Eminence, and I appreciate that. I'm sorry if I seemed to question your prudence, or yours, Mal. That wasn't my intention. And, in case you're too polite to ask, yes, I do want to cover my political ass. But it's more than political. I have kids.'

The two older men exchanged a glance.

'Maybe you should think this through, son,' the cardinal said quietly. 'Nobody here's gonna think any less of you if you just finish up your drink and go home.'

'Believe me, Eminence,' Fox said, with feeling, 'I've been thinking it through every which way since Mal called.' He seemed to mull over something in his mind and his companions waited patiently. 'I first met you two through Sister Kathleen O'Reilly. I – I really cared for her.' Again he paused to gather himself. When he spoke, his voice held an edge of anger. 'She was pushed in front of a train by the Remnant because she held views that threatened their vision of a world order. I don't want something like that to happen to Michael Flaherty or anyone else for the sake of someone's idea of how things should be, even if that someone is the United States.'

He pushed his glass into the middle of the table.

'D'you think you could pour me a half one, Mal?' he asked.

'Mal's Irish,' the cardinal replied. 'He doesn't do half ones. It's against his religion.' The younger man laughed dutifully. Cardinal Wall took the opportunity to nudge his own glass closer to the bottle.

'Okay,' Fox continued, 'I'll keep this as brief as I can. You know all about the rise of the neocons in Washington? We're talking ultra-conservative politicians whose world view is some kind of Fourth Reich with puppet governments in countries strategically important to the United States.'

'You mean countries with oil,' Mal said.

'Yes, I do. Countries with enough oil to keep our military machine greased and rolling right into the next millennium. That's their dream, Mal, part of it anyway. But there's more. We give these countries the hardware to keep their borders secure and their neighbours antsy. So, an expanded Europe babysits Russia, a nuclear Taiwan keeps China guessing. Japan gets the capacity to absorb a first strike from North Korea and fry the Dear Leader's ass with retaliatory strikes. None of this is news. But what about Israel, our favoured nation in the Middle East? Israel gets what it needs before it knows it needs it and keeps the Arab states in line. Act One of the *Pax Americana*. The people in high places who dream of these things are the same people who thought Ike should have rolled on Moscow or that Nixon should have dropped the big one on 'Nam. The only brake on their runaway dream was Russia and her satellite countries.'

Christy Kenneally

'And now Russia has lost her allies and found capitalism,' Wall said.

'Right,' the congressman smiled humourlessly, 'it's a whole new ballgame. I work in Congress and I meet those people. I talk to them and listen to them over coffee. I managed to get appointed vice-chair on the Foreign Affairs Committee and what I hear and read scares me. They're everywhere. They're at every level of the administration and on all the important committees. And, as if their crazy quota wasn't large enough, they're hand in glove with the Christian Right whose vision of a new world order is Old Glory and Mom's American apple pie for all and say, "Thank you, Jesus."'

The two older men smiled at that but the congressman didn't join them.

'Part of the problem is,' he continued, 'that people like you, rational people, smile and think it's too far out ever to happen. The people who court my vote at the water-cooler don't believe that. They're saying it can, will and must happen for the future survival of the United States. Let's get back to Israel. I hear Jerusalem come up a lot in these conversations. Some of it's the usual evangelical stuff, like the Second Coming and the Rapture, stuff that's maybe sort of harmless in the long run. But a lot of it comes from people who see Jerusalem as a touchpaper that could ignite and blow the whole area, and if that happens, guess who rides to the rescue and forgets to go home? And if it doesn't happen, I believe there are people who are ready and willing to make it happen.'

'I can't believe the president would ever buy into this,' Mal said, shaking his head.

'You're right, Mal, she wouldn't. I've known Ellen a long time, even before she was state governor. She can chew iron and spit nails with the best of them but she's not crazy. She wouldn't buy into it

239

but she could be presented with a fait accompli of some sort and, if that happened, her choice would be either to resign or to ride the runaway train in the hope of being some kind of moderate brake.'

Cardinal Wall tapped his finger meditatively against the rim of his glass.

'I hear what you're saying, Congressman,' he said carefully, 'and some of this stuff I've heard before. But I don't believe it's possible for a neo-conservative Christian Right axis to out-punch the White House. You'd have to be talking some kind of coup from outside the administration. The president would see that coming a mile off and slap it down.'

While the cardinal was speaking, Mal was watching the congressman's face. He knew from the expression he read there that he still had something to say. Mal also knew that he didn't want to hear it.

'You're absolutely right, Eminence, if the move came from outside the administration – but what if it came from inside? What if it came from people within the administration and if one of their number controls a vast network of agents and resources worldwide?'

'The Ghost?'

'Yes, the Ghost. I have some friends in Washington who are concerned about the same things we are. I'll see what I can find out and bring it back to the table.'

'Mal?'

'I'm a cop, Eminence. I'll do what cops do – ye know, poke around, ask questions, call in some favours.'

Yeah, the cardinal thought ruefully. Last time you did the cop routine and poked around, you poked a hole right through the hive of the Remnant.

'Well, I think we're adjourned,' he said, draining his glass.

The apartment door slammed and Hanny stuck her head into the kitchen.

'Can I get you guys anything?' she asked. 'Kitchen closes in five minutes.'

'Thanks, Hanny,' the cardinal grunted, hoisting himself out of the chair, 'but we're all done here. How's Raymond?' he asked, as they reversed the overcoat sequence.

'He's okay. Says he was sorry to miss you. Told him to squeeze the trigger next time.'

Baldwin's Mansion, Jerusalem

Cardinal Thomas lay on the bed and stared at the scene painted on the ceiling. It wasn't a Pinturicchio or a Botticelli, he conceded, but it was the only show in town. At its centre, a man stood bulked in armour, swathed in a cloak marked with a red cross. A frail, mitred bishop stood beside him, frozen for ever in the act of placing a crown on the young knight's head. Crowded into the scene were various other knights and their squires, one of the latter soothing a restive stallion. In the corners he could see turbaned figures, bowed to the ground in chains. Among them, a bearded figure stood defiantly, a Star of David on his cloak. The entire group was framed against the looming walls and towers of what was unmistakably Jerusalem. The cardinal's eye was drawn back to the central figure of the Crusader. Blue eyes blazed from a blunt, bearded face. He thought something in the man's expression suggested that the tentative bishop had better get on with the coronation or the Crusader might do a Napoleon and snatch the diadem to crown himself.

He closed his eyes and tried to recall the events leading up to that blissful moment when he had toppled into the embrace of the king-size bed. At Tel Aviv airport, he and the woman … Heck, what was she calling herself now? He suspected she had many names and as many personae as a Russian doll. Even before the props of the giant aircraft had stopped spinning, they had been spirited into a limousine and driven at speed through a guarded gate in the perimeter fence. He had dozed fitfully on the journey, vaguely remembered coming to at some stage and wondering at the ruined trucks that littered the side of the road. The sun was directly overhead when they'd turned the curve of a long avenue to the front of a modern three-storey mansion, brooding in its own shadow. He remembered a young man in a lightweight suit carrying his bag down a corridor to the room he now occupied. The young man had skin several shades lighter than his own and a telltale bulge in the left-hand side of his jacket.

'Sir Baldwin bids you welcome, Bishop Ademar,' the man said, in accented English. 'You will rest now. Later, you will dine with Sir Baldwin and the other guests.'

Who the hell was this Sir Baldwin guy? he wondered. And how come this manservant-bodyguard had got his own name wrong? 'Other guests', he'd said. More than him and the woman?

He must have dozed again. The sharp knock on the door brought him upright in the bed.

'My lord bishop,' a man's voice called from the corridor, 'Sir Baldwin summons you to his presence. I am to escort you. Please dress in the clothes provided.'

As a former head of a Vatican department, the cardinal was no stranger to protocol but the man's archaic phrasing made him uneasy – it was as if he had wandered into a drama and had no knowledge of the script. Pius XII, he remembered hearing from old Vatican hands, might well have 'summoned people to his presence'. In his latter years, they had knelt in that presence until their business was concluded. He had served under a pope who requested meetings. Huffily, he dragged back the covers and froze when he saw what hung on the wardrobe door. He recognised it, almost immediately, as a bishop's ceremonial garb. It comprised a skull-cap, a magni-ficent white surplice bordered with a froth of lace that flowed down over a purple soutane. There was even an ermine-edged cape and a massive pectoral cross, flashing with precious stones. He smiled at the red silk socks rolled and nesting in lustrous buckled black shoes. He thought the whole ensemble looked like something from the wardrobe department of the Cinecittà studios in Rome, some costume designer's idea of how a pre-Renaissance bishop suited up.

Everything was a perfect fit and he dawdled before the full-length mirror, posing like an actor, until he was certain his facial expression matched the hauteur of the costume.

Along the wall of the corridor, portraits bloomed in the candlelight. Each was of a man in armour with a cross-emblazoned cloak. Hurrying to keep up with his guide, Cardinal Thomas hadn't time to read the nameplates hammered into the walls beneath them. Except one: Tancred. He thought he had heard that name before. The last portrait hung over the double doors. The subject was soberly dressed like all the others but his face was thin and sensitive. Someone had cut the eyes from the face so that the backing canvas showed its white coarse grain through the ragged holes. A carved wooden tablet named him as Godfrey de Bouillon. The doors opened inward silently. With a shiver of apprehension, Cardinal Thomas followed his guide into the Great Hall.

It was lit by a galaxy of candles, hundreds of them. Banks of candles stood in lambent pools throughout the room. Wheels of candles hung suspended from the ceiling. As his eyes grew accustomed to their glow, he saw tattered banners spiking from the walls, leading his gaze to an enormous table on a raised dais. A figure sat at the centre, his face a mystery of moving shadows.

'You may approach,' he said, and the cardinal walked forward to stand at the foot of the steps leading up to the dais. The man rose slowly to his feet. Cardinal Thomas stood at over six feet but the other seemed to tower over him. He wore a floor-length black velvet cloak, which rippled as he moved, causing the emblazoned red cross to writhe languidly like a banner in a breeze. Light blue eyes blazed from the bearded face with a daunting intensity.

'So,' he said, 'Ademar returns to Jerusalem. We are well met, my lord bishop.'

Cardinal Thomas considered contradicting the false name and title until he looked into those eyes and thought better of it.

'Sir Baldwin,' he said, inclining his head to acknowledge the welcome.

'Sit at my right hand, Ademar,' his host said graciously, indicating a place at the table. When the Knight was seated again, he seemed to lapse into a state of coiled watchfulness.

'Sir Baldwin,' the cardinal began tentatively, 'there are quest—'

His teeth clicked together audibly as the Knight raised his right hand.

'Peace, Ademar,' he said, 'we await other guests. Soon all will be revealed.' As if on cue, the door at the other end of the hall cracked and swung open. Two figures approached the dais through the gauntlet of tiny flames. The woman, Cardinal Thomas noted, moved with ease as if she had done this before. Her male companion walked a pace behind, his hands jammed into his pockets. He affected a slight swagger, suggesting to the watching cardinal that he masked apprehension with bravado. When they stepped fully into the circle of light before the dais, he was surprised to recognise the woman who had been his liberator, or abductress. The jury's still out on that one, he thought. She was wearing a crimson gown that swept the floor behind her. Around her neck, a cross, studded with red stones, hung from a gold chain. His eyes flicked back to her face and widened. During their journey through Italy, he had seen those unremarkable features flow and meld to form the faces of a subservient nun in the Santa Lucia convent and a feral huntress in Umbria. She looked and moved now like the lady of the manor escorting a guest to the table of her lord. He switched his attention to the other guest and the breath hitched in his chest. He knew that face – a face that had been handsome before dissipation and disappointment had reduced it to caricature. Jack Holland, former President of the United States, met his stare and mirrored his surprise. Instantly, the surprise disappeared, submerged under an expression of boredom. The old political master hasn't totally lost his touch, he thought admiringly. But what the—

The Knight's booming voice interrupted his speculation. 'My lord bishop,' he said, 'I present the Lady Melisande, a staunch ally and the scourge of our enemies, and Mr Holland, the emissary of the West.'

Jack Holland looked as if he might protest but he wrestled his features under control and bowed slightly. When the two men had been seated at either side of Baldwin, with Melisande on the other side of the cardinal, the Knight spoke again.

'There is much we must speak of and you will have questions but I beg your patience. You have travelled far and are hungry. Eat and drink with me.'

He clapped his hands sharply and two men materialised from the shadows. One carried a mounded platter of fresh fruit, which he laid on the table. The other filled their glasses from a crystal decanter.

'To Jerusalem,' the Knight intoned, raising his glass.

'To Jerusalem,' the two men echoed uncertainly.

Somewhere in the shadowed hall, a harpsichord began to play. Did they have harpsichords in the twelfth century? the cardinal wondered, and dismissed the thought. The music was loud enough to excuse the guest from polite conversation and he was famished. The meal progressed at a stately pace to brandy. The anonymous waiters hovered on the periphery, ready to spirit away an empty plate and refresh an empty glass. Finally, the decanter was placed before the Knight and the waiters withdrew.

The Knight began to speak.

'Jerusalem,' he said, so softly that his guests had to lean in his direction, 'is a city divided – divided as the garments of the Lord were among the Roman soldiers. It is my destiny to make it whole again; to plant the Cross of Christ once more in the high places and bring the infidel to heel. You, Bishop Ademar, will once again stand at my right hand. To you falls the duty of Christianising this city. And you, Mr Holland, will be the standard bearer of the Western powers, our defence against the vengeful jackals who will circle our great prize. And you, Lady Melisande, will protect the Companions of the Cross from those who would thwart our sacred mission.'

The cardinal and Jack Holland exchanged a look of mutual incomprehension. The cardinal cleared his throat.

'Sir Baldwin,' he began, 'I'd like to clarify some matters.'

'You may,' Baldwin conceded, leaning back in his chair.

'Church history was never my strongest suit,' the cardinal said self-deprecatingly, 'but I do recall that Ademar was Pope Urban's representative on the First Crusade, which was led by Godfrey de Bouillon. Why do you refer to me by his name?'

'Your recall is accurate,' Baldwin answered softly. 'Ademar was indeed our bishop-companion when we set forth on our sacred enterprise. My brother Godfrey was indeed the one who led our host and, when Jerusalem was ours, refused the crown. My brother was a man of … scruples in some matters. But he lacked vision.'

An image of the eyeless portrait flashed into the cardinal's mind and he pulled his cape more tightly round him.

'It fell to me to take his place. I see scepticism writ large on your face, Bishop. Baldwin, the King of Jerusalem, has been gone to dust these many centuries, you think, and indeed he has. His remains are housed in the vaults beneath us. I am directly descended from Baldwin the First, as is the Lady Melisande. I have vowed to complete the task to which he dedicated his life. You have been chosen to fulfil the role of Ademar.'

Despite his caution, the cardinal laughed incredulously. 'Chosen by whom?' he asked. 'The Pope?'

'Your laughter is fitting,' the Knight replied smoothly. 'You have been stripped of all ecclesiastical privilege by the Bishop of Rome for plotting to set yourself on the Throne of Peter.'

He leaned forward suddenly and blew out the candle before him on the table.

'You are an excommunicate.' He held up an imperious hand to stave off possible protest from the cardinal.

'You think me mad, Cardinal Thomas? You who loosed a murderous madman and his raggle-taggle Remnant on the Church? You who connived in the deaths of priests, who conspired in the death of a pope? You think me mad?'

He laughed loudly and shook his head.

'Appointed by the Pope? What a conceit! You are an embarrassment to Mother Church, Your Eminence. In her efforts to hide your perfidy from the faithful, the Vatican hid you behind the skirts of a convent until such time as they could determine what to do with you. Were they fearful that you might escape? No! Where would you go? Who would give you refuge or succour? And you did not wish to escape, did you? You were content to moulder in self-pity. Oh, you have lived as a prince in Rome but you are no Roman. A true Roman would have sat in his bath and opened his veins. As to who appointed you, let us say that those who gave you covert aid in the past, those who thought your stepping into the shoes of the Fisherman would advance their vision of a new world order, those whom you failed have decided you should have one last chance to redeem yourself. They might well have decided otherwise. There was the possibility that you might throw yourself on the Pope's mercy and unburden your heart of its secrets. The dart shot into your neck by the Lady Melisande could have carried a lethal dose and their worries on this score would be at an end. But they chose otherwise. You are sent to me to be part of my plan.'

'What plan is that?' Jack Holland asked bluntly.

'Ah, the new world,' the Knight sighed theatrically, 'impatient with protocol and the niceties ...'

'Cut the shit, Baldwin,' Holland said. 'Answer the question. What's the plan and how do I fit in?'

'The plan is simplicity itself, Mr Holland. While you are here in Jerusalem, you will establish business links with certain groups and individuals.'

'Why?'

'Because they need to purchase arms I can provide. You will be the broker. Whatever is your normal … consideration will be doubled. And,' he paused to lift a finger, 'you will be acting with the blessing and assistance of an arm of the American intelligence service.' While that sank home, he raised a second finger. 'Should the political situation change, you will have powerful friends in both camps, who will lobby to have you given plenipotentiary powers to act in your country's best interests.'

Holland raised his finger, mimicking Baldwin's gesture.

'One,' he said, 'my country already has an official representative here acting in its best interests, the United States ambassador.' He raised a second finger. 'Two, the President of the United States would never sanction any such powers for me.'

Baldwin nodded. 'As to the first point, His Excellency Herbert Love is the US ambassador. That is true. He is widely regarded as spectacularly ineffective. He was also inherited by the president and not appointed by her. Should a crisis arise, he will be … reassigned. As to your second point, you are correct. If the president had time for deliberation and counsel, she would not appoint you for political and personal reasons. But this is a volatile region, Mr Holland. The political landscape can shift quite suddenly and dramatically. If a former president is in situ when the crisis comes and achieves a high profile, it would seem churlish and politically unwise for the president to resist such an opportunity.'

'You actually think she'd go for it?' Holland said, shaking his head.

'I think she might not have the luxury of choice, Mr Holland. Either way, what do you have to lose? Like His Eminence, you no longer have a reputation worth losing. On the gain side, if you have enough fingers remaining unused to enumerate them, you might consider money, power, prestige – a chance to do more than Carter or Bush ever could to stabilise this region. You could have the chance to be remembered, as Mitchell is for Northern Ireland. You could have it all, including the gratitude of your country – even that of the president.'

He surged to his feet.

'History happens to the great mass of humanity, my friends, but it is made by the few. Enough of business. I would like to show you my home and provide a little entertainment before you retire.'

෨෧෮෫

Locked inside their own thoughts, the cardinal and former president hardly registered the treasures of antiquity on display throughout the mansion or listened to the narrative of their host. When they retraced their steps to the Great Hall, Baldwin rolled back a section of carpet to reveal a trapdoor set in the floor. He swung it open and a stairway led down into the gloom. Holding a seven-branch candlestick, he descended. The two men stayed close to his heels, trying to remain in the circle of light that followed him. The cardinal was aware of the

Lady Melisande bringing up the rear. She moved confidently in the dark, he thought, as if it were her natural element. He was relieved when they left the oppression of narrow passageways and emerged into a large, high, vaulted room. It reeked of damp and mildew. In the centre, the mouth of a well gaped in the stone floor.

'In the original building,' their guide explained, 'this was often the difference between life and death. When the Saracens circled the walls, this water source ensured that the inhabitants would survive for lengthy periods of time. But when the horses, dogs, cats and rats had all been eaten, some resorted to eating their own dead. This is where they made their last stand and this is where the Saracens consigned them to eternal rest. Over the centuries, the well has almost filled with debris.'

The cardinal detected another odour in the room. He recognised it as the sharp, acidic stench of human fear rising from the well. At Baldwin's gesture, they took up positions ringing the opening. Baldwin flipped a switch and the well flowed with artificial light.

The two men were naked, except for loincloths. They sat with their backs against the weeping wall. Startled by the sudden light, they jerked upright, shading their eyes.

'Who are they?' the cardinal whispered.

'They are Mamelukes,' Baldwin replied, amused by the confusion on the cardinal's face.

'But – but Mamelukes disappeared from history hundreds of years ago. They were Christian boys taken by the Muslims and brought up in that faith.'

'Indeed,' Baldwin agreed, circling the pit to join a third man, who had emerged from the shadows. 'Brought up to be assassins and warriors, the shock-troops of the Saracens. Know your enemy, Bishop, and learn from him. I bought triplets and brought them up in the Christian faith. Matthew and Mark you see in the pit. This is Luke, their brother,' he said, indicating the man who stood beside him. 'I taught them all I knew of arms and combat. What I couldn't teach they learned from FARC, ETA and other ... specialist groups. The two you see below have been part of my Praetorian Guard, keeping the enemy from my gates. They have been my vengeance, stretching out to hunt and hinder my foes.'

He stopped walking and gazed almost sadly at the Mamelukes. 'They are my sons,' he whispered.

'You keep your sons in a pit?' Holland spat, making no effort to hide his distaste.

'Only the ones who fail me,' Baldwin answered. 'And now one of them must die.'

He drew a dagger from his belt and dropped it into the well. There was a moment of shocked stillness. It was followed by an explosion of sound and movement as the two men wrestled frantically for possession of the dagger, grunting with effort. Holland saw Cardinal Thomas lean over the lip of the arena, his face suddenly ugly with blood-lust. He turned, and saw that Melisande's face matched the cardinal's for cruelty. Baldwin waited impassively. Sickened by the spectacle and spectators, Holland moved away from the edge of the pit, distancing himself from the death-struggle. Try as he might, he couldn't block his awareness of the animal snarls that rose in volume and intensity until one voice elongated into a scream and stilled.

In his peripheral vision, he saw Baldwin knotting a rope to a metal ring set in the floor and tossing the other end into the pit. The man who struggled out was slick with sweat and blood. He offered the stained dagger, hilt first, to Baldwin.

'Get cleaned up, Mark,' Baldwin said, accepting the dagger and sliding it beneath his cloak. The man bowed shakily and left the room, supported by his brother, Luke. Baldwin picked up the light and led them back to their rooms.

'I will send for you,' he said, and left them fumbling to open their doors in the dark.

&

Jack Holland stepped inside his room and leaned against the closed door. He counted a slow ten after the footsteps had faded before he crossed the corridor to the cardinal's door.

'Cardinal Thomas. Your Eminence,' he whispered, his mouth close to the wood.

The door yielded an inch and Thomas peered at him through the crack. His previous intensity had disappeared and his tone reflected the dullness in his eye.

'What do you want? It's late. I'm tired.'

'Listen to me.' Holland placed his palm against the door. 'This Baldwin is seriously crazy. You must see that. No, no, don't close the door, just listen. Give me one damn minute, okay?'

The pressure from the other side of the door eased somewhat.

'Look, Eminence, Baldwin was right. There's no way back for either of us. The Church doesn't want you, and my wi— the president sure as heck doesn't want me. We're in the shit together, Eminence. Look, whatever cock-a-mamie drama this guy is planning on staging, lots of people are likely to die. You've seen Act One in the cellar, for Chrissakes. Now, you and me are bit players to this guy. I can't see us being in the sequel, can you?'

'I can't talk now,' the cardinal said woodenly, and shut the door. Holland thumped on it with frustration and padded back to his room.

⅏⅏

Beyond a bend in the corridor, Baldwin smiled grimly in the shadows. 'Strike one, Mr Holland,' he murmured.

The White House, Washington DC

'Sit down, Laila. You look like death warmed over.'

The Secretary of State perched stiffly on the edge of her chair. The president plucked off her reading glasses and tossed them onto a mound of papers.

'Let's hear it,' she said. The telephone beeped and she snatched it up. 'Rachel! I want you to hold all calls unti— What? … Okay, send him in. And, Rachel, see if you can find Senator Melly. Thanks.'

She sat back and blew out a long breath.

'Ephrem is on his way, Laila,' she said softly, and pressed on over the distressed woman's protests. 'We're a team. I suspect you two arriving at my door within minutes of each other is stretching coincidence. Let's wait and hear it all together.' The door opened and a flushed Ephrem Isaacson walked in.

'Take a pew, Ephrem,' the president said calmly. 'There's water in the jug.'

The Secretary for the Treasury gestured with a glass towards the Secretary of State, who shook her head. A light tap at the door announced the arrival of the senator.

His glance took in the body language of the others as he eased his bulk into a chair. 'I would bid you all a good morning,' he drawled, 'but I guess that's a matter of opinion.'

'Okay, Laila,' the president said, 'you have the floor.'

Laila Achmed took a deep, steadying breath. 'I have contacts in the … in the press,' she amended, and the president rewarded her circumspection with a small nod. 'The contact called me just fifteen minutes ago. A newspaper will feature a story in tomorrow's edition. It will report on a young man recently arrived in Guantánamo because of alleged involvement with al-Qaeda. He is my nephew – my brother's son.'

She clasped her hands in her lap and struggled for composure.

'I'm very sorry, Laila,' the president said, 'but—'

'No,' Laila interrupted. 'There is no need to apologise, Ms President. I … I understand the implications for someone in my position. My resignation will be on your desk today.'

Ellen Radford leaned forward and fixed her eyes on the Secretary of State.

'Let's get a few things clear, right off the bat,' she said. 'First, I was not apologising, I was commiserating. You have family trouble, I sympathise. Period. Second, the implications, as you put it, for someone in your position are something I will consider with the aid of counsel.' She inclined her head at Senator Melly. 'Are we clear on this?'

'Yes, Ms President.'

'Good. Your turn to bat, Ephrem.'

'I had a call from a relative in New Jersey, who had a call from a relative in Israel. It's complicated.'

'We've got time.'

'The relative in Israel is working in security. The message was "Abba is going to be famous."'

'I thought they already were,' the president said drily.

Ephrem Isaacson attempted a smile and failed. 'Abba is a pet-name we have for our grandfather, Ms President. I made a few calls myself. It seems a film crew showed up at his door and started asking questions. Abba loves to talk – God, does he ever. He told them lots of stuff about running with Menachem Begin and all the things he did for the Stern Gang during the first Arab–Israeli war. Lots of things he never told us. It's going to be wall-to-wall news tomorrow.'

'And you want to fall on your sword as well?'

'No, I don't. But maybe you think I should.'

Ellen Radford leaned back in her chair.

'I think you two did the right thing bringing this here. I said at the start: no surprises. I also think you need to sit in the little drawing room down the hallway while Senator Melly and I have a talk. There's coffee-making stuff there and you won't be disturbed. Hardly anyone goes there. They say it's haunted by President Harrison. Enjoy your coffee.'

When they had let themselves out, she stood and walked to the window. The spike of the Washington Monument looked particularly sharp, she thought.

'I can hear you thinking from over here, Henry,' she said, without turning. 'First off, d'you think this is a coincidence?'

'No,' he said flatly. 'Seems lightning can and does strike in the same place twice. Ask Lee Trevino.'

'Who?'

'Doesn't matter. No, it's too damn neat to be a coincidence. You are under attack, Ms President.'

She turned to stare at him.

'Questions we must answer are,' he continued, 'who's attacking us and why now?'

'Laila's nephew is a story that was leaked, wasn't it?'

'Yeah, I'd say so. Too much of a long shot to think otherwise.'

'And Abba?' She smiled bleakly.

'Of all the doors in Israel, a film crew just happens to knock on mine, oy veh,' he said, returning her smile. 'I think not. To get back to the nephew. Security in Guantánamo knows everything there is to know about the detainees. So how come this piece of information doesn't find its way here? And Abba? Ephrem doesn't spell out that his information comes from someone in Mossad, but you can lay money on it. Why didn't we hear from the security service of our favoured nation? Join the dots, Ellen.'

'Because someone on our side made it so.'

'Yes, Captain Picard,' he grunted, slapping his fist to his chest. 'And who has that kind of access and clout? No need to answer a rhetorical question, girl, but you know and I know.'

'Why is he doing this?'

'No love lost,' he answered. 'Which is a polite way of saying he hates your guts, Ms President. Oh, not just yours. Benson's been a boil festering away on the body politic for a long time. He's got enough pus to go round.'

'Thank you for that tasteful image.'

'You're welcome. He could just be giving you a hard time because he can't bully you or because he wants to divide and conquer your cabinet. Who could even guess at what passes for rationality in that mind? Let's step back a ways from that Black Hole. The real question is, why now? I think it's a feint, some kind of skirmish to keep us occupied while something bigger's going down somewhere else.'

She returned to her desk and placed her palms flat on the papers.

'Okay,' she said. 'One, I need to get those two back in here and sort them out. Two, we need to send out feelers of our own to find out what this "skirmish" is meant to distract us from.'

'This may not be relevant,' the senator said slowly, 'but I hear Jack is in Jerusalem.'

He saw the surprise on her face before she could hide it.

'You didn't know, did you?'

'No,' she answered, 'I didn't know. Nor do I care.'

'Rein it in, bubba,' her old friend admonished her. 'You gotta feel like a person and think like the president. As president, you could expect that kind of information to come from your ambassador in Israel.'

'Yes,' she said, taking a deep breath to calm herself. 'I could reasonably have expected that kind of information from Herbert Love. I inherited him from the previous administration. From what I hear, he can be a little too cosy with the friends.'

'Yep, so I gather, but that's a thought for another day. Maybe he just didn't know. Maybe Jack didn't go through the proper channels. Hell, he can't just go somewhere, anywhere without being recognised.'

'He's not exactly news any more, Henry,' she said stiffly.

Not for the first time, the senator wondered at how she could get so riled up about someone she had cut out of her life. Maybe it's true what they say about phantom pains, he thought, and turned his attention to the matter in hand.

'You're right. He's not headline news but he should figure in a sidebar somewhere. Heck, he's gotta fly in and stay somewhere.'

'How did you know?'

'Got lucky. Old pal of mine from the State Department coming home from over there saw him in the airport. That part of the airport your average passenger doesn't see. This guy happened to be getting the same hush-hush treatment on the way out as Jack was getting coming in.'

'So maybe some of our feelers should go east,' she said. 'Can we do that without certain people seeing our hand?'

'Yep. I got a few favours due for calling in.'

'I think Laila and Ephrem might get a little panicky if I leave them any longer.'

She picked up the phone and gave instructions.

❧❧❧

She thought they looked even more strained that before. Maybe caffeine and the cross-fertilisation of paranoia hadn't been such a swell idea after all.

'Please sit,' she said briskly. 'Here's how it goes. You will, neither of you, tender your resignation to the president. The matters divulged here do not impinge on our country's security or interests. They are personal family matters. I want you to return to your departments. If you come by any further information, bring it right here.'

'But what about the media stories?' Ephrem asked.

'That particular dice has to roll, Ephrem,' she said. 'We can't be seen to tilt the table in any way, shape or form. I'll deal with it at my press conference this afternoon. You two should view the tapes and read the transcripts to be ready for any fallout. That's it.'

'Thank you, Ms President,' they said together.

She softened her expression.

'You two are doing fine. I congratulate myself on your appointments.'

It was the only time they smiled.

Press Room, The White House, Washington DC
The White House press secretary was agitated. 'I didn't hear any of this,' he protested, and gulped as the president skewered him with a stare.

'Cool it, George,' she relented, picking up her glasses from the desk. 'This one caught us all cold.'

'The glasses, Ms President,' he said nervously.

'What about them?'

'You can't wear them out there. And the stylist will have to do something with your hair.' His voice slid to somewhere near the back of his throat and he swallowed it. The stare was back.

'George,' she said levelly, 'we're running against the clock here so I'll make this brief. The glasses stay. Have you any idea how many American men, women and children wear glasses? At my age, reading glasses are normal ... Good word, George, wouldn't you agree?'

As she spoke, she moved to the door, the press secretary back-pedalling before her.

'Think of all the bespectacled kids who get a hard time in school playgrounds. Well, hallelujah, the President of the United States wears glasses, so let's have an end to this four-eyes shit. As for the hair, it's washed and combed and it's mine. Period. This is not a glamour shoot, George,' she said sweetly, 'this is work. Let's go.'

෨෮෬ඏ

'Ms President.'

'It's Helen McCoy, *Boston Globe*, isn't it?'

'Yes, ma'am.' The gratified journalist smiled. 'A story broke this morning, Ms President, concerning an alleged terrorist currently detained in Guantánamo Bay. The story claims a relationship between the Secretary of State and this person. Would you care to comment?'

'Yes, Ms McCoy, I would. I'd like first to comment on your question. The word 'broke' is emotive and might suggest the story was being restrained and somehow had to break free. It was not. That's why it will be in tomorrow's papers. Second, I thank you for respecting our judicial system by using the word 'alleged' before 'terrorist'. Thankfully, we are still a democracy. According to our Constitution, an accused person is assumed innocent until proven otherwise. The law will take its course, hopefully, without prejudicial surmise on the part of the press or prejudicial comment on the part of the president. As to the word 'relationship', whatever Webster says, in today-speak it implies romance. In this case the choice of that word may be construed as titillating or tacky. The facts, as usual, are less romantic or dramatic. A young man has been detained in Guantánamo Bay. He is the nephew of Laila Achmed, Secretary of State. I understand she loves her nephew, and his arrest and detention pending trial is a source of pain to Ms Achmed and her family.'

'Will she resign?'

The president scanned the faces in the front row until she found the speaker. Margaret Harris was the senior journalist on the White House beat. She was known for the acidity of her articles and had waged a one-woman war in print against the election of the present incumbent.

'Why would she do that, Ms Harris?' the president asked.

'Well, surely association with such a person compromises her position as Secretary of State?'

'He is her nephew, Ms Harris. We associate with our nephews at family reunions when they are required to be polite to us and wish they were elsewhere. Ask mine. But we love our sibling's children and care about their happiness. I understand that is the association Laila Achmed has with her nephew. "Such a person", as you described him, implies that he is somehow unsavoury and should be excluded from associating with the rest of us. The law doesn't say that, Ms Harris. If the law decides someone has committed a crime, they will be punished. The laws of the state and the norms of a civilised society nowhere hold that such a person should be shunned. As to compromising the position of the Secretary of State, how might she be compromised? Would she be tempted perhaps to exert influence on the judicial system to aid her nephew? She might, but she won't. Why? Because she is Secretary of State, with all the commitments and restrictions of power that position entails. And also because she is a person of integrity. No, she will not resign. Nor would I accept her resignation if she tendered it.'

'Ms President. John Walker, *Cincinnati Herald*.'

'A documentary programme is to be broadcast tomorrow purporting to reveal the … I was going to say "relationship" but I changed my mind.'

That got a laugh from the press corps.

'Look, ma'am, this press release says that Ephrem Isaacson's grandfather fought with Menachem Begin and had dealings with the Stern Gang during the first Arab–Israeli conflict. Would you like to comment on that?'

'Yes, Mr Walker, I would. Apart from the Native American peoples, the greater part of our population is descended from immigrants or are immigrants themselves. Immigrants bring baggage and their descendants inherit it. I like to blame a Scots great-great-grandmother for my impatience. Some of that baggage is priceless, like culture, ideals and values. When it's invested in the new country, it enriches everyone. Some of it is hateful or hurtful and has to be sorted and discarded in the new country. We have laws to protect our people from carried-over prejudices and we exclude or pursue those who are actively involved in criminality or human-rights abuses in their country of origin prior to coming here. In this country, if I may paraphrase and take a little liberty with the Bible text, the sins of the fathers need not set the teeth of their children on edge. Ephrem Isaacson, our treasury secretary, is just one example of someone descended from immigrants whose hard work, ability and integrity have raised him up to one of the most responsible positions in our administration. Who or what his grandfather was is history.'

'Ms President.'

She couldn't be more than sixteen, the president thought. Probably won some journalism competition at school and her prize was a pass to this bear pit, poor kid. She was tall, willowy and wearing glasses. And she was standing way back in the room.

'I'm sorry,' the president said, 'I don't know you.'

'Belinda Weston, Ms President. *Alabama High School Press.*'

When the good-natured laughter subsided, the president smiled.

'The President of the United States recognises Ms Belinda Weston of the *Alabama High School Press*.'

There were cheers from some of the press corps.

'Ma'am … I mean Ms President, I notice like … eh, you wear glasses … also. Do you like them?'

'No, Ms Weston, I do not. But I need them, like millions of people of all ages do. Need doesn't mean needy, Ms Weston. They don't make me a brainbox, nerdy, owlish or odd. They don't make me anything. They just help me do my job as best I can, so I wear them. Yours shouldn't get in your way of becoming a hotshot journalist like these folks or just President of the United States like me. Thank you, ladies and gentlemen,' she concluded, and left the room.

Warm applause ushered her into the corridor.

'You were wonderful,' George gushed, as he resumed his back-pedalling role down the hallway. 'That comment about glasses was inspired. It'll do a lot to soften your ima—'

He gulped. She had stopped abruptly and the stare was back.

'It wasn't inspired or calculated, George,' she said, 'it was just what I felt and thought. As for softening my image, nowhere in my job description does it say I need an image or the dubious benefits of personality plastic surgery. And, George …'

'Yes, Ms President.'

'You're in my way.'

Bethlehem, Israel

It was early morning, the time he liked best. A cloudless night had sucked the dead heat and most of the smells from the mess of tents and ramshackle shelters that mushroomed on the out-skirts of Bethlehem. Here and there, smoke spiralled up from breakfast fires, rising vertically into a washed-denim sky. Once the sun had untethered itself from the horizon and floated free, the sky would bleach white. It would be hot, very hot. He walked, loose-limbed and confident, through the market, hearing the shutters ratchet up on the stalls, following the odour of fresh coffee to a chair outside Hussein's café. It was shadowed by the canvas awning and angled so that he could look out with his back to the wall. He would see the passers-by clearly. They would see him as an outline in the shadows.

Hussein delivered the coffee cup in a saucer. He mumbled a ritual greeting and shuffled away. The man noted and savoured the small signs of deference. They marked him out in the community as someone ... connected. He inhaled the rich aroma and took a long swallow. His connections sometimes came via the tunnels from Egypt. That they would risk discovery or suffocation in those jerry-built catacombs to pass instructions and hard currency inflated his ego. They referred to him as 'Shepherd' and appreciated the steady trickle of young men he provided as sacrificial offerings to their cause. The money meant he didn't have to stand in line with the others like cattle at the wall. He didn't have to take the bus to Jerusalem and fight his way into a contractor's car for a day's wage. If he was prudent, he knew he could save enough to leave this shit-hole. As long as the present arrangement continued. If the trickle of martyrs didn't run dry ... if ...

Israeli Lookout Post, The Wall

'Sir.'

The young conscript was still raw-bald from the army barber, his uniform still clean and pressed to regulation crispness. The sergeant kept the field-glasses glued to his eyes and a neutral look fixed to his face.

'Call Goliath,' he said. 'I want him to look at something.'

The recruit swallowed and his eyes darted to the other men in the room. Two of the three sitting at the table were playing a languid game of cards. The third was stripping an Uzi, his hands going through the motions automatically while his head tilted back, balancing a cigarette between his teeth. A half-inch of ash threatened to topple on his face. A look ran the rounds of the table.

'Sir, yes, sir,' the young man said, and left the room.

'Like a lamb that is led to the slaughter,' the sergeant intoned.

'He opened not his mouth,' one of the card players answered, sweeping the small pile of coins to his side of the table. 'Double or quits, says Glock,' he said to his adversary.

'On.'

Private Yehudi breathed shallowly through his mouth as he walked the gauntlet of the living quarters. A fug of old smoke and unwashed laundry hung in the corridor that ran to the back of the building. The door at the end was locked. He considered tapping respectfully and calling out but he had already been ragged as a 'regulations mensch'. He eased the door open and approached the figure outlined on the bed.

'Captain, the se—'

The salutation turned into a startled gasp as a hand clamped across his mouth. Through his right eye he saw a man's face in profile. His left eye saw only the blurred tip of a knife poise rock-steady a half-inch from its surface.

'New man?'

He almost nodded until he remembered the knife. He

blinked once. With a snort, the man released him. The knife disappeared into an ankle sheath. The captain, who wore no insignia, drifted by him. Private Yehudi maintained a respectful distance behind as he retraced his steps along the corridor. He noted the five-foot frame of the Special Ops man who had earned him his nickname and the crew-cut bristle of white hair on the small head.

⊱✧⊰

'Take a look, please.'

The sergeant passed the glasses.

'Beside the coffee shop.'

The small man took the field-glasses and fingered the focus wheel.

'Cigarette?'

'Yeah, him. Always a cigarette, sucking away like his life depended on it.'

'It might. Plays hell with night-scopes. Previous?'

'Plenty. Intel thinks he's a groomer.'

'Sex or bombs?'

'Either … both. We don't know. Doesn't work but never short of shekels. Lots of deferential nods. Once or twice, long sessions with young men.'

'Anything from our informers?'

'Nothing. Want us to snatch him?'

'No,' Goliath said, after a long pause. 'Continue the surveillance.'

He handed back the glasses and walked out of the room.

Private Yehudi joined the others in a return to normal breathing.

'Glock or knife?' one of the card-sharps asked.

'Knife.'

'Shit.'

The Camp, Bethlehem

Irritably, the man tossed some coins onto the table and walked away.

His route took him out of the camp and into the narrow streets of the town, which were getting busier as the sun climbed. Men nodded from shopfronts or greeted him respectfully as they passed. He noticed some of the older men look away and sign against the evil eye. To them, he was the Angel of Death, the Taker of Sons. Their reaction reminded him that he was dipping his bucket into a finite well. Every young man who died added to the welling pool of the heartbroken and resentful among the living. His aura of power, even his connections, would not save him should the next martyr or the one after that tip the fine balance between resentment and revenge. He knew he should go before then but the metal box buried beneath his bed didn't contain enough to carry him away and beyond the lethal reach of his connections. His mood soured by these thoughts, he returned home and slumped on his bed.

Something in his jacket pocket twitched and the coffee surged up from his stomach to scald the back of his throat. Snake, some primal part of his consciousness screamed. Snake. He fought frantically to jettison the jacket, sweat jetting from his body. It had been his worst nightmare ever since, as a boy, he had bent to lift firewood for his mother. He flung the jacket to the floor and backed away, his entire body shuddering.

Nothing moved. He edged sideways, never taking his eyes from the jacket, his hand reaching out to grasp the broom handle. Gingerly, he prodded the jacket. Nothing. With infinite slowness, he poked the garment, exposing the maw of the pocket. A blunt metallic object peeped over the flap and he tapped it free. A cellphone slid to the floor, vibrating in the dust. He felt suddenly weak and shaky as the adrenalin fizzled out of his system and he sat heavily on the floor, his hand pressed to the back of his neck until the thunder in his ears faded. Slowly, his brain overrode his subconscious. How had it got there? Who had put it into his pocket? He felt the urge to smash it with the broom handle, to stop that horrible tiny movement. Instead, he stretched out a trembling hand and picked it up, flipping it open.

'Listen carefully,' the voice said calmly. 'Are you listening?'

'Yes,' he gasped.

'It isn't a snake,' the voice said, 'but it might be … next time.'

A muscle twitched in his jaw as the sibilants licked at his ear. 'Who is this?' he grated, trying to flush the terror with anger.

'Listen carefully,' the voice resumed, 'and all will be made plain.'

He listened.

The voice knew everything. In an even tone, it unravelled his story, following the individual threads into the weave of who he had become and what he had done for 'the connections'. The list of martyrs dropped like acid in his ear right up to Haran. Names, dates and times were enumerated clearly and accurately. He shivered and pressed his left palm on the bed to steady himself. The dreadful voice paused finally. 'Put down the phone,' it said, 'and check your assets.'

In a daze, he dropped it onto the rumpled sheets and tugged the bed into the centre of the floor. He fell to his knees and began to scrabble at the earth with his fingers. They touched metal, and he thumbed the lid of the box open. He closed his eyes and wrenched them wide again.

'Allah be praised,' he breathed.

The dollars were clean enough to be suspect. He riffled the edges of the top wad, automatically checking his thumb for ink stains. His brain registered an amount greater than that which he had already hidden. Closing the box, he scuffed earth over it and picked up the phone.

'You have questions,' the voice said. 'They will be answered in good time. For now, it is enough for you to know that there is more, much more – enough to make your dream a reality. But you must do something for me to merit my generosity. Listen!'

His ear turned to ivory under the pressure of the phone.

'And the target?' he whispered.

'Jabal Abu Ghuneim,' the voice whispered back.

'The Mountain of the Shepherd,' the man translated automatically from the Arabic.

'Yes, appropriate, isn't it? The Israelis call it Har Homa.'

⁂

He sat again outside the coffee shop, and punched a series of numbers on his phone, letting them ring three times before disconnecting. He ordered fresh coffee and whispered, 'I am expecting company,' as the proprietor set it before him. The man nodded and disappeared. Shepherd would not be interrupted. He lit another cigarette and waited. Three men appeared at intervals and sat at other tables, their bodies angled away from him. After draining his cup, Shepherd stood and stretched. He slapped some money on the table and sauntered away. The man sitting nearest lifted his foot to the vacant chair to tie his shoelace. He rose and nodded to the others.

They met in a small warehouse, spicy with stored apples, and spread the paper lifted from Shepherd's table. The rough map marked the location of the truck and the launch site. They knew the keys would be in the ignition, the mortars wrapped in oil-soaked sacking under the false floor. The leader read the postscript and cocked an eyebrow.

An hour later, he watched Omar Al Tamari's mother take the twin boys to school. He knew she would detour through the market before returning. The bleary-eyed man who came to the door radiated aggression until he focused on the large bottle. He retreated into the shadows and the visitor followed. Later, while the big man lolled drunkenly on the bed, the visitor carefully pocketed the bottle and glasses. He searched the small shelter with care, homing in on a curtained alcove crowded with two single beds. The one on the right was rumpled and strewn with children's clothes. The other was ordered carefully, a pile of books stacked neatly beside it. He bent and lifted an expensive-looking leather case and clicked it open. The gold-plated pen gleamed in the dim light. He held it close to his eyes and read the inscription etched on the barrel: 'To Omar Al Tamari … The Same Water.'

Shrugging, he dropped the pen into his pocket, closed the case and returned it to the floor.

Har Homa Settlement, outside Bethehem

Deborah knew she should insist but it had been a long day for all of them. She lifted the dinner plates to the sink and rinsed them before loading the dishwasher. 'You buy a dog and bark yourself,' her mother-in-law had said, with a sniff, the first time she'd seen her do that. Sara and Ben laughed in the other room. She hoped they were watching something age-appropriate, but it was good to hear them laugh. She moved to the apartment window and looked outside. Ergud would be home soon, she thought. Her stomach did a slow somersault and she drew a deep breath. He would not be home soon – or ever. Not since the car bomb eighteen months before. 'Phantom pains,' the counsellor said. 'It's normal to have them.' But when do they stop? Down below, an elderly lady's small dog was hitching its back legs to squat under a tree. The old lady stood to one side as if embarrassed. Deborah stepped back from the window and looked up. It's not a holiday, she thought; why fireworks?

☢☤

Tov rubbed the metal disc of the stethoscope against his sleeve, then applied it to the boy's back. Eyes half-closed, to enhance his hearing, his fingers tap-danced over the skin. Older patients would have recognised Tov's father in those manner-isms. He was aware of the mother reading his expression for symptoms of disaster and kept his face neutral. Finished, he dropped the stethoscope around his neck and turned the boy to face him. 'You have an infection, Noam,' he said mildly. 'It's in your left lung. That's why your breath whistles.'

The mother, Martha, gasped but the boy's eyes were unafraid.

'A course of antibiotics will clear it,' he continued, 'but you must take all the pills, even when you're feeling better. Promise?'

'Promise.'

The doctor knew Martha's budget would be stretched even thinner by the expense. He excused himself and went to the locked cabinet in the other room where he kept the free samples from the pharmaceutical companies. Like father, like son, the older patients would have nodded approvingly. He was crouched before the open cabinet, poking through the sample packs on the bottom shelf, when he heard thunder.

⁕✓⁖

The dog began to relieve himself at the base of a tree. Golda turned away, out of modesty. Modesty was something you'd had to work at very hard in the old days when so many lived so close together. She looked away, squinting up at the tall buildings. So many windows, she thought. Someone might be watching.

'This isn't Russia,' her daughter kept reminding her.

The old ladies – she always thought of them as the old ladies – who dressed in black and haunted the park on sunny days knew better. When you live your life in an apartment block where one tenant is paid to watch, you know how to be. You know how to seem, she corrected herself. The old ladies were the last remaining relics of the Jewish diaspora in Russia. Golda knew why Medvedev – Putin Lite, as the young people called him – had let them go. Old ladies remembered things. Old Jewish ladies with long memories made the new order uneasy.

The new apartment buildings in the settlement near Bethlehem were uniformly dressed in yellow stone.

'Government directive,' her daughter said. 'Matches the old with the new.' Her daughter was an architect. She understood such things and approved of them. Golda had walked to the rear of the apartment and pulled back the curtains her daughter preferred closed. Over the rim of the Wall, she had seen the 'architecture' of 'the others'. It reminded her of where she had come from.

On her first visit to the park, she had stopped inside the gate to look around. The old ladies sat in the shade of a huge tree, angled away from each other so that all points were covered by someone's eye. Good. On that first visit, she took a position without greeting or being greeted. Good. Some knitted, some watched, others simply sat with their faces inclined to the sun. One fed stale bread to the pigeons from a paper bag, while another shook her head at the waste of good food. Whenever they chanced to meet outside the park, they behaved like strangers. Safer.

'Grandma, why are your eyes blue?'

'Because I am a Russian. A woman coming to live in Israel must bring something from her own country. I had nothing to bring. I brought the sky in my eyes. You are a *shiksa*; you were born here. Your eyes are black like olives.'

Then she had lowered her voice to a whisper:

'Where do we hide, little one?'

'In the cupboard under the stairs, Grandma.'

'Clever girl.'

'Mamma, what are you saying? I told you not to tell her stories.'

'I told *you* stories.'

'Exactly.'

'I never told you about the Germans.' She stopped and shook her head. It was only in the pauses between actions that she could be ambushed by memory. She tugged at the lead impatiently. How long does it take a small dog to shit? There is so much I don't want to remember. I don't want to remember the heavy boots drumming up the stairs and the screaming that twisted me into a ball buried in old clothes in the cupboard under the stairs. The dog nuzzled her leg and she jumped. Stupid dog. She relented and bent to scratch behind his ears. We had a dog, the ghosts whispered. And when there was nothing left, not even a single potato, we ... She didn't hear the bang. She felt a sudden wind pick her up and tumble her over a low wall.

ജ

Some instinct moved Deborah away from the window. She stood transfixed as it shattered and glass slivers sprouted from the opposite wall as if pounded through with a giant hammer from the other side. Her eyes focused on a tiny sliver of light at the end of her nose. She reached up and tugged it free. When she saw the bloom of blood, she screamed.

ജ

Tov opened his eyes. He was lying flat on his back in a box. I'm buried alive, he panicked, and raised his arms to pound on the coffin lid. Slowly, reality seeped between the cracks of his frenzy. He was littered with pill boxes and rolls of adhesive bandage and there were pressure bands at his chest, waist and ankles. Shelves … the medicine cabinet. He raised it, straight-armed, and wriggled from beneath. The noise battered him into a crouch. It was a sound such as he had never heard before, as if the whole of creation was twisting itself out of true.

Covering his ears, he stumbled upright and limped into his surgery. He saw the hole where the window had been and watched for a moment as fire poured from the apartment building opposite his own. He saw a man hanging by his hands from the railings of a small balcony. The smoke eddied to obscure him and when it ebbed he was gone. Numbed, Tov turned to the mess of glass and timber that had been his workplace. A woman lay spreadeagled on the floor, her back and buttocks shredded raw. He registered it was a woman because a wedding ring gleamed on her flawless left hand … which seemed to point across the spreading stain of blood on the carpet. His eyes followed the direction indicated and he found the boy.

❧❧

The blast that pushed Golda over the wall spared her the deadly hail of debris that screamed like shrapnel over her upturned face. She lay on her back until the thunder rolled away, fading in the distance, and there was stillness before she began to register the screams and sirens. Struggling to her feet, she shook a small avalanche of glass fragments from her coat. She discovered the loop of the dog's leash still circling her hand.

'Home,' she said, and began to walk.

❧❧

Deborah moved like a sleepwalker, sliding her feet along the floor. She turned the handle of the door to the sitting room and opened it. The world ended at her feet. The room where her children had been watching television had disappeared, to be replaced with a vista of burning buildings. Her eyes followed a swirl of sparks funnelling up to a black sky where they twinkled like stars and disappeared.

❧❧❧

Tov clasped the silent boy to his chest and hunched his shoulders to shield him from the burning car and the flaming figure within. His ears registered the sounds of flames like breaking sticks, his nose inhaled smoke, but his eyes had filled with tears so that much of what he saw became a merciful blur. He looked up once and saw a woman silhouetted against an open door. She stood four storeys up, gazing across the space where the rest of her building had been. Someone bumped against him. He stumbled and tightened his grip on the boy. The old woman moved on as if she hadn't seen him. He wondered briefly why she was pulling a dead dog behind her.

❧❧❧

Deborah saw the man, with the bundle in his arms, stagger as the old lady brushed against him. She raised her eyes and gazed again at the sky. Slowly, she took off her apron and wiped her blackened face and hands. She folded it carefully before placing it on the floor. 'I'm coming,' she said. 'Wait for Mamma, darlings.' She stepped through the door.

❧❦❧

The paramedic shot morphine into what remained of the man's leg and strapped him to the stretcher. He slapped the driver on the shoulder. 'Go.' As he reached out to grab the swinging rear door, a man stumbled out of the smoke carrying a bundle. 'Wait! Wait!' the paramedic shouted, and leaped from the ambulance. As the man drew closer, he saw that the top half of his body was white with ash and dust. His trousers were soaked and black in the light of the flames. He placed the boy in the paramedic's arms.

'My name is Dr Tov Schliemann,' he said calmly. 'This boy has a lung infection. He must be started on antibiotics with lots of liquids.'

'Doctor,' he said, and waited until the man's eyes focused on him. 'Doctor, I have injured people in the ambulance. Please can you help me?'

Something like rationality seemed to surface in the other man's staring eyes. 'Yes, yes, of course,' he said hoarsely. 'I'm a doctor.'

The paramedic prayed the doctor would be distracted by the needs of the others and wouldn't see him zip the dead boy into a body-bag.

❧❦❧

Golda saw firemen race up a ladder to the fourth floor of her building. Her chest tightened and she hurried until she stood near the knot of fire fighters at the foot of the ladder. Above, two figures vaulted through the hole in the wall. Almost immediately a radio crackled. 'Nothing and no one left here, Captain. We need to go higher.'

'Tell him to try the cupboard under the stairs,' Golda said calmly.

Four blackened faces swivelled to look at her.

'What'd she say?'

'She's speaking Russian, Captain. She said to try the cupboard under the stairs.'

For a moment, the captain stared at the resolute old woman. For a much longer moment, he looked at the dead dog lying on the pavement behind her. The radio crackled impatiently and he pressed it to his ear.

'Try the cupboard under the stairs,' he mouthed.

Golda watched his face as the radio crackled again. She saw him inhale sharply and a single tear carve a pink trail down his blackened cheek until it nestled in his moustache, like a pearl.

'Woman and girl,' he said, 'in the cupboard under the stairs. Safe.'

Camp A, Bethlehem

Omar Al Tamari woke before dawn and padded outside to wash in the tin basin. As he scrubbed his arms, he pondered the mystery of water. How can two invisible gases come together to make this miracle? Tiny rivulets snaked down his upraised arms to bead at his elbows. He waited for gravity to suck them farther and watched the ripples expand and disappear.

'Where does water come from, Grandfather?'

His grandfather had shifted his rump on the apple crate before replying.

'Such a big question for such a small boy. You know Allah promised the Jews a land flowing with milk and honey? He never mentioned water. The Jews haven't seen the joke yet.'

He shook his grizzled head and laughed softly at his own joke.

'Okay, where does water come from? Water comes from water, Omar. The sun shines, the water steams, the steam rises up, up, up to where the air is cold. The tiny bits of steam huddle together to keep warm and – oops – they are too heavy to rise and they fall again.'

Omar remembered the feeling that had coursed through him like electricity at that revelation.

'It … it's all the same water, then?'

'The same. Think about this, Omar. The water you used to wash this morning could be the same water that came from the rock struck by Moses in the desert. It could be the selfsame water that dropped from Muhammad's beard in Mecca, drowned the Egyptians in the Red Sea and baptised the Prophet Jesus in the Jordan.'

Omar had carried that incredible fact to school and turned it into an essay entitled 'The Same Water'.

Master Shaheen had quizzed him before the other boys until he was satisfied the embarrassed boy had written it himself. Over coffee, some days later, the schoolteacher mentioned it to his former pupil, Professor Sharawi.

'Sounds precocious,' the professor remarked absently.

'Will you read it, Rafi?'

'Master, I have ten theses to mark before Monday. When will students ever learn that bulk does not equal better? My desk is groaning under those weighty works of scholarship.'

'Then you will not notice the burden of two extra pages.'

With an exaggerated sigh, the professor fingered his spectacles from his shirt pocket and shifted his cup on the table to make room for Omar's essay. Eventually he leaned back and returned his spectacles to their roost.

'How old is this boy, Master?'

'As old as you were when you, eh, borrowed a page from my *National Geographic* magazine to read about the Ogalla Aquifer.'

Omar smiled as he dried himself with the thin towel. The professor had become his mentor, librarian, tutor and, finally, his sponsor at the university in Jerusalem. Miracles do happen, he thought, as he salvaged the thin sliver of soap and placed it on the side of the basin. Even to someone like me.

Dressed in a clean blue shirt and carefully patched denims, he took his place at the table. He saw the red smudge in his mother's eyes as she put the bowl of porridge before him.

'The smoke from that fire blinds me,' she said quietly, as she noticed his scrutiny. He nodded and dropped his eyes. Perhaps it was the smoke, he thought, perhaps not. He took her hand and squeezed his thanks. Neither spoke of the explosions the night before.

Omar had risen to calm his brothers when the booming echoed from beyond the Wall. 'It's only thunder,' he whispered, as he tucked the blanket about the twins. 'It's the Angel Gabriel, sending the Evil One back to Hell.'

'Omar, please tell us the story.'

He spun it, slowing the pace and letting his voice spiral down until their eyelids drooped and closed. Silently, he'd edged around his own bed to the window and drawn aside the sacking. He'd watched the mortar shells loft over the camp from the desert and plummet beyond the horizon of the Wall. Shaking his head, he'd climbed into bed, easing down so that the creaking wouldn't rouse the twins.

'Omar?' a sleepy voice whispered.

'I'm here, little brother, standing guard.'

'Like Raphael?'

'Yes, like Raphael who brings thunder and lightning.'

'Eating again?'

He tensed as his father swung his bare feet to the floor and rubbed the stubble on his jaw. Omar didn't reply. He had schooled himself to ignore his father's needling. He shot a warning glance at his mother but it was too late.

'Omar needs to eat,' she protested. 'Our son works hard at the university.'

'University? Pah!'

'Professor Sharawi says Omar will be a hy- hy—'

'Hydrologist,' Omar supplied gently.

'Yes, a hydrologist. The professor says—'

'Professor Sharawi is a running dog for the Israelis. What does he know?'

More than you, Omar wanted to say. More than a man who lies around all day and smells of defeat. He said nothing, only gripped his spoon tighter and worked at keeping his face expressionless. If he should speak, his mother would pay for every word.

'The professor thinks—'

'I don't care what the professor thinks, woman. Does the professor live here? No, he lives in the town and drives to Jerusalem every day. He doesn't have to join the queue to be prodded and searched or stand like cattle in the Jews' market.'

'Omar will never have to do that. He will be educated.'

'It's all he's fit for.'

Instinctively, Omar lifted his withered hand from the table and placed it on his knee out of sight. Why did his father's rages always circle back to his deformity? He had asked his grandfather why Allah had made him imperfect. Sitting at the table, he closed his eyes and conjured up the picture of the old man rubbing his beard before replying.

'Omar, you know that wonderful carpets are made by Muslims all over the world?'

'Yes, Grandfather.'

'And do you know that no carpet can ever show a real bird or flower?'

'Yes, Grandfather.'

'Tell me why.'

'Only Allah can make a real bird or flower.'

'Yes. Very good. You're an intelligent boy. You get that from me.'

Omar had smiled dutifully.

'Now, here is the big question. Do you know that even the most expensive carpet will have one deliberate imperfection?'

'Why, Grandfather?'

'Because the weavers know that only Allah is perfect and only He can make perfection. They make one deliberate mistake to give Him glory.'

He had taken the boy's withered hand in his own.

'Your imperfection is on the outside, Omar. The ones who mock it are imperfect on the inside where their souls should be.'

Omar threaded through the haphazard paths of the camp towards the town. Bethlehem was still mantled in shadow, the twin towers of the mosque and the Church of the Nativity vying to dominate the skyline. He averted his eyes from the posters of the martyrs and from the man who sat smoking in the shadows outside the coffee shop. He knew him; everyone did. But neither the martyrs nor the man were part of his dream. He took a detour that brought him close to the Wall on the other side of the camp. His grandfather sat on the upturned apple crate, riffling his prayer beads through his fingers.

'What are you doing, Grandfather?'

It was a ritual question. He could have recited the answer word for word.

'I am letting the Israelis see me, Omar.'

The old man nodded at the Wall.

'Over there is my father's farm. It belonged to his father, and his father before him. For centuries, we survived the Persians, Byzantines, Crusaders, Mamelukes, Ottomans, Jordanians and the British. We did not survive the Israelis after only six days. You know how the Israelis like to gather at Masada and the Wailing Wall? They say, "We will never forget. We will remember." That is what I do at this Wall. I sit here to let them know I remember.'

'Do you hate them, Grandfather? Even a little?'

'Hate is like cockleweed in a garden, Omar. Even a little will grow and choke the garden. Every day it will spread until it kills the flowers and every other plant. No, I do not hate them. How could I hate the children of my father Abraham? How could I hate the people of Maimonides? The wisest of our ancestors cherished them.'

'What of Dayan and Begin?'

'They have saints and sinners, Omar.'

He lifted his head to the plume of smoke that rose from Har Homa. 'As we have,' he said sadly.

Omar retraced his steps to enter the town, leaning into the

hill that wound up to the cobblestones of Manger Square. Professor Sharawi's two-storey house stood directly across the square from the fortress-like Christian church. Professor Sharawi had taken him there, into the cool shadows, deep down into the rough-walled cave with a silver star embedded in the floor.

'Ignorance is the father of myth, Omar. And myth can lead us to murder. Trust your own mind and the promptings of your own heart,' the professor had said.

He let himself into the Sharawi courtyard and inhaled the perfume of flowers. The door to the house stood open and he rapped politely on the frame.

'*As-salamu,*' a young woman called, and he walked through a short hallway to the kitchen. Nawal Sharawi, the professor's only child, waved him to the table with one hand while she cradled the phone to her ear with the other. She shot him a look of apology, and he smiled. He watched Nawal as she chatted to her friend, her left hand weaving beside her head, conducting the flow of the conversation. Black, Master Shaheen had told them, was not a colour: it was the absence of colour. Nawal's hair was blue-black. Some source of light made it gleam like fish-scales whenever she shook her head. Her face was a perfect oval, her mouth always smiling or about to. But it was her eyes that fascinated him. Nawal's eyes were like perfect black opals, gleaming in a cream sea, reflecting her emotions as she spoke and listened. Her skin was like milky coffee, chocolate brown under her eyes, lightening to translucence over high cheekbones.

'Sorry, Omar,' she said, snapping the thread of his reverie. 'Father's gone walkabout again, and we're trying to trace him. He probably forgot to mention a field trip or something. Coffee or juice?'

'Just water, thank you.'

'But of course.' She smiled and rolled her eyes. 'Hydrologists.'

He had time to avert his eyes from her slim form before she returned from the refrigerator. Somewhere in the house, a phone shrilled and she paused to listen. Someone picked it up and she placed the frosted glass before him.

'He left this for you,' she said, handing him an envelope. It bore the crest of the university and 'To whom it may concern' scrawled across the front in the professor's distinctive hand. It was Omar's passport through the Wall and he put it into his pocket. Only married men with children were allowed through the metal gate to work the fields on the other side or to ride the bus to the building sites around Jerusalem. The Israelis thought such men were likely to return in the evening. The guards knew Omar but he still needed a note from the professor when he was not travelling in his car.

'Thank you, Nawal.'

Saying her name started a melting sensation in his stomach and he sipped the cold water. He knew her parents had named her for an Egyptian doctor who had been imprisoned by President Sadat and had become a cause célèbre internationally. The professor's wife lectured at the university and travelled abroad to conferences. She also ran classes for women in the camp. His mother had wanted to attend. His father had refused permission. Omar sipped water.

'Something to eat?'

'I have eaten at home, thank you.'

It came out sharper than he had intended and Nawal busied herself clearing the breakfast dishes. Omar rose and carried some to where she knelt at the dishwasher. She lifted her head to smile her thanks. He liked the way she looked at him. He liked especially that she didn't look at his hand, ever.

'Nawal!'

Nur Sharawi was a small woman who bristled with energy. Omar had always considered her the perfect foil to her languid, absent-minded husband. He thought she looked distracted: her dark eyes, so like Nawal's, lacked their usual sparkle.

'Mother, what is it?'

'Sit down, dear. I have news of your father.'

'Please, excuse me,' Omar murmured politely, and rose to leave.

'No, sit with us, Omar, and forgive my manners. You are always welcome to our house.'

Her eyes softened for a moment as she glanced at her daughter. Nur Sharawi took her husband's place at the head of the table and Omar's stomach tightened with apprehension.

'I had a call, just now, from – from a friend at the university. My husband has been arrested.'

Saying the word seemed to bring home the reality to her and she dropped her eyes to the table, her strong face straining for composure. Omar saw the mother's feelings reflected in her daughter's face. Nawal opened her mouth to speak and, instinctively, he reached across the table and laid his hand on hers. When her startled eyes locked on his, he shook his head.

Nur Sharawi took a deep breath and continued calmly, 'My friend tells me there was an explosion in Jerusalem, some days past. She says it was in the Damascus Street area. It seems a boy from the camps ...'

She paused and looked uncertainly at Omar. He nodded for her to continue.

'A boy from this side of the Wall was involved. The security services believe he had travelled in the boot of my husband's car.'

'But that's nonsense,' her daughter exploded. 'Why would Papa do such a thing? Also, everyone is searched at the Wall. It just—'

'Nawal.'

Omar squeezed her hand gently. 'Nawal, the professor would never involve himself with extremists, everybody knows that. But he might not have known of the boy.'

'But the soldiers search.'

'The soldiers do not search everyone, every time, Nawal. Sometimes, when the officer is not present and they know the driver …'

He turned to Nur Sharawi. 'What can we do?' he asked calmly.

Even in her shocked state, Nawal's mother registered the young man's quiet strength. She wasn't unaware either that he was holding her daughter's hand and that this didn't seem to bother Nawal. And he had used the inclusive 'we'. There was much she and the professor would have to discuss.

'I will go to some people in Jerusalem and see what can be done. Your aunt will come and stay with you, Nawal. You have been a true friend to us, Omar, we will not forget.'

It was a gracious dismissal but a dismissal nonetheless, and he acknowledged it. 'I will be at the university,' he said.

❧❧❧

Omar joined the queue at the Wall. The line of men shuffled and chatted in low voices, subdued by the three-storey concrete barricade, necklaced along the top with razor wire. At the back of the line, they nodded a greeting to the new arrival. The older ones looked approvingly at the young man who had prospects. The younger ones were more reserved, as if his presence emphasised their own limited options. Beside him, graffiti blocked, swirled and whorled along the Wall, proclaiming emotions and yearnings that couldn't be safely articulated. 'Send help' and 'Freedom of movement' shared the same grey space with 'Jesus is Lord'. Omar distracted himself from the monotony by tuning in to the banter. He thought it was more muted this morning because of the smoke-smudge hanging over Har Homa. A lean, middle-aged man, wearing an American baseball cap and construction boots, sucked on an L&M cigarette, his face split into light and shade by the Klieg lights along the Wall. 'Do you think I want to be here?' he whispered angrily, although Omar hadn't spoken. He knew the construction workers were paid thirty-five dollars a day. It was good money. A job in Bethlehem would pay half that amount – if there was a job. He also knew they were building Israeli settlements on land once owned by their ancestors. He dropped his head and the line inched forward.

'Here we go,' a round-faced, thick-set young man remarked. 'Roll up, roll up, get ready to be printed, metal-detected, searched, stripped and have an Israeli finger up your ass.'

'You'd have to get your own out first,' a companion offered drily, and the queue swayed with good-natured laughter.

At last, Omar found himself confronted by the soldiers. He recognised them as regulars who sometimes joked with the men to relieve the tension. Today he saw they were operating strictly by the book, painstakingly thumbing through documents as if under scrutiny themselves. He switched his attention to the reflective glass window of the outpost. He wondered whose eyes watched from within.

'Next.'

The soldier took his identity card and the letter from the professor, slitting the envelope with his thumbnail. He turned aside to mutter into the radio hanging from his lapel and held his attentive pose until it crackled back.

'Come.'

Omar heard a faint murmur of protest rise from the men behind him as he followed the soldier through the door of the outpost. The interior was army-drab, functional and uncomfortable. It smelled of old cigarettes and strong disinfectant, spiced with the distinctive sweat-tang of tension. A sergeant sat apart at a desk crowded with monitors, sweeping his head to cover the montage of pictures feeding in from cameras on the Wall. Two soldiers stood near the mirrored window, bulked out with body-armour. A man in camouflage fatigues moved his white-stubbled head from side to side as he read the professor's letter.

'What do you study at the university?' he asked, in a whispery voice.

'Hydrology.'

'Captain?' Omar's escort enquired, and the captain, without insignia, waved him back to his duties at the gate.

'Hydrology is what?' he asked.

'Hydrology is the study of water and its properties,' Omar recited mechanically, 'including its distribution and move-ment in and through the land areas of the earth. Primarily, it deals with that part of the cycle after precipitation of water onto the land and before its return to the oceans.'

The captain moved a step closer. 'That's a heck of a

mouthful,' he said, with a humourless smile, 'but, it's textbook talk. Give a rock-head like me long enough with the right book and even I could parrot it.' He took a glass of water from the desk and shoved it at Omar.

'Talk to me about this.'

Omar took the glass in his right hand and looked at the water. The background noise in the room seemed to dip a few decibels as the liquid in the smudged glass worked its magic on him.

'This liquid has no colour, taste, smell or calories,' he began quietly. He lifted his eyes to match the captain's unflinching stare. 'You can see this water. What you can't see is that it's dissolving the molecules of the glass.' He extended his forefinger across the mouth of the glass. 'I can't feel them,' he said, 'but millions of molecules are evaporating up from the surface and around my finger and their bond with each other is so strong that one grips another to pull it up against the tug of gravity. That bonding is what we call surface tension.' He dropped his finger to touch the surface. 'That's how insects can run across the top without getting their feet wet. Once, for my brothers, I put a small darning needle on the surface. It didn't sink.'

He smiled at the memory until he recalled where he was.

The captain held his gaze for a moment, then slowly extended the professor's letter.

'I'm sorry, Omar,' he said gruffly. 'You can't travel today. Best go home and stay there.' He gestured with the glass. 'You want to drink this?'

'I can have water at home, Captain,' Omar said evenly, and put the letter into his pocket.

'Avenging Angel,' the sergeant barked, shoving back from the desk, and the outpost hummed with activity. Isolated and forgotten, Omar looked to the monitor screens for the source of the frenzy. From left to right, they showed swathes of the camps taken from different angles. A single screen, on the extreme right, covered the approach road outside the gate. A soldier paused before the screen and swore. Omar moved his head to see it clearly: a black-and-white image of the metalled road reflecting wetly in the growing light. It stretched straight for a hundred yards before dipping into a deep hollow. As he watched, a turret rose out of the hollow, a man's head haloed by the open hatch. In the wavering air, a huge metal behemoth came gradually into focus, exhaust fumes adding to the mirage effect.

Tank! his brain registered, and adrenalin scalded through his system.

'Let him go,' the captain shouted, as one of the men moved to cut Omar off at the door. He tossed his field-glasses to the bewildered soldier.

'Get up on the roof and keep me posted – now.'

❦

The command boosted the man through the door and up the ladder to the lookout booth.

'What strength?' Goliath demanded of the sergeant.

'Four tanks and fifty infantry back-up. Christ, what's the point?' the sergeant growled. 'The bastards who did Har Homa are home through the tunnels by now.'

Between them, the fax machine grunted and strained to extrude a message. Impatiently, the sergeant held the lengthening sheet until it broke free.

'Roof, tell me!' Goliath snapped into his lapel radio.

'Two tanks peeling away left and two right. Infantry splitting to follow.'

'Going to the camps then, not the town,' the sergeant muttered, scanning the top sheet of the fax as another began to birth.

'Oh, shit!'

'What?'

'"To the commander of Wall Outpost,"' the sergeant began, '"from—"'

'Read the fucking message.'

'"Apprehend or eliminate Omar Al Tamari, Palestinian male, approx twenty years old. Resident of Camp A. Occupation: student at the University of Jerusalem. Previous: none. Distinguishing marks: deformed left hand." There's a photograph,' he added. Goliath snatched the printout and stared at the picture.

'There's more,' the sergeant said, scanning the second page.

'"Mossad located evidence at mortar-site implicating Al Tamari with terrorist action against Har Homa. Al Tamari mentor, Professor Sharawi, currently held on suspicion of complicity with Damascus Street suicide bomber."'

'Doesn't add up,' Goliath muttered, letting the fax message see-saw to the floor. His radio crackled and he thumbed it live.

'Captain, I have the young guy running parallel with the lead tank. Want me to drop him?'

'No.'

'Captain, I have about a ten-second window before the knockdown becomes impossible. Advise.'

'Don't shoot. I'll keep the line open.'

Goliath spun as the sergeant tapped him on the shoulder.

'It's the young guy you were talking to, isn't it?'

'Yes,' he answered irritably, 'but it doesn't stack. No previous. Also, he doesn't run the tunnels with the others. He joins the fucking line at the Wall.'

'We let him go,' the sergeant muttered. 'We had him right here and we—'

'Captain, running out of time here,' the radio interrupted. 'Shoot or no?'

'No,' Goliath said. 'Stand down. I'll take him myself.'

The Camps, Bethlehem

Omar felt as if a small animal, trapped in his side, was burrowing to get out. He tried to ignore the burning stitch, pounding the dusty paths between the shelters, leaping debris and open drains, slaloming around the panicked people rousted by the thunder of the tanks. He risked a glance over his shoulder. Two tanks were grinding along the dusty corridor that ran parallel to the Wall. His brain absorbed the image and projected the possibilities. They would climb a gentle gradient some two hundred yards ahead. His instinct told him they would then swing right and onto the unmetalled road that bisected Camp A. They would encounter no obstacle except one. 'Grandfather,' he gasped.

His foot snagged in some garbage and he fell. The impact drove the breath from his body and tumbled him into a ditch that ran sluggishly beside the path. 'Keep your mouth closed,' he reminded himself. It was a mantra from childhood. 'Don't drink the water in the ditches.' More than one of his playmates had forgotten and shat his way into Intensive Care. He sat up abruptly and spat. Someone was tugging him upright and he skimmed his eyes of foul water to see his helper. The man's reflective sunglasses gave him the appearance of a bug-eyed insect. 'Come with me,' the man urged.

In a fury, Omar spun on his heel and yanked his arm free so that the man lost his balance and sat down heavily. He began to run, ignoring the voice behind him that promised safety before fading into curses. He checked the progress of the tanks and his heart tightened. The collision with the man had cost him. The lead tank had already topped the gradient and its turret was swinging like a predator homing in on its prey. His eyes followed the direction indicated by the metal finger extending from the turret and snagged on a small hunched figure. Ibrahim Al Tarawi sat on his upturned apple crate, watching the Israelis.

෴

Goliath was pounding down the path when he saw the two figures collide and go down. The one with the sunshades seemed to be exhorting the young man to go with him. He saw Omar swing free and begin to run. As he did so, the young man snapped his head sideways and faltered slightly before pounding on, faster than before. Goliath looked to his left at the turning tank and saw a man rise up, some twenty feet before it, his arms outstretched.

'Fuck,' he grunted.

෴

Omar skidded left into the broad path and tried to scream a warning. He had no breath to make the sound and his mouth gaped silently. His grandfather stood, arms outstretched, between Omar and the oncoming tank. He saw the helmeted figure in the turret wave his arms, gesticulating at the old man to move.

❧

'Stop,' Goliath shouted at the figure in the turret. The man snapped his head sideways as if surprised and toppled forward. A sharp crack followed a half-second later and Goliath rolled into a ditch, coming up in a crouch, weapon ready, scanning for the sniper.

❧

Omar saw the man buck and sag bonelessly in the turret. Above the growl of the engine, he registered, without recognising, a sharp cracking sound. His eyes were full of the mottled green monster and the fragile figure in its path. As he lurched forward, someone locked an arm around his throat, cutting off air to his starved lungs. He struggled frantically to break from the nightmare that held him as black spots buzzed at the edges of his vision. Before the darkness consumed him, he saw his grandfather stumble and disappear as the tank tracks dragged him down.

❧

When Goliath looked back, the old man had gone. Savagely, he whipped his weapon to his shoulder, jamming his eye to the scope. The face of the young man he hunted shimmered into focus. He seemed to be in shock or unconscious, his head lolling on the shoulder of the other man. He fingered the focus and the man's face hardened in the scope.

'Groomer,' he grunted.

His anger mounted as he weighed the circumstances that had brought those two together. Leaning back, he steadied his stance and began to squeeze the trigger.

The bullet whipped past Goliath's ear, snarling through the space he had just vacated, venting its fury in the rubbish-choked ditch. He burrowed for better cover. When he looked again, Omar Al Tamari had disappeared.

Church of the Holy Sepulchre, Jerusalem

Tim Conway hooked the filing cabinet open, sighed, and slid it closed again. Jameson whiskey, he concluded, was just fine and dandy for bonhomie among friends or as a lubricant to late-night musings but not just now. He needed a clear head to analyse the phone call.

He had been surprised to pick up the receiver and hear the Father General of the Franciscan Order in Rome enquire if he was alone. A selection of risqué responses had suggested themselves and, prudently, he had pushed them aside. Something in Father General's tone intimated that this wasn't a social call. He liked Carlos Ortiz, even though they had what the cops called previous. More than once, during his term in Rome, he had been carpeted by Ortiz, usually on foot of a complaint from some Vatican department or other. On such occasions, they had hollered and head-butted for the sake of the secretary in the ante-room, then clinked glasses in fraternal solidarity. Ortiz was enough of a politician to play the system and send back the appropriate signals. He was also Franciscan enough to defend and protect his friars, even half-arsed firebrands like Tim Conway. He smiled and steepled his fingers under his chin. Carlos Ortiz had asked him to receive and house a papal envoy and, of course, he'd agreed. Any Franciscan could request bed and board for someone in a Franciscan house anywhere in the world and it would be provided automatically. If not, the Franciscans would organise it with some other religious house. But ... Tim was aware that his superior knew he would read between the lines and figure this request had a whole raft of buts attached to it. He began to tick them off. Father General had made the call himself rather than delegating it to a flunkey. Why would a papal envoy stay in a Franciscan house and not at the nunciature? He suspected the original request had come from above Carlos Ortiz – way above. And the guest's name ... Could it be? He took a deep breath and checked his watch. The connecting flight from Tel Aviv would touch down in an hour.

As he was tidying the papers on his desk, he heard a sharp knock and Brother Werner entered. The Father Guardian continued putting papers in the drawer and concentrated on suppressing his annoyance. Werner might have waited for permission to enter, he thought, but he reminded himself not to sweat the small stuff. Werner's small stuff was quickly building to critical mass.

'Yes, Brother Werner?'

'I must talk to you about repairs.'

'Actually, I'm just going to the airport, Brother, why—'

'Ah, gut, I vill drive you. Ve talk as ve go, *ja*?'

'*Ja* – I mean, yes, of course,' Tim responded, finding himself on the back foot. Put it down to penance, the old friars always counselled, whenever a young friar protested at some unwelcome task or undeserved punishment. Tim considered Werner's offer qualified under both headings and chided himself for his lack of charity.

The drive to the airport was everything Tim had expected it would be. Werner drove with agonising care, grumbling, mostly in German, about money, or rather the lack of it. Tim tried to nod or grunt at what he hoped were appropriate junctures while keeping his foot from pumping an imaginary accelerator. By the time they swerved into Arrivals, he was hunching his shoulders against the procession of irate drivers stacked up behind them.

'Can you find parking, Werner?'

'*Ja, ja,* you get the monsignor, I get the parking.'

❧

The passengers were already streaming through the double doors from Customs when Tim puffed up to the barrier. He swept a fast look around the concourse, in search of a likely suspect, and turned back to the door. Him, he thought, with relief. The papal envoy was a tall, lean man with high cheekbones, prominent in a pallid face. He thought the black suit and Roman collar, with a strip of red beneath, rode uneasily on the rangy frame. The monsignor paused as he entered the concourse and seemed to stiffen. His eyes found Tim's, then angled left over his shoulder. Tim turned to see Werner watching the new arrival. Tim hurried forward, hand outstretched.

'I'm Tim Conway, Father Guardian of the Holy Sepulchre.'

The monsignor took his hand in a firm grip but his eyes remained on Werner.

'Eh, Brother Werner is our driver,' Tim offered, by way of explanation.

The grey eyes swept back to him and the monsignor nodded. 'Thank you for coming,' he said quietly, in the Irish-American accent Tim Conway had grown up with in the Bronx.

The journey back to the Holy Sepulchre was a largely silent one. Werner concentrated on his driving, the monsignor gazed unseeingly at the streets of Jerusalem and Tim worried at something that didn't fit.

'I vill put car in garage,' Werner said, as he pulled up before the entrance to the church. It was the only time he had spoken since the airport and it jolted Tim's memory. There, Werner had mentioned the monsignor. How had he known that? Tim was certain he hadn't mentioned who was being met. He filed it under 'later' and escorted the monsignor to his office.

He offered the Jameson and the monsignor nodded.

'You Irish?' he asked.

'Good as. Pa and Ma were economic migrants to the Bronx. More castaways, really. Always half-hoping to make it back home.'

'Until you showed up?'

'Yeah, a kid anchors you to a place, I guess.'

They touched glasses. The monsignor placed his glass carefully on the desk between them. 'D'you know why I'm here, Father Guardian?' he asked.

'I got a call from the Father General in Rome.'

'I'm sorry to be an imposition.'

'I could have said no.'

The monsignor studied him for a moment and summoned something close to a smile.

'So far, you've exhibited three of the defining characteristics of the Celtic race. Hospitality,' he continued, lifting the glass from the desk, 'mixed with a streak of stubbornness in the face of authority. And what we might call 'the conversational-sidestep'. So, I'll ask again. Do you know why I'm here?'

'No, I don't. They asked, I said yes. You're welcome. That's it, Monsignor. Look, can we drop the titles?'

'I wish you would. I'm Michael Flaherty.'

'Tim Conway. I hope what I'm going to say isn't out of order, but—'

'But you're going to say it anyway. You're more Irish than you know, Tim.'

'Yeah, I guess I am. I was never very good at … games. You're not a papal envoy, Michael. I'd lay a million dollars you're not a monsignor either.'

'That's a hell of a wager for a man with a vow of poverty, Tim, but you'd win it. No, I'm not a papal envoy or a monsignor. I can't say I'm even a priest any more. Can I ask how you worked it out?'

'I've lived in Rome, Michael. I've seen what it can do to guys – decent guys. In my time, a lot of the younger priests working in the Vatican and the various religious headquarters, would meet up in some bar or other, maybe at the weekend. We had a few beers, talked football and bitched about the Church. Time goes by and some of the guys begin to get a bad case of Romanitis, you know what I mean – they learn to walk the walk and talk the talk. They were on their way up at the department or on the hierarchical ladder and the air seems to get thinner up there. Anyways, your old buddy shows up one day with a purple sash and it's bye-bye to the bar and the football, and if there's any bitching about the Church, he ain't talking, just listening. Seems to me a lot of guys lose contact with what's real when they're given a role.'

'You didn't, Tim.'

'You shoulda met my old man. Any time I'm tempted to think I'm something I hear him saying, "Why be something when you can be someone?" Truth to tell, I coulda been sucked into that kind of life, so I took out insurance. I joined the Franciscans. Illusions of grandeur don't hang too well with a brown frock and sandals. Sorry if this offends, Michael Flaherty, but you don't strike me as monsignor or papal envoy material. Anyways, I knew your name before I heard from my boss.'

'You know about … the business in Rome?'

'Let's not do coy here, Michael. I know it's very Irish to understate – heck, my old man could condense eight hundred years of murder and mayhem into 'The Troubles'. I'm talking about the Remnant. Officially, guys in the sticks like me don't get much of a heads-up on what really happened. Happily, the bush telegraph fills in some of the gaps. Way I heard it, Michael Flaherty saved the Pope's life, put a gone-to-the-bad cardinal behind bars and then disappeared. I figured only in Hollywood does a guy like that go home and live happily ever after.'

'I did go home.'

'But, it isn't over, is it?'

'No, it's not. The cardinal I brought down is out and I think he's here. He wants me.'

'And what? The Church wraps you in a monsignor's sash and sends you by Fedex so—'

'Tim, listen. It's complicated, okay? The bottom line is that Cardinal Thomas gets me or other people get hurt, people I care about and maybe, by association, people like you or the Franciscan community at the Holy Sepulchre.'

'We don't stand for much if we can't do something for one of our own.'

'That's a noble sentiment, Tim, and I appreciate it. But these people don't play by the Queensberry Rules. They play for keeps.'

'What can I do for you, Michael?'

'You're already doing it, Tim. I have a roof over my head, a place to rest and think until ... whatever.'

The phone rang and Tim snatched it from the cradle.

'Stall them for a few minutes, Larry, and bring them up the back stairs.'

'Company?'

'Cops.'

&✕&

'Father Guardian, I'm Detective Avram and this is my partner, Detective Goldberg.'

'Please sit down, Detectives, I'm Tim Conway.'

'Pardon my ignorance, Father Guardian,' Goldberg smiled, 'but a Jewish girl like me gets a little confused with all the different Christian groups. You're a Franciscan, right?'

'I'm confused by your confusion, Detective Goldberg. Heck, a Brooklyn girl like you should know a Franciscan when she sees one. Maybe the community in Brooklyn is more modern than we are in the Holy Sepulchre.'

He spread his arms and looked down at his robes.

'You're looking at the vintage version. The newer models come in jeans, T-shirts and discreet Tao crosses.'

'Maybe I was confused by the guy I saw in the hall as we came up. He didn't fit either of the descriptions you've given, so I guess he's not a Franciscan.'

'No, he's a papal envoy, and a guest. Apart from bringing you up to speed on the sartorial evolution of the Franciscans, how can I help you?'

'Father Guardian,' Avram began, 'we have a – a situation. I'm afraid I need your assurance that what is said here stays here.'

'I'm sorry, I can't give you that assurance.'

'Why the hell not?' Goldberg asked, and Avram shot her a warning look.

'It's a fair question, Detective Goldberg. It's like this. I'm the Father Guardian here, which means that for my sins, or theirs, I'm the leader of this community. If anything you tell me affects their safety, they have a right to hear about it and I have a duty to tell them.'

Goldberg looked as if she might argue and Avram interjected quickly:

'Look, Father, why don't I just tell you and you can decide what the community needs to know?'

'Okay, let's hear it.'

Speaking without notes, Avram detailed the serial killings and the locations of the severed heads. When he'd finished, Tim Conway looked a few shades paler.

'How come I never heard about any of this?'

'I think the rabbi and the imam thought it better to keep it under wraps. You can appreciate, Father, there are elements in both communities who'd see this as an act of provocation and— '

'I get your drift, Detective. That kinda stuff is hard to keep under wraps indefinitely.'

'We appreciate that, Father, which is one of the reasons why we wanted to talk to you. Have you any idea why someone would want to stir up trouble between the different denominations in Jerusalem just now?'

'You mean "just now" as opposed to the past thousand years or so?' Tim Conway smiled grimly. 'You both know what Jerusalem's like. I mean, sure, politically it's just a city in a Middle Eastern country. But it's a political symbol for Israelis and Arabs, and a religious symbol for Jews and Muslims. Add in the cocktail of competing Christian sects and it makes for a very volatile brew. Some people think it would take another Six Day War situation to light the fuse under Jerusalem but I don't agree. For what it's worth, I think it's more likely to begin as a religious conflict. The kind of desecrations you've described wouldn't be enough on their own to set it off, but if there were others and it all became common knowledge … I'm not sure where to go with this, Detective. I meet every month with the leaders of the other faith communities. In fact, we're meeting this evening at the Convent of St Mary Magdalene. But I can't see what I can do to help you when I'm not supposed to know.'

'I think Inspector Bernstein thought it better that you did know. Also, he thought you might be able to shed some light on why these things are happening and why now.'

The priest shook his head.

'Bernstein is a good man, respected right across the religious spectrum, but, honestly, his guess is as good as mine.'

'And your guess would be what, Father Guardian?'

'My guess is that someone is trying to provoke a major conflict between the dominant religions in Jerusalem, Detective Goldberg.'

'Who would do that and why?'

'It comes down to the old *cui bono* question, Detective.'

'Cooee who?'

'Sorry, it means 'who benefits?'.' If a religious conflict broke out here, logic and history would dictate that it spread to involve the countries who ally themselves to the various faiths.'

'So, basically, it would boil down to an East versus West scenario, Father?'

'Yes. Isn't that novel? But with Jerusalem and the Jews caught in the middle.'

'Isn't that novel?' Goldberg muttered, but Tim Conway continued as if he hadn't heard.

'But the question is, who benefits? A government, some religious leader or whoever makes big money in wartime? I'm sorry, I seem to be adding to the list of questions instead of providing answers. You did say this was one of the reasons you wanted to talk to me.'

'Eh, yes, Father Guardian. We – that is Inspector Bernstein, Detective Goldberg and I – think this killer will kill again. And if – when – he does, we think it will be here.'

'Here, where … I'm sorry, I …'

'In the Church of the Holy Sepulchre, Father Guardian.'

The Safe House, Jerusalem

'Cappuccino.'

'Cappuccino!'

'And bagels.'

'And bagels!'

'Is there an echo here, Goldberg, or are you just yanking my chain?'

'Oy veh. You go just twenty minutes with a priest from New York and you make like a native already.'

'He got you dead to rights, partner.'

'He's opinionated, suspicious, sarcastic and—'

'So you liked him too?'

'Yeah. He's a feisty guy, smart as a whip and all the other clichés. He's also not telling us something.'

'Okay, impressions time. Give your paranoia full rein, partner.'

'This bagel's delicious. Where's the lox? You forgot the lox?'

'Goldberg!'

'All right already. First off, why the back stairs for the cops?'

'Someone he didn't want us to meet on the regular stairs?'

'Yeah, but we saw him anyway.'

'You saw him. You were rubbernecking like a tourist.'

'Cos you were yabbering with old Brother Larry Whatsisface.'

'Results of yabbering. Ten Franciscans currently reside in friary. The latest addition is, quote, some kind of half-assed engineer, unquote. Visitors come and go, especially around the big occasions like Christmas and Easter. New fella just arrived, quote, some Roman Pooh-bah, unquote. Not expected. Brother Larry expected to organise room for said Pooh-bah by Father Guardian who is, quote, firm but fair, unquote. You gonna choke on that bagel?'

'You wish. Good work on the yabbering, Watson. So a papal envoy arrives out of the blue. What's a papal envoy?'

'A Roman Pooh-bah, according to the all-knowing and talkative Brother Larry. I think it's some kind of messenger from the Pope.'

'Don't they have an embassy? Why's this diplomat staying at the Holy Sepulchre?'

'They call it a nunciature. I'll check it out. I'll run him by Immigration first. Anything gleaned from the rubbernecking on the stairs?'

'About six two, lean, too thin if anything, and tightly wound. Black hair and grey eyes in a pale face. Black suit with that plastic collar thing.'

'Dog collar.'

'Really? Little red strip under the collar.'

'Father Guardian didn't want us to meet this guy.'

'No, and he didn't want to meet us either. It was more than the cops-equal-trouble thing.'

'He seemed affable enough.'

'He was trying too hard, Avram.'

'Could be whiskey-induced.'

'I think it was despite that. Whatever he and the Pooh-bah talked about prior to our arrival did not fill the Father Guardian with good cheer.'

'We're certain they were talking?'

'The second chair was still warm, Avram.'

'He genuinely didn't know about the mosque and Mea Shearim, agreed?'

'Agreed. What about his take on the likely outcome if the killings and desecrations become public knowledge?'

'Logical and credible. The idea that the Holy Sepulchre might be next was a shock.'

'Apart from suggesting he beef up security and call us when he needs us, I didn't know what else to say. It sounded … lame.'

'It was.'

'Thank you.'

'We had nothing else to offer, Avram. We're missing something.'

'What?'

'Something he said after the *cui bono* bit.'

'He said governments and religious leaders.'

'Yeah, that's what I remember too, maybe because that's what we expected to hear. There was something else … What?'

'He asked a question: "Who makes big money in wartime?"'

'Black-marketeers?'

'Yes, who else?'

'Arms suppliers! I'm on it.'

The Apple Warehouse, Bethlehem
Omar woke to the scent of apples and the sound of thunder. He lay on a low cot, like the one at home, and watched faint light sieve through the cracks between the boards a few feet from his face. As the thunder passed overhead, tiny avalanches of dust spiralled down the shafts of light. 'Sleep, little brothers,' he murmured. 'Raphael is standing guard against the Evil One.' A rough hand closed over his mouth and two figures appeared at either side of him in the gloom.

'Give him some more needle, Shepherd,' one whispered, 'or he'll betray us to the soldiers.'

He felt a sudden sting in his upper arm. The apple scent sharpened in his nose and he saw a figure rise up before him. An old man stood in an orchard and raised his arms. Something squat and malevolent drew closer, stalking him. Omar opened his mouth to cry a warning and the vision melted into darkness.

Convent Church of St Mary Magdalene, Jerusalem
Tim Conway turned off the engine and killed the lights. They sat in the sudden darkness, looking through the iron filigree of the gates at the bulbous outline of the convent.

'I expected you to be surprised, Michael,' the Franciscan said quietly. 'I guess someone who survived the Remnant doesn't do surprise.'

'Survived might be a bit premature, Tim. Surprised would be … nice.' He laughed softly.

'What's so funny?'

'I had an old friend who really hated the word 'nice'. He told me to excise it from my vocabulary – his exact words. In the lexicon, according to Father Mack, only Shakespeare used it correctly. In our day, he said, it was used by and about people who were too scared to be real.'

'Insightful kinda guy. Did that usage apply to you?'

'It said a lot about both of us.'

'You said "had" a friend.'

'Yes.'

'Remnant?'

'No, previous.'

'Sorry. Just how far back does all this stuff go for you?'

'Let's just say it's a while since I was surprised. So, no, it doesn't surprise me that there are people out there who want something so badly they don't count the bodies on their way to getting it. Cardinal Thomas was like that. He used people, Tim, used them up and spat them out. Now he's on the loose again.'

Involuntarily, Tim Conway looked over his shoulder.

'How did he escape?'

'He didn't escape; he was sprung. Someone planned,

organised and effected it, and that someone wasn't a fanatic or a flunkey, which means some powerful people are pulling his strings.'

'Ironic, isn't it, that the puppet-master becomes a puppet? So, where is he?'

'I'm in Jerusalem, which probably means he's here. It's all part of someone else's plan. I'm sure of it. If Thomas just wanted revenge, he could have had it on the Island and almost did. You tell me someone's leaving heads as calling cards around Jerusalem, maybe to rattle people into a religious war. So is this a puppet or the puppet-master and how does he benefit?'

'That's the question I asked the detectives – *cui bono*?'

'Usually someone as far from the barricades as they can get. Behind every so-called holy war, there was someone with a political motive, someone who put up the money, provided the arms and, when the bodies were buried, that someone got to redraw the borders and write the history.'

'That's kinda medieval, don't you think?'

'No, I don't, not any more. Maybe it's ancient history for a lot of people in the West, Tim. Most of us take the division of Church and state for granted. Most people, east of where we're sitting, don't see it that way. America is big on the division of Church and state, in theory. In practice, it cosies up to Christian evangelicals and fundamentalists. And what about Israel, slam bang between East and West? Sure, they vote in a democracy but most Israelis see Israel and Judaism as one and the same thing. As far as the East is concerned, Israel is the fifty-first state of the Union. To the West, it's a buffer-zone against the spread of fanatical Islam. Now, if someone was to light the religious fuse here …'

'You really think that's what this is all about?'

'I don't know anything for certain, but I do know religions can be used. It's the oldest ploy in the political handbook. Reagan used a Polish pope to bring down the Berlin Wall. The Elector of Saxony used Luther's little hammer to pound Rome out of German politics. Henry VIII rode the shockwave of a religious reformation in England to a brand-new wife and a bulging property portfolio.'

The engine ticked as it cooled and a scattering of stars blinked behind the convent gates.

'Suppose we said no,' Tim said slowly.

'Suppose who said no?'

'Just suppose, here and now, we, the leaders of the different faiths in Jerusalem, said we're not going to go that road, no matter what.'

Michael pondered the question for a moment.

'I know this is in poor taste, but I think, here and now, the head-count would rise. And the temperature of the various faith members would rise with it until the whole place boiled over.'

He drew a deep breath.

'Okay, let's just say you and the other leaders stood together against the push for war. Who's to say you wouldn't be eliminated or just sidelined? It's been done. Hell, in Germany they got around the Kaiser with a corporal. It's why the Remnant operated just shy of the top. There's never any shortage of disaffection at that level, people who won't go any higher and can't face staying put or going back. The plan was to have their own guy in the top spot and, at the right moment, all their second-string team got to bat.'

'So, Cardinal Thomas would have been pope?'

'He'd have been someone's pope, Tim.'

In the corner of his eye, Michael caught a flicker of movement.

'I think whoever's at the gate is getting anxious, Tim.'

'Wha— Oh, right. You sure you want to be seen here?'

'When Thomas wants me he'll find me. Anyway, it's best to hide in plain sight.'

'Says who?'

'Special Forces manual.'

'You were Special Forces?' Tim croaked, but his companion had already left the car.

⚜

'Father Guardian, you're welcome.'

Tim thought the usually animated novice a little less summery than usual and put it down to his growing paranoia.

'Thank you. This is Monsignor Michael Flaherty.'

'You are welcome, Monsignor,' the young woman said, and bobbed her head. 'Please, will you follow?'

They trailed the white-clad figure through the high-arched doorway. At the end of a dimly lit hallway, she swung open the double doors to the parlour. Tim felt some of his tension lessen as he took in the familiar sorrowful photographs and icons crowding the walls. Antique standing lamps brooded under heavy, tasselled shades that tamed the light into tight bright circles and accented the surrounding shadows. Some of the shadow-pools stirred at their entrance and Tim nodded affably in their direction. He noted how the Chief Rabbi and the Imam seemed locked together in earnest conversation. A secret is something known by one person, he thought, and smiled ruefully. As usual, his brothers in Christ were carefully positioned and angled throughout the room to avoid any possibility of communication. He sighed but brightened immediately as he saw Mother Natasha. She was presiding in her customary spot beside the enormous Russian samovar, bulked upright and regal by the cushions on her high-backed chair.

'I see the brothers are all gathered in fraternal harmony, old friend,' he whispered mischievously, as he bowed over her mottled hand.

'Brothers.' She sniffed. 'Cain and Abel had more in common.'

Her eyes drifted beyond him to where Michael Flaherty stood outside in shadow. 'Come into the light,' she commanded. 'Old eyes see less and less as the years go by.' Michael stepped up to where she sat and bent his lanky frame to take her outstretched hand. Mother Natasha held his firmly in her own and gazed intently at his face.

'Monsignor Flaherty is staying with us at the Holy Sepulchre, Mother,' Tim offered, by way of introduction.

'Go and gather the lost sheep.' She smiled, waving him away with one hand while holding Michael close with the other.

'I'm pleased to meet you, Mother,' he said, as Tim departed. 'Father Guardian tells me this gathering would never have happened without you.'

'Monsignor,' she said, in her papery voice, 'like all true souls of the light, the Father Guardian does not grudge its reflection to the undeserving.'

'I have reason to know that, Mother.'

'Yes, I think you do.'

She reached up and stroked his cheek gently. 'So much pain in one so young,' she whispered. 'Sit with me, child, and be at peace in our house.'

∞❧

Tim Conway managed to corral them all into an untidy circle that included Michael and Mother Natasha. Taking the chair to her right, he began, 'Friends, as usual, we are grateful to Mother Natasha and her community for their warm welcome and strong Russian tea. We have a guest, this evening. Monsignor Michael Flaherty is staying with us at the Holy Sepulchre and I asked him along.'

Some of the assembled men bowed in Michael's direction and smiled, while others inclined their heads fractionally or stared in stony-faced silence. Tim waited until the attention of the room returned to him.

'Jerusalem, as you all know, is a Holy Place for Jews, Christians and Muslims. They've been coming here as pilgrims for almost two thousand years, Jewish pilgrims even longer than that,' he added. The Chief Rabbi smiled and nodded. 'Our job is to meet and welcome those pilgrims and help them, in whatever way we can, to deepen and express their faith. Actually, we all have something in common. I should more correctly say 'Someone', whether we call that Someone Yahweh, God or Allah. And yet what do the pilgrims find when they come to Jerusalem? They find us fighting to preserve our individual pieces of the Holy Places and standing apart from one another as if to say, "I have the whole Truth and everyone else is a liar or, at best, deluded."'

The room rang with the clamour of upraised voices as each

vied with the others to state the primacy of their faith and the historical reasons why their particular sect should have rights and others should not. During the uproar, Michael glanced at Mother Natasha and she leaned closer to whisper, 'Like many a lion, he finds himself in a den of Christians.'

Tim Conway waited until the last strident voice had faded into smouldering silence before continuing so softly that his audience had to lean forward to hear.

'What will it take to unite us?' he mused aloud. 'What does history tell us? It took the threat of a Philistine invasion to bind the twelve warring tribes of Israel together. It took the Persians to bring rival city states into the unit we now know as Greece. Nearer to our own day, it took Hitler to make allies against evil of the UK, the Soviet Union and most of Europe. No, I haven't forgotten my own country. I haven't forgotten either that it took Pearl Harbor to blow us out of our isolationism and into the war. But all that is ancient history, isn't it? We have peace now, don't we? We Christians think so because we look out of our windows every morning, from the Holy Sepulchre, and there are no Saracens circling the walls. The Jews believe it because they can gather to pray at the Wailing Wall without dreading the sound of Roman sandals, and Muslims because the Crusaders are long departed into history and are unlikely to return. So peace has, at long last, broken out in Jerusalem. What we have, brothers, is not peace but tolerance, and peace is surely more than that. Peace is surely more than the absence of war. Peace has to be the building up of brotherhood between those who were divided, because a house divided against itself cannot stand. When – I say "when" not "if" – the next crisis comes, what will we do? Will I go back to being an American and will you,' he said, jabbing a finger at each man in turn, 'go back to being an Israeli, Arab, Armenian, Syrian, Russian and Greek? Will we each ally ourselves with political powers, hoping to be victors not victims? Or will we be brothers, standing together under God and against those who would use our history of division to divide us further?'

He settled back in his chair and Michael saw the sheen of sweat on his forehead. Mother Natasha extended her hand to the Franciscan and he grasped it gratefully as the storm of voices broke about him. Michael saw the old nun bow her head as if she bore the pressure of the raging room. Slowly she straightened and said, 'Enough.' The single word seemed to puncture the inflating anger and the room hummed with tension in the face of the indomitable old woman. 'Enough,' she said again, more quietly, as her gaze swept the circle.

'Each one of you has reason to distrust every other one. We Russians can talk all night long of the hurts we have suffered. How we savour our old pains! We dig up the bones of our martyrs to wave them about and say, "See? We have suffered more than you because of you." We say, like the Jews, "We will remember. We will never forget." We do this to honour our dead but we condemn the living to relive old hurts so that nothing changes from one generation to the next. Are you Jews any different from us? Are you Muslims more enlightened? Adam had two sons who worshipped God in different ways and one murdered the other because of that difference. We – Jews, Muslims and Christians – are children of our father Abraham and we have murdered our own brothers and sisters for centuries. It is enough and more than enough spilling of blood.'

She turned to Tim Conway.

'We are angry because we are frightened. We are frightened of and by the truth. The Father Guardian of the Franciscans has spoken the truth, as uncomfortable as that is for all of us. If you think he lies, speak now or be silent.'

The circle of men stirred uneasily under her stern gaze.

'If no one has a question, perhaps we should turn our attention to—'

'I have a question.'

The circle rippled with surprise at the voice that challenged from the shadows. Sister Raisa moved into the light and stood beside the leader of the Eastern Orthodox Church in Jerusalem.

'You are not part of this circle, Sister,' Mother Natasha said icily. 'I must ask you—'

'Neither is the man who sits beside you, Mother,' Sister Raisa responded, her voice easily overriding that of her superior.

'My question is for this interloper, the envoy of the Roman Pope.'

The Imam and the Chief Rabbi started at this revelation, while the others stiffened with suspicion.

'I did not come to this meeting as a papal envoy, Sister,' Michael said, and the room hushed. 'I am here as a guest of the Father Guardian and of your superior.'

Sister Raisa flinched at the implied censure, and when she spoke again, her voice was laced with venom.

'Are we to believe that?' she scoffed. 'We know, only too well, how the Romans work. Have you not considered other Christian churches inferior to your own? Do you not conspire to evangelise the East and bring us under the rule of the Roman Pope?'

'You may believe that, Sister,' Michael said calmly. 'It is true that for centuries the Roman Church considered itself the only true Church and all other Christian churches were in error. Those who sit here know that this is not the position of the Roman Church today. The most recent Council in Rome, which some of your Orthodox representatives attended, was at pains to proclaim a pilgrim church that walked with brother denominations in search of the truth and considered itself enlightened by those other traditions. If the Roman Church, as you say, considers the Eastern churches inferior, why did no one tell those patriarchs who came to Rome to join the funeral service for the late pope? Did they undertake that journey as inferiors, those patriarchs whose representatives sit here among us? As for evangelising the East, surely you don't wish to diminish the achievements of St Cyril and St Methodius, the apostles to the Slavs, who preached Christianity to the Bulgars and Russians all those centuries ago. Yes, we have had centuries of mutual excommunication, insult and suspicion, and our collective wrongdoing often contradicted the Christian message. And, yes, we have allied ourselves with political powers rather than with one another. That time is past. It seems to me the wheel of change turns and presents an age-old challenge again in our time. The question is, do we have the courage to grasp it?'

Sister Raisa clapped her hands slowly.

'How well the Pope's errand-boy parrots the words of the Father Guardian. How well they work together to spin a web of deceit, to lure us into their so-called brotherhood against some imaginary threat. And will the Jews forswear their history and join this Christian brotherhood?'

The creak of the Chief Rabbi's chair was the only sound to break the profound silence that had settled on the gathering.

'The Jews of Jerusalem have long memories,' he said quietly. 'We have reason to remember the Christians who baptised the Holy Places with the blood of our people. We will not be joining this Christian brotherhood.'

Sister Raisa's face flushed in triumph and she threw a scornful glance at her superior.

'We will not be joining this Christian brotherhood,' the Chief Rabbi continued, 'we will be joining *with* this Christian brotherhood because, as the Father Guardian puts it, we too are pilgrims making our way to God according to our traditions and beliefs, as we believe you are, our Muslim brothers.'

His voice strengthened as he faced Tim Conway.

'I believe the Father Guardian of the Franciscans when he says we stand in grave danger of being used to perpetuate disharmony. That threat, dear Sister, is not imaginary. It is real, I know this to be so. But, above all other considerations, I believe the Father Guardian because I have found him worthy of trust and because what he has said is the truth.'

The Imam rose immediately to stand with the Chief Rabbi.

'As do I,' he said simply.

Sister Raisa's face was a maelstrom of emotion. Imploringly, she turned her eyes to the Patriarch of the Eastern Orthodox Church. The bearded old man stood with difficulty, assisted by the black-cowled Armenian beside him.

'As do we,' he whispered.

Sister Raisa melted back into the shadows and a door slammed.

⧉

As the others queued for tea at the samovar, under the benign gaze of Mother Natasha, or chatted in small groups throughout the room, Tim Conway dropped into the vacant chair beside Michael.

'You sure you're not a papal envoy?' he whispered, smiling.

'You did well, Tim,' Michael said, raising his cup in salute.

'Yeah, you, me and Natasha should form a tag-team.'

'Who was the inquisitress?'

'Oh, that's just Raisa, Rasputin's crazier sister.'

'She knows who I am, Tim.'

Sobered, the Franciscan leaned closer. 'I think Werner does also,' he said. 'It was something he let slip at the airport. Could they be refugees from the Remnant?'

'Could be.'

'That's an Irish 'no', right?'

'Maybe. What's her position here?'

'I guess she's heiress-apparent to Mother Natasha. God help us all if she ever gets the top spot.'

'Amen to that, Tim. And Werner?'

'He handles the money end of things at the Holy Sepulchre. I use the word 'handles' under advisement.'

'If I was a papal envoy, Father Guardian, I would advise you to check the books.'

⊗⊘⊗

Mother Natasha moved from picture to picture in the empty parlour, savouring the company of the heroes and heroines of her youth. She paused briefly before the icon of the Archangel Michael wielding a sword over a writhing dragon. Her thoughts strayed to the young monsignor who had so recently defended the light against the voice in the darkness.

'Dreaming again, old woman?' a voice taunted.

'There are dreams and there are nightmares, Raisa,' she replied, without turning. 'You must choose which to serve.'

The reflection of the white-garbed sister gained substance in the glass of the picture beside her. It was the portrait of their revered benefactress and the old nun shifted her position to remove the stain from her sight. She moved slowly to her chair and gestured to the vacant ones that formed the circle.

'Please sit, Sister, there are matters we must speak of.'

'I would prefer to stand,' the younger woman said defiantly. 'The time for talking is long past. Your precious circle of men is old, as you are old, and clings to the safety of the past, as you do.'

'Being old is hardly a crime, Sister,' Mother Natasha said easily. 'Some of these "old men", as you call them, have lived through terrible times. Perhaps to be old, to have survived, is an accomplishment. I hope you may live long enough to appreciate this.'

Sister Raisa moved to stand before her superior.

'Your day is done, old woman,' she said coldly. 'It would be better for you to prepare yourself for the next world.'

'How young you are, Raisa,' Mother Natasha said gently. 'You think to frighten me with your youth and strength. The young and strong often see no further than their own time. I have seen you before. It was young men and women who put us out in the snow. My father hid us in a barn and went to look for food. He never returned. We ate straw and rats but we survived. I remember the Chekists and the Stalinists and Stalin's pet murderer Beria. I have been hungry and afraid many times, child, but I have survived. The young visionaries roamed all over Russia, Raisa, and, when they had devoured everything we had, they devoured each other. I am an old woman, as you say, child, but I am here and they are not. There is always choice. Even in the gulag there were those who chose to die, those who chose to exist and those who chose to live. You must choose, Raisa, before it is too late.'

She paused to consider the sister's face, then went on, 'Those who have influenced you, what do they promise? Do they promise position, power?' She gestured to the icon of the Archangel Michael and the dragon. 'Lucifer, the bearer of light, was an archangel also. He chose power and fell.'

'You know nothing of those who influence me.'

'I think I do, Sister. I have lived here a very long time. We sisters, as you know, go out to the world only when we must. But the world comes to us. And because they see us as not of this world, they tell us many things they would never whisper outside our walls. Would it surprise you if I told you that General Allenby sat in this parlour and had tea? This was the man who entered the old city on foot in December 1917, the first Western conqueror since the Crusader Godfrey de Bouillon. The old sisters told me when I arrived here that he didn't like our strong Russian tea but he drank it anyway. So very English.'

Sister Raisa showed no reaction but the old woman had seen her eyelids flicker at the mention of the Crusader.

'I think,' she continued, 'this British general was so accustomed to people being other than themselves in his presence that he was surprised by the naïveté of our sisters and so … he talked. The sisters of this convent knew of the Partition of Palestine before the Arabs and Israelis did. A sister told me that T. E. Lawrence came and sat on the floor, Arab fashion. He drank four cups of tea. I suppose he had had worse on the way to Aqaba. She said he was a – a sensitive. When he told her his dreams of Arab unity, she could not reveal Allenby's plan. She said he read her face and sipped his tea in sadness. Before he left, she gave him an icon of St Sebastian as a gift. It was one she had painted herself but, of course, she didn't speak of that. "Judas might be more appropriate, Sister," he said. I remember Golda Meir came here when Saddat invaded and Dayan, her favourite general, was speaking of a new Holocaust. She wept and talked and wept again as we sat with her but I saw her spine straighten as she left our gates.'

Mother Natasha raised her eyes and stared until Sister Raisa was drawn into eye contact.

'Is it likely I would not know if someone dreams of a New Jerusalem – if someone gathers allies to his cause from men and women in Jerusalem already bound by oath to a higher cause – if that someone puts horrors in the Holy Places to further divide Jew from Muslim, both from Christians and Christians from each other?'

'You don't know what you're saying,' Raisa gasped.

Mother Natasha's gaze held her transfixed.

'I do know, Sister, and I know of your part in this, and I beg you now to choose to serve the light, as you are sworn to do as a Christian, and forswear the dark.'

Sister Raisa's face contorted as emotions warred within her. Mother Natasha stared intently at her and saw the flow of anger, hope and fear alter her features. The fear resolved into icy resolution and Mother Natasha's heart constricted with sadness. Sister Raisa stood as if carved from stone. When the old woman spoke again, it was with the calm authority of the superior of the

Convent of St Mary Magdalene. 'It is my decision,' she said, 'as superior of this community, that you must leave Jerusalem. You will return to our mother house in Moscow for a period of prayer and reflection. I will make the arrangements in the morning. May God help you. That will be all.'

Sister Raisa pressed her lips together in a bloodless sneer. She bowed, mockingly, to her superior and walked away.

Rachel's Café, Jerusalem

The young man sat at the back of the café and rested against the wall. He had a clear view of the door. If he was surprised when the big man eased into the chair beside him, his pale, pinched face didn't show it.

'Two Americanos with milk and sugar – lots of sugar,' the big man ordered. 'And bring two glasses of water with two straws.'

The waiter rolled his eyes and withdrew. The big man watched the younger one check the restaurant with restless eyes. 'You haven't forgotten everything I taught you, Uri,' he said quietly.

'I haven't forgotten anything,' the young man muttered. 'That's my problem, Commander.'

'Two very basic things seem to have slipped your mind, Uri,' Avram said quietly. 'The first is always to check the back entrance. The second is never use ranks or names.'

'You used mine,' the young man said petulantly.

'Oh, come on, Uri; it isn't even your real name. We called you that because you bent every damn spoon we ever had.'

'I had a nervous disposition bordering on obsessive compulsive,' Uri said defensively, 'which—'

'Which made you the sanest soldier in our squad,' Avram completed.

The waiter returned and deposited the coffees and the two glasses of water. He placed the straws on the table beside them and left. Avram dumped six sachets of sugar into one cup and filled it to the brim from the milk jug. He dipped a straw into the coffee and put it before his companion.

'You haven't forgotten,' Uri said, with a wintry smile.

'That's my problem, Uri,' Avram grunted, and sipped his scalding coffee. 'Everything going okay?'

'Yes, thank you.'

Uri bent at the waist and sipped his milky coffee through the straw. 'Everything's fine,' he said. 'I have a nice apartment, my books, my music and my job at the Immigration Office, which is not too taxing. I see my counsellor once a week for one hour. She is pleased with my progress. You already know all this, don't you?'

'Yeah.' Avram sighed. 'Look, Uri, it's because I care about you, okay? No big deal. There's a difference between big brother and Big Brother, you know what—'

'I know what you mean. I've read the book but you probably know that too.'

Avram shook out a cigarette and flicked a flame from an army-issue Zippo lighter. The young man shuddered violently and attempted to get up but the detective pressed him back one-handed and pocketed the lighter.

'Uri, Uri, listen to me. I'm sorry, okay? I forgot.'

Gradually, Uri's breathing slowed to normal and the hectic flush faded from his cheeks.

'My reaction is quite normal,' he said steadily. 'Certain stimuli can catch me unawares and I – I breathe deeply.'

'That sounds good.'

'It works for me. What do you want?'

'I want information from Immigration.'

'Without Immigration knowing. I see. And you'd like me to get it for you.'

'Yes … please.'

'When?'

'I'll wait. Look, Uri, it's important, otherwise—'

'No need to explain. It's the least I can do for you. I owe you.'

'You don't owe—'

'What do you need?'

Avram gave him the details and watched him make his way to the entrance. Uri still walked as if he was on a ship, splaying his big feet for purchase. He saw him hover until the waiter opened the door before he stepped out to the pavement. The coffee threatened to come back up and Avram steeled himself, pressing his hands against the table edge until the nausea subsided. Uri wouldn't ever use his hands if he could avoid it, he remembered. Once that train of thought rumbled out from the back of his mind, he knew he'd have to let it run its course.

The squad had ghosted into position around the house targeted by an informer. He had checked his watch and chopped his hand forward. It had been a textbook search-and-rescue operation. Once, an ex-army drinking buddy had told him the military instructors still used it as a model in the Military College, then had stood up and drifted away to a more congenial corner of the bar when Avram had gone very still. The door had flown in before their boots and they had fanned to spray the interior at head height. Four men fell to the floor, shapeless in death. A fifth, bent over, had escaped the scythe of steel and scuttled, crab-like, for the window. Almost absently, Avram had shot him to the right of his spine and splashed bright arterial blood on the far wall. Without breaking his stride, he had knelt by the object on the floor.

'Uri,' he had whispered, 'time to go home.'

An Israeli soldier captured by Hamas would be shot, if he was lucky. Uri hadn't been lucky. His captors had burned his hands until they'd melted into claws. They hadn't been in a hurry; the floor had been littered with cigarette lighters.

Avram sipped the cold coffee and waited, watching the ebb and flow of patrons and staff in the busy café, scanning the traffic that criss-crossed the door for— There! His brain registered the brief glimpse of a familiar blue car and adrenalin rushed through his body. Same car, second time in two minutes.

Uri eased into the seat beside him.

'Back door.' He smiled. 'I'm a fast learner. Immigration has no record of your subject.'

'Nothing?'

'Nothing ... now. Sasha in Records said we had an inspector call immediately after the processing of that flight. Sasha thinks I'm really cute.'

'So do I, Uri. Do me a favour, willya? Wait until I'm on the street and go out the way you came in. There's a door off the hallway to the left, takes you out by the garbage cans in the alley. Get in among the cans and play possum. I'll stall them as long as I can. When it's clear, go. You remember Owl?'

'Yes.'

'He's got a storage business in the Muristan area. You can ask for him using his real name. Stay in storage until I contact you, okay?'

Avram paid at the counter and sauntered out to the street. He turned right and strolled casually along the pavement. The blue car nestled in a parking spot between a black BMW and a vegetable truck.

'Shoe shine?'

A small Arab boy waved a single balding brush without enthusiasm. Avram hitched up his trouser legs and the boy dropped to his knees. The big man bent to inspect the work and whispered in the boy's ear. The boy looked up and his eyes widened. They widened further when Avram dropped some notes and a sodden tissue on the pavement beside him. Briskly, the boy swiped at the dusty shoes and disappeared into the traffic.

Avram walked on and drew abreast of the blue car. The driver's elbow angled through the open window. Cigarette smoke curled out of the interior and vanished in the up-draught from the sun-struck roof. Avram grasped the driver's arm and yanked it back against the door frame. The crack of breaking bone rocketed him into an all-out sprint. Behind him, he heard muffled shouts and the banging of doors as the two men in the car changed places. An engine revved and he risked a glance over his shoulder to see the blue bonnet jerk into the line of traffic and weave in pursuit. Abruptly, he jinked right into a narrower street and pounded furiously past a blur of alarmed pedestrians. The whine of a highly tuned engine waxed louder in his ears and he knew from the change in engine pitch and the squeal of protesting rubber that the car had turned behind him and was gaining. He forced himself to maintain the sprint, eyes and brain calculating his options. And then he heard the engine cough and die. At the next junction, he turned left and lost himself in a maze of alleys.

⊗◊⊗

The proprietor of the corner café brought a tiny cup of pungent Arab coffee to the sweating, red-faced man who sat with his back to the wall. He wondered at the dark stains that fanned down from the armpits of his jacket. He wondered also at the small smile that transformed the craggy features. It is a boy's smile, he decided, a boy who has done something shameful. Shaking his head, he moved back to his stool beside the door.

A wet paper tissue stuffed up the exhaust pipe will do it every time, Avram thought. There are some things you never forget.

⊗◊⊗

Uri crouched between the dustbins and watched the shoes go by. Deck shoes, he registered, ridged rubber soles for grip and canvas uppers stitched around the instep with a leather strip. He practised being still, as he had been taught to do. He let his breathing deepen and his muscles relax so that his body moulded to its surroundings. There are some things you never forget, he thought. A radio crackled and the shoes froze and fled. Uri waited until the slapping sound had faded, then waited some more. Nonchalantly, he eased his way from the bins and began to stroll. He realised he was enjoying this adventure and smiled. You should get out more, he reminded himself. He hadn't seen Owl in a lifetime, but he remembered their shared love of books and his smile widened into a grin. A woman passing him in the alley almost returned the smile. Instead, she tucked her chin into her chest and hurried by.

After all, he could have been anyone. What kind of man walks around with a silly grin on his face and wearing gloves on such a sunny day?

The Nunciature, Jerusalem

Father Joshua Barnett wrapped his handkerchief around his forefinger and ran it around the inside of his Roman collar. He stuffed the sweat-stained cotton into his soutane pocket and took his place at the reception desk in the nunciature. He was a twenty-six-year-old all-American boy with all the accessories – line-backer frame, crew-cut, bleached-blond hair and an abundance of freckles. He was also very hot.

'A soutane in Jerusalem,' Monsignor Denis La Montagne had quipped at the breakfast table, 'is a portable sauna. We're like the Crusaders in full Norman armour. In my opinion, the Saracens just sat in the shade and waited for these morons to melt.'

'Or rust,' Joshua had offered, and they'd both chuckled.

In Joshua's eyes, Denis was a 'lifer'. He had clocked up twenty-five years in the Vatican Diplomatic Service, at least ten of those in Jerusalem.

'Shoulda joined the US Army,' he liked to say, 'one tour of five years tops, then home to Mom and apple pie.'

Joshua, the 'newbie', liked the gangly, cynical monsignor. He was the only member of staff in Jerusalem who didn't treat him like something slightly higher in the pecking order than an altar boy.

'Denis, what am I doing here?'

'Well, let me see. You could be requiting the sins of a past life, or too damn smart for your own good, or your bishop was intellectually threatened by a priest who could walk and talk at the same time. Stop me when I get warm.'

'No, seriously, what do we actually do?'

Denis had lowered his coffee cup and fixed him with a wide-eyed stare.

'That question marks the end of innocence,' he said dramatically. 'Okay, now breathe deeply and relax and I'll take you through it in baby-steps. First, we must make a distinction between priests and us. The blue-collar priest, your average Father Joe, does all the fiddly mundane things from baptisms to burials. We, however, are white-collar priests. We are the ones who 'showed promise' and were plucked like petunias from the onion patches of various hick seminaries to be cultured in Rome. Joy of joys, we were no longer 'the nerd in the herd', the guy who preferred Nietzsche to nachos, Bonhoeffer to beer. Horror of horrors, we were now *primus inter pares*, just another genius among many and locked into a dog-collar eat dog-collar survival of the fittest that would have made Darwin quail. *Quo vadis*, where goest thou? The only way worth going in the Vatican Diplomatic Corps is up, my son. Rome is a thermal. Just angle your wings in an orthodox fashion and soar, boy, soar. But back to basics. Latin was a given for entry at the ground floor but Italian was the visa to sunnier climes. The language of Dante would pick the lock of student Hell and allow us passage through the Purgatory of some musty, minor Vatican department to the Heaven of an overseas posting. That was then. Now, I believe, Spanish has become the new Italian in the service. The entrails augur the possibility that the next pope will be from Rio. Ye gods, how the Empire strikes back.'

He paused to dab his upper lip with a huge handkerchief

and his manic gleam seemed to dim. When he resumed speaking, Joshua had the feeling he was eavesdropping on the private Denis rather than listening to the raconteur.

'That, of course, was the theory. I … One didn't factor in the machinations of those who maintain a stained-glass ceiling to keep certain people in their place.'

His voice trailed off and the usually animated face seemed to sag.

'Where was I?'

'You were telling me what we priests in the Diplomatic Corps actually do.'

'If you don't think it too oxymoronic, my dear Joshua, we do nothing. Ah, I glean from your confusion that we need to take a philosophical tangent. Doing nothing, as I'm sure you've intuited, is actually impossible and the Church rarely expects that of her servants, particularly her civil servants. Doing nothing is actually doing the something that is least likely to lead to anything, particularly to anything like nasty repercussions for the doer to the point where he gets done and is done for.'

'I'm sorry I asked.'

'Ignorance is merely a door to knowledge, Father.'

೭ഠയ

Joshua sat at the desk and ticked off the list of people he'd dealt with that morning. There had been the Irish priest, with the lobster complexion and rheumy eyes, enquiring as to the location of St Anne's Church, and would there be a bar anywhere in the vicinity of the nunciature because his aged mother was a martyr to the heat? Joshua had spread his map of Jerusalem on the desk and actually found St Anne's near the Bazaar. Flushed with this minor triumph, he had admitted ignorance of local bars and was left with the feeling that he had failed this particular pilgrim. There were the two young females from California enquiring, 'Like, where's Jesus' body on display? You know, like the mummies in Egypt, 'n' all?'

'There is no body.'

'No body? So who took it? I guess it was that Carter guy on the Smithsonian Channel.'

'Eh, no. Jesus ascended into Heaven.'

'Reeeally! Isn't that a bummer, Arlene?'

'Whatever. Can we go back to the hotel now? I'm all cultured out.'

And there was the irate Jewish male objecting to the proximity of the Church of the Holy Sepulchre to the Wailing Wall. He had produced a tattered map of Jerusalem and pointed to where the Church should be moved.

'Excuse me, sir, but isn't that the Dome of the Rock?'

'So?'

Joshua had referred that particular client to the Father Guardian of the Franciscans at the Holy Sepulchre, acting on the belief that misery should be spread. Denis would be proud. He looked up to see a gamine young woman, in a too-large jacket, fatigue pants and sensible walking shoes, gazing at him with perfect green eyes. He noticed she had close-cropped red hair and …

'Father!'

'What?'

'Father, I was asking you if you have a papal envoy staying here.'

'Sorry, I just … lost my place. Miss … ?'

'A papal envoy – here.'

'Ah, I don't … wouldn't know. Do you have some identification, M—'

'You wouldn't know! You live here, right?'

'Right.'

'And you wouldn't know if you have a papal envoy on the premises. Like, at the breakfast table you might happen to glance up and see – wow – a tall, thin, good-looking guy with black hair, grey eyes and a haunted expression and this little strip of red running under his dog-collar, like someone had just cut his throat with a very sharp knife, and think, Omigod, I've never seen this guy before.'

'I'll ask.'

'You're a sweetheart.'

Joshua closed the door to the reception area behind him and leaned his forehead against the cool wood.

'Even a small, run-down parish in the Ozarks, Lord,' he prayed fervently. He straightened his soutane and made a beeline for Denis.

ଚଚ୍ଚ

Goldberg eased back in her chair and took a lazy look around. No cameras. She ignored the disapproving stare of the current pope from the large framed photograph on the wall as she concentrated on reading the young priest's notes. Reading the wrong way up was a skill she had developed in her dysfunctional home all those years ago. Okay, so the kid's notes were a lot of nada. She sat and waited.

ଚଚ୍ଚ

'She asked what?'

'She asked if we had a papal envoy.'

'Like on special offer, buy one get one free?'

'Denis, please.'

'God, give me patience. Stand there and don't touch anything, okay?'

'Okay, okay.'

Monsignor Denis La Montagne stepped into a small annexe where a computer monitor glowed a cool blue. He sat at the keyboard and typed a password, drumming his fingers until the screen went blank and a twinkling cursor invited him to type a message.

'Enquiry re papal envoy,' he typed, and pressed Send. Carefully, he checked the outbox to confirm that this particular model had done exactly what it said on the tin. Bingo! He forced himself to sit quietly and wait. Within seconds, the computer chirped and he pricked Send/Receive with the little arrow to list all incoming emails. They marched in bold ranks from the top of the screen and he scanned impatiently through offers of an intimate nature until his eye hit 'Crusader'. His fingers slipped on the slick mouse and he rubbed them dry on his shirt before opening the file. It displayed a one-word message: 'Delay.' Quickly, he went through the process of closing the whole thing down. He was the only member of staff with the password to this particular computer but it didn't hurt to be cautious. If the time ever came when his contact could no longer ensure his position in Rome, he was resolved to donate the machine to the Sea of Galilee.

'What's the story, Denis?'

'Oh, small earthquake, only a few killed.'

'Denis!'

'Joshua, my son, hie thee to the kitchen for a Coke, okay? I'll handle this one.'

'Gosh, you're a pal.'

'That I am. Now get thee hence and let a real diplomat strut his stuff.'

He flourished himself into the black soutane with the red piping and the galaxy of unnecessary buttons and left for Reception.

'What's this? Good cop bad cop?'

'Father Barnett has other duties, miss, and—'

'You're a monsignor, right?'

'Eh, yes.'

'Been here long?'

'Fift— Miss, I understand—'

'Detective.'

'Oh.'

'Do you or do you not have a papal envoy here, Monsignor?'

'We don't divulge that kind of information to just anyone.'

'Depends who's asking, doesn't it?'

'Yes, yes, of course it does. Naturally I'll have to see some form of identification. I'm sorry. It's not that I disbelieve you, Detective; it's just how things are done around here.'

'The photograph isn't the best, but ...'

'It's undoubtedly you, Detective Goldberg. Thank you. Now, if you'll just fill in this form ... I know it's tedious, but who knows more about the winding ways of bureaucracy than the police?'

Goldberg's alarm bells were ringing at such a pitch she expected to hear dogs barking. She didn't like this guy, hadn't from the minute he'd walked in, from that half-second inside the door before he'd had time to adjust his diplomat's face. There was something in the way those cold eyes had frisked her while the even teeth were already smiling. Something!

'You know, I think maybe I got the wrong end of the stick here, barking up the wrong tree, so to speak,' she said, and began to back away. Get out, girl, she told herself. He was coming out from behind the desk, his face suddenly over-anxious. Please could she just give him two minutes to check? Don't show your back to him. Where's the goddamn door? The door behind the advancing monsignor opened and she saw the young priest enter. His jaw dropped as her pistol came up.

'Down on your knees, hands on your heads,' she hissed.

The monsignor stiffened. The young guy began to sidle to the desk.

'Press that button, Father,' she said calmly, 'and the monsignor gets his wings. On your knees, both of you – now.'

Her left hand scrabbled behind her and found the brass door handle. 'While you're down there, boys,' she said sweetly, 'say one for me.'

'Walk, don't run,' she murmured, over and over, and the mantra carried her all the way across the drive and through the gates. She turned right, where a few parked cars dotted the kerbside. Better than nothing, she thought, and moved away from the solidity of the boundary wall to walk beside the cars. Where is he? she wondered, as the prickle at the back of her neck began to wind up into an itch. He could be in the park at the other side, tracking her as she walked. He could be hidden in the bushes or lying just beyond that grassy knoll … Don't go there, Goldberg, she cautioned herself. A gateway loomed closer and she saw a lady emerge and slide behind the wheel of a black Mercedes. Goldberg blocked the closing door with one hand and flashed her ID with the other.

'Madam,' she said, to the well-dressed, middle-aged woman, 'I'm a police officer, I need to use your car. Move over.'

The high-powered round shattered the side-mirror on the passenger side and pocked a hole in the gate pillar. No report, Goldberg registered, silencer. The woman was already scooting across the seats and Goldberg was behind the wheel, revving the engine to a roar.

'Better keep your head down, madam,' she growled, and spun them out into the avenue, weaving as she accelerated to make it difficult for the gunman.

'Get your damn head down,' she yelled, yanking the steering wheel hard over and correcting the fishtail motion with a stamp on the accelerator.

'That is not necessary,' the woman replied calmly. 'The windows, they are bulletproof.'

'Well, praise the Lord and pass the basket.' Goldberg grinned. 'You got a cellphone? '

'Of course.'

'Dial this number. Tell Avram we're on the avenue going north from the nunciature and have a shooter.'

She glanced at the rear-view mirror and watched a pick-up truck inflate to fill the mirror as it closed.

'Perp in truck,' she added, and floored the pedal as the woman repeated the message.

'He seemed so calm,' the woman remarked, as a heavily laden lorry loomed and they slid by close enough to register the driver's dental problems.

'Turn right after fifty yards,' she said crisply.

'What?'

'Do it,' she snapped. Again, the tyres protested, spat gravel and gripped to launch into another straight avenue. Behind them, the truck hit the bend, tilted on two wheels and slammed down in pursuit.

'He's getting closer,' the passenger said calmly. 'Take the next right and the first entrance in the wall on your right.' She tapped her phone and spoke tersely in German.

'Lady, that brings us full circle.'

'I know. Trust me. Coming up – now.'

The truck slammed them in the rear and the Mercedes began to spin. Goldberg angled the wheels to follow the spin and used the traction to launch them right before wrestling the gears to power them through the hole in the wall.

'Drive around the house,' the woman directed, and Goldberg obliged, braking in another shower of gravel. She rolled out of the car and was up, feet spread, gun arm extended, when the woman said behind her, 'Security closed the gates after us. Please come inside.'

She turned and climbed the steps to the double doors that opened as if by magic. Goldberg caught up with her hostess at the foot of a broad staircase. She was folding her phone and smiled.

'Avram will be here shortly,' she said.

'Gee, I'd better drop my glass slipper.'

'He sounds like an interesting man, your friend.'

'He's my partner,' Goldberg muttered, as they climbed the stairs.

'And your friend, I think,' the woman said, as she led her into an office. 'Please, sit – Detective Goldberg, isn't it?'

'You have a good memory.'

'Sometimes, when the stakes are high enough.'

They sat in soft armchairs, either side of a heavy mahogany coffee table.

'I'm sorry, I don't know your name,' Goldberg said.

'I am Hannah Klinsmann. Now you, Detective Goldberg, must tell me, as the Americans say, what the hell that was all about.'

Someone knocked politely and a maid entered with a tray, followed closely by Avram. He stood just inside the door and stared at Goldberg. 'How difficult can it be?' he growled. 'You go to the nunciature, you ask, they answer, and you leave.'

'Have they complained?'

'No.'

'Guess why not?'

'You okay?'

'I'm okay.'

'Please, Detective, tea or coffee?'

'Coffee, please. I'm Detective Avram,' he said gruffly.

'And I am Hannah Klinsmann, and now that you are both here, perhaps you could tell me what happened.'

'Well, Ms Klinsmann, we're very grateful—'

'For all your help, especially letting me have the car.'

'But, you see—'

'Sorry about the car, by the way.'

'This is a police matter—'

'And strictly on a need-to-know basis—'

'No offence intended—'

'If you follow me?'

Hannah Klinsmann looked from one to the other.

'I follow you both,' she said. 'Now, I will speak for myself. I left the office at approximately ten a.m. As I sat in my Mercedes car, a young lady identified herself as a police officer and, very politely, requisitioned my vehicle. My mind was made up, rather more quickly than usual, by a shot fired, I believe, from under cover of the foliage in the park opposite. There was no sound of a gunshot so, I presume, the assailant used a silencer. There followed a rather exciting pursuit during which we were rammed by the following vehicle, a tan pick-up truck, registration number JX 75973.'

'I'll get on it,' Avram said, and flipped open his phone.

'My staff are already on it, Detective. I think it's a waste of time. The plates will be untraceable, and the truck will be burned out or disappear.'

'Did you see the driver, Ms Klinsmann?'

'Yes, Detective Goldberg. He was a medium-sized man with a sallow complexion, tight-cropped black hair and high, prominent cheekbones. You don't seem surprised.'

'No – I mean, no, I'm not surprised. You were, eh, extremely calm under pressure.'

'Thank you, but that's not what I meant.'

'Look, Ms Klinsmann—'

'As we've already said—'

'Please!' Hannah Klinsmann raised a palm. 'I don't think I could survive another of your duologues. The last one made me quite dizzy.'

'Sorry,' they said in unison.

'Let us be clear. I want to know what happened – now, please.'

'Ms Klinsmann,' Avram began, 'we are police officers. We can't just divulge that kind of information to anyone. Why don't you ask your embassy to contact Inspector Bernstein and—'

'My dear young man,' she said, placing her cup firmly in its saucer and sitting erect in the armchair. 'I am not just anyone.

I am the German ambassador to Israel. This house has been in my family for generations. I come here from the embassy in Tel Aviv when I need to relax.'

'Oh.'

'Shit.'

'Exactly,' the ambassador said firmly. 'Can I freshen your coffee, Detectives?'

Without waiting for an answer, she began to pour. Avram turned slowly to glare at Goldberg.

'You hijacked the German ambassador.'

'The British were busy.'

'You took the ambassador with you under fire.'

'I woulda taken her anyway. She's a game gal.'

'Thank you, Detective.'

'No, I mean it, you were really great.'

'You are such a good driver.'

'Helluva car.'

'But of course.'

'If you two are finished with the mutual admiration spiel, maybe—'

'Maybe we can what? Detective Avram?'

'Sorry, ma'am … Ambassador.'

'You must teach me how to do that,' Goldberg said admiringly.

'Happy to.'

The ambassador leaned back in her chair.

'Perhaps you are right and I am wrong,' she said quietly. 'There are some matters that cannot be divulged, even to the German ambassador. What can I do to help you?'

'Thank you, ma'am. You could get us out of here quietly.'

'That would be very boring but, yes, Detective Avram, I

can do that. I don't think our marksman friend will be watching, but we will take precautions. Happily we have two Mercedes here at the house. Identical, of course, apart from the rear of mine.'

'Sorry.'

'It was a joke, Detective Goldberg. We Germans do have a sense of humour, you know, even if we take it very seriously. The simplest plan is for one car to exit the front of the grounds and the other the rear. You two will lie on the back seat of one car, covered with a blanket. I hope that is not too much of … an inconvenience?'

Avram cleared his throat.

Goldberg stacked the tray.

Bethlehem

'Where am I?'

The old man paused before placing the tray on the table.

'I cannot tell you that, little brother.'

The affectionate term flooded Omar's eyes and he turned his head away. After a short while, he drew his forearm across them and his voice was steady when he spoke.

'My grandfather's dead, isn't he?'

The old man moved to squat on his haunches before him.

'Yes. It is a great sadness. I knew him. We were friends many years ago.'

'You say "were"?'

The old man sighed and rubbed his face.

'We had different ideas about how to deal with the Israelis and so we parted. I never stopped loving him. He was very brave and wise. Will you eat?'

'I can't eat. I will drink the water.'

'You must eat also. The living must go on living. If they do not, the sacrifice of the dead will have been for nothing.'

Omar began to cry. He screwed up his face and tensed his body to hold back the tears but to no avail. The man leaned forward and tucked his head beneath his chin. The young man thought he smelled like Grandfather and his tears flowed faster.

'A true man knows there is a time for tears,' the man said gently. 'Weep now, little one, while there is time.'

�

Shepherd opened a small box and took out a syringe with a bottle of clear liquid. 'I don't want that,' Omar said.

'You will be in a small space for a long time. It will be dangerous. If you should cry out …'

'I will not cry out. I have done with crying. Tell me about my parents and my brothers.'

'They are in the prison. Your home has been flattened. It is what the Israelis do.'

'And Professor Sharawi's wife and daughter?'

'Under house arrest.'

'Why am I here?'

'The Israelis are looking for you. I am taking you to someone who will explain everything to you.'

Omar shook his head in disbelief.

'Please leave me now. I wish to sleep.'

Military Outpost, the Wall

Goliath sat on the edge of the bare mattress and cleaned his weapon. Only his hands were involved in the process, the stubby, manicured fingers doing automatically what they had been trained to do until they did it in the dark and under fire with the same detached precision. He wondered if that reflexive response would spread like a cancer to other areas of the body until the entire organism began to function on instinct. 'Reflection is what separates us from the animals,' the voice of the squad philosopher echoed in his head. He couldn't recall the soldier's name or even the squad name he had been given. It was some kind of bird, he thought. The stillness of his hands brought him back. He checked the magazine before slapping it home, then swung the weapon into the firing position and checked the scope. The long canvas sheath he had laid out on the bed swallowed the weapon and he pressed home the brass fasteners. 'Zips and sand don't mix, soldier.' Who had said that? Probably the squad commander, he thought, the most efficient fighting machine he had ever served under. Sometimes he wished he had killed him when he'd had the chance. To deflect that thought, he let his eyes quarter the tidied room until they found the book that had slipped behind the bedside locker. He took the well-worn copy of the Qur'an and put it into the small front pocket of his rucksack for ease of access. Four seconds to the knock, he estimated.

The knock on the door came five seconds later.

That kind of day, Goliath thought.

'Come in.'

The new recruit stopped just inside the door, his hands hanging at his sides in plain view.

'You're learning,' Goliath grunted.

'I – I just came to say good luck, Captain.'

The captain nodded his thanks.

'Wall duty isn't what you wanted, is it, soldier?'

'No, sir.'

'The Wall is just a different kind of front line,' Goliath continued softly. 'Both sides, people and soldiers, are on a hair trigger. Every rough search, every small disrespect adds an ounce of pressure to that hair until an ordinary man with a wife and kids can't take it any more and becomes something else.'

'Do you mean the men in the queue, Captain?'

'Yes, and you. Did you ever shoot a man, soldier?'

'No, sir, never.'

'In a war, "never" means "so far". I hope you never do. But you can kill a man a little every day without shooting him. Understand?'

'I ... I think I do, sir.'

The new recruit followed Goliath to the guardroom, keeping his distance, planting his feet firmly on the floor. He was learning.

⟡

The guardroom smelled of resentment. The card players sat at their usual table, the cards fanned out before them, untouched. Some soldiers, who normally took queue duty at this time, sat on the edge of plastic chairs or shuffled near the window, bulked up in full duty kit. All dressed up and nowhere to go, Goliath thought. Bethlehem was in lockdown. 'Purgatory is a waiting room,' his squad companion with the bird's name had concluded.

'They want you,' the sergeant said.

The sergeant's small eyes flickered and found purchase somewhere to the left of Goliath's shoulder. Goliath turned his back on him and stared appraisingly at the two civilians. The clothes told him nothing. Men like them didn't clothe themselves: they covered themselves. Their sartorial choice, he thought grimly, had long ago been refined to clean or dirty, damp or dry. He tried the eyes and read nothing there, no anger, fear or any of the other normal emotions – it wasn't that they were concealed, just absent. Some men had the eyes of people who stack shelves or shift rubbish for a living, people whose real lives are somewhere else. These men had the hard, emotionless eyes of people who had spent years working in an abattoir. He walked outside, letting the door slam behind him.

ಬಿೋಚ

Goliath watched the two-tone surface of the Dead Sea emerge from the heat-haze, the dull metal of the northern section contrasting with the vivid turquoise of the evaporation pans at the other end. He craned his neck to catch a glimpse of Jericho as the helicopter angled to the left and set a course parallel to the Jordan river. Mount Nebo, where Moses had caught his first glimpse of the Promised Land, jutted up to the right. From this altitude, Goliath thought, it didn't look very promising. He wondered if that was why Moses had stayed on the mountain. Before him the thin blue ribbon of the river curled down the Perspex window. The plains, on either side, were bracketed with green squares, cultivated fields that mottled both banks of the river valley. The guardroom at the Wall had been an almost book-free zone but a coverless and dated copy of *National Geographic* had temporarily sated his thirst for knowledge. He remembered a contributor noting that Israel and Jordan both drank from the Jordan river and were consequently sucking the Dead Sea dry.

He tuned his hearing to a frequency below the racket of the rotors and concluded that his minders in the back were taking turns sleeping. That was something he'd learned to do with the squad, he remembered. Old tapes, soldier, he chided himself. Nazareth relieved the monotony of brown to his left and the cool blue of the Sea of Galilee beckoned in the distance. It would be left to Tiberias, where kids rode the water-chutes and Christian pilgrims embarked on the 'apostle' boats to marvel at the water Jesus walked on, or right to a different world, the other Israel.

The helicopter banked right and the high ramparts of the Golan humped up over the pilot's shoulder. The Six Day War had brought the Golan Heights back into the Israeli fold and trapped more than half a million Arabs on the wrong side of the new border. Almost an equal number of Jews lived down there, Ashkenazim of European origin, Sephardic from North Africa and the Middle East, Jews from America, Iraq, the Caucasus and Russia. There were even black Jews from Ethiopia. Some were ultra-religious and some so secular they wouldn't know the inside of a synagogue if it fell on them. Goliath was aware, from various sorties the squad had made into Galilee, that the glue that bound this disparate band of Jews together was the real or perceived threat they saw in their Druze and Muslim neighbours.

'Ninety-five per cent of the people here co-operate reasonably peacefully,' the commander had informed the squad. 'We're here to keep an eye on the five per cent, the five in a hundred, who take things beyond talking ill of their neighbours to killing them.'

Goliath knew now that statistics always boiled down to one. It took just one kid in a blue Opel car packed with explosives, gas canisters and a bag of eightpenny nails to target a local bus and bring crowds on the streets shouting, 'Maret la Mavim' – Kill the Arabs. The snow-streaked enormity of Mount Hermon broke through his reverie and, as if in solidarity with him, the helicopter baulked at the nine-thousand-foot hurdle and began to descend.

The two-storey farmhouse shone in the dull hillside, the whitewashed walls reflecting the sunlight. Scattered randomly around it, he saw the gapped teeth of ruined dwellings, destroyed in 1967 when more than seventy thousand Arabs had fled before the Israeli expansion. The helicopter settled close enough to a small olive grove to startle the sombre green leaves into showing their pale underskirts. One of the minders pointed to a path that meandered through a vineyard. 'Roof,' he said, and turned away to light a cigarette. Goliath checked for security as he negotiated the path and saw no one. He rated them ten out of ten.

The old woman swept the khamsin-borne red dust across the tiles with a defeated-looking broom. He judged her to be on the charitable side of five feet tall. She wore a khaki shirt and a pair of khaki trousers tucked into well-worn hiking boots. His eyes roved over the silver stubble on her head and he wondered if she was one of those ultra-Orthodox women who shaved her hair and kept her good wig in the kitchen drawer for special occasions. She stroked a few more times with the broom before giving up and leaning it against the low wall that hemmed the tiled roof.

'The dust,' she said, over her shoulder, as she looked east from the parapet, 'is just another nuisance sent by the Syrians to try us. I suppose we should be grateful. Before the Six Day War, the Syrians sat up there on the Golan Heights in their concrete bunkers and amused themselves by shelling our farmers in the Hula valley. When they were especially bored, they would take turns at knocking a farmer from his tractor with a high-powered rifle. Bad times,' she said, almost to herself, 'bad times for everyone. Now we have listening posts up there which can hear them sneeze in Damascus.'

'I think it puzzled them when we didn't leave. They couldn't understand why we buried our dead, filled in the craters and put another farmer on the tractor the next day. They never quite grasped the fact that we couldn't leave – we had nowhere else to go.'

She sat on a plastic chair and gestured for him to sit on the one that faced it from the other side of a plastic table. She looked at Goliath for the first time and he was struck by the intensity of her gaze.

'You must excuse me,' she murmured. 'I should have welcomed you to Nimrod. A fitting setting for a mighty hunter, wouldn't you agree?'

'That would depend on which one of us is the hunter, madam,' Goliath said coolly.

She clasped her gnarled hands on the tabletop.

'I am the director of Mossad, Captain,' she said quietly. 'A very small number of people know that. Should you ever feel tempted to reveal it to anyone and succumb to that temptation, then that small number will be reduced by one. As a soldier, you will accept that we are all expendable in the service of the nation.'

'I've always accepted that one of the strongest reasons for creating our nation was to ensure that no one would ever be expendable again, Director.'

She held his gaze for a moment, then dropped her eyes to a folder on the table and flicked it open at the back page. He watched her head move from right to left over the document and wondered what his dossier looked like in Hebrew.

'It seems your reputation as a hunter has been somewhat tarnished of late, Captain. This report from the Wall states that you interrogated a young man and released him. You were subsequently informed that he was to be apprehended or eliminated. Despite this, you refused permission for a knock-down, choosing to pursue and lose him yourself. Is that a fair summary?'

'Yes, except for "interrogate". I did not interrogate him, I questioned him.'

'And your questioning led you to what conclusion?'

'That he was, as he claimed to be, a student of hydrology and posed no threat to state security.'

'Because he had a piece of paper signed by a man who is now held by state security?'

'No, because of the way he spoke … about water. It was a judgement call and I stand by it.'

'Do you think your reading of the Qur'an might have influenced your judgement, Captain?'

'Yes, as a matter of fact, I do. As I think it was influenced by my reading of the Torah, the Talmud and the army manual on the interrogation of suspects.'

She sat back and looked at him searchingly.

'As it happens, you were right, Captain. Our intelligence is that the young man is not and never has been a terrorist. In fact, he has no previous connection with terrorists.'

'The document faxed to the Wall said there was evidence linking him to the Har Homa shelling.'

'Planted, we are almost certain.'

'You said he had no previous connection with terrorists?'

'I did. We think someone may be trying to use him, groom him in—'

'Groomer.'

'Yes, the man the sergeant brought to your attention at the Wall, the man you saw with the boy before he disappeared. We want you to find this Omar, Captain, and protect him.'

'From whom?'

'From anyone who might harm him or compromise him. We think he will lead us to others.'

'Like a lamb that is led to the slaughter …'

'Captain, think for a minute about where you are. You are sitting less than sixty miles from Damascus, the capital of Syria. To get here, you had to fly on one side of the Jordan river because our marginally less hostile neighbour would have shot you down on the other. If your pilot had overshot Nimrod by a mere five miles you would have been in Lebanese air space. We are a small nation with our backs to the Mediterranean and bordered on three sides by hostile nations. And those are just the enemies we can see. From this roof you can see two Druze villages where the people dream of our disappearance. Dotted in the hills around us are Arabs, even Bedouin, who share that dream, not all of them but enough to keep us on a permanent war footing. When we identify the people who do more than dream, who strike at us with bombs and bullets, what do we do?'

'We hunt and kill them.'

'Yes. We send search-and-destroy squads, Phantom bombers,

gunships, drones. We kill them any way we can. The finger that pulls the trigger, the hand that plants the bomb can be amputated, but the men and the money behind those people recruit a new gunman, a new bomber.'

'People like Groomer.'

'Or whoever controls him. We know him also as Shepherd. We'll kill him, of course, but not yet. Nothing must happen to alert our real targets. I must tell you, Captain, that Mossad is not the only arm of the security services involved in this affair. Unfortunately, the Jerusalem police are investigating some criminal activity that may involve persons we have an interest in. It is possible that the goals of the police will conflict with ours and they refuse to withdraw. Should the two detectives involved compromise our operation, they must be eliminated.'

She took two photographs from the file and placed them before him. Goliath saw only one and his face became stony.

'I understand you reported your former Special Forces commander for the torture and murder of a terrorist,' she said.

'I did.'

'He was court-martialled and dismissed from the army. Did you consider his punishment too lenient?'

'I did … at the time.'

'Yes, he has been … punished since, but you know of that. You may have to kill him.'

Goliath didn't reply. He stared at the photograph of his former commander, mentor and friend, Ari Avram.

Piazza Spagna, Rome
Giuseppe Fermi strolled along the via Condetti and inhaled with pleasure as he passed the Caffè Greco. Keats, Byron and

Goethe had all sipped the famous brew in the establishment, founded by a Greek. Don't forget Liszt, Wagner and Bizet, he reminded himself. He wondered what eccentric former patrons like Casanova and Ludwig, the mad King of Bavaria, would have made of the early-morning patrons who stood in the crowded foyer sipping espressos before rushing about their business.

The Piazza Spagna never failed to raise his spirits and he savoured the tall, shuttered houses painted in muted shades of ochre, cream and russet. As an amateur historian, he loved the layered story of Rome, and the Spagna, shaped like a crooked bow-tie, had been the haunt of wealthy tourists as far back as the seventeenth century. The Spanish ambassador to the Holy See had lived here and the area around the piazza had been deemed Spanish territory. He was amused to think that the tourists who flocked here from all corners of the globe might well have been dragooned into the Spanish army had they come a few centuries earlier.

Earlier that morning he had kissed what his mischievous daughter called 'the two other women in his life' goodbye. Cybele and Sister Eileen were off to meet Dr Emilia Spenza who ran a women's refuge in Trastevere. The good doctor had long been looking for an extra female medic to share her workload and Eileen longed to be useful. Cybele, as usual, was the catalyst who would effect change for both women. His smile faltered as he remembered Monsignor Sebastiano Spenza, brother to Emilia, who had been executed in the Colosseum by the agent of the Remnant. The wheel turns, he thought, and his optimism reasserted itself.

He perched on the rim of the Fontana della Barcaccia, at the foot of the Spanish Steps. It was still a little early for the young people to flirt, preen or bask along the famous steps and only pigeons fussed there, like the scolding grandmothers of his childhood. The tall young woman paused to consult her guidebook before easing herself onto the rim of the fountain, a few feet away from the detective. She tilted back her head and stretched her legs – long, he noted, clad in tan slacks. She wore a cream blouse under a fawn linen jacket, loose enough to conceal the shoulder holster from any casual observer. Reflections from the fountain shimmered over a strong profile.

'Can this possibly be by Bernini, Signor?' she enquired, gesturing at the fountain.

'Oh, yes, Signorina,' he replied, his eyes still scanning the piazza. 'I believe it is. But the scholars argue whether it is by Gian Lorenzo Bernini or by his father, Pietro.'

'I suspect you have an opinion on this, Signor.'

'As I have on most things, Signorina.'

She smiled and nodded.

'I believe it is the creation of Pietro, the old man, for two reasons. The first is that the boat in the centre of the fontana, from which it gets its name – Barcaccia – is leaky and useless.'

'And the second reason?'

'The water comes from an old aqueduct, Signorina. There is not enough pressure for a big fountain, like the ones in the Piazza Navona. So I would guess it is the work of an elderly artist for an elderly Barberini pope.'

'Thank you, Signor, that was most enlightening. Now, if you'll excuse me, I think it's time for tea.'

She sat at a small table in the rear of Babington's Tea Rooms, framed by a window that made a perfect silhouette of her profile while effectively dazzling anyone who might glance her way for more than a moment. Giuseppe was impressed by her professionalism. As he eased himself into the other chair, he remarked, 'You are most certainly your father's daughter, Signorina.'

'Antonio is most certainly my father, Signor,' she replied, and poured him a cup of Earl Grey.

'It's been a long time, Signorina. How did you recognise me?'

'I think you'd better call me Antonella, Signor Fermi. My father said you would sit on the rim of the fountain like a teenager. He said you would seem dreamy and abstracted yet miss nothing and ...'

'And?'

'And you would know more about everything than was good for you.'

'My old friend Antonio knows me only too well,' he said, and coughed into his handkerchief to conceal the catch in his voice. 'How was the dig in Umbria?' he asked abruptly.

Taking her cue from his brisk businesslike tone, she answered in a formal voice:

'There were a number of interesting finds, Signor – the remains of a male in the latrines, shot in the head, eh, in situ, if you'll pardon the pun.'

'You are most certainly your father's daughter,' he said wryly, and sipped his tea.

'The quality and style of clothing suggested an American,' she continued. 'This was reinforced by a tattoo on the right shoulder, which indicated that the deceased may have served in the American armed forces. There were tyremarks in the picnic area that matched those taken outside the Santa Lucia convent.'

'*Brava.*' He toasted her with his cup.

'It makes things easier for Forensics when criminals

accelerate from the scene of a crime,' she said modestly. 'The bin in the picnic area yielded two sets of clothing. The male set comprised plain black trousers and white shirt, scarlet socks and black slip-on shoes. The shirt collar exhibited a small bloodstain. Interpol have drawn a blank on the blood.'

'I don't suppose they have the College of Cardinals on file,' Fermi grunted. 'And the other set of clothing?'

'A female religious habit of the Franciscan sisters on Cenci Street.'

'Brother Sun, Sister Assassin,' Fermi murmured.

'Pardon?'

'Sorry, Antonella, I tend to indulge in stream of consciousness.'

'My father mentioned that.'

'Yes, I'm sure he did. I tried his patience more than once … Now, where were we? In summary, there is a body, presumably an expendable member of the group so, most probably, the driver. There is a blood spot on the shirt collar, which means Thomas was most likely shot with some kind of anaesthetic dart. Neither the body nor the clothing is concealed. Why not, Antonella?'

She leaned back into the shadows as if weighing her answer.

'In recent times, at certain of our airports, there are people who have joined the usual plane-watchers outside the perimeter fences. They come from various human-rights groups who monitor certain aircraft chartered by the US military.'

Fermi nodded to confirm he understood the meaning camouflaged in her terminology.

'We have some of our own people among them, of course. A report from Florence details the arrival and departure of a

US Hercules aircraft. The observer recorded the embarkation of a Caucasian female lieutenant and an African-American flight assistant.'

'Destination?'

'Our information is that the aircraft flew to Israel.'

Detective Fermi folded his napkin and placed it on the table.

'Please tell your father I am in his debt,' he said formally.

'He said you'd say that, too,' she said, gathering up her guidebook. 'He said to tell you there is no owing between friends. He said you told him that after Caracalla.'

She paused, and he could read the question in her eyes.

'He'll tell you what that means himself, Antonella,' he said gently. 'When he's ready.'

Her eyes misted, and as he extended his hand, she leaned forward and kissed him lightly on both cheeks.

'My mother and I have never forgotten, Uncle Seppi,' she said huskily.

He watched her walk away until she was hidden by the turn of the stairs before sitting and refilling his cup. Absently, he stirred and sipped the tepid tea.

They had been unlikely partners, the handsome bon viveur and the bookish Giuseppe. Antonio had been the powerhouse of the partnership, always bristling with energy and enthusiasm, always eager to kick down doors and take risks. Giuseppe, on the other hand, had been the forensic, analytical one, the one who calculated the odds and rarely acted on impulse. That innate caution had informed his every move that night in Caracalla. It hadn't been enough to save Antonio. The bullet intended for the Prime Minister had lodged in Antonio's spine and the Red Brigade would learn from that experience to kidnap and kill an Italian prime minister later. What had once been a vivid and detailed memory of that night had faded with the passage of time. Giuseppe could remember pacing the empty stage, before the arrival of the audience, checking for lines of fire to where the Prime Minister would sit. Typically, Antonio was flouting regulations with another cigarette and teasing his partner.

'C'mon, Seppi, what's so wonderful about opera? The fat lady sings, dies, sings, dies …'

'You're a barbarian, Toni. You wouldn't know an aria from your—'

'Please, Seppi, explain to me why you must know the history of the Caracalla amphitheatre all the way back to the third century to stop someone taking a pot-shot at the Prime Minister.'

It hadn't. Giuseppe's knowledge of the opera *Aida* led him to believe an assassin was more likely to strike at the beginning of the Grand March when the music built up in triumphal volume and live elephants rumbled onto the stage. Alone among the thousands in the audience that night, he was not watching the action. At the moment when the audience drew a collective breath at the familiar first bars of the Grand March, he had seen a sudden commotion erupt at a small table far back on the left side of the amphitheatre. He was already drawing his weapon and pivoting to the right from where, instinct told him, the shot would be fired. He opened his mouth to shout a warning and everything began to run at half speed. In his peripheral vision, he saw the conductor begin the uppercut movement that would bring the cymbals together and had known it was too late. He swung his head to see Antonio register his partner's alarm and begin to launch himself at the Prime Minister. The shot came like some dissonant percussion and he watched the bodies tumble to the floor, Antonio's curled protectively around that of the politician. Armed police were already wading through the panicked opera-goers, following the shot to its source, swamping a young man and kicking him senseless among the smashed wine bottles and scattered food.

'Don't touch him! Don't touch him!' the detective had screamed at the people who moved tentatively towards the stricken Antonio. He had pointed the gun steadily at the Prime Minister's own paramedics until they deserted the shocked dignitary and strapped Antonio to a stretcher. They had run it to the helipad where the mad gunman had cleared a helicopter of journalists so that they got Antonio to Santo Spiritu in time to save his life.

Giuseppe sighed and held the napkin to his forehead. The memory of the aftermath was all too clear. There had been a backlash of complaints from the paramedics and the press, and only the gracious intervention of the Prime Minister had kept him out of jail and in his job. And Antonio? Giuseppe remembered the long nights in the hospital waiting room with Francesca as her husband fought his way back to life, then wanted to lose it when he discovered just how limited that life would be. There were even longer nights when he talked his partner through the dark depressions, and walked the floor of their apartment with the baby Antonella while Francesca and her husband sobbed in the other room, sifting through the shattered pieces of their lives trying to find enough to make continuing worthwhile. He had held the baby's head nestled under his chin as he paced the apartment, crooning the tunes of operatic arias into her tiny ear, every opera in his repertoire except *Aida*. And then Cybele had come to take him home, knowing, before he did, that there was a time for friends to leave. Some of the old normality had returned to their relationship but there was too much in Giuseppe that reminded Antonio of what he'd lost and they'd grown apart. Giuseppe knew that Antonio had found a position in Intelligence where his fine brain more than compensated for his useless legs. He knew Antonella had followed in her father's footsteps and excelled in forensics. He knew that whatever he asked of them would be given and so it had been. For both their sakes, they couldn't afford to meet, even casually, especially on this matter. Antonella had been the go-between.

'Will there be anything else, Signor?' the waiter asked cautiously.

Giuseppe Fermi, amateur historian, archaeologist, opera buff and lover of spaghetti westerns, never missed a beat.

'You bet your bottom dollar, hombre,' he growled, and left to phone Mal O'Donnell.

The O'Donnell Apartment, New York
'Hi, Tony, it's Mal.'

'There's a blue moon? I'm gonna buy big in the lottery.'

'Very funny, Tony. Now, listen up, pilgrim, I gotta job for you.'

'Three things, Mal. One, I don't do that western thing any more, okay? I've moved on – I'm more a Crouching Tiger kinda guy these days – more culturally appropriate, ya know, me being half-Chinese 'n' all. Thing number two, I gotta job and I'd like to keep it, so no more sitting in my damp underwear while you insult the Mafia. No more swapping Shakespeare with generals before they blow their brains out. No more—'

'Tony! You remember Michael Flaherty?'

'The priest! Listen, Mal, if there's one guy scarier than you in this world—'

'They're going to kill him, Tony.'

'Why didn't ya say so?'

'I just did. Okay, now, all you have to do is sit at the computer. You know the thing that looks like a television? You call up all the stuff we worked on under 'South of the Border' and you send it to this email address. Get a pen, Tony. Memorise the address and eat the paper.'

'Mal, I … Jeez, I mean they can trace things like that. What—'

'Tony, clear your mind of guys running in the bamboo forest. The guy at the other end talks to God and God doesn't dare interrupt.'

'You saw the movie, Mal. Wow! You actually saw *House of Flying* …? Mal? Mal!'

ℬℭ

'Terence, it's Mal O'Donnell.'

'It wasn't me.'

'Terence, I just—'

'No, no and no, Detective. All that is behind me. I've been to the top of the mountain, seen the light and been washed in the Blood of the Lamb, so—'

'I want you to do a little hacking for me.'

'What? Wash out your mouth. Get thee behind m—'

'You'll love it.'

'"So saith the serpent unto Eve and she did succumb to his blandishments and—" What is it?'

'Nah, maybe you're right. Now that you've gone legit, working for the bank and all, maybe you can't—'

"Can't' is not a word in my vocabulary, Detective. There is no 'can't' in cyberspace.'

'Still, you know what they say, use it or lose it. You've been out of the loop too long. Maybe the old black magic doesn't weave so well no more.'

'Don't make me mad, Detective. You know I can hook you up to the talking clock in Timbuktu until your phone bill comes in its very own truck. I can—'

'Okay, okay. I just wanted to be sure the old hunger was still there. Heck, if the best don't practise and keep the hand in—'

'Talking clock, Detective, twenty-four/seven.'

'You've convinced me. Two things to do and the first is easy. Some time around now a file marked 'South of the Border' should be coming up in your mailbox. I want you to send it to Congressman Fox in Washington.'

'Done.'

'The second thing is a bit more challenging. You sure you can—'

'Talking clock twenty-four/seven. Fox News on every channel, for ever, Detective, and a lifetime subscription to *The Watchtower*. You know I can make this happen. So, what d'you want me to do?'

'I want you to haunt a ghost.'

CIA Headquarters, Washington DC
The red light blinked alive and burned balefully on Catherine De Lancy's desk.

'Yes, Mr Director.'

'There's a problem with the phone. Can you get someone from Maintenance?'

She tapped on the door and entered. 'May I?' Catherine leaned across and pressed the speaker button. A tangled Australian accent filled the room.

'It's twelve midnight in the Kakadu region of north-western Australia, the top end of Down Under.'

'How extraordinary! I'll call Maintenance from my phone, sir.'

'Turn that thing off before you go.'

'Yes, sir.'

The Ghost swivelled away from the offending instrument and booted up his computer.

'Catherine!'

The bellow from the inner sanctum snapped every head from their consoles in the outer office. At a glance from Ms De Lancy, they bowed in unison. As she made her way to the door, the sudden hush behind her slowed her steps.

'What is it?' she asked.

'Ms De Lancy.'

'Yes, Charlotte?' God, the girl talked like she had a mouthful of molasses.

'Ms De Lancy, you need to come and see this, ma'am.'

Charlotte's usually expressionless face was working its slow way to a scowl, and Catherine felt her stomach tighten. A manager manages, she reminded herself, and took up a position behind Charlotte's ample shoulder.

'Now, what seems to be—'

Benson's voice boomed from his office.

'Catherine, get the hell in here.'

She couldn't tear her eyes off the cartoon ghost that wafted across Charlotte's screen. 'What is that ... thing?' she hissed.

'Why, it's Casper the Ghost, Ms De Lancy,' Charlotte drawled. Then her eyes began to widen in shock. 'He's not the, eh, real thing, ma'am; he's just one of those cartoons.'

'That will be enough, Charlotte,' Catherine said. She walked around the desk and clapped her hands for attention. 'Everybody else, log off and close down, now.'

They bowed to obey. Only Charlotte stayed upright, staring over Catherine's shoulder.

'Oh, Lordy.' The big girl quivered.

Catherine faced the Director.

'We have a malfunction—'

'In my office, now,' he grated, and turned on his heel.

It took every last ounce of her self-control to stand calmly before his desk as the speakerphone drawled out the time in some god-awful part of Australia and two newscasters exchanged inanities on the large television screen. Benson thumbed the remote only to have the carefully coiffed mannequins come back, smiling, again and again. Reluctantly, her eyes switched to the computer console on his desk. The ghost figure wafted left and right across the screen. On the director's computer, the little wraith emitted an eerie 'whoo' sound that was followed immediately by a burst of manic laughter.

'I – I don't understand, Director.'

'Find someone who does,' he said, and shut down the appliances.

In the abrupt silence, she imagined she could hear her own heartbeat.

The O'Donnell Apartment, New York

'Tell him it's Mal O'Donnell … Yes. I understand that when you say he's unavailable. it's because you've never heard of me and I don't exist on the list you've just checked. That's okay, I know you're just doing your job. Now, before we move on to the next stage where I become insistent and confirm your suspicions that you're dealing with a nut, consider this. How did I get this number? All you gotta do is say, "Congressman, there's a Mal O'Donnell on the line." If he says, "Mal who?" hang up … Yes, I'll hold …

'Congressman, is this a secure line? … Okay. The computer in your office is about to receive material that is strictly for your eyes only … Oh, yes, it can happen, Congressman … Let's just say he's a hacker of my acquaintance. Everything else is need-to-know and you're better off not knowin'. You'll read it now and I'll be by later. Where can we meet?'

CIA Headquarters, Washington DC

It took her just thirty minutes to send the girls packing and rescue the maintenance man from the wrath of the director.

'Ev'thin' 'lectrical workin' jus' fine, Ms De Lancy,' he whined, as he trailed her to the door of the outer office. 'I ain't no computer whiz, 'lectrical what I do 'n' there ain't no call for name callin'.'

'Thank you, Mr Lucas,' she said. 'I'm sure you did everything you could. It was good of you to come so promptly.'

'Well, thank you, Ms De Lancy. Anythin' I can ever do to oblige you, ma'am, you know you just gotta say 'n'—'

'I know that, Mr Lucas,' she interrupted. 'Please, excuse the director – he's under a lot of strain, right now.'

'Maybe he is 'n' maybe he ain't. All I'm sayin' is manners don't hurt none.'

'Yes, of course,' she soothed, and closed the door behind him. Plan B, she thought and plucked up the telephone from the nearest desk.

'The time in Kak—'

'Fuck!' She dropped it back on its cradle.

∞∞

'We've got a hacker, sir. A hacker is—'

'I know what a hacker is, Agent Howard. Are you telling me some nerdy kid is doing this?'

'Can't say it's a kid for certain, sir, but it could well be. Things some of these kids get into. I hear the Pentagon's been hit a few times. NASA's had some near misses. Jeez, last time some crazy kid threatened to land a space shuttle in Burkino Faso or some such 'cause his momma had grounded him and he was pissed. Sorry, sir.'

'This is all very … instructive, Agent. What happens when we trace them?'

'Well, it depends, Director. Most of them are just kids and all, so they go to juvie court and get some kind of community-service time.'

'And the others?'

'Pardon?'

'You said most of them. What happens to the others?'

'Well, if they're good enough, we give them a choice, sir – jail or job.'

'We hire them?'

'Yes, sir.'

The O'Donnell Apartment, New York

'Hanny, I'm goin' to Washington.'

'Whatever you say, Mr Smith.'

'You're showin' your age, Hanny.'

'The black-and-white movies were better, Mal. They stuck to the script, no colourful distractions. Get my drift?'

'Subtle and you are strangers, Hanny. If your drift was any deeper, they'd be sendin' the dog with the brandy barrel.'

'This another need-to-know, Mal?'

'Yeah.'

She sat at the other side of the kitchen table – sat there until his eyes had exhausted all the alternative focal points in the small room and returned to hers.

'I need to know something, Mal, even if it's not the whole truth, so help me, God. Otherwise I start imagining and, believe me, old lad, I can imagine far worse than you could ever tell me.'

He thought she looked tired and scared, and it burned him. Hanny didn't do scared, not even when a crazy, knife-wielding priest came through the front door that time. Unless, of course, it involved Michael Flaherty and then Hanny's wise-cracking, ball-busting schlep began to lose the beat.

'I didn't want to scare you, Hanny.'

'You been scaring me for almost fifty years, old man. It's been one of the best things. And I'm still here, ain't I? There was only me and you for a lot of those years, Mal. We got, well, I suppose you could say we got comfortable. Then Michael turned up at our door and … I never wanted him to leave. Oh, I'm over that now. I don't own him, never did. But once you feel that way about someone, everything changes. It's not comfortable any more but it's—'

'I know, Hanny.'

'I guess you do. Otherwise, you wouldn't be fartin' about makin' all those calls to Tony and the congressman and Whatsisface, the computer fella.'

'Hanny!'

'The walls are thin, Mal. Think I put on a jazz record every time you start in on the phone? Now, tell me, what are we going to do?'

'We?'

'God almighty, deaf and slow – my mother warned me.'

'We're going to rattle someone's chains, Hanny.'

CIA Headquarters, Washington DC

Catherine held the door as Agent Howard ushered a young man into the director's office. He had a scholar's stoop that made his height difficult to determine and two black eyes that shifted nervously in an alabaster face. Black, curly hair overflowed his large head and foamed at the neck of his T-shirt. The logo on the front declared that somebody's cat was dead. As he was manoeuvred to the edge of the director's desk, she saw that the logo on the back contradicted that.

'No handshake,' the agent said hurriedly. 'Timothy doesn't like to be touched.'

'Just wind him up and get him working,' Benson growled. He gathered papers from his desk and swept them into a briefcase. ooooo'I'll be at the house,' he muttered, and left.

'Would you like something to drink, Timothy?' Catherine asked.

The black eyes bounced left and right a few times. 'Coke … please,' he mumbled.

When she returned with the tumbler, the agent was sitting motionless, out of sight of his charge. His eye caught hers and he made a slight patting gesture with his hand. She slowed her walk and placed the glass on the desk within Timothy's reach. She was familiar with some of the expressions popular among young people and 'in the zone' came to mind when she read his face. She sat quietly to the left of the watchful agent where she had an unobstructed view of the computer screen and Timothy's profile.

She thought it was like the piano recital her friend Dora had dragged her to some weeks before. The audience then had been cowed into silence as the latest wunderkind had stepped up to the dais and taken his seat before the gleaming Steinway. The pragmatic office manager in Catherine had fought against the urge to holler, 'Just play the damn thing, fella. If it's what you do, do it, for God's sake. Enough of the mystique, already.' Mystique, she knew from her job, was a colourless, odourless gas, exuded by people in power simply to promote that power. Under its insidious influence, she knew high-flying people who stepped into Benson's office and seemed to have left their brains in the foyer, bright people who became uncritical and compliant in the presence of the director, people like … Like you, Catherine, a small, inner voice suggested. Like hell, she thought fiercely, and was immediately aware that she protested too much.

Timothy raised his hands and long delicate fingers danced over the keyboard. The cartoon ghost froze on the computer screen. Catherine saw the owl-eyes widen, then the figure spun in a slow circle while two bony hands materialised to lift its cloak and flash its cartoon ass. Timothy stood up abruptly, gathered his Coke and went to sip it at the window.

Catherine raised an eyebrow at the agent, who shook his head. She sat back in the chair and waited. Timothy returned to the computer and played another arpeggio on the keys. The cartoon ghost blinked out and Catherine breathed a huge sigh of relief. She looked triumphantly at the agent. His expression wilted her smile and spun her head back to the computer. Pages of text were rolling up the console before the young man's impassive face. She hurried to stand at his shoulder.

'Oh, my God!'

Her lips formed the words but no words escaped her. With a sudden push, she swivelled Timothy away from the screen.

'Get him out of here,' she barked at the agent.

She sat in the still-warm chair and scanned the pages as they unspooled. It was all there, details of the top secret special unit recruited by Major Devane for insertion into Colombia, details of the bloodletting initiated by their selective strikes against the drug lords and their families, graphic details of garrottings, crucifixions and summary executions designed to destroy the cohesion of the cartel and allow another agency to control the flow of white powder. Her eyes widened as the screen revealed the fate of the Special Forces unit that had been parachuted in to hunt the hunters, and the subsequent rescue, repatriation and confinement of the only survivor, Michael Flaherty. Hardly breathing, she absorbed the minutes of the meetings convened by a committee to determine the fate of Michael Flaherty, and the terse memos that chronicled the violent deaths of the renegade major and his assistant on an Irish island. With mounting revulsion, she read the bloodless prose reporting the death by suicide of the general deemed responsible for the entire operation. She clicked the mouse and the screen went blessedly blank. Take it as a given, she told herself. This material is ready to roll on every screen in the office. Catherine breathed a prayer of thanks to whichever divine mentor had prompted her to evacuate the staff. Which left only Agent Howard and Timothy.

The young man sat slack-faced and unmoving beside the agent in the outer office. She took the third chair and a deep, steadying breath.

'Timothy, can you please tell me what's happening?'

The darting black eyes were suddenly still, as if he had processed her request.

'Someone has planted a virus in your computer system,' he said calmly, and his eyes flickered again as if his thought processes had been unplugged.

'Who did this, Timothy?'

'Untraceable.'

'Can you fix it?'

'Yes.'

'How long?'

'Twenty-four hours.'

She switched her attention to the agent.

'Did you see any of the stuff that came through?'

'No, ma'am.'

'Sure?'

'Timothy was blocking my view of the screen, ma'am.'

'I believe you,' she said, and the big man flinched.

'Now, the question is: how much does our young friend here remember of what he read?'

'Our young friend remembers all of it, ma'am,' Timothy said quietly, 'but he doesn't comprehend it.'

The agent's face had lost its colour.

'Do you understand the phrase need-to-know, Timothy?' she asked softly.

'Yes, ma'am.'

'Good. The material you've seen is classified, understand?' He nodded.

'If anyone, and I mean anyone, should ask you what you saw, you must say you saw nothing.'

'You – you mean tell a lie?'

'I mean need-to-know, Timothy. The only people who need to know what this is about are right here.'

'Yes, ma'am.'

The agent was dabbing his eyes with a very large handkerchief. He looked blearily at her when she spoke and she was sickened by the fear in those eyes. 'Listen carefully,' she said. 'I want you to stay with Timothy.'

Her cellphone buzzed and she saw her own shock mirrored in the man with the frightened eyes.

'Yes, Director. Everything's fine, sir. Timothy says he can clean out the virus in twenty-four hours … Yes, sir, 'fraid so. I thought he could start right now and Agent Howard could stay with him … Yes, of course, sir. I'll be ready.'

She folded the phone and slipped it into her jacket pocket.

'The director would like you to continue, gentlemen,' she said.

The agent nodded, his eyes never leaving her face. She inclined her head and he followed her into the corridor.

'It is imperative that Timothy doesn't reveal anything of what he saw,' she said.

'He's cleared for a pretty high level of sec—'

She stepped closer, her eyes boring into his. His teeth clicked together audibly.

'Don't be a goddamn fool,' she hissed. 'He can't see what he saw and live. And you, Agent, by association ...'

She let him fill the gap for himself and was relieved to see determination replace fear.

'You can count on me, ma'am,' he said earnestly. 'I'll see he sticks to the script.'

Vietnam Veterans' Memorial, Washington DC

Mal walked along the path beside the Vietnam Veterans' Memorial, moving west towards the Lincoln Memorial. He found himself stepping slowly, placing his feet almost reverently, on the walkway. A tired sun sent yellow streaks along the ten-foot wall of black marble and, against the sunset, he saw a tableau resolve itself from silhouette into a woman and girl. The woman sat on her heels before one of the seventy-four panels. The girl, earthed by the woman's lap, was intent on the rubbing she was making with crayon and paper. At least one name among almost sixty thousand, he thought, would be copied with bright crayon and brought home from the cold marble. The thought warmed him and, rather than just pass by, he paused for a moment and held his hat in his hands. The woman seemed to sense his presence and surfaced from her reverie long enough to bless him with a faraway smile. It buoyed his steps for another forty yards to where a man was straightening a small, framed photograph against the base of a name-filled panel. Mal doffed his hat again and waited. His eyes roved down the list of names etched on the wall in light grey until they found 'Fox'.

'I hope you don't mind meeting here, Mal,' Congressman Fox said, as he stood. 'I like a memorial that remembers people rather than wars.' His eyes were drawn back to it as if some thought process hadn't been completed. When he spoke again, Mal had the feeling he was eaves-dropping on some internal conversation. 'Hell of a waste,' the congressman said. 'Johnson knew from as far back as '64 that it couldn't be won. He claimed he was surrounded by advisers who thought otherwise.'

'I seem to remember one of our generals in the Second World War got himself surrounded, Congressman,' Mal said softly. 'Germans sent him a message askin' for his surrender. He sent back a one-word reply. "Nuts." I guess you have to have them to say that.'

'Point taken, Mal. Let's walk.'

As they made their way west, their ghosts kept pace with them from one reflective panel to the next.

'You got the stuff?'

'I got it. I won't ask where you got it. So, what's the game-plan, Mal?'

'Let me back up a little. Friend of mine, in Italy, says Cardinal Thomas was most likely spirited away by people funded from our taxes, the kind of people who drop a body along the way to avoid excess baggage. Same people organised a Hercules at Florence for one African-American male and one Caucasian female. They were both in airforce uniforms.'

The congressman snorted in disgust.

'Headed where?' he asked.

'Israel. From here on, I'm flyin' on conjecture, Congressman. You already know the connection between Michael Flaherty and Cardinal Thomas. Now we have both of them in Jerusalem. Coincidences don't stretch that far. This is part of someone's plan. That someone is way beyond the reach of my jurisdiction, maybe even of yours, I don't know. I thought I'd slow him down a little. You're a historian, Congressman. You know what the Continentals did against the British during the American Revolution? Farm boys with muskets couldn't go toe to toe with crack troops and cannon. They picked them off from the trees, sniped and scooted. Targeted the officers until the Brits got frustrated and demoralised. I figure it might distract him a little to have all that stuff rolling up on his computer and on the computers of some armchair heroes who sent men to die in the Colombia business. Apart from that, I wondered if you could bring this higher. I know I'm asking you to put your head above the parapet on this one but—'

'I agreed to do that the last time we met, Mal,' he interrupted. He turned to look back at the wall of names that seemed to stretch into infinity towards the Washington Memorial.

'I did my doctoral thesis on the eighteenth-century Neapolitan scholar Vico. Yeah, I know, you never heard of him. No one has. He was standing on Plato's shoulders when he said that there were organic phases in human society. History shows we go from chaos to theocracy to aristocracy to democracy. Then, when republics begin to lose the plot and become imperial and tyrannous, we go right back to chaos and the wheel begins to roll all over again. Vico was looking back on the Roman republic when he wrote that. If he had looked over his shoulder, I don't think he'd have been surprised to see the same cycle coming up roses again in ours. I decided to become a congressman to put a brake on that wheel, Mal. Heck, we like to demonise the theocrats in Israel and Afghanistan but—'

He broke off and looked again at the wall.

'You know why this memorial is reflective, don't you?' he asked.

'Yeah, I think I do.'

'I'll do all I can do, Mal, I promise.'

Mal looked back once on his way from the memorial. He saw the young man standing with his hand outstretched, touching the wall. There was just enough light left in the sky to make out the ghostly image reaching out to make contact from the black marble.

CIA Director's Residence, Washington DC

There had been five telephone calls, ranging in tone from querulous to shrill. The Ghost had listened, grunting at appropriate intervals, letting them talk themselves down from righteous indignation and hollow threats to the realisation that they were merely forts on the edges of his empire. Should they fall to a vengeful band, there was another circle of defence and yet another and another, rippling all the way to Washington. The bottom line, and he heard and savoured it in their eventual silence, was that foot-soldiers were expendable. At least three of them had been generals, men whose lust for power or money had lured them into the secret cabal that had planned and effected the Colombian incursion. And now, when their computers treacherously made plain what had been hidden …

Benson checked his garden for signs of his guardian agents and, finding none, allowed himself a small nod of satisfaction. He returned to his desk and sipped his drink, lapping with his tongue at the rim of the glass before setting it aside. Wife

number three, he remembered, had actually listed that
mannerism in her affidavit at the divorce proceedings. It had
appeared almost halfway down a long list of 'disgusting and/or
provocative acts intended to cause mental suffering'. Of
course, it had been a throwback to nurture not nature, he
concluded. Maman would insist there could be no unsightly
residue on a cup or glass.

He pondered another example of 'unsightly residue' and
calculated how it could be lapped up without repercussions.
The agent, he agreed, had simply done his job by unearthing
the computer geek to solve their problem. If Catherine was to
be believed, the young man would complete his task in
twenty-four hours and would return to doing whatever it was
such people did. Or maybe not, considering their little
tripartite tête-à-tête in the office. Amazing what can be
gleaned from an open line, what people will say when they
don't notice a handset sitting slightly askew on a secretary's
desk. 'Remember but don't comprehend', indeed. It seems
even geeks have a survival instinct. When the task was
completed, he would negotiate with one of that small band of
psychopaths who specialised in 'accidents'. He might even
haggle the assassin down to doing two for the price of one ...
or should that be three? His mood darkened and he repeated
the sip-lap ritual before sitting back to brood in his chair.

The others were mere ciphers. Catherine had moved into
the inner sphere. He had revealed more of himself to the
dutiful Ms De Lancy than he had ever done with another
human being.

'"There's no art to find the mind's construction in the
face,"' he quoted aloud from *Macbeth*. That would have
pleased Jones, he thought. The murderous little bastard had

delivered his message to the Island and disappeared. Probably lying low, he concluded, among the other bottom-feeders.

�⚜�

'Good afternoon, Director.'

'Is it?'

He had closed the heavy drapes and turned on the desk lamp. It was angled so that he sat in shadow. She saw only his outline while she sat full-square in the unforgiving light. Catherine De Lancy had been through those types of hoops before and concentrated on steadying her breathing. Let the games begin, she thought.

'Timothy, the young computer expert, says it's a virus, sir. He can clear it in twenty-four hours.'

'Dead air' was such an old interview trick, she thought, as the director sat in silence. Now I'm supposed to find the silence oppressive and fill it by talking until, eventually, I say something best left unsaid. She blanked her face and sat him out.

Benson blinked first.

'And that's it? End of story, case closed, good night, America?'

A hand reached across the desk and took the glass into the dark. She heard a sip followed by that horrible lapping sound.

'You know that's not how it works, Catherine. You, of all people, should know that someone can't just ...' Sip and lap. 'No, we are the ones who hack and bug. We, Ms De Lancy, are the ones who do. We are not done to. And when anyone, for whatever reason, assaults our citadel, even with a pea-shooter, we visit our wrath upon them, we bring them down to rubble, plough the rubble under and sow that place with salt.'

She heard him take a steadying breath and braced herself.

'I want you to go back to the office and light a fire under that whiz kid. I want you to lean on him until he scours our system clean, you got that?'

'Yes, sir.'

'You know what we must do, Catherine. When the task is completed, I want you to contact the systems provider and get him to replace our system. You know who to call. Tell him, from me, it's a do-it-or-lose-it scenario. As soon as the idiot savant is finished, call Scylla. We need to sanitise.'

'Sir?'

'Jesus Christ, Catherine, what's the problem here? The kid and his keeper know we've been breached. This is not a situation we can tolerate. Scylla will know what to do, that's all.'

'But, Mr Director, surely there are other ways. Timothy is just … a child, a very brilliant child, who has no—'

Benson's head loomed into the light, his face freighted with cruel shadows.

'You think we can let some dumbass kid know what he knows? You think we can let that agent walk?'

'I – I don't understand. I remember we—'

'What? What don't you understand?' he shouted. 'What do you remember and not comprehend? This is not some kind of Disney fantasy, like your fucking hero boyfriend in Vietnam. You don't have to understand. You just do. Now do it.'

※

The car smelled of Perry's gum. The big man drove with his fingertips while his jaws moved up and down. Catherine leaned back against the leather upholstery and struggled for calm, but her mind chewed on the conversation with the director. She knew – had known from the instant he had given his instructions – what fate lay in store for Timothy and the agent. She had received that kind of order before from previous directors, orders that led directly to the elimination of perceived threats, and had carried them out without compunction. But he was only a kid and— 'Oh, Jesus!' She didn't realise she had spoken aloud until the voice rumbled from the front.

'You okay back there, ma'am?'

'Yes, Perry, everything's fine, thank you. And how's Michelle?'

'Oh, ya know, empty-nest syndrome. Rattlin' round the house now that Lucy's gone to Caltech. Told her she should …'

She tuned him out and replayed the mental tape of her conversation with Benson. He had said, 'What do you remember and not comprehend?' Suddenly she felt cold.

'Should take up some classes,' Perry continued, as his passenger ground her teeth together to stop them from chattering.

He knows, she thought, and that shocking realisation seemed to free her. There was something else he had said at the height of his angry outburst. That's for later, she told herself.

'Life goes on, don't it? Well, here we are, Ms De Lancy.'

'It certainly does, Perry. Things change but life goes on.'

'That's what I told her, ma'am.'

He was out of the car and holding the door open.

'Your Michelle is very lucky to have found such a gentleman,' she said.

Perry's big face took on the flustered look of a man who must struggle with compliments.

'Well, eh, I guess I was lucky to find one heck of a lady,' he said gruffly, 'like you, Ms De Lancy.'

CIA Headquarters, Washington DC
She stood inside the door of the office and watched the young man bowed over the computer. For a few moments, she allowed herself the pleasure of observing someone at one with their work. Timothy's hand skipped over the keys, his head nodding to some cerebral music. Agent Howard placed another glass of Coke within his reach and caught her eye. She motioned him to follow and waited with her back pressed against the wall of the corridor.

'Are you married, Agent Howard?'

'Eh, no, ma'am.'

'Good. Can you disappear for a while?'

He held her gaze for what seemed like a long time.

'I reckon I can but what about the kid?'

'The kid isn't deaf or stupid,' Timothy said, from the doorway.

'You both have to leave now,' Catherine said urgently. 'You have to find somewhere where he – where you can't be found for a time. I'm afraid I don't know for how long. I wish I could do more.'

'I appreciate what you're doing, Ms De Lancy,' Timothy said. He turned to the agent. 'Where would you like to go?'

'Huh?'

'I asked where you would like to go.'

'I dunno – I guess somewhere in Europe would be nice. Always wanted to see Scotland. Can't go there or anywhere without a passport, and they can trace that.'

'If you'll excuse me for a moment, please.'

After Timothy had left, they stood in awkward silence for what felt like a long time until he returned.

'There's a flight out of Washington at five thirty in the morning with a connection to Edinburgh. You're booked first class. A gentleman in Barbados has paid for it with his credit card. You will be met at check-in by a courier with a passport made out to Ryan Ford. I had to get into your personnel file to get your picture – I hope you don't mind. The request to the Passport Office originated from the FBI Procurements Division, so there wasn't a problem.'

The agent nodded his thanks.

'What about you, kid? Can you get a flight someplace?'

'Yes, but that's need-to-know, Agent Howard.' Timothy's mouth curved into a small smile.

'Can I do something for you, Ms De Lancy?' he added.

She hesitated and then shook her head. 'You are a very remarkable young man, Timothy,' she said. 'In other circumstances I would have been honoured to know you.'

Tentatively, he stretched out his hand.

❧❧❧

Catherine avoided the cabs on the Avenue and took a bus to the centre of town. In a bar, near the university, she scanned the patrons with a shrewd eye before approaching a young man who sat alone at a table reading a book, seemingly oblivious to the raucous cheer of the students at the other tables.

'May I?'

'Wha— Oh, yeah, sure.'

He swung his owlish gaze back to the book.

'I see you read Dante,' she said. 'Do you think he's really buried in Ravenna?'

Two eyes surfaced over the top of the book.

'No, ma'am,' he said. 'I think the Florentines brought him home.'

'So the oil sent from Florence every year for the eternal flame is what? Some kind of joke?'

A smile creased his face. 'Yeah, wouldn't that be so typical? I think he'd have loved that.'

'I agree,' she said, smiling, 'very Machiavellian. May I ask your name?'

'John—John Jordan, ma'am.'

He offered his hand and she shook it.

'John Jordan,' she said quietly, 'I would like to make you an offer you have every right to refuse.'

'That's one hell of a genre switch, ma'am,' he said, and his smile widened.

'I have a situation,' she began, and broke off to beckon a passing waiter. 'Same again?' John Jordan nodded. 'And a glass of the house red wine,' she added.

'If you don't mind me saying so, ma'am,' he confided, when the waiter had left, 'I hear the wine in this place never saw a grape.'

'Thank you, John,' she said. 'I don't plan on drinking it. As I said, I have a situation. A gentleman of my acquaintance, and I use the word 'gentleman' rather loosely, insists on paying me some attention – unwelcome attention, I assure you. He's got my cellphone number and … well, I was wondering …?'

Twenty minutes later, Catherine De Lancy ordered coffee in a café a few blocks away. John Jordan had listened to her proposition and promptly exchanged his battered phone for her BlackBerry. He had further promised to book a seat on the Greyhound bus departing Washington for New York one hour later and disembark at the first stop. It was mutually agreed that the BlackBerry would continue the journey, hidden on the overhead rack. John Jordan would return to his studies, refreshed by the short bus journey and the two thousand dollars the lady had pressed him to accept. She punched some numbers into her new phone.

'Dora? Remember you said if I was ever in trouble I should call you? I'm in trouble. No, don't say anything; just write this down.'

She had finished the refill when the sedan eased to the kerb.

'Is it a man?' Dora asked, as Catherine got in beside her.

'Well, yes, sort of,' Catherine replied.

'About time,' Dora grunted, and floored the accelerator. 'I've always said you were a dark horse, Catherine.'

'So I believe,' Catherine replied. 'Harry still visiting with his mother in Florida?'

'Gawd, yes. Whoever said flying the nest was a one-way trip never met Harry's mom. So, where we going, Catherine?'

'Can you swing by my place? There are a few things I want to pack.'

'Pack?'

She asked Dora to park a few blocks away and walked to her house. Halfway through packing, she sat on the edge of the bed. Am I being paranoid? she wondered. Wishful thinking, Ms De Lancy, she told herself. Benson had been right. She did know how things worked and what happened when they malfunctioned. Benson had introduced a replace-versus-repair policy at the agency. Time to get your ass in gear, girl, her pragmatic self prompted, but Catherine the Doubter needed more: some tangible proof. She'd never done 'The Tommy Test'. She hadn't dated agents; hadn't dated, period. Tommy had sort of dropped by a few times for coffee and company. He was scrawny and balding and, as her mother would have said, 'unprepossessing', but he'd been fun. He had a personality made up of two parts black humour and one part paranoia. When she'd remonstrated with him about his irreverence for the Agency in general and Benson in particular, he'd said, 'Catherine, there's always a priest at Delphi who knows the Oracle is out of her skull on drugs, always one cardinal in the Consistory who just knows the Italians have rigged the vote – again. That's me, Catherine. It's my genius and my cross. Every time I read something from the agency, my crapometer goes off the scale. Every time I come within a mile of Benson, I smell sulphur. If you doubt me, do the Tommy Test.'

'What's that?'

'Do unto thyself as we do unto others.'

They'd laughed, opened a bottle of good Burgundy and toasted all the famous nay-sayers and doom-vendors from Cassandra down. And then Tommy had gone to Waco and taken a 'friendly' bullet from some gung-ho trooper. She shook her head to dislodge the hurt and marched into the hallway.

'Phones,' Tommy had said. 'Someone is always listening. Why not to you?'

Using an antique letter-opener, she prised the little box from its moorings under the telephone table and stared at the tiny disk, stuck like a parasite among the wire intestines. In a frenzy she attacked every phone outlet in the house until the blade snapped, then rocked back on her heels. She unclenched her fist and four tiny disks dropped to the floor. She looked at the four perfect dimples imprinted on her palm and went to throw up in the bathroom.

⁂

'Right here, Dora, will be fine.'

'You sure?'

'Yes, I'm sure. You've been a friend indeed, Dora. I won't forget it.'

'Sure you don't want us to hightail it to the boondocks – ye know, like some kinda Thelma and Louise?'

Catherine looked at Dora's pink jumpsuit, straining in all the wrong places, and patted her plump cheek.

⁂

'You sure, ma'am? It's just that it ain't no neighbourhood for a lady.'

The cab-driver scratched under his cap and inspected his fingernails.

'I'm sure, and, please, don't call in on the radio. I'll make it worth your while.'

The city unravelled outside the window, fading from bright lights and tall buildings to the ragged, gap-toothed architecture, broken glass and security shutters of the poorer districts. This is Dante's journey in reverse, she thought grimly, and hoped John Jordan was as good as his word. The building that slid into and halted in the cab window was an urban fortress, three storeys of solid brick, caged windows and what Dora would have called a 'fuck-off' metal door. She tried to palm the driver a hundred-dollar bill but he brushed it aside.

'Lady,' he huffed, 'if you need to come here, your need is greater than mine. I'll just wait a whiles till you get inside.'

She pressed the bell and sensed someone on the other side of the spy-hole. Bolts rattled and locks clicked and she was in. Behind her, the door encored its repertoire of noises as it shut out the street. The African-American lady stood barely five feet tall but her stare seemed to give her stilts. Her lined face was a map of places she had been, places where few would ever wish to go.

'Think you might have taken a wrong turnin', honey,' she said, with a small smile that didn't displace the question in her eyes.

'I'd like to see Sister Agnes,' Catherine said.

'Doan ev'ybody?' the little lady said, and inclined her head for Catherine to follow. They walked along a dim hallway, past an open door to a room lit largely by a TV. Instinctively, Catherine glanced inside as they passed. She saw the outlines of four or five women, perched or sprawled on a large couch. One seemed to have a bandage around her head. None of them returned her glance. The old lady stopped at a door and turned.

'Agnes an ol' lady now, like me. You keep that in mind now, ya heah?'

She knocked and shoved it open.

'Agnes, honey, you got company.'

A single desk-lamp uplighting the white head reflected, like twin moons, in the spectacles.

'Thank you, Shonda. Now, who have we here?' the sister said. 'Step into the light, sweetheart.'

'It's Catherine De Lancy, Sister Agnes,' Catherine said, as she approached the desk.

Sister Agnes rose with difficulty and came to meet her.

'Miss De Lancy,' she said warmly, 'this is a pleasant surprise.' She took Catherine's outstretched hand and held it while she scanned her face. 'You've got trouble.'

'Yes. I need somewhere to stay for a while.'

'Long as you like,' Sister Agnes said, without releasing her hand. 'If it hadn't been for your generosity ...'

'Please, Sister Agnes, I don't want that to be an issue.'

'No, it's not an issue, it's a fact. And the fact is that no woman who needs us is ever turned away. It's just that I like the idea that we can do something for you.'

She linked her arm through Catherine's and led her out of the room and up a short flight of stairs.

'This is a little apartment we set aside for visiting priests – when there were priests. It's self-contained with its own bathroom, kitchen and such. No, you're not getting the Dorchester Suite because of who you are. We don't work that way. Trouble is a great leveller. I'm putting you here for the sake of the other guests. What they don't know won't hurt them. Will it?'

The United States Senate, Washington DC

'Senator Melly.'

'Senator Clarke.'

Henry Melly slumped on the armchair beside the senator from Virginia. The speaker had just called a recess and the ante-room was already filling up with those members who prized coffee and conversation over their offices and constituency business. Melly supped his coffee and cast an appraising eye over his colleague. Frank Clarke was the Father of the

House, clocking in at eighty-two. Among the members, he was generally regarded as a benign old bore, always ready to steer the conversation back to an era he found comfortable. Melly knew that much of it was affected: under that silver fringe ticked a steely brain. Behind the folksy down-home façade, Frank Clarke was a formidable politician. He was conscious of the twinkle of mischief in the childlike blue eyes peering at him from under the twin pelmets of carelessly thatched eyebrows.

'Still workin' on the book, Frank?'

It was an attempt to steal the old man's thunder and Melly saw the recognition and futility of his gambit in the bright eyes.

'Yeah, Henry, John Quincy Adams still whispers in my ear and guides my quill. You know he died in Congress?'

'That could be said of a wagonload of the present incumbents, but they still sit in the chamber, Frank.'

Frank Clarke tilted his coffee cup in mock salutation.

'Good one, Henry, and tragically true. Voted against the war with Mexico in '48, signalled he wished to speak, then just toppled right over.'

'Mighty close call for California and the south-west.'

'Yeah, you could say that. Still, how many former presidents came back to Congress to fight the good fight on behalf of "we the people".'

'Only John Quincy Adams?'

'You always were a bright one, Henry.'

He leaned forward to shovel an extra spoon of sugar in his cup.

'Your little girl gonna save us from ourselves, Henry?' he asked softly.

'You've been around a long time, Frank, what d'you think?'

The senator's eyes crinkled to acknowledge the evasion, then sobered.

'You know, Henry, we expect too much of presidents, always have. Harry Truman accused FDR of lyin'. In time, old Harry found himself similarly accused. What a pair. Franklin had to know about Pearl Harbor – I mean beforehand. Heck, old Hirohito offered to hand over his sword far back as '41. And Harry? Old Harry does a double-drop with the A bomb. Just the same as reversin' over a guy you've just run over. And why? Ike sure didn't want it, said the war was over. That was before he became a politician, of course. No, Harry Truman wanted to send a message to Uncle Joe.'

'Joe Stalin?'

'No, Joe DiMaggio – crank up the old brain here, Henry. Well, let's on with the mendacious dance. Ike shafts Eden over Suez and JFK makes a stand over Cuba, only he don't. He makes a sly deal with Khrushchev and the problem goes away. Sorry, but a lot of the guys since are a bit of a blur – one of the few pluses of old age. It takes big bucks and big business to get to the Oval Office, these days, Henry, so I'll ask again. Have we a Joan of Arc or an Imelda Marcos?'

'Neither, Frank. So far, no bells, no visions, and whatever she's got in the closet, it ain't slingbacks.'

'Maybe it's Jack Holland, then?'

'Jack is a problem, Frank, I won't tell you otherwise. Former presidents are an embarrassment, for the most part – ya know, forgotten but not gone. Carter was the only former to make a fist of it.'

'Ain't that the truth!'

'Yep, and the truth is she's feisty 'n' smart 'n' she's got backbone.'

'She's gonna need it, Henry. Girl's got enemies nearer home – the agency, as I hear. New breed on Capitol Hill too. Young 'uns round these parts have a longin' for empire. Lots of bomb-'em-back-to-the-stone-age kinda guys. They think American foreign policy was summed up by Kissinger when he said, "Let's act ferocious." She'll have just one turn at bat, Henry.'

'Know what you're sayin', Frank,' Melly said, putting his cup in the saucer as a prelude to leaving.

'And what about you, Henry? Thinkin' about doin' a Cincinnatus any time soon? Ya know, goin' back to the farm 'n' all?'

Henry Melly moved to open one of the lockers that lined the ante room. He took out his coat and hat and the scrap of paper he hadn't put there. 'Me,' he answered absently. 'I'm more a Cicero kinda guy, Frank. I have a mind for long, thoughtful evenings with a good book.'

The old man laughed knowingly.

'You know what Emerson said about Adams, Henry? He said, "He is an old roué who cannot live on slops, but must have sulphuric acid in his tea."'

'So, we've come full circle to John Quincy Adams, Frank?'

'Have we?'

The White House, Washington DC
Special Agent Joshua Harley opened the door to the Red Room and stood aside.

'Congressman Fox to see you, Senator,' he intoned, and withdrew, closing the door behind him. The two politicians eyed each other warily. Fox knew the senator was regarded on the Hill as an affable and hard-working member. He knew for a fact that the senator was Ellen Radford's mentor, chosen as her confidant for more than his genial, old-world courtesy. The younger man had no doubt that under the velvet exterior there was a razor-sharp mind and a spine of steel. Melly knew the congressman as capable and idealistic, with a softness for minority causes. He knew also that the premature death of his wife had left him as sole parent to two young daughters. He thought the young man looked worn beyond his years.

'Thank you for agreeing to this meeting, Senator,' Fox said, and held out his hand. They seemed to weigh each other's before releasing them.

'Let me warn you, Congressman. Eleanor Roosevelt liked to caution visitors that when FDR said, "Yes, yes, yes," it meant he was listening, not that he agreed. I'm here to listen, boy. Let's sit.'

Without reference to notes, Congressman Fox outlined his meeting with Mal O'Donnell and gave a synopsis of the documents Mal had sourced and sent to Benson's computer. The senator listened attentively and sat forward when he had finished.

'I took a look at the material you left in my locker,' he said quietly, 'and … what can I say? Rumours of Benson's dark arts have been rumblin' round Washington for some time now. If my memory serves me right, this is the first piece of hard evidence to see the light of day. Don't know rightly if it'll stand up in a court of law, but …' He heaved himself upright. 'Will you excuse me for a few moments? I'll be right back.'

As Senator Melly left the room, Agent Harley stepped inside and took up a position beside the door.

'First time, sir?' he asked.

'Oh, yes, it's my first time in the White House.' He waved his hand at the décor. 'Obviously, this is the Red Room,' he said, smiling.

'Yeah, we got one hundred and thirty-two rooms, all told. This here room is where Mrs Kennedy met lots of important people after her husband's funeral.'

The agent cleared his throat and shifted his feet.

'Thank you for sharing that, Special Agent,' Congressman Fox said, with a tired smile.

'Welcome, sir.'

The Oval Office, The White House

'Come right in, Congressman. President'll be by shortly.'

Fox walked into the Oval Office and stopped to look around.

'It's bigger than I imagined,' he said, and the senator smiled at his hushed voice. 'Has to be,' he shot back. 'Lots of big egos to accommodate over the years.'

The younger man took a few steps forward and reached out to touch the desk.

'I've only ever seen this in photographs, Senator, but I always thought there was an opening under here.'

Melly chuckled and sat on one of the chairs dotted around the wall.

'Bet you're thinking of young John-John Kennedy pokin' his head outta there. Didn't do no harm to Jack's image to reveal he was a family man. Franklin Roosevelt was the first to have a panel put there, to conceal his wasted legs. Image is kinda important to some presidents.'

'Why did President Radford have the panel put back?'

'So she can kick off her shoes when her feet get tired,' Ellen Radford said, from the door, where she stood shadowed by the Secretary of State. She crossed the carpet displaying the Presidential Seal and shook his hand.

'Welcome to the Oval Office, Congressman Fox. I think you know Laila Achmed. Won't you sit by the senator? I always wondered what it would look like to see a Republican and a Democrat share the Oval Office. Senator Melly's given me a heads-up on why you're here and I've read the documents. Who's the Deep Throat guy?'

'Pardon?'

'Mal O'Donnell?'

'He's a New York cop who headed up a special unit monitoring drug movements from Colombia, Ms President.'

'What's his connection with Father Michael Flaherty? Is he family?'

'No, no, ma'am, no blood ties that I know of, but I gather they're like father and son.'

'You included some extra material with the documents to Senator Melly covering Flaherty's hospitalisation and demob. How did O'Donnell come by that material?'

'Mal O'Donnell went to Virginia to meet with the people responsible for the insertion of Michael Flaherty's unit and for his subsequent hospitalisation. He saw for himself what 'hospitalisation' really meant. To all intents and purposes, it was imprisonment. Flaherty was the only survivor of a secret mission, the only one outside a select military group who knew what had happened down there. They were deciding on whether they should release him or ...'

'Or?'

'Or not, ma'am. Mal O'Donnell made them an offer. Basically, they would release Michael Flaherty into his care and the secret would remain intact.'

'He had to offer more collateral than that.'

'Yes, ma'am, he did. He suggested that if Michael Flaherty had his freedom, it was likely that the major and sergeant who had responsibility for the illegal unit in Colombia might … hunt him down.'

Ellen Radford sat forward and placed her palms flat on the desk.

'So, Flaherty was to be a stalking horse?'

'Yes, ma'am. And it worked. The major and the sergeant were killed and the general in the Pentagon who had liaised with them took his own life.'

'I get the feeling that happily ever after isn't how this story ends.'

'No, ma'am. Michael Flaherty was an assistant to Cardinal Thomas in Rome. I … I don't know how much you know about the activities of a right-wing group in the Roman Catholic Church called the Remnant?'

The president exchanged a glance with the Secretary of State.

'We know of the Remnant, Congressman,' Laila Achmed said carefully. 'We also know of the actions they took to bring about a situation where Cardinal J. Arthur Thomas would be elected pope.'

'What about the involvement of the US government in that matter, Madam Secretary?' Fox said, leaning forward so that he could address her across the bulk of Henry Melly.

'There are reports on file, unconfirmed reports, that a

branch of the security agencies may have aided and abetted Cardinal Thomas and his organisation. We have no proof, Congressman.'

'A source in the Italian police suggests that Cardinal Thomas is now in Jerusalem, aided and abetted by a branch of our security agencies. I imagine you've got no proof of that either, Madam Secretary. Maybe if this administration leaned on the Italian government, that proof might be forthcoming and you could actually do something.'

''Scuse me,' the senator said mildly, 'I'm beginning to feel like Belgium sitting between the warring powers of Europe. Correct me if I'm wrong, Congressman, but it seems to me like Mal O'Donnell is tilting his lance at two separate windmills. We got the person or persons unknown who authorised the illegal unit in Colombia. We have another individual or group who sent in Michael Flaherty's clean-up squad of which he's the only survivor. They stake him out to lure the first group into the open. Three people bite the bait and die. Okay so far?'

'Yes.'

'Riddle me this. How come he's jabbing his lance at the second group?'

Congressman Fox exhaled his tension.

'He suspects, Senator, that they represent two factions in the Pentagon. He figures if word gets round, as it does in all organisations when there's a hunt on, it might just flush someone from cover. It might also distract whoever's masterminding this long enough for Michael Flaherty to figure out a way to survive. Thomas was part of a plan to take the Papacy. We know he had the Remnant behind him because they thought he'd advance their careers in the Church if the plan succeeded. It failed, largely because of Michael Flaherty. Thomas is in Jerusalem and so is Michael Flaherty.'

'Why are you here, Congressman?' the president asked.

Fox sat back for a moment and closed his eyes as if considering his answer. When he opened them, he fixed them on the president.

'O'Donnell might sound a little like Don Quixote, ma'am, but he's realistic enough to know when he's out of his league. He said whoever's behind this is way out of his jurisdiction. He asked if I could take it higher. That's why I contacted the senator and that's why I'm talking to you, Ms President.'

Ellen Radford held his gaze for a few moments and nodded. She pushed a button on her desk and Special Agent Harley stepped into the room.

'Congressman,' she said, 'I need to talk with the Secretary of State and Senator Melly. Would you oblige me by waiting in the Red Room? Agent Harley, can you ask the chef to rustle up some lunch for our guest? I think we could do with some coffee for ourselves.'

Laila Achmed waited until the door closed before letting out a long breath.

'Feeling a little bruised, Madam Secretary?' Melly asked impishly.

'The phrase 'shoots from the lip' does come to mind, Senator.'

'Yep, he's a straight talker all right. I knew his daddy – decent man, good local congressman but always played it safe. Son was a shoo-in when the old guy passed away. Coulda done what Daddy done, as they say, but …'

'When it comes to incomplete sentences, Senator, you are the original 'hanging judge'.'

Melly smiled in acknowledgement.

'Of course there's a but – isn't there always? But he stuck his neck out for unpopular causes, the ones that risk losing you votes and don't gain a nickel in contributions from the big corporations. Boy's had a rough time, lost a wife and then I heard he was friendly with that young nun in New York – feisty girl with a great brain and lots of ideas about things less than right with the Roman Catholic Church.'

'Seems like a recipe for a short career as a nun.'

'Yeah, she got pushed under a train by one of them Remnant bozos.'

The president cleared a space for the coffee tray as the maid entered. As soon as the maid closed the door behind her, she began to fill the delicate china cups.

'I see you rescued Nancy Reagan's coffee service from the warehouse, Ellen,' Melly said.

'Yep, only things did any regular work in that particular administration.'

'And how.' He laughed. 'Nancy and Betty Bloomingdale got through more politics over coffee than Ron ever got round to in cabinet. Lots of political secrets in that coffee pot.'

'Usual sugar mountain?' she asked.

'I support the Southern cane growers, ma'am, so pile it in there.'

'How's about eye of newt and toe of frog?'

'Pass.'

He gestured at the fourth cup.

'Who's the fourth horseperson of this particular Apocalypse?'

'Attorney general's coming in.'

The senator tried, unsuccessfully, to smother a smile.

David Duke stepped into the room and stopped, peering through impossibly thick spectacles. The president thought he looked like someone who had submerged himself in a book and surfaced some time later in Atlantis. Duke was a man whose dress sense challenged the thesaurus to come up with a term between 'dishevelled' and 'unkempt'. At the moment, he wore a suit jacket he had buttoned unevenly so that a small flap of excess material bulged above his waist like a marsupial's pouch. The trousers were in the same broad colour range as the jacket and overflowed his shoes. Even someone like Ellen Radford, who favoured functional over decorative when it came to clothes, wished he would put on his glasses before he dressed.

He had been a child prodigy, the tenth offspring of a Virginian couple who had been too tired to do other than let him be. What he had done was read – everything. He had read himself to scholarships and Harvard Law School, the top of his class. Head-hunted by the State Justice Department, he had proved to be a lethal prosecutor in the Columbo mode. Seemingly distracted and unfocused in the courtroom, David Duke had conned more than one expensive defence team into underestimating him. He seemed to have found his perfect niche when Washington University had wooed him to a professorship. His tempting initials and seeming abstraction had quickly endeared him to the student body, who labelled him Daffy. Ellen Radford was among the few who knew of his pro bono work for small rural groups who couldn't afford to take on the water companies or the big utilities. He had never forgotten his roots among a people who spoke disparagingly of the 'guv'mint'. The clincher for her in choosing him as attorney general had been an erudite and hard-hitting paper he had published on the runaway powers of the various security services, entitled 'Perpetual War for Perpetual Peace'.

She ushered him to the chair recently vacated by Congressman Fox and placed his coffee on a small table beside him. Daffy's clothes, one long-suffering secretary had remarked, were the sum of all his spillages.

'You had time to read the material, David?'

'Yes, ma'am.'

Briskly, she brought him up to speed on the congressman's contribution.

'I'd like to tighten the screw on those who were behind the Colombian business,' she concluded. 'What I need to know from you, David, is if it's possible to do that within the law.'

David Duke blinked a few times. 'As the law stands, ma'am,' he answered, 'you can do pretty much as you please.'

'Specify,' she said, 'and, David, English is the preferred language of this meeting.'

'Okay, here's how it goes. In time of war, the office of the president takes on a whole range of powers.'

'But – but this isn't a wartime situation,' Laila Achmed interrupted.

The attorney general pushed his enormous spectacles a notch higher on his nose as if lining up a gunsight on the Secretary of State.

'Actually, Madam Secretary, as things stand, we are involved in two ongoing wars right here and now: the war on drugs and the war on terrorism. It could be argued that, constitutionally, the United States can only go to war with another country, but—'

'David!'

'But we won't go there.'

'Thank you, David.'

He continued as if he hadn't heard her.

'Because we have those two ongoing wars, any American citizen can have his or her telephone tapped, house searched, computer confiscated, goods impounded, habeas corpus suspended, and be eligible for immediate deportation if suspected of even the most tenuous links with illegal drugs or terrorism.'

'So,' the president interrupted, 'I could order some or all those agencies to investigate the people mentioned in those documents?'

'Yes, you could, ma'am.'

She heard the reservation in his tone and responded to it.

'Look, David, I know your views on all this and I share many of them. One of the reasons why I included you in the team was because of the reservations you have about the overreaching power of the agencies and the erosion of constitutional rights. You know I'm committed to redressing that imbalance.'

'Yes, I do, ma'am; that's why I'm here.'

She sat forward, resting her elbows on the desk.

'What we're dealing with now is evidence of a group, probably made up of factions within the Pentagon plus one or more of the security agencies, who ordered a military hit-squad into a foreign country with the express purpose not of taking out the drug cartel but of taking over the process themselves. Second, a legitimate if secret military unit, sent in to cancel out the first group, ended up as their victims. Which brings me to the immediate problem. The only survivor of that unit was held against his will in a military institution and released as a 'tethered goat' only to attract the bad guys. Same person is now in Israel under some kind of fatwa from an American cardinal. I want to do a few things here. I want to do all that can be done by this administration to preserve the life of the citizen and ex-serviceman Michael Flaherty, who is in clear and present danger. I want to poke a sharp stick into the Pentagon and security agencies to root out whomever was responsible for violating the borders of Colombia. Hopefully, something or someone will give and the buck will boomerang all the way and stop with the person who is behind this. Can I do this within the law?'

'The short answer, ma'am, is that you can. The only question is how. Can you give me, say, fifteen minutes? I need to check some stuff.'

When the attorney general had left, Ellen Radford turned her attention to the senator and the Secretary of State.

'I think we can push on here,' she said. 'Laila, what's the word from Jerusalem?'

'I think you're already up to speed on the Har Homa incident and the Israeli retaliation beyond the Wall.'

'Yes,' Ellen Radford said. 'This eye-for-an-eye diplomacy is just keeping the damn cycle going round and round.'

'We're low on specifics, ma'am,' Laila Achmed continued. 'What's coming in from the CIA is just low-grade stuff. The reports from our own people suggest the tension is being ratcheted up. They're talking about when, not if, we have a major blow-out in the region. Word from the neighbouring states is that everyone's stepped up to a higher level of military readiness, lots of state-of-the-art hardware appearing near the front lines. We got this intel from the satellite.'

'That bothers you?'

'Yes, it's a lucky strike when someone's careless with the camouflage. We would expect more intel from the fixed assets on the ground. Even our eyes and ears in Mossad are drawing a blank. It scares them. They think someone may be flying solo.'

The final sentence hung heavily in the silent room. Ellen Radford sat back in her chair.

'Tell me some good news, Laila,'

The Secretary of State glanced at her file.

'Michael Flaherty is still alive. He's located in the Franciscan monastery at the Church of the Holy Sepulchre. Attended a meeting of an inter-faith group at the Russian Convent of St Mary Magdalene in the company of the Father Guardian. Surveillance is ongoing.'

'Step it up, Laila. Henry, want to have your dime's worth?'

The senator hunched forward, a worried expression erasing the lines of good humour from his face.

'I got a gut feeling we're on the verge of some kind of black hole here,' he growled. 'You know, like lots of people being pulled over the edge and disappearing … like Thomas, Flaherty and former President Holland.'

'Can Flaherty take refuge in our embassy?' the president asked Laila Achmed.

'No For two reasons. The first is I think it's pretty clear he wants to see this Thomas thing through, and the second is I think our ambassador is compromised.'

'Should I pull him out?'

'No, I don't think so,' Laila said thoughtfully. 'Not right now anyway. It might send the wrong kind of message to the Israelis, might even prompt them to go pre-emptive. Also, it might seriously compromise the assets we've got.'

The tap on the door alerted them to the Attorney General's return.

'You ready to shock and awe us, David?' the president asked, with forced good humour.

'Pardon?'

'What's the plan, David?'

David Duke hitched his spectacles a little higher and nodded, as if he was shaking his thoughts into a logical sequence. He drew a steadying breath.

Potomac Heights, Washington DC

The doorbell rang. God, he hated that twee faux-carillon sound, another of Susan's must-haves since they'd moved into this upmarket neighbourhood. It tinkled again and Lieutenant Colonel Drew Hunt turned down the television and called, 'Suze, could you get that, honey?'

More bells!

'The bells of bloody Saint Mary's,' he grunted and swung his legs out of the La-Z-Boy.

The two men at the door wore identical suits and sported Mormon-tight haircuts.

'What is this?'

'IRS, sir,' the smaller of the two said, flashing ID. 'May we come in?'

The Pentagon, Washington DC

'Anything else, Bill?'

'Just this, General. It's marked private and confidential, so I thought it best you opened it yourself, sir.'

'Probably my son Adam, currently saving the damn whale somewhere and playing fast and loose with his old man's money in the process.'

'It was hand-delivered by military messenger, sir.'

General R. H. Highlander laid his glowing briar in the tray and slit the buff envelope with his thumbnail. He flattened the letter on his desk and angled the desk-lamp. He read it through once, ignoring the tightening in his chest, and started again from the top. Second time around, his vision seemed to waver and strange blank spaces occurred in the text. Only the words 'Colombia', 'Special Unit' and 'Investigation' stayed visible, burning into his staring eyes.

'General, sir, you feeling okay?'

'Yes,' he grunted, with a massive effort. 'That'll be all, Lieutenant.'

He didn't return the subordinate's salute, keeping his hands beneath the rim of the desk. When the door closed, he raised his hands to put the letter back in the envelope. After the second failed attempt, he rested them on the desk, where they drummed softly in time with the shudders that racked his body.

Military Medical Facility, Virginia

The doctor washed his hands thoroughly and elbowed the spigot until it settled to a drip. He tore a length of towel from the dispenser, blotted his fingers dry, then tossed the sodden paper into the trash bin. Involuntarily, he looked into the mirror over the washbasin.

'All files pertaining to the case of Michael Flaherty to be forwarded immediately to this office,' he recited in his head.

'They know,' he whispered, and leaned his forehead for solace against the cool mirror. 'They know.'

CIA Director's Residence, Washington DC

Benson pressed the disconnect button and flung the cellphone against the wall. On impact, a thin metal sheath popped loose and a battery dropped gently onto the carpet. 'Cowards,' he ground out, through clenched teeth. 'One sniff of a hunting dog in the cover and they're ready for flight. It's what they want you to do, goddamnit. Once you break cover – boom, one by one.'

'I take it that particular metaphor wasn't for my benefit, Benson.'

The man who stood inside the door was dressed conservatively in a navy wool suit that accentuated the brilliance of his white shirt. He was wearing a silk tie that shifted colour, like oil on water, every time he moved.

Benson hadn't heard him enter. If he had, the other wouldn't have been Scylla.

'How long have you been standing there?'

'Which translates as, how much did I hear?' Scylla said, revealing strong white teeth in a saturnine face. Although of medium height, he radiated a sense of self-possession that was almost hypnotic. It had often proved lethally attractive for those the assassin hunted.

'Drink, Scylla?' Benson asked, to break the tension.

'Why not? I'll have what you're having, Benson.'

Benson upended the decanter, giving it no time to catch its breath, until the two tumblers brimmed with amber liquid. He placed one glass on the far side of the desk and raised his own.

'I asked how long you'd been there,' he said evenly, and forced the neat Glenfiddich past his lips, holding it on his tongue until it burned, to cauterise his anger and centre him.

Scylla slipped smoothly into a chair and stretched a languid hand for his drink.

'Let's just say I was here long enough to deduce there's some huffing and puffing going on and some of the little piggies are beginning to squeal. Cheers,' he said, in the same calm tone, and sipped his drink. He sat back, placed his palms on his knees and waited.

How does he do that? Benson wondered. How does he switch off and become immobile as a damn rock? Good metaphor for a man with his code name, he thought, and ran with it because why settle for one metaphor? Should have called him Crocodile ... lying half-submerged like a flaking log for hours on end and then – snap. It only ever took one bite.

'It seems Ms President has rented a pair of balls,' Benson said.

'Pithily put,' Scylla said, through lazy lips. 'And ... the ramifications?'

'Depends. The little piggies, as you call them, are running in panicked circles. Panic spreads, my dear Scylla, as I'm sure you know.'

'And are you huff-proof, Benson?'

'That's why I called you,' Benson answered, and tossed a folder to the other side of the desk.

Scylla teased it open with the tip of his forefinger.

'Surely not,' he said tonelessly, and shook his head as if he was puzzled by the vagaries of fate. 'Naughty Catherine. Whoever would have thought?'

Benson dropped his eyes to the desk and concentrated on a matter-of-fact tone.

'Why take chances? She's been around for ever.'

'Well, nothing lasts for ever, does it, Benson? And the other two?'

'You can have them for dessert.'

'You do know this is going to be very expensive, Benson?'

'I'm worth it.'

☣

Benson checked that the little box of tricks attached to the desk phone was operational before dialling.

'Come on, Baldwin,' he muttered, as the phone rang and rang. 'Bastard's probably laying siege to Dammiato . Answer the fu—'

'Language, Benson. Is there a problem?'

'Why the hell don't you answer the goddamn phone, Baldwin? You think it's fucking charades we're playing here? You think you can go camping around in armour waving your shiny sword? Be delusional in your own time, Sir Knight.'

The silence from the other end buzzed like a mosquito in his ear.

'You there, Baldwin?'

'Yes.'

He heard the menace in the flat answer but the rage wouldn't release him.

'I want you to bring the next stage forward.'

'To when exactly?'

'To seven a.m. tomorrow – exactly.'

'But, Benson, I—'

'Don't but-Benson me, Baldwin. The bitch in the White House thinks she can play hardball with me from her fucking Oval tower. Well, it only takes one bullet.'

Part of his brain became alerted to the fact that he was screaming and his entire frame shuddered as if in shock. He was bent double, the phone still clutched to a face engorged with blood. A long swaying loop of saliva hung from his chin.

'Benson? Benson?'

Benson swiped his sleeve over his mouth and straightened slowly.

'Tomorrow, Baldwin,' he said, in a hoarse whisper. 'Tomorrow.'

Baldwin's Mansion, Jerusalem

Jack Holland moaned in his sleep and held a hand over his eyes as if shielding himself from some horror. The nightmare was the one that had disturbed his rest since he was a boy. The word 'boy' triggered some neural mechanism and a picture of two boys came into sharp focus in his head. The older one, twelve going on thirteen, was gliding over a frozen pond as if the skates were part of his feet. His brother turned a frost-burned face in his direction. 'Chicken, chicken,' he taunted.

'I ain't no chicken,' he murmured, as the smaller boy dragged a foot sulkily in the snow at the edge of the ice. He felt hate boil in his belly as he watched his brother skate so effortlessly. 'William did everything good,' the sleeping man murmured, 'better 'n me. Pop said no goin' on the ice. Gonna tell Pop.'

'The fuck you will.'

'Tell him you said "f—" what you said.'

Nothing could delay or halt the inevitable. The boy in his dream sucked in a breath as the ice popped and blasted it back out as the pond swallowed his brother.

'William,' the man whispered breathlessly, 'William.'

He was sliding on his belly to the grinning hole, calling, calling. Inches from his face, his brother looked at him from under the pale blue ice. He started to scream.

'Mr Holland.'

'Wha' … What time is it?'

'It's five thirty, sir.'

Jack Holland licked dry lips and focused on the Mameluke standing beside his bed. 'Well, thanks for the time-check, watchman,' he growled, and rolled over.

'Mr Holland, Sir Baldwin would like you to shower and get dressed. Breakfast is served in fifteen minutes.'

'Tell'em to go back to Hell.'

He felt a sudden chill as the blankets fled the bed.

'He said you should come or I was to bring you, sir.'

'Okay, okay.' He swung his feet to the floor and glowered until the door closed.

He felt as if he'd run a marathon. He tried to distract himself from the acid residue of the dream that lingered in his belly. 'How ya doin', Jack?' he asked himself. 'Tired.'

'Ah, c'mon.'

'Okay, exhausted.'

'Shouldn't that be 'emotional' as in 'tired and …''

'I know how it goes, damnit. Hollands don't do emotional, except for Momma.'

'Daddy? Well, here comes good ol' Abe fresh arrived from Mount Rushmore with the tablets of wisdom.'

'Be a man, Jack. Straighten your spine, boy. Your brother is dead – accident. Life goes on.'

'But I dream, Daddy.'

'Work hard and play hard, Jack. You've a helluva pair of shoes to fill. William would have—'

'Yeah, William would have been top of the class, summa cum laude, youngest congressman on the Hill, married to a smart and beautiful woman, President of the United States. I was all those things, Daddy. But I was not William. I was …'

He felt the urge to roll back into the sweat-damp bed and draw his knees tightly to his chest.

'Jack and the Beanstalk, honey.'

Momma sitting by the bed, turning the pages carefully, so the tremble didn't show. Momma reading the story really slowly, so her words wouldn't slur, riffling his hair good night 'cause if she kissed him he might smell her breath.

'"Jack killed the Giant and came home to his mother with great treasure and they lived happily ever after."'

What a crock!

Baldwin sat at the table in the light-washed breakfast room, the pale Mameluke still and attentive at his shoulder.

'Ah, Mr Holland, I trust you slept well?'

'Your trust would be misplaced.'

'Only in this particular instance, I hope?'

Careful, Jack, he told himself, the Giant can smell your blood. At least it's 'Mr Holland' today, he mused. Fantasy setting's turned to low. Thank you, Jesus. Go with the flow, Jack.

'Good news, Mr Holland. Remember I said you would meet with some people to discuss matters of, eh, mutual benefit? Well, today's the day. Mark will drive you and—'

'Who are those people?'

'Why, pillars of the community – men who command respect, patriots one and all, Mr Holland. Just like you.'

Jack Holland looked at Baldwin and saw his father – same hectoring voice, same bully-boy tactics.

'Bullies start out by pulling the wings from butterflies, Jack. Then they move on to little kids. Find a place to hide, son.'

'Where, Momma?'

'Inside, honey.'

Bethlehem

As the car exited the Damascus gate, the guy playing the drums in Jack Holland's head shifted to brushes on cymbals behind his right eye. By the time they reached the Wall, the drummer had packed his kit and gone. The soldiers wore the blank mask issued as standard equipment to the military worldwide. Holland observed as the Mameluke flashed the papers. The soldier scanned them slowly and turned away to the glass booth. Ten minutes is a long time to wait in the sun, he thought, sitting in the air-conditioned car and watching the Mameluke, as he knew someone in the booth was doing. He watched him as he had watched supplicants in the Oval Office. Most people just couldn't help themselves. Sooner or later they would touch the face, shift the feet and go through an entire repertoire of non-verbal signals an astute observer would place in the scales against the weight of their paper. The Mameluke was a pro, he conceded grudgingly. When the soldier turned away, the guy seemed seemed to slip into standby mode. Even in the refrigerated car, Holland felt a bead of sympathetic sweat swell and slide down his back.

The metal gate inched upwards and they were through. Holland exhaled a breath he hadn't realised he'd been holding. The car wound up through narrow streets made even more cramped by single-storey stalls that jutted out to crowd them. He noted the profusion of brightly coloured plastic utensils, imported fabrics and the empty spaces on shelves in the food-stalls. Women passed slowly, most carrying a basket or plastic shopping bag and wearing the heavy shapeless burka. Men stood singly in the stalls or sat in silent clusters outside coffee shops. Only the kids stared. If he could have smelled the place, he knew it would have that dead-air odour he had encountered in small-town America where local industry had gone belly-up and the shopping mall was three miles down the highway. It was the unmistakable stench of disappointment.

'Here.'

They climbed out before a high courtyard wall. He noted the absence of graffiti and the wary body language of the men who flanked the door. Someone with clout owns this place, he thought, and the guards ain't locals. Jack Holland flexed his hands, straightened his spine and stuck out his chin.

'Showtime,' he murmured.

He was taken into a spacious, high-vaulted room, bordered on three sides by silent men in upright chairs. His politician's eye swept over them. Local folks, he concluded, probably representatives of the community except for the man who sat beside the little guy in the white robes and skull-cap.

'*As-salamu 'Alaykum,*' he said, placing his right palm over his heart.

'*Wa 'Alaykum as-salaam*,' they chorused, except for the guy in the tan slacks and buttoned-down cream shirt who sat by Skull-cap. He's the man, Holland concluded, and the ritual dance began. There was a vacant chair to the left of the man in the skull-cap, who, Holland guessed, was the local imam. When he was seated, a round-faced man took the floor. Jack Holland had heard it all before in town halls, lodges and hotel function rooms. Mentally he ticked off the items on the agenda. Jobs, living conditions, education – the usual recipe, lacking only the essential ingredient: Israel. He marvelled at the ability of successive speakers to ignore that 'elephant in the room'. He assumed a listening posture, smiling and nodding when appropriate. He was on cruise-control right up to the moment when a young guy rose and introduced himself as the local teacher. He continued in careful, slightly archaic English, detailing the inadequacy of the space available, lack of books and materials, opportunities for access to higher education, then stopped. Holland sensed a quickening of interest – or was it apprehension? – in the room as the teacher seemed to wrestle with something inside himself. When he raised his head, there was a resolute expression on his face that stiffened Jack Holland in his chair.

'Former President Holland,' the young man began, 'we say our children are our future. Perhaps you also say this in the United States. There are those among us who do not value education, those who say it is worth nothing, that books do not feed a family. There are also those who say that our children should only be instructed in the Holy Qur'an.'

Holland felt the old man beside him stiffen and saw a ripple of unease spread around the room.

'We are descended,' the teacher continued, 'from those

who gave mathematics to the world. We are the heirs of those who mapped the stars when Europe was in darkness and America undiscovered. We are of the bloodline of those who preserved not only the holy books and teachings of Islam but the books of the Christians and the Jews so that we would understand the world. What man would deprive his children of those treasures? What man would bend his child's head from the stars and command him to be satisfied with the sight of sand?'

The unease in the room was almost palpable. Jack Holland was convinced that the teacher would have been shouted down if not for the presence of the illustrious visitor.

The teacher resumed with the same quiet intensity:

'Without education, our children are not innocent but ignorant. Ignorance is a room without the light and furnishings of truth. It is an empty room kept swept and ready for untruth. The truth is that our children are penned here like sheep and there are wolves among the flock.'

A low rumble of anger sounded in the room and the teacher raised his voice to override it.

'It is written in the Holy Qur'an,' he said, and the rumble subsided, 'that if anyone kills a human being, except as a punishment for villainy in the land, it would be as if he had killed the whole people. We are putting weapons and not books into our children's hands, Mr Former President. If the killing continues it will never stop until we are all dead. The Israelis have taken many things from us, but what are things? We can survive the loss of many things but we cannot survive the loss of hope. They must not take away hope for the future. You must say these things to the Americans and the Israelis, Mr Former President.'

He sat down and all heads swivelled to Jack Holland. Holland had the reputation of a man who could do a presentation on auto-pilot. The cynics argued that in Congress and the Oval Office he had amassed millions of frequent-flyer points by winging his way through recycled speeches. He knew he could do it now: he could weave their straw into tinsel and be the hell out of there before the shine wore off. He looked again at the young teacher sitting absolutely alone in the crowded room and stood.

'Some things are important,' he said quietly. 'Things like sanitation, clean water, good housing, because people who must worry about the basics have no energy to spare to create something better. They spend their lives locked into the present moment and that becomes their legacy for their children and their children's children. Yes, some things are important because they're basic, but some things are important because they're better, like jobs. I've heard it said that a man can't have dignity without a job. I don't agree. The way I see it, there is no dignity in a job. There is dignity in the human being and that human gives dignity to whatever he does. That dignity doesn't come with the job or disappear with it. At least, I hope not, speaking as a former President of the United States. Jobs are good for many reasons. They give us a chance to make our mark, to do something for ourselves, our families and our communities. They give us a sense of owner-ship over our lives. It's hard to develop that if someone else is feeding your children, although, in times of crisis, relief is necessary. It's hard to develop it when you live on charity, although there are times when charity is necessary. Your Holy Book and mine and the one held holy by the Israelis all agree on the virtue of charity and that the giver and receiver are both blessed. But what is best? This young man has said it better than I can. You once led the world in mathematics, science and astronomy. The journey back to eminence begins with a child with a book and a hope for a better future. What man among you would deny his child that opportunity?'

He paused and delivered his final line.

'I promise to bring your voice, your hope and your dream to the people of the United States and Israel.'

The teacher stood and applauded enthusiastically. The others clapped politely, except for the man with a wolf's eyes, in the tan jeans and button-down shirt. One vote is one more than I had coming in, Jack Holland thought ruefully, and sat down.

❧

He was left with Wolf-man and the two heavies who had come in from the gate.

Time for hardball, he thought. Bring it on.

'Perhaps Mr Holland wishes to see where the dream will happen,' Wolf-man said.

It was everything he had seen in newscasts and documentaries with the added element of smell. They stepped over sewage ditches to enter plastic lean-tos and shake the limp hands of idle men. The women, as he had seen in parts of Africa, moved busily in the background, working hard at making some kind of normality and security for their families. He was shown the bloodstained tracks where an Israeli tank had chewed an old man to death and the razed site of a suspect's home. Although weary to the core of his heart, he was sharp enough to notice a bunch of cameramen circling their little party. Al Jazeera? Mossad? He couldn't tell and didn't ask. He thought he knew how this particular drama would play out. He felt certain there would be a palaver with the hard men and braced himself to listen to details of armaments required to pursue the glorious struggle. He felt dirty, a fraud, a man who spoke of books and haggled over the price of bombs. It didn't pan out that way. They escorted him back to his car and the imperturbable Mameluke.

The car corkscrewed down the narrow streets and picked up outriders as it went, kids with tiny American flags, young men shouting and punching the air. He didn't feel remotely threatened: young and old were smiling. At the Wall, the soldiers waved them to a halt while others took up positions facing the crowd. The Mameluke was arguing, more animated than he had been before.

'What's the problem?'

'They want to search the car.'

'Go ahead.'

He heaved himself out of the back seat and a hundred pairs of hands sprouted from the crowd. He was doing what he loved to do, pressing the flesh, patting babies, going grin-to-grin with kids and old men. The shot flash-froze the scene. A heartbeat later, it dissolved into bedlam. Fathers swept their children into high embraces and lunged to safety. Old men tottered uncertainly or fell beneath the feet of others. He saw soldiers fan out, looking for the source of the bullet and, in a fleeting instant, he saw a guy with a camera, rock-steady in the maelstrom. A strong arm gripped his shoulder and spun him into the sanctuary of the car. The driver revved and leaned on the horn until the gate rose and they were through. He turned to look behind and was surprised to see a guy flatten himself over the handlebars of a motorbike to avoid decapitation from the descending metal gate. He angled himself on the back seat to track his progress in the wing-mirror and saw him appear and disappear as he rode the security dips. At the first junction, the biker peeled away. Holland was willing to lay good money that he had been one of the camera-jockeys recording his movements beyond the Wall.

ॐ

Goliath disassembled the weapon and stored it in his camera bag. He slung it over his shoulder and kick-started the bike, accelerating, heading straight for the Wall. He had deliberately aimed high, socking the high-velocity round into the masonry, ten feet above the former President's head. In the ensuing panic, he had seen the military hustle the car to safety through the Wall. Mission accomplished. The Mossad ID evaporated any delay at the military checkpoint and he was already gaining speed as he bent to avoid the descending gate. Technically, he had played his part but a niggle of unease refused to let up and he gunned the bike up a ramp and back onto the highway. In his side-mirror, he saw the former president's car lean out to overtake a truck. Goliath surged ahead to keep a good distance, and a line of other vehicles, between them. Security drivers, he knew, tended to keep one eye for a tail and the other on the bumper before them.

On the outskirts of Jerusalem, he swerved into a filling station and hoisted the bike onto its stand, well away from the station-cum-cafeteria. It took him ten seconds and a small lock-pick and he was driving a nondescript Fiat when the target car swept by. Slotting into the traffic stream, six cars back, he watched for their indicator and followed its blink winding away from the city and working up the Mount of Olives. On the way, he stripped off his jacket and popped his sunglasses into his shirt pocket. Gradually, he nosed closer to the lead car as it topped the rise. The viewing area to the left had the usual throng of tourists and he watched for a parking space.

The taxi driver jolted awake as the back door slammed.

'Straight ahead, I'll tell you when,' the passenger said.

Baldwin's Mansion, Jerusalem

Inside, the air was blessedly cool and Holland mounted the stairs, eagerly anticipating the longest shower in history. The dazzling strip of sunlight on the carpet at the turn of the stairs narrowed his eyes. His attention moved to the arrow-slit window and the view beyond. He put out his hand to steady himself against the banister. Through the narrow window, he saw his driver pop the trunk of the car. He squinted against the glare for a clearer look.

'Ah, Mr Holland.'

He jerked around to see Baldwin stride from the top of the stairs to place his bulk between Holland and the window.

'A very successful trip, I believe,' Baldwin said, watching Holland very closely.

Any doubts Holland had entertained went west as he saw the mocking smile twist the man's mouth. He had spotted the lower half of a man emerge from the trunk of the car.

Baldwin seemed to savour the disgust that washed over Jack Holland's face.

'As they say in America, Mr Former President,' he said, 'you really delivered.'

He slammed the heavy door and flung his jacket onto the bed. Any residual good feeling he carried from his experience beyond the Wall soured into self-loathing. A mule, he thought. Yeah, one of those hard-up bastards who let the drug lords shove condoms packed with cocaine up their butts so they can earn a few bucks when they come out the other side of Customs. When they deliver, he thought, and the phrase burned his brain so that he dropped his head into his hands and squeezed his temples.

'Hey, Jack,' a voice whispered from the past, 'What's the problem, kiddo?'

He hadn't thought of Gillespie, the old ward boss, in a lifetime. That had been when he was the fresh-faced congressman, new to the Hill, full of spit and vinegar and all the other clichés. And then some whoreson journalist had done a number on him. He had to admit it had been a classic of the genre: Jack the Lad had segued into 'usually reliable sources', spiced with a plethora of half-truths and a soupçon of speculation.

'The result, Dizzy, my old friend, is that he kicked me in the ass.'

'Take it from one who knows, Jack,' the old politician had murmured, around his cigar, 'gettin' kicked in the ass means you're out in front.'

Even now he had to laugh. It was the kind of laugh that could have elongated into tears, and he snapped his jacket off the bed, rummaging for his cellphone. 'Kick ass, Jack,' he muttered, as he prodded the numbers. 'Operator, could you connect me to the embassy of the United States, please?'

US Embassy, Jerusalem

Avery Young, first secretary at the embassy, watched Ambassador Herbert Love glad-hand his way around the group of visitors in the large reception room. He flicked open a folder to check their provenance and smiled. Yet another batch of Baptist pilgrims from Alabama, he noted. They were led by a senator, a dead-ringer for an MGM Moses, complete with flowing white locks and sepulchral voice. The file said they were foundry workers and their spouses. Probably served their time in Hell already, he mused. He checked his watch and raised an eyebrow at the catering manager, who nodded. It was time for the Rapture Folk to move on, and the staff began to remove the coffee pots and biscuits. Ambassador Love, framed by two large ladies, struck a final pose for the photographers.

'Excuse me, Mr Young.'

Abigail Hubble inclined her head from outside the open door, and Young eased himself gratefully out of the room.

'Sorry to bother you, sir, but I have a gentleman on the line who insists on speaking to the ambassador.'

Young touched her elbow and steered her into an alcove lit by a tall window.

'Would that be insists as in "I am the chosen of Yahweh with a message from Mount Sinai for the ambassador" or "I am Hashid the wrath of Allah with a truckload of Semtex parked in your driveway" or …' She began to smile. '…"I'm from Pennsylvania and I've lost my passport"?'

She covered her mouth for a moment before replying. 'Actually, it doesn't fall into any of those categories. He's very insistent, sir. I tried to ask a few questions but he cut me off. He said, "Tell them it's Jack Holland."'

Avery Young felt sweat bloom on his forehead and angled his body so that the strong sunlight came from behind him.

'Ask him to hold for the first secretary,' he said calmly, 'and put him through to my office.'

Young waited until she was out of sight before he pressed a handkerchief to his forehead. 'Oh, Jesus, God,' he muttered.

The insistent burr grew in volume as he entered his office and locked the door. He slid into the chair and took a steadying breath before he lifted the receiver. 'How can I help you, sir?'

He listened intently, then spoke in the robotic voice favoured by public servants all over the world.

'You'll understand, sir, that for security reasons this call may be recorded. Have you some means of verifying who you claim to be?'

He held the receiver away from his ear as a stream of invective crackled from the other end. Good, he nodded, rant your way into the file marked 'Nuisance'.

'That may very well be, sir,' he interrupted smoothly, 'but you'll appreciate I have no way of verifying who you claim to be. I should also point out that it is a serious offence under Israeli law to—'

Excellent, he thought, as the receiver buzzed in his hand: from irritated to apoplectic in two seconds flat.

'Sir … sir, I really want to help you here. Sir, perhaps you could give me a message for the ambassador. Unfortunately he's occupied right now but I could get a message to him. If you could give me your number he'll call you back … Thank you, I've got that … Yes, directly, sir. And thank you for calling, sir. If there is any way the United States embassy can be of assistance in the—'

He listened to the disconnect tone for a few moments before dropping the receiver.

'And have a nice day, sir,' he muttered.

⁂

Avery Young checked the visitor roster again, then slipped inside the reception room. The Hallelujah Chorus from Alabama had been replaced by a group of community leaders from Gaza and the temperature in the room had dropped accordingly. Young had written the brief and should have been included in the meeting but the ambassador was much too politically astute to include anyone at a meeting like this. Love had been the political choice of the Jewish lobby in the United States and the appointment of a president who owed them. Young knew that 'Herbie the Hawk', as he was known to the junior staff, was a raptor resting on the wrist of the Israeli government. He would greet this group formally, listen attentively, parrot the government line and show them the door.

'Your Excellency,' he whispered in his ear, 'if I could speak to you privately.'

'Not unless we got a missile inbound from Iran, Avery,' the ambassador grunted, leaning back in his high-winged chair.

'No, sir. We just had a call from a gentleman who claims to be Jack Holland.'

'*The* Jack Holland?'

'That's who the caller claimed to be, sir.'

'We have any intel to say Jack Holland is in Israel?'

'Nothing in the official communications, sir.'

The ambassador glazed over.

'Write me up a memo, Avery,' he said dismissively.

Avery Young clicked the cellphone closed and dropped it into his shirt pocket. Baldwin had appeared unsurprised at the news – in fact, he'd seemed amused. 'Strike two,' he'd said, and hung up. The first secretary turned his attention to composing the memo re one Jack Holland and his mysterious call to the embassy. By early afternoon the matter would be academic.

Washington University

'You're sure everything's ready, Marjorie? Run it by me one more time.'

Marjorie shifted her glasses from the top of her head to read the itinerary – again.

'Presidential motorcade arrives before the Administration Building. You greet President Radford and escort her to your office for refreshments.'

'Shouldn't we take the elevator?'

'No, White House Security said no elevator. Guess it wouldn't do to have the president trapped between floors while the red phone rings in the Oval Office.'

'Marjorie!'

'Course, it would give you the chance to come the heavy about the lack of federal funding, captive audience and all that.'

'Thank you, Marjorie. I gather the answer is no elevator. Have you seen Professor Hancock?'

'He's in his department with some of the postgrads.'

'Is he dressed?'

'Unfortunately.'

'Oh, for Heaven's sake, I meant is he dressed ... appropriately?'

The phone burred and Marjorie swept it up. 'President's arriving in thirty seconds, sir.' She smiled.

'Oh, God,' James J. Ford, President of the University of Washington, flapped, 'do I look okay?'

'Yes, sir, extremely ... appropriate. Very ... presidential, sir.'

❧❧❧

Ellen Radford allowed the little man to shepherd her to his office and accepted his offer of coffee. She patted the chaise-longue beside her and he perched like a nervous sparrow.

'Mr President,' she began, and saw him swell at the title. 'I know you were ... not amused when I poached David Duke for my cabinet.'

'Well, Ms President, it is a great honour when one of our professors attains such high office but ...'

'But it's a headache finding a replacement of similar stature.'

'Yes, it is.'

She placed her coffee cup on a nearby table and gave her full attention to the academic.

'I think I may be able to make some form of restitution,' she said, smiling. 'I want Professor Hancock to head up a new government department.'

She saw confusion in his face and pressed on.

'You're thinking this sounds more like academic larceny rather than restitution, right?'

'Right.'

'The new department would be based here,' she said, 'completely funded from the public purse and under the direct patronage of the President of the United States. It would attract students of hydrology and allied disciplines from all over the world. The basic brief would be to harness cutting-edge technology and expertise and put it at the service of developing countries.'

'It sounds wonderful,' President Ford breathed. 'I'm sure Professor Hancock will be honoured and, ah, thrilled by your proposal, Ms President.'

Hydrology Department, Washington University
'No!'

President James J. Ford looked as if he'd been punched in the stomach. Ellen Radford stared at Professor Hancock. He was wearing drab olive trousers, an open-necked green shirt and a stubborn expression. She sat upright on the folding metal chair amid the mayhem that passed for his office.

'Why not?' she asked.

'Because when government funds a university department there's always a quid pro quo. Sooner or later the pressure starts to build on the faculty to dance with the Pentagon.'

'Not on my watch,' she shot back.

'Your watch lasts all of four years, ma'am, eight tops. You're asking me to set up a department, recruit staff, attract students and liaise with governments in the developing world. If I do all that and some politico in the Oval Office decides to pull the plug, whatever standing we'll have built up internationally will be shot. We could never get our credibility back.'

'You're right.'

'What?'

'I said you're right. The strength of the proposal is that the President of the United States can make it happen. It's also its weakness. What can be made by a president can be unmade by a successor, unless …'

'Unless what?'

'Unless between now and the end of my four-year term, someone can come up with a cast-iron way to guarantee independent funding for the department. That would make your reservations about the Pentagon and my successor baseless.'

'Who's the someone?'

'It looks like there are just two principals involved in this venture, Professor, and one of them has a country to run.'

She stood up to leave and Special Agent Harley materialised at her side. She stepped away from the two academics and Harley leaned close. 'Secretary of State wants to talk to you, ma'am,' he whispered, handing her a cellphone. He positioned himself out of earshot and in the eyeline of everyone else in the room.

❧❦

John Hancock saw her in profile as she lifted the phone to her ear. He saw her face tighten and took an involuntary step forward, only to be frozen by a stare from the special agent. When he glanced back, the phone had disappeared and she seemed lost in thought. Abruptly, she turned and strode back to where the two academics stood together. He thought she looked uncharacteristically fragile and immensely attractive. He wondered what it would feel like to put his arms around her. It would feel like being dead, the special agent's eyes signalled, as if he had read his mind.

'Thank you for your time, gentlemen,' she said.

Bodies began to move in the choreographed dance designed to protect her, and she was gone. Hancock heard a wheezing sound and turned to look down at the livid face of the President of the University.

'You,' the old man managed, 'you … buy yourself a goddamn suit.'

The Oval Office, The White House

'This is a recording sent over by CNN, Ms President. The original broadcast went out on Al Jazeera. Thirty minutes back, it started airing on the major US networks.'

Ellen Radford sat behind her desk as the intern loaded the disk, handed the remote control to the Secretary of State and left the room.

Laila Achmed checked that the president and Senator Melly were ready before she pressed the button.

A carefully coiffed and smiling anchorman swung to the autocue.

'Former President Jack Holland made a surprise visit to Bethlehem today,' he intoned, 'crossing the controversial Wall that separates Israelis from Palestinians to meet with leaders of the local community. After the meeting, Mr Holland was brought to the camps on the outskirts of the town to see at first hand the hardships of those who live in a stateless situation.'

Ellen Radford shook her head. How could Jack be so dumb? she wondered. How could he let himself be paraded like this?

'The people of Bethlehem showed their appreciation of the visit as his car wound its way back to the military checkpoint at the Wall.'

This was illustrated by footage of the car being escorted by smiling children and young men pumping the air and chanting.

'But at Checkpoint 300, the only crossing in the Wall between Bethlehem and Jerusalem, things began to get out of hand.'

The Safe House, Jerusalem
'Avram, get the hell in here.'

'What is it?'

'C'mon,' Goldberg urged, crabbing sideways on the sofa to give him room. 'Get this,' she said, around a mouthful of bagel. On the television a soldier argued with the driver of a car at the crossing in the Wall. A thick-set man emerged from the rear and the camera zoomed in to focus on him.

'Who's he?' Avram asked.

'He's Jack Holland, former President of the United States. You missed his meaningful-walk-and-sincere-face routine in the camps.'

'For this relief,' Avram began, 'fuck!'

There was no mistaking the pop of the gunshot and the shockwave of humans that raced back from the car. The detectives sat on the edge of the sofa as the American was bundled into the car and it accelerated through the gate. A scared-looking journalist came to camera to intone, 'Yet another outreach in the name of peace is spurned at the concrete wall that runs like a fault-line between Israel and the

Palestinians. How much pressure can it take before we have the earthquake of a new intifada … or worse?'

'God, I hate clichés like the plague,' Goldberg quipped, swinging her legs up beneath her and settling back comfortably. Her partner stayed erect, staring at the final sequence before the anchorman segued into speculation about the build-up of nuclear arms in Iran.

'Earth to Avram, what's the big deal? It's a quiet news night, so what are the stories? Former president not shot, there might be nuclear arms in Iran, give me a break he—'

'Goldberg, is this live or recorded?'

His tone snapped her head up.

'Recorded. I set it automatically in case we were late ho— late back.'

'Rewind it, will you? I want to see it again.'

The Oval Office, The White House
'You sure you don't want to see it again?'

'I'm sure, Laila, thanks.'

The Secretary of State flicked a button and the television blanked.

'What's coming down the track, Laila?' the president asked.

Laila Achmed sat on a chair beside the senator and took a second to gather her thoughts.

'The Israeli government will protest,' she said simply. 'They will ask why a former President of the United States shows solidarity with the Palestinians while the present incumbent maintains a policy of support for the integrity of the Israeli state. The ambassador will be here tomorrow, latest.'

'Home front, Henry?'

'Political pressure from our opponents in Congress and the Senate. One or more of the usual mouths for hire will pop up on television – usual script. What is Jack doing there? Did you know? Did you send him?'

'I'm not getting into that dog-fight.'

'Then you should think of a press release, something short and to the point. And no RSVP, thank you. You will definitely not be taking further questions.'

'What was he doing there?' she asked.

Senator Melly sighed. 'From what we know, we can say with a fair degree of certainty that Jack didn't just develop itchy feet in Africa and decide the scratch was in Israel.'

'Colloquial overload, Henry,' the president said tiredly. 'Run that by me again.'

'Meaning,' Melly said, 'he didn't just go off his own bat. Someone asked him or someone sent him.'

'You thinking the same someone I'm thinking?'

The senator nodded grimly.

'Best scenario is that Benson is using Jack to keep you unsettled. After Laila's nephew and Ephrem's granddaddy, this is his second pitch, Ellen. You called Benson on the Colombian thing and, hey presto, Jack steps up to bat.'

'What's the worst scenario?'

'Well, I hope I'm wrong, but …'

'I hate when you say that, Henry. It always means you're pretty sure you're right and want to soften the blow. It's a kind thought, Senator, but candour is what I need right now.'

'Yes, ma'am. The worst-case scenario is that Benson is using Jack—'

'To embarrass me?'

'Yes, that too. I keep asking myself, why is Jack in Jerusalem? Jack doesn't need to be anywhere outside Washington to cause embarrassment, if you get my meaning.'

'Loud and clear, Henry.'

'I think what we've just seen is a side-show, Ellen. Maybe like an hors-d'oeuvre to the main course. Okay, okay, I forget everybody's gone linear these days. I got a gut feeling that Jack is being used. Whether he knows that or not, I can't say. What I can say is that he can't be in Israel without a helluva lot of people knowing.'

'Like who?'

'Like the Israeli government for a start. They must know he entered the country. Who gave him the damn papers to cross the Wall? Someone like Jack could be used by parties unfavourably disposed towards the Israelis so, why risk shooting themselves in the foot? It doesn't pan out. So, let's go back to first principles. Let's assume Jack is there because Benson wants him there for a reason that's more important than distracting you from the Colombian affair. The Israelis want him there for reasons of their own, so they allow him to go where he shouldn't and kick up holy hell when he does.'

'Can we bring him out, Laila?'

'Yes, we can. The question is, should we? It might imply we sent him there in the first place and, as a US citizen, he has the right to decide whether to stay or leave. We can't force that issue.'

'Anything from our embassy?'

'Nothing. The ambassador is on my list to call after this meeting.'

'I'll be here.'

When the Secretary of State had left, the silence was broken by the sound of shoes striking the panel under the desk. 'That's better.' The president sighed. 'Suppose I draft the press release and you vet it, Henry?'

'Okay, but the White House press secretary ain't gonna like it.'

'The White House press secretary can take a long walk off a short pier, Henry,' she said firmly.

'Can I get you some coffee?'

'Would you? Bring a big pot for the both of us. It's shaping up to being that kind of day.'

The Safe House, Jerusalem

Avram watched the footage of the confrontation at the Wall. The two-shot showed the driver present his papers to a soldier and an angry, silent interchange. As the driver walked back to the car, the camera zoomed out to include the man climbing out of the rear. Quickly, the camera operator zoomed in and sharpened focus to provide a close-up of the man's face. The American's head masked the driver until he gave a half-turn and the driver's face was revealed. Immediately the camera operator thumbed the focus-ring.

'Freeze,' Avram barked. 'Back it up a few frames and replay.'

Goldberg had taken up a position at his elbow and she reversed the sequence to the point where the car stopped at the gate in the Wall. She scrutinised the images as they flicked by and jumped when he said, 'There.'

'Him?'

'Yes, he's a dead ringer for the guy in my apartment, but it's not him. Could be his brother, though – same features, same outfit.'

Avram leaned forward as though he might see something beyond the dimensions of the screen.

'Anyway,' he said, sitting back, 'the whole thing stinks.'

'What stinks in particular?'

He lurched up from the sofa and grabbed a beer. He raised an eyebrow in her direction and she shook her head.

'Soldier wanted to search the car,' he said. 'I'm sure of it.'

'Oh, come on, Avram,' she said. 'He's going to search the car of the former President of the United States? Yeah, right. And tomorrow he's herding goats in the Negev.'

"Former' is the operative word here, partner,' Avram said quietly. 'That Holland guy is out of the diplomatic loop.'

He moved to stand before her.

'What happened next, Goldberg?'

'The shot.'

'And?'

'And … there was panic. Someone shoved the former President into the car and they were hurried through the gate.'

'And?

'And … Jesus!'

'Not exactly, partner,' Avram said, with a small smile. 'I'm not saying it was baby Jesus born in Bethlehem who was smuggled out in the boot of that car.'

'I think I'll have that beer, after all,' Goldberg said wanly. She took a sip. 'Avram,' she said quietly, 'there was something else.'

'What?'

Goldberg snatched up the remote control.

'Maybe because you were watching for that guy with the car you missed it.'

'Missed what?'

'It's coming up. I'm just running it on.'

The screen flickered to show surging bodies and a soldier milling his arm to urge the car through the gate. The camera operator couldn't resist the perfect end-image. Avram and Goldberg watched as the picture zoomed in to catch the receding car being gradually occluded by the descending metal door. Something blurred in the frame and she froze it.

'It's a guy on a motorbike going through after them,' she said. 'Lucky not to lose his head.'

'Tasteless, Goldberg,' Avram muttered, but his eyes were riveted on the screen. She flicked it on to the final frames, letting them run in slo-mo. As the motorcyclist bent his body under the door, he angled his head back so that he was facing the camera.

'Jesus!' Avram said.

'I thought we'd sorted all that?'

'No, Goldberg, listen.'

He was beside her on the sofa, his face just inches from her own.

'You know you're amazing?'

'I am?'

'Absolutely! I'd missed it.'

'That's a first?'

'The guy on the bike. I know him. Isn't that wonderful?'

'Terrific,' she said. 'Hey, where are you going?'

'Gotta make some calls and track him down,' he said, and left.

Goldberg realised she hadn't been breathing for a while and drew a long breath. She looked at the face frozen on the television screen.

'I don't know who you are, fella,' she muttered, 'but you'd better be worth it.'

Archaeological Dig, Valley of Kidron
Brother Juniper followed the young woman into the hut beside the dig. She was dressed in khaki shirt and shorts, like the others he had seen in the long trench outside. 'You will wait here for Fra Pablo,' she said, directing him to a metal folding-chair beside a trestle table covered in small cardboard boxes.

'There is beer in the refrigerator,' she added.

He guessed from the accent that she was German.

'You find all this stuff here?' he asked, waving at the contents of the boxes. She gave him a frank stare and he felt like a very small boy who had just asked a particularly dumb question.

'But of course,' she said curtly, then seemed to relent as she took in the sweat-stains on his dusty brown habit.

'It is a midden.'

'A midden?'

Her cornflower eyes revolved at his ignorance.

'A midden is a place for rubbish,' she explained. 'Two thousand years ago people threw "stuff", as you say, in the midden. It can tell us much about how they lived.'

'Wow,' he said, and bent over one of the boxes.

'Do not touch,' she barked.

He had to struggle with the urge to reply, '*Nein, nein, mein Kommandant.*'

Brother Juniper opted for a bottle of cold water and settled to wait. Waiting had never been his strong suit, he reflected.

Engineers had a strong urge to be up and doing; an urge that had brought him into conflict with his novice master.

'You must pray for one hour every day, for the virtue of patience, Brother.'

'You mean like "God give me patience and I want it now", Father?'

'Perhaps two hours of prayer would be better, Brother,' the novice master had sighed, 'and two days of putting out the rubbish.'

Tim Conway had been sympathetic. 'Horses for courses, lad,' he'd said brightly. 'Some guys have a gift for preaching or contemplation or whatever. What's your gift?'

'I fix things.'

'So, go fix! This whole excuse for a building is falling down around our ears. You're a kid in a candy factory, Bob.'

'Will they let me do that?'

'By 'they' I take it you mean our Brothers of the Sacred Demarcation Line, the Armenians, Orthodox and all the rest.'

'Yes, I don't feel exactly welcome anywhere outside our own patch.'

Father Guardian had taken up his pondering pose, which involved having his feet on the desk.

'You know,' he mused aloud, 'that the Pope gave Francis permission to preach pretty much anywhere? Now, that was a big deal at the time. Only bishops had that right. Oh, they could delegate it, but their lordships weren't big on delegation. *Plus ça change*, huh? Francis, under all the meek-and-mild, was a wily old dog. He asked permission every damn time, really pumped up the episcopal egos. If he was refused or insulted, he said, "God give you peace." What a pain in the butt. You curse a guy and he blesses you back. Wore them down eventually.'

He swung his feet off the desk.

'Now, get the hell outta here. I've got some hotshot accountants coming in to untangle Werner's accounts. Go be a Franciscan – shoo.'

Juniper had tried it the Franciscan way and had been rebuffed and insulted in at least four languages. But he had kept coming back and, grudgingly, the Syrians had allowed him to talk them out of removing a retaining wall. Word spread that the beanpole American Franciscan didn't seem to have an agenda riding on his offers of help. The big breakthrough came when the Armenian Patriarch had confronted him while Juniper was balanced on a stepladder inspecting a sagging arch.

'Why do you do this?' he demanded.

Juniper had wiped a few thousand years of dust from his eyes before replying, 'Because I can.'

'And what do you want in return?' the bearded old man had asked suspiciously.

'It is written, "Charity is its own reward,"' Juniper had said, and gone back to measuring the arch for a brace. When he climbed down later, a cowled Armenian priest had beckoned him to follow and led him through a series of carpeted and lamp-filled shrines to the patriarch's quarters.

'Sit!'

He tried to whack most of the dust from his habit before occupying the plush chair. The Patriarch had gazed at the grimy Franciscan for a long time before reaching under his desk and conjuring up a bottle of Armenian brandy.

'Charity is its own reward, Brother,' he'd said, with a small smile, 'but, is it not written, too, that "The labourer is worthy of his hire"?'

'It is also written,' Juniper had countered, 'that "The one

who has should share with the one who has not. By this shall they know that you are followers of mine." You got two glasses?' he added.

'Brother Juniper?'

Juniper started and stood.

'I am Fra Pablo,' the wizened man said, offering a dirty hand. 'You have workman's hands,' he said happily, as he grasped Juniper's calloused one in a firm grip. '*Bueno*, I like that. Please, sit. What can I do for you, Brother?'

Briefly, Juniper told him of his interest in the Crusades. The old priest smiled indulgently until the Franciscan mentioned the Tears of God.

'Others have searched for Lacrimae Dei, Brother,' he said cautiously. 'Perhaps they thought it was something of great value. In my experience, true relics are of value to none but believers.'

'I've never believed the Holy Grail was studded with precious stones, Fra Pablo,' Juniper said earnestly. 'It seems to me that a poor preacher from Galilee would have drunk out of something more ordinary. Nor do I imagine that a supper cup in a tavern was preserved for two thousand years because someone knew all those years ago that the man who drank from it was special.'

He shook his head.

'I think it's more likely that, sooner or later, it went into the midden like everything else.'

The old Dominican nodded thoughtfully, never taking his eyes from the younger man's face. 'As I have said,' he continued quietly, 'others have searched for what you seek and have met misfortune. Some think there may be a curse attached to the Lacrimae Dei.'

Brother Juniper wiped his sleeve across his forehead.

'I don't go with the curse theory, Fra Pablo,' he said. 'Maybe people thought a curse would keep grave-robbers out of the pyramids and ancient tombs but I don't buy the story that Carter and the others were fated to die because they opened Tutankhamun's. I guess if people really believed that stuff today, there wouldn't be any archaeologists and we'd be missing out on what previous generations can teach us.'

Fra Pablo seemed to weigh Juniper's words for a long time. He stood abruptly and walked to a filing cabinet. When he returned, he cleared a space on the cluttered table and spread a parchment on the surface.

'I did not show this to the others,' he said. 'Perhaps they were too zealous in their search. Dominicans like me are cautious of zealots ever since our brother Dominicans, Torquemada and Tetzel.'

'What is it?'

'It is a copy of a letter sent by Godfrey de Bouillon, the crusader, to Pope Urban II. I came across it while I was researching Urban's letters when I was a young man. It seems Urban and Godfrey did not trust the Crusader's brother, Baldwin. Godfrey was a true knight, in the Romantic mould. He was also a true believer, a humble man who refused the Crown of Jerusalem. I think his experience of Jerusalem changed him. The letters to the pope show that he had set out to drive the infidel from the Holy Places. When this was accomplished, he began to appreciate that those Holy Places were also held holy by Judaism and Islam. He urged the pope to make Jerusalem an open city for all three faiths.'

'And what happened?'

'He died,' the old man said softly, 'or was poisoned, and

Baldwin, his brother, took the crown and lost Jerusalem. It has been lost to all of us ever since. Please, pardon me, I tend to wander.'

He pointed at the parchment.

'How is your Latin?

'*Un pocito*, a very little.' Juniper smiled.

'Allow me to translate for you. It is written as a poem, perhaps because letters could be read and resealed.'

He pulled a pair of wire-framed spectacles from his shirt pocket and shook them open.

'This is the relevant verse,' he said, bending over the parchment. '"As I stand, where stood the Tree of Life,/I give glory to God who sustains us with the fount of the Son's tears./The Lacrimae Dei that dwell in darkness." 'I'm sorry,' he said, straightening, 'my English is not so good.'

As Juniper finished scribbling the translation, a young man poked his head inside the door.

'Fra Pablo, can you come?'

'Ah, Jacob, this is Brother Juniper, a true searcher like ourselves.'

As the two men shook hands, the Dominican added, 'Jacob is the curator of this dig, Brother. The young are truly wonderful, no?'

He shook hands warmly with Juniper.

'*Vaya con Dios*,' he said. 'And good luck with Lacrimae Dei.'

Juniper made his way carefully along the boardwalk beside the trench. Behind him, the young curator held a ladder while Fra Pablo stepped gingerly into the midden. Jacob walked into the shadow of a twisted olive tree. Looking at the receding figure of the Franciscan, he put a phone to his ear. He didn't see the man who set aside his shovel and lifted a cellphone to his ear at the other end of the dig.

'Inspector Bernstein, please,' Jacob said.

The Safe House, Jerusalem
Avram picked it up on the first ring.

'Suffering from cabin-fever yet, Avram?'

'Sharpening the axe, Inspector.'

'Goldberg there with you?'

'She's in the other room watching television.'

'Avram, if you were my son, I'd slap you.'

'Inspector, if you were my father, you'd try it.'

'We've got a lead on the Tears of God,' the inspector said.

✿

Juniper stopped at Muhammad's coffee shop and lowered himself gratefully into a chair in the shade outside. The coffee was aromatic and sweet and he stretched his legs, letting his eyes wander over the piggy-back buildings and winding alleys of the Arab Quarter. His emotions fluctuated between terror at the haphazard nature of the structures and admiration for the human beings who had cobbled homes out of the rubble of antiquity. He was surprised when Muhammad stopped at his elbow and began adding milk to a jug already two-thirds full.

'You are being watched, my friend,' the slight man murmured, while concentrating on his task. 'I will call Father Guardian. When you finish, come inside to pay.'

Juniper resisted the urge to look around and waited a few

moments until the excuse of lifting his cup allowed him to survey the street. A woman, in a burka, glided by on the far pavement towing a reluctant child. Two Orthodox Jewish men argued and gesticulated as their reflections mimicked them in a shop window. His eyes trawled back to the window and fixed on the faint outline of a man standing just ten feet away from where he was sitting. Juniper rose slowly and sauntered inside. Immediately, Muhammad grabbed his elbow and hurried him through a plastic-strip curtain into a steamy kitchen. He barked something in Arabic and a young man, with frightened eyes, took the Franciscan's hand and hauled him through a door into the alley at the back of the café. He pointed right and whispered, 'Run!'

⁂

'Talk to me, Avram,' Goldberg whispered, as she cruised the most direct route from Kidron to the Holy Sepulchre, scanning the pavements and resisting the urge to floor the pedal.

'He's a Franciscan, Goldberg, about six two in a brown skirt. He should be as obvious as a Harlem Globetrotter in Tokyo.'

'Sporting allusion not helpful.' She glared at a guy with a cellphone glued to his ear who stepped right in front of her hood. 'I need to lose this car,' she muttered, 'too many distractions.' She swerved into a space.

'Complications,' Avram's voice whispered in her ear, and his tension stilled her. 'Father Guardian's just been on. Our man is being tailed. Remember, walk don't run,' he counselled. 'If you spot the target, scan his tail and stay back.'

'I hear you, Papa,' she grunted, and flung herself out of the car.

At the end of the first block Avram's voice crackled in her ear.

'I'm on foot in the alleys to your left.'

She stepped under the awning of a cornerstore and stood. One of Avram's maxims, she remembered, was 'Stand in shadow.' Another was 'Keep still and watch the flow.' Avram and Confucius, she fretted, as she watched the passage of people, men of a thousand maxims. The Franciscan was walking away from her about two blocks up, his height and brown garb identifying him easily in the crowd.

'Avram, subject two blocks ahead of me coming up to the Maccabee butcher shop.'

'On my way.'

She moved at a brisk pace, staying on the edge of the pavement near the road so that she could step out and run if need arose. As she drew closer, she could see the tension in his shoulders and felt a stab of sympathy for the lumbering, hunted man. 'Stay aloof and detached' – Avram-maxim number four popped into her head.

'Yeah,' she muttered, 'like the world needs loofs. As for detached …'

'Goldberg, I can see and hear you. Watching your back from the other side. Stop and go, okay?'

She stopped abruptly and checked a shop window, watching the reflection for anything suspicious. Nothing.

'He's going to make it to the Holy Sepulchre,' Avram's voice whispered in her ear. 'I'm on the entrance, you're inside.'

Avram watched the Franciscan bow his head to enter the doorway, like a runner breasting a tape. He saw Goldberg follow at twenty paces and moved diagonally to lounge against a corner where he could cover the entrance.

∞✕∞

Juniper hurried towards the Chapel of the Crucifixion, standing aside to make space for an Orthodox procession. He leaned against the cool stones and tried to stop panting. A number of the Orthodox priests smiled in his direction and he bobbed his head in acknowledgement. The chapel began to fill with the sounds of sonorous chanting and the clashing of thuribles. On impulse, he retraced his steps to the tiny chapel nearer the entrance: the actual site of the Crucifixion.

Brother Athanasius sat in his usual chair, scanning a Greek newspaper with one eye and keeping the other fixed irritably on a pair of female pilgrims. The original Athanasius, Juniper knew from his history studies, had argued so energetically against the Arian heresy at Nicaea that he had earned the nickname Athanasius Contra Mundum – Athanasius against the world. Coiled on his rickety chair, Brother Athanasius regularly cast a cold eye on the world and usually found it wanting. If he had a weakness, it was for American cigarettes; a weakness Brother Juniper, in his one-man crusade for brotherly accord, was only too happy to cultivate. He followed the old monk's baleful stare and watched the pilgrims. The younger of the two women began to weep silently. The older woman placed the palm of one hand against her back in a simple gesture of solidarity. Juniper found himself moved by the tableau. He saw a tear slip from the older woman's eye and drop to the floor. For a moment, he stood paralysed as a light seemed to flash behind his eyes. He eased a hand into the deep pocket of his brown robes and withdrew the wrinkled sheet of paper. Holding it between thumb and forefinger, he scanned the contents. "As I stand where stood the Tree of Life,/I give thanks to God who sustains us with the fount of the Son's tears./The Lacrimae Dei that dwell in darkness."

He took a deep breath to control the excitement that threatened to rob him of it. Was it possible? Surely the Tree of Life was an allusion to the Cross of Jesus. Could the Tears of God be here? But where? In his peripheral vision, he saw Athanasius raise his head from the newspaper and smile at him. Automatically, Juniper bowed in the old man's direction and, as he straightened, he saw Athanasius do likewise. Behind him, on the wall, he saw the faint outline of a door, like a door to a cupboard. His brain raced and his hand dug deeper in his other pocket as he closed the distance between them.

'Brother Juniper, *kali mera*,' the old man whispered, through his beard.

'*Kali mera*, Brother Athanasius,' he replied softly. 'You must be tired with watching, Brother. Wouldn't you like to walk outside for a while?'

He couldn't be sure how much of what he'd said was actually understood, but the concerned expression on his face, allied to the nod at the door and the appearance of the packet of cigarettes in his hand seemed to bridge the language gap. Athanasius crinkled his eyes almost closed with pure pleasure, palmed the cigarettes and hobbled away. Juniper slumped onto the chair and tried to relax. Presently the pilgrims crossed themselves devoutly and left. He swivelled in the chair and examined the door. The lock on the bolt looked brand new, but the bolt could have been there since … Since Adam was a boy, his father said, in his memory, and he smiled. He braced his knee against the door, grabbed the lock and pulled. There was a heart-stopping moment of resistance before the entire apparatus came away so quickly that he almost overbalanced. Tentatively, he pushed the door and it moved inward. He wormed his way inside and stood in a small stone chamber. Carefully, he eased the door flush with the wall and waited for his eyes to adjust to the dark. As his pupils expanded, he examined the small space. It seemed rectangular, but a deeper shade of shadow in the far right corner piqued his interest and drew him to investigate. It was an opening to what seemed like a passage leading away at an angle from the chamber. Juniper took two slow steps into the darkness and on the third his foot found air. Frantically, he jammed his palms against the walls to stop himself from falling headlong. Shuddering, he waited for a moment before sliding his right foot forward and down … Steps.

❧❧

'Goldberg?'

'Nothing. You?'

'Same.'

'Avram, we knew where the Franciscan was going, right?'

'Right.'

'If we hadn't been watching for a tail, we could have come here directly and waited for him.'

'Damn. Look around the hallway for a map. Check out the Franciscan area. I'm on my way.'

❧❧

Juniper padded cautiously down the steps, sliding his palm along the wall beside him for balance and comfort in the semi-dark. He felt a cooling flow of air and smelled dust and decay overlaid with a darker, dank odour. I do not want to find the remains of the last Franciscan who came wandering down here and was lost for ever, he thought. Cut it out, he remonstrated with himself. You're an engineer, damnit. You had your imagination removed at bir—

The small scraping sound came from somewhere in the rear. He felt his neck muscles tighten, drawing the small hairs upright. Athanasius? Had he noticed the missing lock? Would he follow me down here in the dark? The second sound seemed to come from somewhere closer. It was the kind of sound someone might make sliding a foot along a floor; someone in pursuit, who would become immobile and watch to see if the quarry took flight. Hide, his brain commanded, and he looked around for a refuge.

❧❧❧

'This is the Calvary Chapel?' Avram whispered.

'Yeah, bare minimalist meets Baroque,' Goldberg muttered, taking in the austere Franciscan section cheek by jowl with the Byzantine excess of the Orthodox shrine. 'I have a hunch he wouldn't come here for sanctuary. Wait up a minute.'

She stood in thought for a few seconds.

'Back this way, towards the entrance. I think we passed it,' she said. She led him up some steps to a tiny chapel resting on a hewn rock. It was empty, except for a single chair and the temporal anomaly of a carefully folded newspaper. Avram circled to the right, keeping an eye on the entrance, while Goldberg moved to the chair. She bent to check the newspaper.

'Avram.'

৪৩৫৩

Juniper's hand slid from the smooth wall into an alcove and he followed it. After three paces, his extended fingers encountered rock and he turned to press his back against it. Instinctively, he brushed his fingers against his habit, wiping them of the film of algae that covered the surface of the wall. Rising damp, the engineer registered. He had seen some signs of it already in the upper structures. The dank smell seemed to be magnified in the cramped space and he breathed through his mouth, listening.

৪৩৫৩

The Mameluke lifted his head and sniffed the air like a hunting animal. He analysed and dismissed the odours of age and decay until he fastened on a faint scent of human sweat; a single vivid thread in a drab weave. His foot slid forward and found the floor at the bottom of the steps. Slowly, he moved his head from side to side, maximising the available light. Before him, he was aware of a circular chamber with a high, vaulted roof. To his right, the wall was divided into three alcoves, vertical slashes of shadow in the smooth stone. He brought the silenced pistol upright beside his cheek, locked his left hand over his right wrist and moved.

⁖✮⁗

Juniper sensed a change in the quality of the darkness before him. He was unconscious, at a rational level, of his heightened spatial awareness. Somehow he just seemed to know when the curve of an arch or the line of a wall was off. Something was off in his immediate surroundings. He sensed it in his belly and adrenalin surged through his system so that his body was charged with energy and the surrounding walls seemed to press on him. I'm standing in an upright coffin, he thought, and ran.

⁖✮⁗

Something flickered on the far side of the chamber and the hunter swivelled on the balls of his feet. As he did, the scrape of a sandal came from behind. He swung back that way, marking and following the shadow that scrambled across the chamber in search of deeper shadow. His right arm straightened and he sighted, his finger already exerting pressure on the trigger. Something brushed against his right leg and instinctively he lashed out with his foot. He realigned his aim and ignored the sting in his right ankle. The phut of the silenced gun followed fractionally on the grunt from his quarry and he saw the shadow tumble to the chamber floor. The Mameluke remembered the fate of his brother in Baldwin's pit. There could be no room for error. Again, he sighted along the weapon at the prone form.

He never heard the sound of the bullets that killed him. He felt two sledge-hammer blows to his back and had a brief illusion of flight before the darkness swallowed him.

'Am I dead?' Juniper croaked, as Goldberg turned him over onto his back.

'I'm no angel,' she said, sticking her gun back in its shoulder holster. She offered him her hand and tugged him upright.

'I tripped,' he said.

'Guess that saved your life, Brother,' she said, easing his head to one side to inspect the graze on his cheek. 'That, and a little black cat.'

'Gehenna,' he breathed. 'I always thought black cats were unlucky.'

'For some,' she said brusquely, and turned away.

'Avram?'

'He's dead,' Avram said, from the gloom. 'Same guy we saw on the news.'

'Maybe we should get you to Father Guardian's office, Brother,' she said. The Franciscan was wandering around the chamber, bent double.

'You gonna be sick?'

'No. I lost my sandal when I tripped.'

He scanned the floor for a few seconds and picked it up. Still holding it, he traced further along the floor.

'Here,' he said.

Goldberg moved up beside the squatting Franciscan and saw a hole in one of the flagstones. A rusty iron bar bisected it. As she watched, Brother Juniper lowered his face to the hole and inhaled. 'Well, I'll be damned,' he whispered.

'Obviously not today,' Goldberg said soothingly, taking his arm and leading him back to the steps. 'My partner, Avram, on the other hand …'

Father Guardian's Office, The Church of the Holy Sepulchre
'And that's it,' Juniper concluded, and reached for his glass.
Tim Conway raised his in a half-hearted toast and was joined
by Goldberg.

'Only the good die young, Juniper,' he said. 'Any clues on
the – the other guy?' he asked soberly.

'Yes and no,' Avram said. 'We've seen him before and someone like him. There was nothing on the body to identify him.'
Father Guardian nodded.

'I want to thank you for saving Brother Juniper's life,' he
said. 'At some cost to yourselves,' he added.

The two detectives locked eyes with him and nodded.

'He's not saved yet,' Avram said quietly. 'We have no
guarantee that whoever sent the first shooter won't send
another. We were lucky this time. If it hadn't been for my
partner …'

Goldberg felt her face redden and took a long pull from
her glass. Immediately she regretted it as the fiery liquid
napalmed her trachea. She could only nod dumbly as the
blurred shape of Father Guardian raised his glass in her
direction.

'I'd like to stay in Jerusalem,' Juniper said to Tim Conway.
'I'd prefer not to be sent out of the country, Tim. I feel I'm
just a gnat's whisker away from cracking this Tears of God
thing. Can you hide me somewhere until this blows over?'

'I can,' Avram said.

Mea Shearim, Jerusalem
Goldberg figured they were driving north. Avram had insisted
on taking the wheel.

'Brother Juniper has had his brush with death for today, partner,' he'd joked.

She wanted to work on a huff but the glow of his earlier compliment still warmed her and she sat in the back of the car behind Brother Juniper. Over his shoulder, she saw high, blind walls looming up before them.

'Where are all the windows?' the Franciscan asked, out of professional interest.

'On the inside,' Avram said.

'So, what is this place?'

'Mea Shearim,' Avram answered, easing the car into a parking space in the shadow of the wall.

'Don't remember ever being here,' Brother Juniper said, awed into whispering by the forbidding buildings.

'I have,' Avram said shortly, and began to walk.

They walked on either side of Goldberg along a cobbled street. She saw children with sidelocks and skull-caps pause at their play to watch them pass. Men in long black coats, hanging open over striped kaftans, turned their heads under broad-brimmed hats to track their progress. The older ones turned away angrily.

'Boy,' Brother Juniper whispered, 'this is what Israel must have looked like a hundred years ago.'

'Eighteen seventy-four, to be exact,' Avram said. 'It was built by the Ashkenazi Jews from Europe, mostly Hasidic and ultra-Orthodox. And by the way, Brother Juniper,' he added, 'this isn't Israel. The people here don't recognise the state of Israel and won't until the Messiah comes.'

The man who opened the door, Goldberg thought, could have stepped straight out of the Bible. He was a tall man whose broad shoulders filled the door frame. His white skull-cap was almost invisible in the thatch of grey hair that coiled in two locks at either side of his face and cascaded into a prophet's beard. Stern black eyes stared at the trio. Abruptly, he turned and walked into the house.

His place was taken by a matronly woman wearing an ill-fitting wig.

'Come inside,' she said, and led them into a dining area warm with the smell of freshly baked bread. As they sat at the table, she began to ferry place settings from the kitchen.

'May I help?' Goldberg offered.

'You are a guest,' the woman said, but she granted Goldberg a small smile of gratitude. When she returned to the table, she touched Avram's arm and inclined her head. He stood immediately and tapped once on a door beside the kitchen, then entered.

Goldberg and Brother Juniper exchanged a puzzled glance and sat in awkward silence. The woman returned with platters of food. She sat at the head of the table as they helped themselves. Goldberg looked her way and saw her glance anxiously at the closed door.

❧❦❧

'I want you to hide this man,' Avram said.

'Why?'

'Because there are people who want him dead. They tried once already today.'

'And you saved him?'

'I shot the man who would have killed him.'

The man sitting in profile at the other side of a small table stiffened.

'You come into my home with blood on your hands?'

'You'd prefer me to have stood by while an innocent man was slaughtered?'

'Why did you bring him here?'

'There was nowhere else. Also, I knew that if Mea Shearim took him no one else would.'

'The Israelis took you,' the man said vehemently.

'No, they didn't,' Avram said calmly.

'Is his presence here a danger to our people?'

'Yes.'

'I will have to consult with others.'

Avram nodded.

The old man rose and fetched a black coat and hat from a wardrobe against the wall. He walked out of the room without looking at Avram. When he heard the front door close, Avram rejoined the others at the table. The woman hurried to bring another plate and mounded it with food. They ate in silence. Later, when she stood up to carry the empty soup bowls to the kitchen, Goldberg gathered the plates.

'Where do I put these?' she asked.

'Here will be fine,' the woman said, edging sideways to make space at the draining board. They washed and stacked in companionable silence until the sink was empty.

'I'd better go and join the other two,' Goldberg said.

'In a while,' the woman said. 'Please, sit.' They sat on either side of the scrubbed wooden table.

'My name is Esther.'

'I'm Goldberg. That's what Av— what everyone calls me.'

'Were you born in Israel?'

'No, I'm … from America but I live in Jerusalem now. I'm a detective. Avram is my partner.'

The woman raised an eyebrow.

'No,' Goldberg said hurriedly, 'not like that.'

'Do you like him?'

'He can be a total pain in the bu— He can be difficult.'

'You didn't answer my question.'

'Esther, are you sure you were never a detective? Ya know, like in a former life?'

Esther shook her head.

'I was a lecturer in Jewish Studies,' she said. 'In America,' she added, with a twinkle.

'You were?'

'I was.' Esther nodded. 'I came to Jerusalem to do some research for my doctorate. I needed to interview some Hasidic scholars and came to Mea Shearim.'

'That must have set the cat among the pigeons.' Goldberg laughed. 'Sorry,' she said, 'I don't mean …'

'Actually, it was the other way around,' Esther continued. 'I felt like a sparrow among crows. All those men in black with long hair and pale faces really scared me. Most of them wouldn't even talk to me.'

'But not all?'

'No. I remember Rabbi Zephaniah spent a considerable period of time explaining why the state of Israel was a blasphemy to the Hasidic and ultra-Orthodox.'

'So, the rabbi converted you?'

'No, he did not,' Esther responded spiritedly. 'He married me.'

'Wow!'

'Yes, "wow" is probably as good a word as any for what happened,' Esther said wryly. 'There were all those meetings and all sorts of looks and dark mutterings, but Zephaniah wouldn't be dissuaded.'

'He must have loved you very much,' Goldberg said wistfully.

'Yes, he did,' Esther said. She leaned across the table and took Goldberg's hand.

'And do you love my son, Goldberg?' she asked.

⁂

Rabbi Zephaniah hung up his hat and sat directly opposite Brother Juniper.

'I am Rabbi Zephaniah,' he said. 'What are you called?'

'I'm Brother Juniper,' the big man said. 'I'm a Franciscan in the Holy Sepulchre.'

'You know Francis went to Sultan Malek Al-Kamil,' the rabbi said. 'He wanted to convert him to Christianity or die in the attempt. He succeeded in neither. Will you try to convert me, Brother Juniper?'

'I won't if you won't,' Brother Juniper said, smiling.

The rabbi's face softened a fraction.

'Our experience of the Franciscans,' he said thoughtfully, 'is that they have been the most Christian and the least Christian of all the religious groups who settled in Jerusalem. Do you understand?'

'I think so.'

'It is agreed,' the rabbi said, rising. 'You will live here as a member of my family until it is safe for you to return.'

'Thank you, Rabbi,' Juniper said. 'I'd like to be of some use.'

'What can you do?'

'I'm an engineer. I fix things.'

'Good. I will show you the roof of the synagogue.'

⁂

'He's your son?'

'Yes, he is our only child. Ari was born in Mea Shearim and, when he was seventeen, he decided to go to Israel and join the army.'

'Is this why your hus— I mean the rabbi finds it difficult?'

'Yes. The rabbi feels his son has died to him. But Zephaniah …'

She dabbed her eyes with a handkerchief. 'I see him watch the door as if he's waiting. I hear him, at night, walk in Ari's room.'

'What do you think of Ari's decision, Esther?'

'I think my son was true to his heart, as his father was when he married an outsider from America. Ari has lost so much. You know what happened?'

'I know.'

'He deserves—'

The door opened and Rabbi Zephaniah stepped into the kitchen.

'The Franciscan is staying,' he said.

'He is welcome,' Esther replied, rising to face her husband. 'As are all who come to our home,' she added. 'Come,' she said, taking Goldberg by the hand, 'I will say goodbye to my son.'

⊱✖⊰

Brother Juniper shook Avram's hand and hugged Goldberg awkwardly.

'I don't get to do that very often,' he said shyly.

'Practise, big boy,' she said, and hugged him back.

Esther took Avram and Goldberg's hands and walked them to the terrace outside. She kissed Goldberg on both cheeks.

'You are very beautiful, Goldberg,' she said. 'Come back to us soon.'

Goldberg turned away to give mother and son some space.

The Safe House, Jerusalem

They were sitting at the table nursing cold beers when he broke the silence that had settled between them as they left Mea Shearim.

'What?'

'What?'

'Is there an echo here, Goldberg?'

'Okay, Avram,' she said. 'I'm shocked, stunned, traumatised and almost at a loss for words to discover you have a mother. Satisfied?'

'What did you two talk about?'

'Fashion, movie-stars, diets …'

'Goldberg!'

She leaned across the table and stared into his face.

'I'll tell you what we talked about, numb-nuts,' she said furiously. 'We talked about men. And, in particular, we talked about an all too common sub-species known as *Homo ineptus*, you know, the big, strong, silent hominids who wander the world in a daze wondering where they put their fucking emotions. And …' she said, stabbing a finger in his chest '… and I'm going to bed. Goodnight!'

He sat for a long time after she'd left the room. He contemplated having another beer and decided against it: drinking a beer alone was just drinking, he thought. Finally, he buckled his beer can and lofted it into the bin.

At four in the morning, he woke suddenly and sat upright

in the bed. 'Hello, Goliath,' he said quietly. A shadow detached itself from beside the window and sat on the end of the bed.

'Put the light on, Avram,' Goliath whispered.

Avram squeezed his eyes shut against the sudden glare. When he opened them he was unsurprised to see the gun in Goliath's hand.

'Don't make any sudden moves,' Goliath said.

'Took the words right out of my mouth, bozo,' Goldberg said, from behind him, touching the cold muzzle of her firearm to the nape of his neck.

'She's very good, Avram,' Goliath said calmly.

'Yes, she's the best,' Avram agreed, 'although most people who pull a gun on me tend to discover that posthumously. Put the gun down, Goldberg,' he added.

'Are you crazy? He's going to kill you!'

'If Goliath wanted to kill me, I'd be dead,' he said reasonably. 'Put it down.'

Goliath felt the muzzle press once before it pulled away. Very slowly, he slipped his weapon into the shoulder holster.

'Let's make it unanimous,' Avram said, smiling grimly. He lifted a snub-nosed handgun from under the blankets and placed it on the bedside locker.

'Now what?' Goldberg muttered.

'Now you go and put some clothes on, partner,' Avram said, without inflection.

'We saw you on the news,' Avram said, tossing a beer to Goliath. 'You were doing a Steve McQueen under the gate at the Wall. Too many cameras there, soldier, shouldn't have looked back.'

'You know how it is in the movie business, Avram, stunt-rider never gets his face on the screen. So, you started making calls.'

'Yes. I called all the usual suspects and then a few I knew would call you.'

'They did. I'm here. So talk.'

Avram told him everything. Goldberg rejoined them as he started and chipped in occasionally with what Avram called 'colour' and she called 'context'. Avram took the story right up to the newscast he had watched with Goldberg.

'We saw the Holland guy at the Wall with a driver and the usual rigmarole about papers. Next he's doing the camps, pressing the flesh. Then we have rent-a-crowd running the car to the gate. So far so what? I'm thinking. Here's where it gets interesting. The driver is the same guy or a clone of the guy who tried to cancel my ticket, definitely the same guy who tried to take down the Franciscan. He's out of the equation but the link is the Tears of God, whatever that is. Goldberg saw you gurning for the camera and that set me pondering.'

'That was always your strong suit, Avram,' Goliath said drily.

'Not always,' Avram said, and sipped his beer. 'I figure it this way. You fire the shot, the car goes through and you follow. My guess is that there was someone in the trunk the former President didn't know about. He was the fall-guy; so what was your role, Goliath?'

'Pieces of a jigsaw,' Goliath said, and went on to add some of his own. When he'd finished, Goldberg looked at him in amazement.

'You met the director of Mossad face to face? Wow!'

'What my partner means,' Avram said, 'is that when the director allowed you to meet her, she was handing you a death sentence.'

'Actually,' Goliath said equably, 'she handed me yours as well, Avram. And yours, Ms Goldberg. This was after she gave me her Masada speech.'

'You never did like that speech, Goliath,' Avram said.

'Pardon a mere cop interrupting you old army buddies,' Goldberg said sweetly, 'but can you cut the happy-days routine, Goliath, and explain this Masada stuff?'

'Whatever happened to 'bozo'?'

'He's on probation,' she said darkly. 'Talk!'

'Masada was where a bunch of zealots held out against the Romans. Rather than go into slavery, they killed their wives and kids and fell on their own swords. So, Masada is where some army groups make their passing-out pledge. It's where they hear the Masada speech: no surrender, death before dishonour, thank you for coming and please leave your brain in the bin on your way out.'

Goliath stretched in the chair to ease some of the tension in his shoulders.

'Thing about zealots is they're Armageddon freaks, the kind of people who get antsy with trivia like diplomacy and democracy. If the end of days is slow to arrive, they're apt to give it a nudge.'

'Meaning what exactly?' she asked.

'Meaning everything seems to suggest that someone or a group of someones is pushing us helter-skelter towards a cliff edge and anyone who gets in their way …'

Avram and Goldberg filled that gap for themselves.

'So, what do we do?' she asked.

Goliath looked at Avram.

'I don't think Goldberg and I have much to go on, right now,' he said. 'It comes down to you, Goliath. Do you think you can suss out the place where the former President is holed up?'

'I can try.'

'Watch your back,' Avram said.

'I'm sure Detective Goldberg is watching that already.'

'Took the words right out of my mouth, bozo,' Goldberg muttered.

Church of the Holy Sepulchre, Jerusalem

Michael Flaherty paced the Spartan room – again. Walls closing in, Flaherty? he thought. Won't be long now. He stopped beside the small window and watched the pre-dawn limn the Jerusalem skyline. The Dome of the Rock almost filled the frame with its bulbous crown. Tim Conway had left some histories of Jerusalem and a few magazines as antidotes to boredom. Amazing what kind of knowledge a man can amass when he's waiting to die, he thought. He knew the Caliph of Damascus had raised the shrine in 691, marking the spot where legend held Muhammad began his journey to Heaven. Before that, it had been the site of Solomon's first temple. The golden dome sparkled in the first light and he smiled. Nothing in Jerusalem is as it seems, he mused. The books claimed the original dome was covered with ten thousand sheets of brass-gilt, sheathed with pure gold. It had duly collapsed, in 1016, and was rebuilt in dull lead. And today? Today the reflected light that caused him to squint was bouncing from gold-plated aluminium.

He paced again.

He ransacked his memory, trying to recall what Father Mack, his old priest-mentor, had said all those years ago when he was a boy on the Island. Suddenly the orator's voice sounded clearly in his head and he stopped to savour it.

'We live on an island, Michael, a knuckle of stone sticking up out of the Atlantic. An island can be a prison or a paradise, boy. You get to choose which one it is for you. Some men spend their days like greyhounds in a pen, racing from one side to the other, whining for the horizon. Others can inhabit the smallness and discover worlds beyond the horizons of themselves. What was it Hamlet said about space?'

'"I could be bounded in a nutshell and count myself a king of infinite space,"' the boy quoted.

Father Mack had nodded approvingly.

You never mentioned the next line, Father Mack, Michael thought sadly, the one that mentions 'bad dreams'. Surprisingly, the dreams had stopped since his arrival in Jerusalem. Nightmares enough during the day, he concluded. Even the twinges of his old wounds rarely bothered him, as if his body felt secure enough to disarm its warning system.

A sharp rap at the door interrupted his reverie and his shoulder hurt like hell.

'Come in, Brother Werner,' he said.

Werner entered warily and closed the door quickly behind him.

'How did you know it voss me?' he asked suspiciously.

'I knew it would be you from the day at the airport, Brother. What do you want?'

'I have a message for you,' Werner panted. 'It is time to go vither you vould not vish to go.'

'Ready when you are, Brother,' Michael said easily.

'Vait. Someone comes for you,' Werner said, and left the room. He returned momentarily, followed by a nun in a Carmelite habit. She kept her head bowed as she entered.

As soon as the door closed, she looked at Michael directly.

Her face was a stiff, blank mask. He had no doubt that she could arrange those features to simulate human emotions but her eyes would play no part in the charade. They might reflect as a mirror will but they could never reveal anything but the vacuum inside.

The eyes are the windows of the soul, his mother liked to quote. This particular soul seemed to have put up the shutters long ago.

'The sister vill bring you,' Werner said, as he stood beside her.

'Actually, there has been a change of plan,' she said. 'Cardinal Thomas has been encouraged to defer his … gratification. It seems Michael Flaherty is to make his way by a more circuitous route. That journey begins now.'

Her right hand blurred in a short vicious arc and struck Werner's throat, just above his Adam's apple. As the stricken man wheeled away, her left hand swept up to shoulder height holding a gun which she levelled at Michael's head. He could only watch in horror as the man with the crushed windpipe fell writhing to the floor and drowned in his own blood.

'Such a tragedy,' she said mockingly. 'But, then, you were a member of Special Forces, Michael Flaherty, trained in hand-to-hand combat. Perhaps Brother Werner was marginally more obnoxious than usual. You have twenty-four hours to elude the police and find Cardinal Thomas. If you fail, my instructions are to take an Island holiday. No,' she snapped, as he took a step forward. 'You know the odds.'

She backed slowly to the corridor outside and disappeared. Immediately, he pressed his fingers to Werner's neck in search of a pulse. He took his hand away and, using finger and thumb, closed the dead man's eyes.

Father Guardian's Office, The Church of the Holy Sepulchre
Tim Conway opened the door and looked at Michael Flaherty.
'Come in, man,' he said. 'You look like you've seen the devil.'

Michael waved away the offer of a drink and Tim refrained from filling his own glass.

'I want you to hear me out, Tim,' Michael said slowly. 'When I've finished, ask me any question you like but we won't have much time. Do you understand?'

The Father Guardian nodded bleakly.

In the same steady voice, Michael recounted what had happened from the moment he'd heard the tap on his door. For a full minute after he had finished, the Franciscan sat in stunned silence. His mouth worked a little before he was able to speak.

'What should I do, Michael?'

'As soon as I've gone, go to my room and discover the body. Don't touch anything. Come back here and call the police. Tell them ... tell them whatever you like, Tim, I release you from any bond of confidentiality.'

'Where will you go, Michael?'

'Better you don't know that – and, Tim, I'm sorry.'

Tim Conway looked suddenly aged beyond his years as if he had deflated inside his habit. He roused himself from his stupor, showing some of the old fire.

'I'm sorry about Werner too,' he said. 'I always suspected he was a thief, and the accountants tell me he's been reaming us financially for years. Obviously, he was a traitor as well, handing you over like that to ... them. It's important we tell the truth here – you don't need to carry more than you must. I'll do as you say. If I can do more, you'll ask.'

Tim Conway had placed the slim leather notebook on his desk blotter and opened it with trembling fingers. It contained a series of names and numbers, written in Brother Werner's Gothic script. He didn't need a facility with foreign languages to deduce that the names were of financial institutions. They were based in places like Zürich, Liechtenstein and the Cayman Islands. He guessed that the numbers unlocked various accounts. On impulse, after he had called the police, he had gone to Werner's room and rummaged among his papers. A bottom drawer in the desk had yielded the notebook and he had pocketed it without reading it. As he sat waiting for the arrival of the police he wondered if he had failed Werner. Perhaps if he had tried a little harder to like the man, he might have come to him when he had been tempted. You're beating yourself up unnecessarily, he chided himself. Werner was into his scams long before you got here.

'Father Guardian?'

Avram and Goldberg stood tentatively in the open door. Tim Conway slid a sheet of paper over the notebook while gesturing to them to take a seat. He rose to greet them but Goldberg pushed him gently back into the chair. 'You've had a shock,' she said. 'Is there anything you'd like me to get for you?'

'Yes, there is,' he said, smiling wanly. 'It's amber and aged for ten years in oak but, under the circumstances, I think I'll pass.'

'We don't want to make this any harder than it already is, Father, but we need to ask you a few questions.'

'That's your job,' he said. 'Let's get it over with.'

'Let's start with an easy question, Father,' Goldberg said, as Avram clicked his pen and opened a battered notebook on his knee.

'What can you tell us about Michael Flaherty?'

Fifteen minutes later, Tim Conway stopped talking. Goldberg sat on the edge of her chair, a dazed expression on her face. Beside her, Detective Avram still held his pen poised above the notebook. He hadn't written a single word. Goldberg was the first to recover.

'I got to ask, Father, but is there any chance he could be, you know, delusional? I mean, could he have made this up as a cover story for killing Brother Werner?'

'No!' Tim Conway said flatly. 'Everything he told me about himself could be a fantasy but the call from my superior in Rome was legit when he asked me to give him sanctuary here. The original request came from the Pope.'

'And all this Remnant stuff and the American cardinal, that's all kosher?'

'Yeah, it is, sad to say.'

'You say he's got twenty-four hours to get to the cardinal,' Avram said.

'That's what he said, Detective.'

'Do you have any idea where he might go?'

'Your guess is as good as mine, I'm afraid.'

Which, Goldberg noted, wasn't answering the question but she decided not to push it. Father Guardian looked as if the slightest nudge might topple him.

'He's got no transport or money and we have a pretty good description of him,' Avram said, pocketing his notebook as a prelude to departure.

'Shouldn't be too hard to find him.'

471

'Did I mention he served in the United States Special Forces?' Father Guardian enquired.

Jerusalem

Michael Flaherty stood at the side of the street with his arm outstretched, thumb extended. He was wearing a Franciscan habit over slacks and a shirt and the heat seemed to radiate in waves from the pavement beneath him. He mopped the long sleeve over his eyes, and when his vision cleared, he was looking at an army truck.

'Where you going, Father?' the moustachioed driver asked.

'Mount of Olives,' he replied.

The driver jerked his head back at the raucous troops in the open-sided truck.

'They're on their way to Hell,' he said happily. 'Maybe you can save them.'

Willing hands hoisted him among the heavily armed soldiers and the truck sailed on through every checkpoint.

⊗⊗⊗

The young novice peered at him through the bars.

'Monsignor?' she asked uncertainly.

'Could I see Mother Natasha, please, Sister? It's urgent.'

Mother Natasha looked shrunken in the huge chair. 'What a pleasant surprise,' she said, rousing herself to offer him her hand. 'Sister, can we have Russian tea for the visitor? It's obligatory,' she confided, in a whisper.

He sat beside her as the novice served tea in translucent china cups. When she had left, the old nun looked at him searchingly.

'You have not found the peace I wished for you,' she said sadly.

Haltingly, he told his story while the old voice crooned in sympathy, the aged hand caressing his own, unravelling the knots in his mind and heart. When he was spent, she spoke softly.

'Stay with us tonight,' she urged. 'Perhaps I will think of something – who knows? You will need your rest for whatever must be done.'

⁂∞

He rose up from just beneath the surface of sleep, irked into wakefulness by a ticking clock. He angled his watch to check the luminous dial. Four a.m., the witching hour, the hour at which, tradition claimed, most souls loosed their hold on life. His shoulder spasmed suddenly and he was wide awake. Someone or something was hunting in the dark.

'Use your senses,' the Special Forces instructors said. 'Aborigines smelled for rain, Bushmen watched for a single stalk of elephant grass moving contrary to the wind, the Iroquois listened to the forests before they hunted. You punks are deaf, dumb and blind in the world. Sharpen your senses or die.'

He took a deep breath and let it go, slowly stretching his senses like an invisible web. Something snagged his hearing. He resisted the urge to tighten, instead loosening his limbs and chest, breathing slowly to the pit of his stomach, in, out, in, out. The sound came from outside the window. His room was at ground level. This wing of the building was skirted by a narrow gravel path, beyond which a small brown lawn petered out among the trees that stood like a palisade inside the wall. Slowly and smoothly he eased from the bed and wormed into his shirt, trousers and socks.

'You got a weapon, grunt?' the instructor asked.

'No, sir.'

'You got two on your feet, asshole. Four if you got laces.'

Carrying his shoes in his left hand he felt his way with the right, reading the Braille of the furniture until he found the wall and slid towards the window.

'Light before is the enemy's friend, light behind is yours.'

'Yes, sir.'

An invisible moon shone a fitful cold light from the other side of the convent roof. He kept his eyes fixed, letting the scene imprint itself so that the slightest change would register through his optic nerve.

There! A blob of shadow, beyond the moon-slicked gravel, split like an amoeba. He tracked its trajectory, keeping his head immobile until the blob coalesced with the dark shadow of the gable. Slowly, slowly, he submerged beneath the level of the window and crabbed to the door, which he opened. He let his eyes travel low and from left to right down the corridor until they encountered a line of light. He tapped lightly on the door.

'Who is it?' a young voice asked. There was no trace of fear in it and he exhaled with relief.

'Michael Flaherty, Sister,' he said, keeping his mouth close to the door and enunciating very clearly. 'There is danger.'

ଚ୬ଓଷ

Christy Kenneally

Mother Natasha was dreaming of Aunt Olga's farmhouse. She
thought she could see it from above: a sturdy house buttressed
by a barn and shielded from the west wind by sentinel spruces.
From her vantage point, she saw the old dog stretch from the
mouth of the kennel and pock a path through the snow to
squat by the gate. He turned and started to pad back. When
he stopped again, he turned his head, neck stretched. It was
then she heard the rumble of engines. She was unsurprised to
wake with someone's hand over her mouth.

'Come, Mother,' the novice whispered.

⁓⁓⁓

Michael calmed his breathing and let his memory spool back
to the Special Forces night-fighting exercises.

It was midnight in the brightly lit gymnasium. The
instructor was a guy who looked as if he'd been poured into his
perfect uniform.

'Gentlemen!'

That raised a few snickers.

'Gentlemen, I want you to look at the gymnasium for a few
moments.'

There was the usual crap, guys striking poses and shading
their eyes, guys making exaggerated owl-eyes.

'Thank you,' the perfect man in the perfect uniform said.
'Now, where would you hide?'

Big Kowalski, who would die in Michael's arms, looked
baffled.

'Ain't no place to hide here, sir. Place is bare as a baby's butt,
sir.'

The instructor rode out the laughter.

475

'Quite right, soldier.'

He strode to the box on the wall and pulled a lever, flooding them with darkness.

'Now, gentlemen,' the voice said, 'find me.'

After fifteen minutes, the light flooded back on. Michael saw that at least two-thirds of the squad were wearing bang-bang-you're-dead adhesive stickers.

'I've left some books on the table outside, gentlemen,' the instructor said. 'I suggest you read them.'

Michael caught up with him at the door to the officers' mess.

'Sir,' he asked, 'what happens if the other guy's read the book?'

'What's your name, soldier?'

'Flaherty, sir, Michael Flaherty.'

'You didn't rush off right away to find me, did you?'

'No, sir.'

'Why not?'

'My eyes weren't accustomed to the dark, sir.'

'And when they were?'

'It wasn't all dark. There were pockets of it in the corners.'

The man nodded.

'To return to your question, soldier. If the other guy's read the book, forget it. The book, I mean, not the encounter. Books are for people who don't trust their instincts.'

He had tried it and found the instructor the second time.

There would be no second time tonight, he sensed. He followed the odour of incense to the little chapel and scooped charcoal from the thurible, rubbing it in streaks across his face and neck. Silently, he slipped his feet into his shoes. He would need both hands.

❧❧❧

The novice led Mother Natasha through a labyrinth of passages to a small door. Noiselessly, she drew back the bolt and pulled the door closed behind them. 'This way, Mother,' she whispered, keeping them close in the shadow cast by the moon shining from the other side of the convent. An owl ghosted past and they froze. When they came to the gravel strip, the young woman placed her lips close to her superior's ear.

'Put your feet down firmly on the stones,' she whispered. 'Take one step at a time and do not hurry.'

The old nun plodded carefully across the narrow strip, remembering crossing ice-bound rivers at another time in another place. The spruces rustled a welcome as they reached the wall.

'There is no door, Sister,' Mother Natasha panted.

'There is a little one behind the garden shed.'

'It has been overgrown for many years,' Mother Natasha protested.

'Not any more, Mother.'

As they passed through the door in the wall, Mother Natasha reflected that it wasn't the first time the novice had come this way. For the first time since their adventure had begun, she smiled.

❧❧❧

Moving bodies displace air, he thought, and was rewarded by the slightest twitch of a curtain at the far end of the reception room. He relaxed, leaning against a black shutter, letting his body sag into shapelessness. He began a slow count, and when he had reached three, he kicked out sideways and felt a satisfying connection. The shadow tumbled and rolled, coming up crouched in a knife-fighter stance. Michael circled away from the knife hand, making the striking arc longer. His opponent leaped forward, swung down and up for his belly. Michael spun sideways, grasped the knife hand by the wrist and tugged back. He heard the weapon thump to the carpet. At the same moment, his legs were swept out from under him and it was his turn to roll. A foot blurred past his face as he came to rest and instinctively he clutched and twisted. There was a loud crash followed by utter silence.

∞∞∞

Three small cottages huddled companionably together beside the road. The novice knocked on the second door. A light wavered and leaked over the doorstep from inside as someone approached. Mother Natasha heard a voice enquire in Arabic and the novice replied. The door opened immediately and a man raised a lantern to inspect them.

'Sister,' he said, 'a thousand welcomes.'

∞∞∞

Where? A shadow loomed to his left and he had raised his hands before he recognised the outline of the samovar. Instinctively he dropped them and the garrotte looped over his head.

∞∞∞

They were seated on cushions before an open fire, sipping mugs of scalding tea. The man sat respectfully, at a distance. A woman flitted between the kitchen and the table, ferrying plates of oaten cakes. Mother Natasha bowed her head in the man's direction.

'May God reward you for your kindness,' she said.

'God has rewarded us many times through our little sister,' he said simply.

'Who are you, sir?' she asked gently.

'We are Arab Christians, Sister,' he replied, lifting a small crucifix on a leather thong from inside his shirt. 'We had farms until the Israelis came. Now we have gardens. We grow as much as we can,' he said, 'but often there is not enough. Without little sister it would be hard. You must rest,' he admonished her.

'I fear we may have brought danger to your home, sir,' she said. 'Perhaps we should move on.'

'No, no,' he protested, patting the air before him with his palms. 'We have sent word to our neighbours. They will guard us.'

'Are they also Arab Christians?'

'No, Sister, they are Muslims. They have also known the kindness of little sister. They will guard us well.'

❧❧

He resisted the urge to surge away from his assailant – the instinctive response to an attack from behind. As the cord bit into his throat and began to constrict his air supply, he stepped back and stamped down hard with his right heel. He heard a grunt as it connected with his opponent's instep and the noose slackened. He swung his right elbow and sent the attacker stumbling against the samovar. Samovar and adversary crashed to the floor. Despite this setback, he saw the other man race for the door.

At last they were alone, lapped in the warm light of the fire. Mother Natasha felt deeply weary but she was not ready to sleep.

'It seems you are well known here, Sister,' she whispered.

'Yes, Mother.'

The young woman's face was a mere six inches from her own and she saw it stiffen.

'Tell me, child,' she said.

'I was in the garden,' the young woman began. 'I heard children laughing on the other side of the wall. It was how my brothers and sisters laughed.' Her eyes glistened in the faint light and she rubbed them with the heel of her hand before continuing.

'I opened the door just to see them, Mother. Later, we spoke and I learned of their difficulties. We have so much …'

'You know it is not our way to go out to the world, Sister,' her superior said. 'The world comes to us and we share our quiet to nourish souls.'

The novice looked around the room.

'This is not the world that comes to us, Mother,' she said. 'When we have shared our plenty with them, perhaps they will come to us to nourish their souls.'

The silence was broken only by the soft sounds of settling embers.

'If I have done wrong, I will do penance, Mother,' she said, in a small voice.

Mother Natasha had not experienced the gift of tears for a long time and she let them run their course.

'It seems to me,' she said finally, 'that the novice has

discovered something hidden from the superior. You share the laughter of children and the extra in our store. "By their fruits you shall know them," the gospel says. What are the fruits of your actions? We receive welcome and hospitality from the poor, and people of different faiths come together to protect us from evil.'

She extended a hand and touched the young woman's face.

'Am I at fault, Mother?' the novice asked.

'You are the future, Sister,' Mother Natasha answered.

∞✠∞

He tracked the wraith around the shoulder of the hill, dodging from one dark pool of shadow to another until a wall loomed before him. His quarry had disappeared. Probably through a door, he thought, which would now be locked. Five frustrating minutes passed before a leaning tree helped him over the wall. He stayed in the cover of the shrubbery bordering the drive. Two cars sat in their own soft shadows beside an imposing building. He rocked the smaller car on its springs until the alarm protested. Then he sprinted to the rear of the house. Timing his move to the whoops of the siren, he slammed his elbow against the glass of a ground-floor window. He was in. As his feet touched the floor, the room filled with light. A tall man, dressed in chain-mail, stood before him, hefting a wicked-looking broadsword.

'You precede expectation, Michael Flaherty,' he said, and swung.

Baldwin's Mansion, Jerusalem

Michael Flaherty knew it was a dream; the neural DVD that clicked into 'play' when he sank into REM sleep. Most often, it was a collage of seemingly unrelated images, as his conscious mind winnowed the happenings of the day. Thankfully, the horror-series, featuring walls of green water and the drowning face of his brother, seemed to come less often to drench the sheets and bring him gasping back to the light. A face resolved behind his eyelids and a familiar voice began to speak.

'Tonight, we'll take a tour of the chessboard, Michael.'

'Yes, Father Mack.'

The Island priest disinterred the chessmen from a carved wooden box. The boy was surprised to see cheap plastic figures stored in such a fine piece of workmanship and the priest snorted as he read his expression.

'When men take the time to make chessmen,' he said, with mock solemnity, 'that usually means there's peace in the land and the possibility of civilisation. When they start carving in ivory and fine woods, it's a sign that civilisation has peaked and started on the slow, sordid slide into decadence.'

'Where does plastic feature in that continuum, Father?' the boy asked, smiling.

'Somewhere beyond irony and beneath sarcasm, boy. Now, pay attention.'

He leaned forward and put a stubby finger on the castle.

'In this game, castles are just walls on wheels,' he said dismissively. 'This wall rolls forward or sideways. It stands out there on the edge of the board, guarding the four points of the compass because beyond that point be demons. What is the purpose of protective walls, Michael?'

'To keep people out, Father,' he replied promptly.

'Aye,' he nodded, 'and to keep them in. Remember that.' Then Father Mack shook his head as if to shift a mood that threatened to turn sombre.

'Example of a defensive wall, boy?'

'The Great Wall of China, Hadrian's Wall …'

'One example is an answer, two is a boast,' Father Mack admonished him lightly. 'Don't gild the lily. As you'd expect,' he said, moving his finger to the next piece, 'the knight stands in the shadow of his castle, represented by the figure of his horse, because the animal is marginally more intelligent than its master. A knight usually wears armour – portable walls, same strengths, same weaknesses. He's a man weighed down by his own protections, can't take two steps but he has to take one step sideways, for a rest.'

Again, the finger moved.

'In the shadow of the castle and under the protection of the knight, we find the lord bishop. He's the sidewinder of the board, always going off on a tangent, always calculating the angles.' He huffed angrily, 'Don't get me started.' He leaned back and took a long swallow of neat whiskey. 'Where was I?' he asked, thumbing his spectacles higher on his nose.

'The queen, Father.'

'Yes, of course, the queen. Women, boy,' he sighed, 'a species of which I know little and you know less. The queen, the woman, can do everything the men can, except the knight's sidestep. She wouldn't lower herself. She's adaptable, Michael, able to operate outside the rigid rules of the others, and she's suspected and even persecuted because of that. Example, please!'

'The witchcraft trials, Father.'

'Yes,' Father Mack said, roused again, 'the old toss-the-witch-in-the-river trick, sink and drown or float and burn.

Infallible logic, isn't it?' He snorted. 'Example of a woman who could outman the men?'

'Joan of Arc.'

'Delusional!'

'Boudicca.'

'Bloody Brit!'

'The Amazons.'

'Ah, well done, boy. The Amazons were the perfect example of the man-made myth, the personification of all their prejudices. According to the myth, they were man-haters who cut off their right breast to make it easier to draw a bow. D'you get the point, boy? The myth disfigures their femininity and reduces them to being more like a man.'

'Really?'

'It's a bloody myth, Michael,' the old priest said sternly, 'and don't go repeating that at home.'

'No, Father.'

Father Mack raised his finger and dropped it dramatically on the piece in the centre.

'And here,' he said sarcastically, 'at the centre of the universe, we find the king. Big fella, isn't he? So damned big he can't shift himself more than one step at a time in any direction. So, what strikes you about the great and the good lined up there before you, Michael Flaherty?'

The boy brooded over the chessboard in silence.

'They … they're all at the back, Father.'

'Damn right,' Father Mack said intensely. He continued speaking as if thinking aloud. 'That's where the so-called leaders tend to stay, isn't it? Napoleon, Haig and Hitler, leaders behind the lines with their dry maps and toy cannons, pushing the little man to die at Borodino and the Somme and

Stalingrad. And here are the little men,' he said, waving his
hand at the double phalanx of pawns, 'the over-the-top lads,
the run-at-the-guns lads. Cannon fodder.'

He reached behind him again for liquid sustenance.

'They're called pawns,' he said tiredly, as if worn out by the
injustice of it all. '"Pawn',' he continued, 'is a word that can
refer to something used, or to the act of trading something. In
either case, redemption can be costly. How do they move?
They move like the Assassins, Berserkers and Celts, in just one
direction – forward.'

He placed his finger horizontally on the board behind the
pawns and marched them forward.

'Like the Roman phalanx, they move forward one step at
a time, and they kill sideways.' He rubbed his nose with his
baton-finger. 'Truth is, pawns rarely kill anyone and, because
that's a given, they're often forgotten. But they're stubborn
little bastards, if you'll pardon my French, and sometimes …
sometimes they get between their powerful enemies and …'

The finger shot forward and toppled the king.

Michael heard someone call his name.

'I have to go, Father Mack,' the boy in the dream said.

'Yes.'

'You know,' Michael Flaherty said, as he hung suspended
between sleep and waking, 'that I never wanted to let you
go?'

Father Mack was fading as the voice called Michael's
name again.

'You didn't,' he said, 'not in any way that matters.' His
voice grew softer. 'Always with you, boy.' When he was
almost gone, he whispered, 'Love you, son.'

He woke and touched the welt on the side of his head where the Knight had struck him with the flat of the blade. He was sitting with his back to the wall of a sunken circular chamber. It was bare but for a black stain in the centre of the floor. He thought it looked like dried blood. Carefully, he raised his head to look at the circular opening above him. A man stood there looking back at him. He was dressed in an ermine-edged cloak and an antique pectoral cross hung from his neck.

'Have I missed the fancy-dress party?' Michael said, and saw Cardinal Thomas' face turn ugly with anger.

The cardinal fought to control his rage, and when he spoke, his voice had all the rich, hypnotic bass tones Michael remembered so well.

'Why, no, Flaherty,' he said, smiling humourlessly, 'how could we have the party without the entertainment?'

'The party already had a fool, Eminence,' Michael said. 'I'm sure they'd find your fantasies endlessly entertaining.'

'You thought you'd finished me in Rome, didn't you?' the cardinal said.

'Oh, no, Eminence. The history of the Church shows that bad bastards are like boomerangs – they keep coming back. Ever read Shakespeare? Read *King Lear*, Eminence, and Prospero's speech in *The Tempest* – they could have been written for you.

> *Our revels now are ended. These, our actors,*
> *As I foretold you, were all spirits, and*
> *Are melted into air, into thin air;*
> *And, like the baseless fabric of this vision,*
> *The cloud-capped towers, the gorgeous palaces,*

The solemn temples, the great globe itself,
Yea, all which it inherit, shall dissolve,
and, like this insubstantial pageant faded,
Leave not a rack behind.

'Sound familiar? You're Shelley's Ozymandias, Eminence, a 'colossal wreck'. You're Crassus choking on gold, the last pathetic remnant of the Remnant. You wanted the papacy so badly. Even Pacelli, who was groomed for the top spot, had the decency to have doubts when he got it. But not you. You wanted me and you couldn't have me until someone said so – until someone smuggled you here and tarted you up like some bit-player in their farce. You know what the nun-with-the gun said, Eminence? She said you'd been persuaded to defer gratification. It means keeping the kid from the biscuit tin until Mom or Pop says it's okay. It's supposed to build character, develop self-restraint, help with the maturing process. Too late for you, Eminence; you wanted it all and you wanted it now and hundreds of people danced to your tune. Well, the puppeteer has finally become the puppet. What does it feel like to have someone pulling your strings, Eminence?'

The cardinal clapped mockingly. 'You know you'll never leave here alive, Flaherty,' he said.

'And that's the only thing we have in common, Eminence,' Michael said. He turned away and closed his eyes. 'Now run along,' he added. 'Massa maybe got something else for you to fetch.'

When he opened his eyes again, the assassin stood on the spot vacated by the cardinal. She was looking into the sunken chamber like a cat looks into a fish-pond. She moved to be in his eyeline and he noticed she favoured her left foot.

'I suppose a cup of strong Russian tea is out of the question, Sister?' he said.

Her expression didn't change. Her voice was dust-dry and emotionless when she spoke.

'You were lucky in the monastery, Flaherty.'

'Maybe,' he conceded, 'but I wasn't the one who ran. You know, you're pretty effective against elderly Franciscans, I'll give you that. But you couldn't take me face to face, Sister. Whoever holds your leash won't forget that.'

'My task was to bring you here. I did that.'

'No, Sister, you did not. I followed you here. There's a difference.'

'That puzzles me,' she said, inclining her head as if she was examining an interesting specimen. 'Even with your limited skills, you could have disappeared.'

'I got tired of disappearing,' he said, and she left.

⊗⊙⊗

'Hey, fella, wake the fuck up.'

The man who stood on the rim of Michael Flaherty's world appeared blessedly ordinary. He was dressed in black slacks and a white shirt. He looked like Joe Average except that Michael knew differently.

'You're Jack Holland,' he said. 'What are you doing here?'

'Exactly the question I was going to ask you, buddy.'

'You're definitely Jack Holland,' Michael said drily. 'I'm Michael Flaherty.'

'Guilty as charged and nice to meet ya,' Holland said, easing himself down on the rim and letting his legs dangle in space. 'First off,' he said, 'I gotta check something and don't lie. Remember, I'm a politician, I hold the copyright, okay?'

'Okay.'

'You know a guy called Benson?'

'No.'

'Don't ever play poker, kid. If you don't know Benson, then keep it that way. We don't have much time here so I'll keep it short. Let's just say I was persuaded by the director of the CIA to come here and meet up with this Baldwin fella. Met him yet?'

'In a manner of speaking,' Michael said, feeling the bump on the side of his head. His fingers came away dry.

Holland shook his head.

'Guy's loco enough to make a loon look sane. Bad-mad, ya follow?'

'Lead on.'

'Naturally, he's got a master-plan – don't they all? Heck, I even had one myself once but ... Anyways, best I can figure, the plan involves some kind of crisis in Jerusalem. When the dust settles, the West will rule the roost with Baldwin, the Knight, as number-one nabob and this cardinal fella as the local patriarch.'

'And you?'

'I'm cast to play Washington's man in Jerusalem, something like Mountbatten in India. You get my drift?'

'Yes.'

'You don't seem surprised by any of this, kid.'

'Mr Holland,' Michael said, smiling, 'I was involved in the Remnant business in Rome. Within the space of a very short few hours I've been hit on the head with a sword and had a cardinal and an assassin standing where you now stand. I'm beyond surprise.'

Jack Holland swung his legs up and stood.

'First chance I get, I'm gonna bring the cavalry,' he said. 'Can I do something for you?'

'You got a ladder?'

'Sorry – anything else?'

'Yes! Why, Mr Holland, did you get into this?'

Jack Holland shuffled his feet and scratched behind his ear.

'Heck, I dunno.' He gave a lopsided grin that made him seem both boyish and sad. He looked into the hole for a long time and nodded as if he had come to a conclusion. 'We're never gonna get out of this alive, anyway,' he said.

'It's been said.'

'When I was a kid,' Holland began, 'I thought I'd killed my brother. Now, is that weird or what?'

'Painful, not weird,' Michael said softly.

The man continued as if he hadn't heard. Michael suspected this was one of those rare times when the politician needed to hear his own voice.

'I thought if I did what William would have done, my parents would, you know, cancel the debt. I damn well did it too, and some. I wanted to be number one. It was one heck of a ride to get up there, son, and an awful long way down. Too far to pick up the pieces I broke along the way. Too far … way too far inside to find Jack. I think Ellen knew that.'

His voice had been fading and now was little more than a whisper.

'I had nowhere else to go,' he said, and Michael lowered his eyes to respect the man's privacy. When he looked again, Jack Holland had gone.

Some time later, a plastic water bottle and some pieces of cooked chicken fell out of the sky. 'Vote Democrat,' a voice murmured.

Omar sat at the table and tried to calm his mind. He had been bundled into the small room and held down by the driver on the bed. A man with piercing blue eyes prepared a syringe. When he had finally clawed his way back to consciousness, his first thought and need was for water. It was the sweetest he had ever drunk. He felt it on his tongue and savoured its cool passage to his belly. Refreshed, he replaced the carafe with a steady hand and explored the room. There was no window and the heavy wooden door was locked solid. For a brief moment, he felt the stirring of the claustrophobia he had suffered in the car boot and braced himself against the door until it subsided. Now he opened the copy of the Qur'an he had found by his bedside. He began to read the Al-Fatiha, the Opening. The seven short lines were as familiar to him as his mother's face and he felt the tension ease. 'Show us the straight way. The way of those on whom you have bestowed your grace, those whose portion is not wrath and who go not astray.'

Unbidden, the image of his grandfather standing before the tank loomed large in his mind. He felt rage pulse and closed the book.

The slamming of the door bolt jerked him upright. The man who stepped inside was tall and powerfully built.

'*As-salamu 'Alaykum*,' he said, in a deep voice.

'*Wa 'Alaykum as-salaam*,' Omar replied automatically.

'You do not know me, Omar. I am Baldwin,' the man said, taking a chair at the other side of the table and waving Omar back to his own. 'I know you,' he continued. 'I know of the boy who wrote an essay on water, an essay so full of promise that Professor Sharawi was moved to encourage that promise.

I know of that boy's growth to young manhood and of the flowering of friendship with the professor's family to the point at which the young man was cherished in their home.'

The man's hooded eyes burned with a hypnotic intensity but Omar met his stare unflinchingly.

'Do you also know of my family?' he said evenly. 'If you do, please tell me.'

'Your grandfather is dead,' the man said brusquely. Omar felt his heart stall in his chest. 'He was murdered by the Israelis,' the man continued. 'The same Israelis who bulldozed your home and put your parents and brothers in their prison.'

'Why did they do this?' Omar asked.

'Because you are a terrorist.'

Omar felt as if he had been punched in the stomach.

'I,' he gasped, 'am not a terrorist.'

'They have proof,' Baldwin said emotionlessly. 'Your pen was found at the mortar-site used for Har Homa.'

'My pen?'

'Yes, the one given you by Professor Sharawi, the one with the inscription.' He raised his palm to stifle further questions. 'You were seen with Shepherd.' He read the young man's incomprehension. 'In the camps, he is known as Groomer,' he explained. 'It was he who helped you escape.'

Omar closed his eyes and swayed on his feet.

'Who brought me here?'

'I did,' Baldwin answered. 'I brought you here to protect you from the Israelis.'

'Why?'

'Because I want to help you avenge the blood of your grandfather and the shame of your family.'

Omar digested this slowly, then leaned across the table and looked Baldwin in the eye.

'I am no longer a boy,' he whispered fiercely. 'I am a man. I am an educated man. I am not someone to be fooled by Groomer or by you. You did not help me escape out of the goodness of your heart.'

'No,' Baldwin said calmly, 'you are correct. I want to use you.'

Omar was thrown off-balance by the man's candour.

'What?'

'I don't repeat myself,' Baldwin said. 'You are, as you say, an educated man, therefore I will speak plainly. I can put you in a position where you will be able to bargain with the Israelis for the release of your family and friends and a guarantee of safe passage for yourself. I will do this because part of the bargain will be the release of men who are important to my business. I am a provider of arms, Omar. To whom? To whomever can pay for them. The threat that will bring the Israelis to bargain with you will also provoke the Arab states to a higher level of readiness. I will provide what they need in their time of crisis, and when the crisis has passed, they will not forget.'

He crossed his arms.

'Your family and friends are nothing to me,' he said. 'What I'm proposing is a business arrangement. I will leave you to consider it.' He rose to go. 'My servant will be outside. When you wish to speak to me, knock on the door.' He bowed stiffly and left the room.

Immediately, Omar began to tremble. The iron hold he had struggled to maintain against the gravitational pull of the powerful man collapsed. He fell to the floor, drew his knees up to his chest and ground his teeth to stop himself crying out.

Behind his eyelids, images burned his mind: his brothers, his mother, his grandfather and Nawal clamoured for his attention. With a huge effort, he wrenched his eyes open and focused on the light directly overhead. You are an educated man, he reminded himself. You have been taught to think. Grandfather said that to be a man is to think and take responsibility. For a moment, the loss of his grandfather threatened to drown him in tears. Later, he promised.

He sat at the table and fixed his gaze on the bare surface. Slowly he brought his mind into focus. He concentrated on putting the details of the conversation with Baldwin into some kind of order and analysing them.

'We are scientists,' Professor Sharawi liked to remind his students. 'We deal with the evidence.'

The evidence Baldwin had provided to convince him of why the Israelis hunted him was:

His pen was found at the mortar-site.

He had been seen in the company of Groomer/Shepherd, who had helped him escape.

Omar was by nature a trusting person but he was not naïve. Since he had not been involved in the terrorist attack, the logical conclusion was that his pen had been planted to incriminate him. Also, Groomer/Shepherd was someone he had avoided. The man had approached him in a crisis and taken him to safety. It was a set-up – but set up by whom? By Baldwin? Why? According to Baldwin, to free his friends and improve his business. Perhaps! He had no way of verifying that.

'Put it all in a single drop of water,' the professor liked to say, when a student submitted a lengthy paper. 'One drop can contain and explain all the properties of the lake. If you can give it to me in one drop, I will happily wade through your lake. If not, rework the paper until you can.'

'I have no choice,' Omar muttered aloud.

'There is always choice,' his grandfather's voice chided.

Yes, he agreed, in his mind. I can say no. Whether or not that will affect my family or the Sharawis, I have no way of knowing. What I do know is that Baldwin cannot hear me say no and let me live.

The breath caught in his chest. I can only say yes, he thought. The professor was back on the podium. 'The reasons why we begin and experiment,' he was saying, 'don't always hold good to its conclusion. We study water and we should learn from it. We accept certain truths when we begin our studies: water is heavier than air and always flows downhill. But as we progress we learn that water flies and climbs trees. A man with a set store of knowledge is tempted to defend it against anything that might contradict it, as the Creationists tend to do. A scholar sees contradictory evidence as a door to increased knowledge. Start with what you know and be ready to adapt. Remember, nothing in the world stays the same.'

Omar walked to the door and knocked.

'I have decided to do this,' he said calmly, when Baldwin sat before him. 'I have some questions. What is the nature of this threat you spoke of and where will the threat be made?'

80G8

Jack Holland had never suffered from indecision. In his Oval Office days, he'd liked to boast he'd been vaccinated against vacillation. Having made up his mind to escape from Baldwin's mansion, he'd gone into game-plan mode. Mentally he plotted the route that would take him to and through the front door. The shrubbery would shield him down the drive and when he came to the wall he'd think of something. His body tingled with a thrill of excitement. He had been on a high ever since he'd visited the Flaherty guy in the hole. Hadn't even known the guy was there but he'd followed Thomas on a hunch and enjoyed hearing Flaherty yank the cardinal's chain. Some instinct had kept him in the shadows after Thomas had departed and the crazy lady had glided by within feet of his hiding place. Again, Holland had to admire the way he'd played the woman. Divide and conquer, boy, he cheered, way to go.

His own audience with the prisoner still troubled him. Flaherty had managed to do something in thirty seconds tops that lifelong friends and even Ellen had despaired of doing: getting Jack to let down his guard, drop the mask and allow them to glimpse the man who moved so fast to stay a step ahead of himself. He shook his head and narrowed his focus to a slender beam of concentration. 'Okay, Jack,' he said aloud, in the hubba-bubba voice of a football coach. 'Get suited up, boy.'

The black slacks stayed. The white shirt missed the laundry basket and lay deflated on the floor. He struggled into a black cotton shirt and looked at himself in the mirror. Black pants, black shirt and a shock of white hair! You look like a pint of Guinness, Jack, he told himself. What the heck? It was too late to do anything about that. He'd always liked his white hair; thought it gave him a certain gravitas.

'Should I keep it like this, Ellen?' he'd asked.

'Absolutely, Jack; it gives the illusion of wisdom.'

For a second, he lost the beat and felt a twinge of regret. Fuck it, he thought, maybe I'll wear one of these bandannas and an eyepatch and … Enough, Jack, the rational side of his brain counselled. Okay, I'll settle for the peg-leg and stuffed parrot.

'Mr Holland.'

He wasn't sure if the voice was coming from inside his head. The Mameluke stood inside the door.

'Hi there,' Holland said, beginning to unbutton his shirt. 'Thought I'd turn in early.'

'Mr Holland, Sir Baldwin will see you now.'

⁕✕⁖

The Great Hall looked formless under the dust-cover of darkness. In the distance, a small candle warmed a circle on the varnished table. As Jack Holland approached, shadowed by the Mameluke, Baldwin leaned into the light.

'Mr Holland,' he said, in little more than a whisper, 'it seems I have been mistaken about you. I thought you had the potential for greatness, that you would seize the day and—'

'And all the other bullshit clichés,' Holland said calmly. 'As for your glorious Crusade, your loony ancestor tried that on over a thousand years ago. It was dumb then, it's even dumber now. Let's move on here.'

'You disappoint me, Mr Holland.'

'That's the nicest thing anyone's said about me in the longest time.'

'Then let it be your epitaph.'

The Oval Office, The White House
Special Agent Frawley inclined his head and pressed two fingers to his ear.

'Kosher pizza delivery coming through in twenty seconds,' his partner whispered from the hallway outside.

Suppressing a grin, Frawley approached the desk.

'Israeli ambassador on his way, Ms President.'

'Thank you,' she said distantly. Ellen Radford took a deep breath, straightened in the swivel chair and placed her palms on the desk.

Fire in the hole, Frawley thought. He glanced quickly at Senator Melly and the Secretary of State hunched forward in their chairs flanking the desk, angled towards the empty chair set in the middle of the carpet. The three stony faces in the room looked as if they were carved on Mount Rushmore. He felt the tiniest twinge of sympathy for the Israeli ambassador as he opened the door.

Chaim Baruch was a tall, cadaverous man with a scholar's stoop. Intelligence-gatherers were unanimous in their assessment that he spent more time agonising over nuances in the Talmud than he did over affairs of state. He was normally diffident, almost abstracted, and the president was surprised to see the agitation evident in his walk and in the two hectic spots that rode high on his cheekbones. The ambassador bobbed a small bow and perched on the edge of the chair. Ellen Radford skipped the formal preamble and went straight to attack mode.

'Mr Ambassador,' she said coldly, 'I want to know how a former President of the United States got permission from your government—'

'Madam,' he interrupted.

'I was not finished,' she enunciated icily. 'Someone was stupid enough …'

Her voice tailed off as the ambassador lurched to his feet.

The vivid spots on his cheeks had disappeared and his face was bleached white by his distress.

'Madam,' he croaked, 'I must inform you that minutes before I entered the Oval Office I received some information from ...' his mouth worked through a number of alternative titles before his voice joined it on '... the Israeli security services.'

The president saw her advisers lean forward apprehensively.

'Continue,' she said.

'Madam,' the ambassador quavered, 'I am advised to inform you that a special broadcast is to be made on Al Jazeera at ten a.m. Washington time. The caller used the correct code and the Israeli Prime Minister strongly urges that you watch it.'

She glanced at her watch. It was ten minutes to the hour. She pressed the button on her desk and Agent Frawley appeared instantly.

'Please accompany the ambassador to the Blue Room,' she said briskly. 'Inform my secretary that I want the Secretary of the Treasury and the Attorney General here in five minutes, latest. Thank you.'

The ambassador, already forgotten, beat a grateful retreat.

The trio sat frozen, as protocol demanded, until the door closed behind him, then dissolved into action. As the minute hand on the tall clock standing against the wall jerked to mark five minutes to the hour, a White House aide muted the Al Jazeera station on the large TV and handed the remote control to the Secretary of State. A half-circle of chairs was already arranged on the carpet arcing around the Presidential Crest. Laila Achmed snatched the phone from the president's desk with her free hand and put the Joint Chiefs of Staff and the directors of the security agencies on standby. Agent Frawley listened to his instructions and fed them through his lapel microphone to his partner, who relayed the message to the White House Tourist Department. All non-White House personnel to be escorted and excluded from the building – now.

Radios crackled in the unmarked security cars cruising Pennsylvania Avenue and echoed back in a ripple effect through the cadre of visible and covert agents in the grounds. The shockwave of heightened awareness swept through internal security, telephonists, carpool drivers and catering staff all the way back to its source in the Oval Office.

At nine fifty-nine a.m., Laila Achmed activated the remote control and the voice of the Al Jazeera announcer sounded in the still room.

'He's just concluding this item,' she translated, in a calm, carrying voice. 'Should be coming up now.'

The president sat in the centre chair, flanked by Senator Melly, Ephrem Isaacson and David Duke on her right. Laila Achmed sat on her left and gasped when the pictures began to come through. She composed herself quickly and began to translate. The president heard only snatches of the narration as her eyes locked on her husband.

Jack Holland sat in a straightbacked chair, holding a folded newspaper in his lap. He was framed by four men wearing balaclavas and carrying an assortment of automatic weapons. Snatches of translation penetrated the president's shock:

'Disk arrived one hour ago at this station … time to verify the code … group claiming responsibility not Hamas or any of the other …'

The camera zoomed to the newspaper.

'Shows today's date,' Laila continued. 'Former President Holland will now make a statement.'

He looks old and beaten, Ellen thought. She wondered if the splotches on his face …

Jack Holland's eyes darted sideways as if he had caught a signal from someone off-camera. 'My name is Jack Holland,' he said, in a voice barely above a whisper.

Ellen heard the sharp intake of breath from those around her. His eyes flicked sideways again and he cleared his throat.

'I am a former President of the United States. A list of political prisoners has already been sent to the Israeli government. If the prisoners are not released by twelve noon, Washington time' – he paused and the watchers held their collective breath – 'I – I will be executed,' he said, in a rush.

The presenter returned to the screen, speaking animatedly in Arabic. 'We will keep our viewers informed as the situation develops,' Laila whispered.

'Turn it off,' the president said quietly.

She stood and went to sit behind her desk as the others turned their chairs to face her.

'Laila,' she said, 'I want you to organise the joint chiefs and security heads for one hour from now. Check with your own people and tell them to have the latest intel here in thirty minutes. I want the ambassador back in here when … just tell him to wait.'

Laila Achmed left the room.

'Henry?'

'Press Office already under siege,' Melly said. 'The choice is between a press conference and a statement.'

'Maybe later,' she said. 'I have to see how this pans out. The time for talking to the press is after a decision is made. The floor is open, gentlemen. Let's hear it.'

'Ms President.'

David Duke rarely spoke at meetings unless he was asked a direct question and the others looked curiously at him. He had a reputation as someone who came at things from what Senator Melly described as 'left field'. Laila would have said 'from a different field entirely' and Ephrem would have amended that to 'a different planet'.

'It really boils down to a fundamental question,' he said.

It was a preamble that tightened the others in their chairs. They sensed that he was about to name the elephant in the drawing room, the huge issue that others strained to avoid and worked hard at pretending wasn't there.

'Do we comply with their demands or not?' David said.

Ellen Radford allowed a few seconds to tick by before she replied.

'They're not demanding anything of us, David. As I read it, their demands are directed to the Israeli government.'

'With respect, ma'am,' the attorney general said stubbornly, 'that boils down to the same thing. In this case, they've taken a prominent American citizen. Jack Holland is a former President of the United States and—'

'And what, David?'

A more politically savvy person might have engaged reverse gear at this point, but David Duke had been busy somewhere else when 'political savvy' was distributed. That's why he's in my cabinet, the president thought, anticipating what he was going to say.

'And,' David ploughed on, 'he's the husband of the President of the United States.'

'He was in Israel as a private citizen, David.'

'That's neither here nor there, ma'am,' he said doggedly. 'The terrorists did not lift John Doe of Delaware, they took Jack Holland for who he was and is. True, they made their demands of Israel, but they know and the world knows that Israel is effectively our protectorate.' He paused for breath. 'This challenge is directed at the US in general and at you in particular, ma'am.'

Ellen Radford lifted her right hand to her head and tugged her fringe into a clump. God, she thought, how her mother had hated that mannerism. 'You look like a startled porcupine, dear.'

As a girl, she had done it to anchor herself in her head. She knew that what David had said was the plain unvarnished truth and tugged hard one last time to feel some pain.

The room was deathly quiet. She looked at the senator and had to look away quickly from the sympathy in his eyes.

'Thank you, Ephrem and David,' she said levelly, 'I'll need you back here after my meeting with the Brass and Spooks.'

Ephrem nodded and left. David Duke stood uncertainly and took an impulsive pace forward. He held out his hand and she took it.

'I'm very sorry this happened to Mr Holland,' he said quietly.

His hand felt warm and surprisingly strong.

'Thank you, David,' she said. 'So am I.'

Senator Melly waited until the door had closed behind the attorney general.

'Laila won't be back for a few minutes,' he said softly. 'You have some time.'

She knew what he meant and took the time to search her

feelings. Had she ever loved Jack? Yes, a long time ago. Maybe the studious Methodist girl had fallen in love with the bright, brash and scary Jack, the Jack who leaped first and looked later. Except he didn't look later. Jack seemed to have an aversion to reflection, a mental block that closed him off from introspection. Sometimes he could be caught off-guard and lapse back to being a boy, an earnest, insecure and scared little boy, wonderfully naïve in his enthusiasms and revelations. But those times had come around less often until the boy disappeared. I loved the boy and married the man, she thought sadly. Even now, especially now, she found it hard to feel anything deeper than sympathy for the man.

Laila Achmed's return interrupted her reverie.

'They're filing into the Cabinet Room right now, Ms President,' she said. 'Latest intel from the Middle East is that Israel and its Arab neighbours have stepped up to Code Amber. Our embassy reports they had a call from someone claiming to be Jack Holland but it was filed under 'Nuisance'. Apart from that, nothing. Assets on the ground have nothing on the location or identity of the terrorists. Oh, and Michael Flaherty's disappeared – there's a warrant out for his arrest.'

'For what?'

'Suspicion of murder.'

'And the Israeli ambassador is waiting.'

'Let him wait,' the president said brusquely. 'I want lie-of-the-land stuff from you two before I go into this meeting. Laila, you know the Brass.'

'The forces chiefs fall into two categories,' Laila replied promptly, 'the Hawks and the Lesser Hawks. Watch for Admiral Daniel F. Berman, a.k.a. Nuke-'em-Danno. He's the leader of the extreme flock. Davis and Proctor are army from way back. Started out bagging bodies in Vietnam. You could regard them as doves in hawks' plumage. Reilly is air force – sees everything from thirty thousand feet and doesn't get the point of the other services.'

'Thank you, Laila. Henry?'

'Benson, first and last,' the Senator said firmly. 'The other agencies follow Benson's lead like a flock of damn sheep because they're scared he'll pick them off singly. He'll push your buttons, Ellen,' he added.

'It's been tried,' she said.

Agent Frawley tapped and entered.

'Time, ma'am.'

Baldwin's Mansion, Jerusalem

Omar drank some water and placed the tumbler on the long table. His eyes were drawn to the tattered banners that hung from the high ceiling and the rows and rows of candelabra planted like young trees throughout the Great Hall. Reluctantly, his gaze returned to Baldwin, brooding in silence at the centre of the table. I am in the belly of the Beast, he thought, and felt the stirrings of fear. He was distracted by the sound of soft leather slapping on stone and watched a man approach the dais. He was tall, black and broad-shouldered. He was dressed in strange robes and wore a Christian cross around his neck. Power seemed to radiate from him but, Omar thought, he had angry eyes and a cruel mouth.

'Where is Flaherty?' the man demanded. 'You promised me—'

A low guttural growl from Baldwin cut him short.

'I promised you the keys to the kingdom of Jerusalem,'

the Knight rumbled, 'and you badger me for a toy, a plaything.'

'Flaherty is mine,' the man insisted.

The Knight shook his head in mock-sorrow.

'How hard it is for those who have riches to enter the Kingdom,' he said softly. 'Come, Ademar,' he coaxed, indicating the chair beside him. 'Sit here at my right side that I may make my enemies thy footstool. This,' he added, with the merest nod in Omar's direction, 'is our Archangel Raphael, the one who brings thunder and lightning.'

He lifted his head abruptly, and looked to the rear of the Great Hall.

Omar saw two men approach through the shadows, one staying a distance behind the other. The man in front moved awkwardly as if he was carrying something that skewed his balance. As they drew closer, Omar saw that the man behind carried a weapon.

Baldwin sat back, a huge grin of satisfaction on his face.

'I said you would threaten the Israelis, Omar,' he bellowed.

'You said you would be giving me a bomb,' Omar replied. 'Where is this bomb?'

'He's right here,' the Knight answered.

Omar turned and froze. The man who stood before the dais had what looked like white slabs strapped to his upper body.

'He is your bomb,' Baldwin said to Omar. 'And your satisfaction, Cardinal Thomas,' he added. 'Satisfied?'

'Yes,' the cardinal breathed, his eyes devouring Flaherty.

'Omar will bring his bomb to the Dome of the Rock,' Baldwin said. 'When he is ready, the demands will be sent to the Jews. What are they to do? Fight or flight? If they are desperate enough to assault this holy place of Islam, will the Arab states stand idly by? If they hold back and let it come to ruin …'

The cardinal nodded admiringly.

'My servant will go with them,' Baldwin said softly, 'as a guide and as insurance against betrayal. Cover him,' he commanded.

The servant dropped a Franciscan habit over Flaherty's head and let it envelop him. Omar watched the man's head emerge from the neck of the garment. He wondered how he could be so calm and felt ashamed of his own fear.

The Cabinet Room, The White House

She liked the Cabinet Room. The Red Room gave her headaches and the Blue Room was a little too glacial for comfort. The Cabinet Room made a stab at triumphalism with its little copse of standing flags, but the dark brown leather chairs bordering the thin strip of bare table signalled its real function. This was the arena where the *mano a mano* of decision-making happened. The gladiators rose to their feet as she entered. As the daughter of a four-star general, she wasn't fazed by the array of braid.

'Thank you, gentlemen,' she said, sitting at the centre of the table where she would be flanked by the flags. 'You've all seen the broadcast. You know the time constraints. What are our options?'

Immediately the hawks closed their wings, extended their talons and dropped out of the sky. The first wave of contributions fell into the shock-and-awe category. Air Force argued for gunships and search-and-rescue. Navy proposed carriers with Cruise missiles ready to target Arab capitals unless their governments ordered the terrorists to 'cease and desist'. She looked at the men who tried to outdo each other in what her father called 'bellicosity'.

'Bella who, Daddy?' she'd asked.

'Bellicosity, honey. It means war-talk.'

She knew that this war-talk was backed up by six hundred and six billion dollars' worth of war-toys and these men were keen to use them. She had a sudden flash of Jack Holland's slack face and hopeless eyes. She raised a hand.

'Thank you, gentlemen,' she said firmly, nodding to the contributors from the navy and the air force. 'I'd like to hear from the army.'

General Davis, like his colleague General Proctor, propped his elbows on the table.

'Jimmy Carter went for the search-and-rescue option to free the embassy hostages in Iran back in 1980,' he said slowly, 'and we're all old enough to remember wreckage in the desert. We could threaten the Arab states with retribution in the hope that they'd influence the terrorists, but threats before means action after – if you say you will, then you gotta follow through and take the consequences. All the hardware in the world ain't worth spit against a small group operating in their own country. We shoulda learned that from 'Nam. The Russians sure did from Afghanistan. As I see it, the bottom line here is time. The hard fact is that there isn't enough of it to search and snatch Jack Holland or squeeze the Arab paymasters.'

'So, what do we do?' the president asked.

'With respect, ma'am, it's not about us, it's about you. You've got two options. You can lean on Israel to deliver on demand, but last time I looked, Israel is not a state in the Union. It's a sovereign state with the right to take appropriate action on whatever's happening inside its borders. Ossetia or the Ukraine or Belarus it ain't.'

'What's the second option?'

'To say no, ma'am.'

Nothing prepares you for this, she told herself. A president can mound up a bunker of reports and position papers and advisers but when the crunch comes …

'Thank you, General Davis,' she said.

'No is not an option.'

Heads swivelled to the turn of the table at the far end of the room where Benson lounged alone.

'No is not an option,' he repeated, when he had their collective attention. 'Truman could have said no to Hiroshima and Nagasaki and we'd have scraped dead Americans off every square foot of the Japanese mainland. Kennedy could have said no to the blockade and Cuba would be red and ready today instead of all washed up economically and praying for Castro's death. What we have here is not an option but an opportunity: an opportunity to stop talking and actually do something. Talk is cheap, Ms President, and we've cheapened ourselves for far too long. A whole ragbag of terrorists and factions and loonies out there loves to hear us talk. While a predecessor of yours was talking, they drove a bomb-boat into a navy ship. While our negotiators were palavering, they blew our embassy in Nigeria to kingdom come. While our negotiators were talking in Geneva, the Vietcong were planting booby-traps and *punji* sticks and keeping our boys in cages. Talk is for the weak and timid; they know that. It's time to act. The motto of our country is '*e pluribus unum*', out of many, one. The strength of the many is made up by this coming together of individuals. The security of the many comes down to the security of that individual American. They've got one of ours, Ms President. If we let them keep that one, what's to stop them coming for another one and another one until there's no one left to say, "Enough"?'

Benson sat back in his chair and the president scanned the room for reaction. Navy and Air Force looked grim and purposeful. Admiral Berman appeared ready to applaud.

Army General Proctor stood slowly. He turned and looked the length of the table at Benson.

'That was one hell of a speech, Mr Director,' he said. 'The kind of speech that might have been given to the cavalry before the charge into the valley of death or to the Aussie boys before they ran at the Turkish machine-guns in Gallipoli. Interesting, but factually flawed, sir. You mentioned Truman and the bomb. Fact is, he could have accepted the Japanese surrender some months before and didn't. He wanted to make a stand, make a point and, boy, did he ever. He took the short view. If he had taken the long view and seen the inevitability of the Cold War and the arms race, I wonder if he would have decided differently. You cited the example of Jack Kennedy and Cuba. Fact is, he made a deal with Khrushchev rather than convert half of America and Russia into glass. You see, Mr Director, rhetoric stirs the passion but logic, negotiation and talk save lives. I could have let you run with these examples. I could have sat here and thought, Heck, that's just the CIA blowing its war-trumpet and justifying its black budget, but I couldn't do that once you mentioned Vietnam. You see, Mr Director, some of us sitting at this table were actually there. And when you've lived through taking bits of boys out of the water like the navy people, or hung your Huey over a jungle full of missiles to evac the wounded like the air force, or shared a cage with a rat for three months in the Mekong Delta, as I did, sir, then, with respect, you don't actually know what you're talking about. Rhetoric is for armchair generals. Real generals call it bullshit. As for going back for the one, I was that one, Mr Director. I never expected my superiors to risk the lives of my comrades to bring me home. In the real world that's not how it works. It wasn't the cavalry coming over the hill that freed me from the cage; it was politicians talking in Geneva.'

He turned and looked directly at the president.

'Ms President, he said, 'you're the Commander-in-Chief, the highest-ranking officer in this room. What you say stands. You have to do what you think is best for all of us, whatever the cost.'

Baldwin's Mansion, Jerusalem

Baldwin led them from the Great Hall through long passages down darkened stairs into the bowels of his mansion. He herded them into a high-ceilinged, echoing chamber and flicked the switch. Omar and Michael froze in the sudden brilliance. When Omar's eyes adjusted to the light and focused on what lay before them, he turned aside to be sick.

Sister Raisa hung by her wrists from manacles embedded in the cold, bare stone. Her face was streaked with blood and contorted by the agonies she had suffered before death had released her.

'She failed me,' Baldwin said.

Michael took a step forward and found himself looking at the muzzle of the gun held by the Mameluke. He stared into the man's implacable eyes and shrugged his lethal burden a little more comfortably on his shoulders.

'Better try for a head-shot, friend,' he said coldly, 'If you do happen to get lucky,' he added, 'no me, no bomb.'

Michael saw the man's eyes flicker uncertainly to Baldwin and brushed past him to close the nun's with his thumb.

The Oval Office, The White House
The four members of the cabinet stood when she returned from the Cabinet Room to take her place behind the desk.

'Please, sit,' she said, 'the Israeli ambassador is on his way.'

They had ten seconds to register her stony face and rigid posture before the tall man entered.

'Mr Ambassador,' she said, 'if former President Holland entered Israel without the knowledge or permission of your government, then you must consider that he was brought there by a person or persons inimical to Israel or …'

She allowed the pause to linger until the ambassador felt he could hold his breath no longer.

'Or,' she continued coldly, 'by someone within the state apparatus who is pursuing a private agenda. You will urge your prime minister to investigate and act.'

'Yes, ma'am,' he breathed. 'With regard to the demands of the terrorists, Ms President?'

'We do not trade with terrorists,' the president said tightly. 'We gave our word on this. We will not go back on it.'

'So, Ms President?' he faltered, as if he had difficulty understanding the implications of what she'd said.

'So the answer is no.'

The ambassador sat as if carved from stone. After a few

moments, he shook his head and looked around at the members of the cabinet, whose faces mirrored his own profound shock. Shakily, he rose to his feet.

'I will convey your message to my government, ma'am,' he whispered, and bowed.

Ellen Radford forced herself to look at the clock in the corner. It was five minutes to midday.

The Arab Quarter, Jerusalem
The car pulled into a parking space at the edge of the Arab Quarter. Michael had puzzled throughout the journey at the light flow of traffic and the scarcity of pedestrians on the streets. A single, lightly manned roadblock had barely interrupted their progress. The policeman had scanned the papers offered by the Mameluke driver, glanced at Michael in his Franciscan habit and waved them through. Michael caught a brief glimpse of a small television flickering in the guardhouse before the Mameluke had driven on. He counted four policemen standing in a huddle, their attention locked on the tiny screen.

They left the car and approached a door set in the street wall. It swung wide to a coded knock and he bent his lanky frame to negotiate the low entry. The Mameluke chivvied them across a cobbled courtyard to the house, and someone carrying a lantern led them through a kitchen to where two children sat at a table drinking milk from Disneyland mugs. As the strange procession passed, their eyes widened and their milk-moustached lips pulled wide with surprise.

The basement smelled of damp and decay. Their guide set his lantern on the floor and hauled at a trapdoor.

'Down,' the Mameluke ordered.

The Oval Office, The White House
'Laila!'

'Yes, Ms President.'

'Would you tune into the Al Jazeera station, please? I need to … to see this through.'

Laila Achmed looked at Senator Melly and he nodded.

'I want to thank you all for your support,' the president said. 'We'll meet back here in thirty minutes.'

Nobody moved. She raised an eyebrow at the senator.

'With your permission, Ms President,' he said formally, 'we'd like to stay.'

Ellen Radford stood between Henry Melly and Laila Achmed with David Duke and Ephrem Isaacson at either end of the line. Laila translated the presenter's introduction in a faltering voice, then gulped and was silent.

It was mercifully quick. Jack Holland knelt on the floor wearing a black blindfold. His wrists seemed to be bound behind his back and his body was bowed forward. The executioner was a broad-shouldered man, anonymous behind a black balaclava. He read a short statement, then extended his hand and fired a single shot. Ellen Radford had steeled herself against the moment but she couldn't suppress a shudder at the flat crack of the pistol. The presenter returned to the screen and Laila Achmed turned it off. The senator's large hand enclosed her own while Laila's small one crept into the other. The clock ticked on in the corner, suddenly loud in the hushed room.

She released them and turned to the senator.

'I'd like to make a broadcast some time this evening,' she said. 'Can you organise that?'

He nodded and stood aside as the secretary for the Treasury

and the attorney general approached. Ephrem Isaacson kissed her on both cheeks and she felt his tears transfer to her face. David Duke held her hand awkwardly for a few moments. She allowed herself some time to take comfort from it. Laila touched her cheek gently to the president's.

'*La illaha illa Allah*,' she whispered brokenly. 'There is no God but God.'

Finally she was alone with Henry Melly.

'I think you made the right decision,' he said gruffly.

'It was the only option, Henry.' She sighed.

'Yes,' he agreed, 'but someone had to take it.'

He cleared his throat before continuing. 'You know I never had kids, Ellen,' he said, and she saw his eyes mist. 'Often wished for them, to tell the truth,' he continued softly. 'If I could have had a daughter, I would have been real proud if it could have been you.'

'What does a president have to do to get a hug?' she said.

It was only when she was snuggled in under his chin and he was stroking her hair that she could weep.

The Cavern, Jerusalem
Omar looked around in amazement at what was revealed by the lantern.

'What is this place?' he whispered.

Michael had been thinking of ways to initiate conversation and blessed Tim Conway mentally for the cache of books he had left in his room.

'I've read a little bit about it,' he murmured, as they followed the receding light. 'About two thousand years ago, King Herod's masons quarried limestone here for the temple.

Some people think Solomon did the same nine hundred years before that.'

'Where does it lead?' Omar asked, and the Mameluke flicked a warning look over his shoulder.

Michael waited until their guide was temporarily hidden behind a limestone pillar before replying.

'Under the Old City.'

'Where Haram As-Sharif stands?'

'Yes.' Michael hefted his harness a little higher for comfort. 'The Dome of the Rock. History says it was built by one of your ancestors, Abd Al-Malik. Legend says it's where Adam rose out of the dust, the Ark came ashore and Abraham almost sacrificed his son Isaac. Do you believe that?'

Omar looked at him uncertainly.

'My grandfather ...' His voice wavered and steadied. 'My grandfather told me once that seventy thousand angels guard the Rock.'

'Let's hope they're awake,' Michael said, and Omar smiled.

The Oval Office, The White House

Agent Frawley didn't like media people. He snorted as a young woman in a skimpy tank-top and frayed jeans balanced her bottom on the edge of the desk to check the angle of the lights. Agent Grant poked him lightly in the ribs. 'Hold your fire, Josh,' he said, out of the corner of his mouth. 'Old Resolute there's seen a lot of bums in its time.'

'The desk's got a name?' Frawley asked, distracted from the mayhem he wanted to visit on the 'hippie-types' who had reduced the sacred precincts of the Oval Office to a chaos of cables.

Kenneally

'Sure it has,' his partner said soothingly. 'That old desk's been around long enough to draw down a pension.'

'More'n that sucker ever will,' Frawley growled, as a young man with a blond ponytail flopped into the swivel chair.

'Easy there, old hoss,' his partner whispered. 'Guy's gotta sit there to check lights and camera angles and such.'

'Yeah,' Frawley huffed, shrugging the tension out of his shoulders, 'so how come you know all this stuff, Mr Spielberg?'

'Steven's a good kid,' Grant said, stony-faced. 'Respectful, you know. Calls me Mr Grant.'

He patted his partner's arm.

'I'm going outside to give you the heads-up when she's on her way. Promise me you'll be a good Dobermann while I'm gone.'

Joshua Frawley was impressed, though he worked hard at maintaining his scowl. Since his partner had gone to recce the president's arrival, the 'hippie types' had scurried like ants and the chaos had resolved itself into taped or coiled cables, camera operators leaning attentively into their eyepieces and a sound operator, lost in the zone between her earphones, tweaking the levels on her little box of tricks.

'Seems like we're ready here, people,' Ponytail announced. 'Lady should be arriving any moment now. Make nice, okay?'

Frawley pressed a finger to his ear, nodded at the message and strode across the carpet to stand before the desk.

'Listen up … people,' he said, and all eyes swung his way. 'We got twenty seconds before the president arrives.' He placed a heavy emphasis on 'president' while shooting a disapproving look at the ponytailed director. 'When the president comes in, y'all stand. You remain standing until she is seated. You call her Ms President if you need to talk to her.

If you don't, you stay shtum. My name is Agent Frawley. Anybody breaks the rules, I get to shoot them. Thank you and have a nice day.'

With his hand on the door handle, he strafed the room one last time with a fierce look.

'Ladies and gentlemen,' he said, 'the President of the United States.'

❧❦

Ellen Radford sat behind the desk and watched the crew ease out of the erect postures they had frozen into as she entered. Some glanced nervously in Agent Frawley's direction and she suppressed a smile.

'Ms President,' the young woman said, 'I'm Grace Connors. I'm going to dab a little make-up on you, ma'am.'

Seeing the President's eyebrow quirk, she hurried on: 'It's just that the lights are so strong, ma'am, and they'd bleach you right out. Wouldn't do to have you looking, you know, like death warmed over ... or anything.' She gulped, and her eyes grew enormous.

'Grace,' the president said softly, 'you go right ahead and do your job.'

She closed her eyes and willed herself not to wince as the small sponge slid over her face. It felt cool and clammy and she was relieved when Grace Connors murmured something and left.

When she opened her eyes a young man with a ponytail stood before the desk.

'Ms President,' he said nervously, 'I, ah, understand you won't be using an autocue.'

'That's right.'

'Ah, will you be using notes, ma'am? It's just that if you are, we got to change the camera angles a little.'

'No, I won't be using notes.'

'Ah, right, no notes,' he said. 'I'll give you a five-second signal and point right at you when it's time to go, okay, ma'am?'

'Okay,' she said, and placed her palms flat on the desk.

8003

Jeff Symes subscribed to the old gag that politicians and babies' diapers had one thing in common: they should both be changed regularly and for the same reason. As a television director, he'd seen them appear before the camera and mutate into something other than themselves. He had a rep in the trade as someone who could 'handle the talent' – flatter their egos and put them at their ease – apart from that one time when a vain state governor had instructed him to get a big close-up of his face and the young director had asked, 'Which one?' That Freudian slip had landed him in the gulag of indie movies until the network relented.

No notes, he thought. Okay. Okay for a recorded session when we can afford umpteen retakes until the penny drops and we wheel in the autocue. But this is live, baby. Either Ms President is a one-take wonder or … Before he could tease out the awful implications, the camera operator nudged his shoulder. Jeff fanned his splayed fingers in her eyeline, just below the lens, and began the countdown. When his pinky finger joined the others in a fist, he shot out his index finger and cued the president.

❦

Senator Melly sat unobtrusively in the shadows and watched as she raised her head. He had always known Ellen could 'do' television. She seemed to grasp instinctively that she wasn't on the stump or at the hustings but was talking to a maximum of four people in an American living room.

'This is my first time talking to you since the Inauguration,' she began. 'I wish it was in happier circumstances.'

No preamble, no grandiose 'my fellow Americans', he thought approvingly. Go, girl!

❦

Jill Summers adjusted the sound level and nodded as the needle flickered mid-dial. The president had a strong, steady voice that didn't need tweaking up from the black or down from the red. She had disciplined hand movements so there was little chance she would bash the microphone and deafen America. Jill checked the ambient sound nobody ever heard because they weren't listening. Listening was her job and, undistracted by the visual element, she gave the president her undivided attention.

❦

Grace Connors, the make-up artist, was deaf to anything the president was saying. Her own voice ran on a loop in her head repeating the same line over and over. Like death warmed over. Oh, shit, I can't believe I said that.

It was Joshua Harley's job to watch everyone in the room except the President. He'd positioned himself so that everyone stood or sat in his line-of-sight. Or line of fire, he thought grimly, and hitched his shoulder holster a little higher. The sound operator arched an eyebrow in his direction and he stopped moving. Contrary to all his training, his attention swung to the woman behind the desk.

'Revenge is something I don't want,' she said, 'and something the world can do without. Revenge makes terrorists of all of us – no difference, except we've got bigger guns and are likely to kill more people. But justice is a wheel that always comes full circle eventually.'

Jeff Symes' total attention was focused on the tiny monitor set at his feet. The picture flickering on that screen was the one millions of Americans were looking at right now and, for him, nothing outside that frame mattered. Except that something tugged at his attention and drew him to cast longer and longer glances at the president. At first he thought it was just her easy verbal flow that attracted him. Usually professional presenters could make a prepared script sound spontaneous. Amateurs, he knew, tended to work from memory, reading an internal autocue that glazed their eyes and killed their contact with an audience. This lady, he thought, was all of a piece, her voice and vocal expression coming from somewhere in her subconscious. She was riveting television, he admitted, and winced at his own cynicism. This was real. She was real.

'We spend billions on preparing for war,' the president said, 'and small change on maintaining peace. You don't need an accountancy degree to figure out the sum. The bigger the push for peace, the smaller the chance we will backslide into war.'

❧❧

Jill Summers listened. The professional part of her brain was still attuned to the dials and her fingers hovered, almost of their own volition, ready to adjust if necessary. But her listening had moved way beyond the wavelength of her technical ear to the heart of the message the speaker embodied and articulated.

'If we are attacked, we will defend ourselves. That's something presidents have said and you've heard so often that we've all lost sight of what it really means. It means reaction and, yes, if you add a few extra letters you get reactionary. In a world of reactionaries, the wheel of violence goes round and round. It's time to put a brake on that wheel, time to ask questions, like what brings people to despair of ever having food for their families, education for their children and the chance of a job – all the things we take for granted – and pushes them to destroy what we have?'

❧❧

Grace Connors' mantra couldn't compete with a stronger stimulus and she was lured into listening.

'Sending aid is the right thing to do in a crisis,' the president said. 'But aid doesn't tackle the root causes of a problem. Sending aid is like blocking a leak in the dam with your finger and waiting until the pressure punches another hole and another. In the long term, sending dollars and food just doesn't work. The crop fails, the famine comes, the children starve, over and over again. If we share our technological and agricultural know-how and our experts, the people who know how, then there's some chance the day will come when the cycle of helplessness and hopelessness will be broken.'

⚮

Jeff Symes sensed she was coming to an end. He caught the camera operator's eye and signalled for a close-up shot. Symes knew this was the critical moment in every broadcast. People who made good presentations didn't always know how to end them effectively. They wandered off the path into a swamp of 'therefore' and 'finally' until the impact of their message just weakened and died.

'You're on the green, lady,' he prayed quietly. 'Sink the putt.'

And she did.

Ellen Radford held the lens with steady eyes until the director signalled they were 'off-air'.

'Thank you, ladies and gentlemen,' she said to the crew, and stood.

A tall young woman wearing headphones over her long hair unclipped the lapel microphone.

'Thank you, Ms President,' she said, with shining eyes. She stepped back and began to applaud. Her colleagues took it up.

Flanked by Senator Melly and shadowed by Agent Harley, the president walked to the door.

⚮

'Coffee?'

'Water,' she said, 'lots.'

'You really turned up tonight, Ellen,' Senator Melly murmured, as he passed the glass. She nodded, and he saw the fatigue that pulled the skin tightly across her cheekbones. 'Why not lie down?' he added. 'If something comes up, we'll call you.'

'I might just do that.' She sighed.

Agent Harley appeared at her side.

'What is it, Joshua?'

'Something you should see, ma'am,' he said.

'Problem?'

'No, I wouldn't say that.'

'What would you say?'

'Come and take a look,' he said.

The crew had packed up and gone, leaving the Oval Office as they'd found it.

'Over here, ma'am,' Harley said, directing her to the window behind her desk. He pulled the drapes open slowly and she saw the illuminated monuments that glowed in the window frame. In the foreground, pinpricks of light moved to and fro like a shifting stream of stars.

'What is it?' she asked.

'Folks, ma'am,' the agent whispered. 'They've been coming since your broadcast finished. Security says it's the same on Pennsylvania Avenue.'

'Why?'

'Why?' he repeated. 'For you, ma'am.'

She took his arm and they stood together, watching the fire-fly glimmers in the dark.

The Safe House, Jerusalem
'Avram?'

'It's Goldberg. Who is this?'

'Bozo.'

'Okay, Goliath, shoot.'

'Maybe next time, Goldberg. Can you drag the old man to the phone, please?'

'Goliath, Avram, what is it?'

'I followed a car from that place we talked about. I'm in the Arab Quarter. Three guys exited the car and disappeared inside a house.'

'You get a look at them?'

'Couldn't get too close. I think one of them was your driver. Another guy was tall, bulky-looking, wearing one of those priest robes. Third was a young guy, maybe five eight.'

'Name of the street, Goliath?'

Avram scribbled on a notepad beside the phone as he listened.

'No, don't go in,' he murmured, 'I'll call you back.'

He ripped out the page and automatically ripped out the next sheet.

She knew him well enough to give him space. Avram paced the small kitchen, pondering the scrap of paper as if the address scribbled there was the key to the Rosetta Stone. She eased a cup of coffee to the edge of the table and he lifted it without looking.

'Jesus,' he whispered.

He stopped pacing and let the crumpled paper drift from his hand.

'Avram?'

His raised hand struck her dumb.

'Map,' he grunted.

Goldberg rummaged in her shoulder bag. *One of these days I'm going to hire an archaeologist to sift and sort the layers of rubbish in this …*

'Here,' she said, and planted the tourist map flat on the table. They hunched over it, heads almost touching. His stubby finger hovered and dropped on the paper. Slowly, it began to move. It traced a path across the mazy lines and stopped. When he lifted it, she was alarmed to see it tremble slightly before he hid it in his fist.

'We need to go,' he said, turning away to whirl his jacket from a chair.

'Where?'

'Home,' he said.

Goldberg drove the only way she knew how – flat out. For once, Avram refrained from his usual commentary and his silence sawed at her nerves. Jerusalem seemed eerily quiet, even at such an early hour, and she took advantage of the sparse traffic, feathering the wheel with the tips of her fingers and keeping the pedal to the floor.

'Left,' he called, and they fishtailed off the main thorough-fare. 'Right at the next junction,' he murmured.

'I know,' she said, more sharply than she'd intended. She did know. They had swung north – to Mea Shearim.

⊰⊱

Esther looked curious but controlled when she opened the door.

'This is a sur—'

'I want to talk to him, now,' her son said tensely, as he strode inside trailing an apologetic Goldberg in his wake.

Goldberg thought Rabbi Zephaniah looked no less imposing in a dressing gown.

'I need some information,' Avram said.

'Why would I give information to an Israeli policeman?' the big man rumbled.

'Because if you do, we might be able to avert a disaster.'

'And if I do not?'

'Then this Israeli policeman will arrest you for withholding information.'

Standing beside Esther, Goldberg felt the tension that crackled between father and son.

'You made your bed among the Israelis, Ari,' the Rabbi hissed. 'Go lie with them.'

'You made your bed with my mother, Zephaniah,' his son growled back. 'We both made choices.'

Goldberg thought the rabbi would strike her partner and, instinctively, her hand moved to cover her weapon. The rabbi wrenched his head around to glare at the women.

'Leave us,' he said.

'No,' Avram said. 'You may instruct your wife as you see fit, Rabbi. Goldberg stays with me.'

'So do I,' Esther said firmly. 'Oh, Zephaniah,' she said, smiling at her furious husband, 'it's your own fault for marrying an American. You should have listened to those greybeards all those years ago. Now,' she added, 'we will sit at the table like civilised people.'

There was a moment when the other three gazed at her with varying degrees of surprise and then they sat.

'Remember when the group from Mea Shearim decided to retake the Rock?' Avram pressed his father.

'There was no such—'

'Yes, there was,' Avram insisted. 'I was there.'

'You?' the rabbi said dismissively, 'You were just a little boy.'

'So, there was such a time.' He ignored his father's head-shake and continued: 'Yes, I was a little boy who went to the synagogue with his father, the rabbi, a little boy who sat on his father's lap while the plan was made.'

'I don't remember you being there,' the rabbi said, perplexed.

'I was with you everywhere,' Avram shouted in his face. 'You took me to the synagogue. I was a boy and I didn't understand and I asked you to explain. You said you would when I was a man. I am a man now, Father.'

Goldberg's eyes misted and she felt Esther's calming hand on her arm. Rabbi Zephaniah sat immobile. Abruptly he lurched to his feet and walked stiffly to a small bookcase in a corner. When he returned, he pushed a folded document across the table. Goldberg moved behind Avram and scanned it over his shoulder.

'Oh, shit,' she said quietly.

When Avram and Goldberg had left, Esther wrapped the seated rabbi in her arms from behind and leaned her cheek against his beard. His sidelocks tickled her face and she smiled.

'I didn't remember, Esther,' he said softly. 'I didn't remember that my son sat on my lap that day.'

'He was your shadow, Zephaniah,' she murmured. 'A man doesn't notice his shadow.'

'Or his son,' he said sadly, 'until he steps out of it.' He was silent for a long time. 'Do you think he'll marry this Goldberg?' he asked.

'Who knows?' She laughed. 'But that sort of thing seems to run in your side of the family, Zephaniah.'

He raised his palm and pressed her cheek to his.

'Happily, it does,' he said.

The Cavern, Jerusalem

'I smell water,' Omar said quietly.

They had walked through the cavern behind the Mameluke's lantern until a huge slab of rock loomed up to block their passage. They huddled together as the Mameluke quested back and forth before the obstruction.

'Where?' Michael asked.

Omar tilted his head from side to side, like a dog seeking a scent.

'There and there,' he said, pointing left and right. 'The water on the left is still, perhaps a cistern. The water on the right flows quickly and … falls.'

'You have a gift, Omar,' Michael murmured admiringly.

'Yes, I have,' the young man said simply.

The Mameluke paused in his search and lifted the lantern.

'Up!' he said.

In the light of the lantern, Michael could make out a series of shallow steps cut in the rockface.

'Jacob's ladder, Omar,' he whispered. 'Maybe your grandfather was right about those angels after all.'

The Safe House, Jerusalem

Inspector Bernstein looked dapper and wide awake. Goldberg wondered briefly if he showered and dressed before he went to bed. Avram brought him up to speed on Goliath's call and produced the rabbi's document. He didn't mention where he'd got it and Bernstein didn't ask.

'Some years ago,' Avram said carefully, 'a group of ultra-Orthodox Jews decided to retake the Dome of the Rock. They claimed it was the site of Solomon's temple.'

'I remember,' Bernstein said, shaking his head. 'None of us got much sleep then either,' he added drily.

'This is their plan,' Avram continued, unfolding the yellowed paper. 'This is the Dome,' he explained, stabbing his finger at a crude drawing, then sliding it down and through the flat line that marked the base of the mosque. 'This,' he said, pointing at a white space beneath the floor, shaped like a genie's lamp, 'is a cave. The Muslims call it the Well of Souls. Ever since the Orthodox attack it's been sealed off from this lower cave.' His finger travelled to the lower cave and kept moving. 'This cave is linked by a channel to the ancient water system that runs under the old city.'

'Yes,' Bernstein said, 'there's a labyrinth down there. It was supposed to have been closed off years ago. That lower cave, Avram, what's it called?'

'The Abyss of Chaos.'

The inspector digested this.

'You two had better come down to headquarters,' he said.

Police Headquarters, Jerusalem
The phone rang as they entered Bernstein's office. He waved at them to sit and plucked the receiver from its cradle. Bernstein had always appeared unflappable to the partners and they were surprised to see him grimace.

'*Toda*, thank you,' he said eventually and put the phone

down slowly. He shoved his hands deep in his trouser pockets and rocked on the balls of his feet.

'What?' Goldberg blurted.

'You should take out a patent on your hunches, Avram,' Bernstein said humourlessly. 'Demands from terrorists have just come through. They're in the Dome of the Rock.' He drew a deep breath. 'They've got a bomb in there,' he said, 'in the Abyss of Chaos.'

He sat down at his desk and regarded the detectives.

'You two probably missed the previous episode,' he said. 'The former President of the United States made an appearance on Al Jazeera with the usual supporting cast of terrorists. They made the usual demands as well – release of political prisoners, or else. Our masters,' he continued grimly, 'consulted with the White House. The president said no.'

'No?' Avram echoed. 'Isn't she Jack Holland's wife?'

'Actually, he's her husband,' Goldberg amended mildly.

'She's also President of the United States,' Bernstein said, with undisguised admiration, 'and she proved it.'

'They kill him?' Goldberg asked.

'In full living colour on prime-time television,' he answered. 'Now, I wonder …'

'What?' Avram asked.

'I wonder if it was a feint, some kind of side-show set up to test the spine of the American President.'

'And this is another?' Goldberg offered.

'No, I don't think so,' Bernstein answered, and pressed the tips of his fingers to his temples. 'I think this is what you Americans would call the real deal. If they blow the Dome of the Rock, all bets are off. The hawks will have their day.'

'Try English, Inspector,' Goldberg pleaded.

'War,' he said simply.

He checked his watch. 'Jerusalem will be locked down solid in about thirty minutes,' he observed to no one in particular.

'On our way,' Avram said.

The White House, Washington DC

Ellen Radford lay on her bed and let the events of the day unfold behind closed eyelids. It was something her general-cum-philosopher father had taught her.

'Plato always did it, honey,' he'd assured her. 'He figured you could review and learn from the past day and be better equipped for the new one.'

It was a worthy pursuit but she felt only relief when the phone rang.

Déjà vu, she thought, when the doors to the Oval Office swung open and she saw her cabinet assembled. As soon as everyone was seated, she began to issue rapid-fire instructions.

'Laila, I want you in Jerusalem today. Bring some of your own people to man the embassy in Tel Aviv. Get that jerk Love and his staff on a plane back here. David,' she said, turning to the attorney general, 'get the FBI to meet and debrief them. The issues are lack of intel flow to this office in general and the call from someone claiming to be Jack Holland in particular. Let's trace how that was handled.'

She turned back to the Secretary of State.

'Assure the Israeli government that we have their back unless they go proactive. They've got to keep their nerve, whatever the provocation. Lebanon, Syria, Jordan and the other Arab states need to know that as well. If they escalate military readiness above Code Amber, we'll know from our satellites and the Israelis will know from us.'

'Yes, ma'am.'

'Henry, I want the Republican and Democrat leaders of Congress and the Senate in the Cabinet Room for a briefing, soonest. Get the Chiefs of Staff back in here as well – I need to be brought up to speed on our military assets in the Middle East.'

'What about the security agencies?' Henry Melly asked.

'Oxymoron,' she growled, 'we'll get around to them later. Ephrem, keep an eye on the stock market. The message is we're not going to war.'

'What can I do, ma'am?' the attorney general asked.

'How are you at praying, David?' she asked, with the hint of a smile.

'Rusty,' he admitted.

'Okay,' she said, 'let's not go there. As long as this lasts, I want you to act as the sensible side of my brain. I'm all pumped up right now, so I need someone to balance me, someone to play the devil's advocate. How does that grab you?'

'Maybe I undersold the prayer bit,' he said.

The Women's Refuge, Washington DC

Shonda Baines turned off the television, tidied the limp magazines and closed the sitting-room door. She listened for a moment outside the bedrooms in case any of the ladies was restless. Satisfied, she murmured aloud, 'All the birds in their nests, ol' girl. Time for you to follow.'

Automatically, she checked Sister Agnes' door and frowned at the crack of light beneath it. She knocked and entered to find the old nun asleep, at her desk, her head pillowed on a pile of papers.

'Bills, most likely,' she clucked, 'always bills.' She shook her gently and saw the eyes widen in the lined face.

'Oh, it's you, Shonda,' Sister Agnes said sleepily.

'It's always me,' Shonda chided. 'Been me finding you like this for nigh on twenty years. You need your sleep like any other body or you gonna get sick or die, and then what?'

'I could get some real rest,' Sister Agnes said, smiling.

'Don't you sass me, Agnes, I—'

The shrill sound of the doorbell cut her short.

'I'll get it,' she said.

'Bring her here, will you, Shonda?' Sister Agnes said, stifling a yawn. 'I like to greet our guests.'

Shonda shook her head and padded to the door. She slipped the eyepiece and stretched up on her toes. In the distorted orb, she saw a policeman standing outside, supporting a woman.

'Trouble never sleeps.' She sighed and started on the locks. 'What we got here, Officer?' she said, as he manoeuvred the woman into the hall and propped her against the wall.

'We got a whole mess of heartache, little lady.' He grinned, placing the muzzle of a pistol against her temple. 'Unless,' he added, 'you co-operate, dig me?'

'I dig,' she whispered.

The unconscious woman slid down the wall and curled up on the floor.

'What about this lady here?' Shonda protested, taking a step forward, making to help her.

'Let the trash lie,' the man grunted. 'That hooker's played her part. Who's here?' he demanded.

She hesitated just long enough to look into his eyes. She had looked into eyes like that before and her chest constricted.

'All the guests in bed,' she said sullenly, ''cept Sister Agnes. She in her office, yonder.'

'And?' the man prompted.

'And Ms Catherine,' Shonda answered.

The old nun looked up as the door opened. 'Lord, have mercy on us,' she whispered.

'Let's not put Him to the test, Sister,' the man said, shoving Shonda into a chair. 'You ladies just sit there and be comfortable,' he said. 'Ms Catherine and I would appreciate a little privacy.'

The door clicked behind him and they heard his steps ascend the stairs.

Sister Agnes lifted the telephone and let it fall from numb fingers. 'Nothing,' she said.

They sat staring at each other until Sister Agnes cleared her throat and said, 'I have a gun in my desk drawer.'

'What? Where you get that?'

'Well, it's a long story, too long to … What are we going to do, Shonda?'

⊰⊱

Catherine De Lancy looked at the policeman sitting astride the chair.

'Hello, Scylla,' she said calmly.

'And hello to you, Miss Catherine,' he said, in a cultured voice. 'I regret my unexpected appearance and my, ah, purpose. But you know better than most how these things go.'

'I do.' She nodded. 'I'm your target, Scylla. There's really no point in involving the others.'

She hated the note of pleading that had crept into her voice.

'Sorry, Miss Catherine,' he said, with mock regret, 'I was instructed to use my discretion – you understand.'

'I understand.'

She sat erect and folded her hands in her lap.

'Whenever you're ready,' she said.

'Always a pleasure dealing with a professional, Miss Catherine,' he said admiringly, and raised the gun. 'Oh,' he said, 'how remiss of me. Benson did ask me to relay a final message. I was told to tell you that your fiancé exhibited such stupidity in the execution of his duty in Vietnam that his squad had no other recourse but to shoot him. Fragged, I believe it was called,' he said helpfully.

She was suddenly distracted but forced herself to concentrate.

'Where was he buried?' she asked, ignoring the trickle of sweat that had begun a slow journey between her shoulder blades.

'It seems he wasn't,' Scylla replied. 'They dumped his body in a village refuse pit. I'm not sure if that qualifies under dramatic irony. It was never recovered.'

The distraction clamoured for her attention and it took all her willpower to remain impassive.

'Did Benson say anything about Jack Holland?' she asked, and had the satisfaction of seeing his stupid smile falter.

'You do know too much,' he said, and sighted down the barrel.

She shut her eyes tightly. The explosion sounded as if some giant had clapped his hands against her ears. When she opened her eyes, Scylla lay slumped over the back of the chair. A rope of thick blood oozed from the corner of his mouth and swayed to the floor. Over the dead man's shoulder, she saw Shonda holding an enormous pistol in both hands.

'You killed him,' she whispered.

'Not so bad second time round,' the little woman said, and fainted.

⑬

Shonda lay on the couch, eyes closed, while Catherine held a cold compress to her forehead.

'Just shock,' she said, as Sister Agnes returned from re-assuring the other guests.

'I called the police on my little phone,' Sister Agnes said quietly. 'Never thought of using it when … To tell the truth, I don't like these new—'

'Sister Agnes,' Catherine interrupted, 'may I use your cellphone?'

'Of course, my dear. You do know the police will be along shortly?'

'Yes, I know,' Catherine said sadly. 'I'll be gone before then.'

She stood in the hallway and pressed the numbers.

'Who is this and where the hell did you get this number?'

'One question at a time, Senator,' she said. 'I am Catherine De Lancy. My, ah, former employer had lots of numbers.'

'What can I do for you, Miss De Lancy?'

'"Ask not what your country can do for you,"' Catherine quoted, '"ask rather what you can do for your country."'

The Cavern, Jerusalem

Michael surfaced from the shaft into a space that smelled of must and mildew. The lantern, rising through the hole in the floor behind him, revealed a wide, rock-walled chamber, brooding under a low concrete ceiling. Moisture glinted from the walls as the Mameluke placed the lantern in the centre of the floor.

'Sit here,' he said, gesturing to a spot beside the lantern. Michael sat, exposed in the glow. He raised his eyes and scanned the concrete ceiling. Directly overhead someone had hacked a hole in the concrete. From the lack of light coming through, he guessed it was covered on the other side by a thick carpet. The Mameluke fanned the gun at Omar.

'Sit beside him,' he said.

After a beat, the young man hunkered down.

'Sir Baldwin wishes you to know the demands have been sent to the Israelis,' he said.

'Suppose they refuse?' Michael asked.

'I do not answer questions for you,' the Mameluke said dismissively.

'Then answer for me,' Omar said. 'What happens if they refuse?'

The Mameluke's mouth curled into a cruel grin.

'Boom,' he said, lengthening and savouring the word. 'The force of the blast will be compressed by the chamber and channelled through the hole. It will be enough to destroy the Dome of the Rock. There will be war.'

'How is the bomb exploded?' Omar asked.

'By a timing device,' the Mameluke answered. 'It is built into the harness.'

He dug in his pocket and dangled a small remote control at the end of a cord.

'Where will we be?' Omar persisted.

'My young friend,' the Mameluke sneered, 'we won't be anywhere. You and Flaherty will disappear in the explosion. I will be far along the cavern.' He smiled at the confusion on Omar's face.

'Did you really think Sir Baldwin would allow you your freedom? However, he is not without mercy. I am to kill you both three minutes before I detonate the bomb.'

'To give yourself plenty of time to escape,' Michael added.

The Mameluke didn't reply. He went to the lip of the opening in the floor and peered down into the cavern. Michael had always known he was on a one-way ticket but the young man beside him seemed to have believed there was hope. His head had dropped and his body seemed to have folded in upon itself.

'Omar,' he whispered. 'Omar!'

'Yes.'

'Have you someone to live for?'

'Wha— Yes.'

'Who?'

'My mother, my brothers and – and another person.'

'Focus on them,' Michael whispered urgently. 'See their faces in your head. Omar?'

'Yes.'

'When the time comes, run, okay?'

Omar did not answer. The Mameluke was back.

The Arab Quarter, Jerusalem
'I have a lock-pick here somewhere,' Goldberg whispered, as she rummaged in her pocket.

'I have one right here,' Goliath said, and kicked the door. It smashed back against the wall of the courtyard and Avram was already in and moving right, fanning his gun for targets, while Goliath ghosted left.

Goldberg took the direct route across the cobbles to the door of the house. Goliath is right, she thought. We're way beyond subtlety here. The second door suffered the fate of the first and they thundered down wooden stairs to a musty basement.

Avram put his back to the wall and step-measured to a count of three.

'Map says here.'

It took mere seconds to sweep back the flimsy carpet covering. Avram bent and opened the trapdoor a fraction.

'Stairs down,' he whispered. 'Goldberg, on a count of three.'

She sailed through the opening as her companions bent into the space, covering her left and right. She was crouched and pivoting when two soft thumps announced their arrival in the cavern.

'Go slowly, wait for night vision,' Avram whispered. 'Me on point, Goldberg on my left shoulder, Goliath sweeps the rear.'

'You two make what speed you can,' Goliath said. 'I have your back.'

Goldberg thought of a phrase that included 'rock' and 'hard place' but wisely stayed schtum.

Seconds seemed to tick fast and furiously in her head as they planted their feet carefully, making slow progress across the rubble-strewn floor. At least we can see more, she thought, and immediately collided with Avram's broad back. He swivelled his head around to whisper in her ear, 'Wall, ten feet ahead.' Her eyes saw it as a deeper shade of black until she looked up and saw faint light coming from an opening in the roof.

৪০৫৪

The Mameluke's shadow loomed monstrous on the wall behind him and Michael tracked it as it paced back and forth, shortening its journey by a pace every pass, like a pendulum swinging down to rest. He read the tiny unconscious tics of a body under pressure, smelled the sharp tang of sweat emanating from the Mameluke and decided. Slowly, he stretched his arm and touched Omar.

'Ready?' he breathed.

The Mameluke stood still and cocked his gun-hand to check his watch. He saw a light bloom suddenly in its glass and instinctively raised his arm to protect his head. The lantern smashed into his elbow and fell quenched to the floor. Ignoring his numbed arm, he crouched, brushing the floor with his right hand, questing for the fallen gun.

Michael was already scurrying away from Omar while the lantern was in flight. He was relieved to see the young man go the opposite way before the darkness became total. The gun spat and he heard the complaint of the bullet as it whined through the space he had just vacated. Before it had spent its spite, chewing stone from the back wall of the chamber, he was edging back to where he had been. The second bullet passed him on the left as the Mameluke grasped that the target had moved and corrected his aim. Michael hunched forward and gathered his strength to make a headlong charge.

৪০৫৪

Avram was the first to react. His eyes had been glued to the faint patch of light, and when it wavered, he ran to the wall beneath the opening and bent double. Almost immediately, he felt Goldberg's foot stamp on his back as she trampolined up into the shaft. Clinging to the lip of the opening in the floor above with one arm and braced by her legs, she saw the muzzle-flash of the second shot and fired. It was a short, staccato burst that bisected the space occupied by the after-image in her eyes and she had the satisfaction of hearing a grunt and the thump of a falling body before her left foot lost its purchase and she slid down the shaft. Avram flattened himself against the wall as his partner went past, digging his fingers into the horizontal crevices that gouged the rock at regular intervals. Before she struck the cavern floor, he was climbing.

❧◆❧

Michael registered the burst of shots and heard the Mameluke exclaim and fall. Immediately, he heard the growing sound of scraping from the shaft and called out in the darkness:

'Two friendlies, unarmed, and one hostile down.'

'Status of hostile?' Avram barked.

'Unclear,' Michael answered.

Michael winced from the sudden sting of light and shaded his eyes with his hand. In the beam of Avram's torch, he saw the Mameluke curled on his side, unmoving, and a man, made huge by the torchlight, emerging from the mouth of the shaft to approach the prone figure.

'I'm Michael Flaherty,' he said. 'There's a young guy back there called Omar.'

'Detective Avram.' The man never took his eyes from the

figure on the floor. He covered it with his handgun and nodded. When Michael rolled the Mameluke over, he saw the terrible wound in his chest and shook his head. 'Detective Avram …' he began, and stopped. He heard the wet sucking sound of a chest wound and turned to see the Mameluke's eyes flicker open and lock on his. The stricken man's bloody lips stretched into a smile that widened into a grimace as he tried for another breath and failed.

'Detective Avram,' Michael said calmly, 'check the back of this harness for a timing device.'

'It's here,' Avram said.

'Okay,' Michael breathed. 'We had three minutes tops from the time the first shot was fired.'

He glanced at Goliath and Goldberg, who had emerged from the shaft to flank Avram.

'Help me back down the shaft,' he said, 'and get as far away as you can. Omar,' he added, turning to the young man, 'show me where the running water is in the cavern. I want to be well away from under the Dome when …'

Two precious seconds ticked by as they absorbed the implications. Avram was the first to break the silence.

'Let's do it,' he said.

'Wait,' Omar said, when they reached the cavern floor.

'There's no time, Omar,' Michael said urgently. 'Get me to the water and leave.'

'What tools do you have?' Omar asked Avram.

Quickly, the detectives and Goliath pooled their resources. Omar plucked a Swiss Army knife and the tiny torch from the small stock in Goliath's hands. 'Now, go,' he urged them.

'You too,' Michael urged. 'Take the boy with you, Avram,' he pleaded.

'I am not a boy,' Omar said calmly. 'I am a man and I am training to be an engineer.'

Reluctantly, the two detectives began to make their way back through the cavern. Goliath stayed.

'You'll need someone to hold the torch,' he said.

⊗⊃⊂⊗

'I can't dismantle the bomb,' Omar confessed, after a brief examination of the harness.

'Okay,' Michael said. 'Now will you two get the hell out of here?'

They were sitting near a deep trench at the side of the cavern. Omar could hear the running water chuckling as it tasted the air briefly between one underground channel and the next.

'There is more than one way to skin a dog,' he muttered, weighing the knife in his hand.

'Cat,' Goliath corrected, holding the torch rock-steady.

'Whatever.' Omar deepened his breathing, drawing in huge draughts of water-flavoured air. Water always finds a way, he reminded himself, and repeated the mantra as he traced the wire tributaries that criss-crossed the deadly harness. He saw the slabs of explosives as rocks and dams that thwart the stream and force the water to probe and push until it finds the point of least resistance and …

His finger paused in its passage where a thin wire jointed with a leather pad that nestled under Michael's arm.

'You think this is the place?' Goliath whispered, leaning closer with the light so that a drop of sweat falling from his chin flashed and disappeared like a meteor in the beam.

544

'*Inshallah*,' Omar murmured, angling the heavy blade against the spot where the metal and leather conjoined.

'Yes, God willing,' Goliath agreed. 'Now, in the name of God, do it.'

Michael heard the snap and felt the harness shift slightly. He started to wriggle frantically as the two men worked it up from his torso.

'Do not push,' Omar urged. 'Flow.'

Michael relaxed his muscles and the harness began to move more easily. It caught, for one agonising second, as it angled over his head, and then he was free. Goliath was already swinging it away in the direction of the trench as Omar burst into a run.

'This way,' he gasped.

In the half-dark they stumbled over the stone-strewn floor. Goliath and Michael followed the young man without hesitation, veering when he did, following his every direction, caught up in the wild flight and the exhilaration in his voice. Suddenly he disappeared and they checked their mad scramble, standing uncertainly, wheezing in great gulps of air.

'Down here,' a voice called.

Michael jumped and cleared his eyes of water as Goliath splashed down beside him. He had time to notice the pale chisel-strokes that had hollowed out the cistern they stood in before the world began to shake itself to pieces.

☤☣

Avram and Goldberg were running, flat-out, oblivious to the debris on the cavern floor that threatened their every step – a minefield, Goldberg thought, and felt a surge of giddy excitement, heightened by her awareness of Avram's hand under her elbow, lifting her almost off her feet so that she seemed to be … flying. It was an unbelievably thrilling and painfully brief sensation. A hot wind lifted the pair and tossed them forward contemptuously. She was aware that the floor was sandpapering her outflung palms and she was rolling. Suddenly she was still. Her brain registered that Avram was curled protectively around her, but before it could spark any response of pain or pleasure, the sound came.

The earth seemed to cough – the kind of cough that came up from the toes, what her mother would have called a 'graveyard cough' – and every bone in her body rattled in sympathy. A hot exhalation of air whipped over the prone pair, peppering them with grit and then – silence.

&

The three men in the cistern clung to each other as the thunder rolled over their heads and showers of stones pelted from the roof. Instinctively Omar tugged his two companions under the surface and the water insulated them against the deadly hail. When the shaking stopped, they surged up, gasping for air. Michael cleared his stinging eyes to see Omar struggling to support Goliath. They hauled the unconscious soldier over the side of the cistern and laid him on the floor. In the thick murk of dust, Michael trusted his fingertips to assess the man's condition.

'His pulse is strong,' he said.

Omar read his lips while waiting for the bells to finish their carillon in his ears. Wordlessly, they hitched their arms under Goliath's shoulders and dragged him across the floor.

'Avram. Avram,' Goldberg shouted frantically, pressing her palms against his cheeks. 'Don't you dare die on me, you bastard,' she hissed, checking his breathing with her ear stuck to his chest. She tilted his head back, pinched his nostrils closed and placed her lips on his, urgently forcing air into his lungs. He coughed into her mouth and she pulled back to spit. When she hunched forward again, he was looking at her with amusement.

'That was gross.' She was trying to wipe her mouth and eyes at the same time.

'It wasn't that bad,' he said hoarsely.

The sounds of the others approaching broke the moment.

Between them, they hauled Goliath into the basement of the house, helped by a squad of Israeli police. Michael checked Goliath's vital signs, relieved to find his pulse still strong. He touched Avram's arm and inclined his head. He was unsurprised when the female detective appeared at his shoulder.

'I have to get out of here,' he said. 'Can you arrange that?'

'Father Guardian told us about you, Michael,' Avram said. 'You can relax, it's all over.'

'It isn't over for me,' Michael said. 'While Cardinal Thomas is on the loose, my family are in danger.'

'If you go after him, they'll kill you,' Goldberg objected.

'I'm not that easy to kill.'

'So we've gathered,' Avram said, shaking his head.

He walked away and, when he returned, he offered a pistol, butt first, to Michael.

'I don't think Goliath will be needing this for a while.' He grinned.

'There's one more thing,' Michael said, as he tucked the gun into his waistband.

᠎᠎᠎ৰুৎৡ

Omar sat quietly in the kitchen as armoured bodies milled around him. The euphoria had leached from his system and the reality of his situation was seeping back into his consciousness. Suddenly a strong hand pulled him upright and he was face to face with Michael Flaherty.

'I wanted to run away,' he whispered. His eyes began to leak slow tears that carved brown channels through the dust-mask on his face.

'But you didn't,' Michael said gently, using the flat of one palm to wipe the young man's face. 'You didn't,' he repeated, 'and you saved my life. You know what the Holy Qur'an says about someone who saves a man's life?'

Omar nodded, his mouth working to form the quote.

'"It is as if he has saved a whole people,"' he murmured.

'You may have done that also,' Michael said. 'The detectives will take you to Father Guardian at the Holy Sepulchre. He's a good man, Omar. He'll know what to do.'

He took the young man in his arms for a few moments, smelling the dust and sweat in his hair.

'And you?' Omar asked, against his shoulder.

'My journey isn't over,' Michael said, and released him.

The Oval Office, The White House
Agents Frawley and Grant did what Americans, outside the White House, had been doing ever since the situation in the

Middle East had escalated to prime-time media coverage and therefore qualified as a crisis. They speculated.

'You think the Secretary of State got what it takes to bump heads with the Arabs?' Frawley asked.

'Yeah, sure.' Grant nodded. 'You remember when Condi went to see Gaddafi that time? I was on that one.'

'I remember. You pulled the short straw.'

'Did I ever! Man, it was so hot. We're in this big marquee, right, and she's wearing a black pantsuit and just a hint of rouge. Gaddafi's wearing a kinda portable tent, very Lawrence, all the way to the eyeliner. So, here we are in this damn Bedouin tent in the desert. It's so damn hot the camels have heatstroke and we're all juiced up to enjoy Arab hospitality, and guess what?'

'What?'

'There's no water on the table.'

'No water. You sure?'

'Sure I'm sure. I was there. No water. But in pride of place, smack-bang on the table between him and her, there's this box of tissues.'

'Just plain tissues?'

'The plainest! We're talking motel-cheap, budget-airline tissues. But, as it happens, these cultural anachronisms have huge symbolic implications.'

'And the tissues?'

'Peasant! The point of the whole thing is who dabs first. Who feels that little bead burgeon above an eyebrow, dangle from an earlobe. Beads of perspiration attract other beads, brother, until they coalesce and we're deep into trickle territory. So, who cracks and reaches for a tissue?'

'Did she?'

'Did she hell! She laid it on thick and fast about what a good boy he'd been, a marked improvement from that time we nearly put a Cruise missile up his keister to attract his attention in class. And all the time she goes with this reasonable tone of voice, like Hannibal Lecter giving a recipe for grilled liver, and Gaddafi knows whose liver we're talking about here, and—'

'And what?'

'And she offered him the damn tissue-box. Game, set and match to the piano-player.'

Frawley shook his head admiringly, then tilted it back at the door behind him.

'You think the, uh, present incumbent can chill this one out?'

'Sweat-glands removed at birth, partner,' Grant said confidently. 'Put the house on it.'

⟡

'God, it's hot.' David Duke sighed and mopped his forehead with a wad of tissues. He looked around for a bin to dump them in and settled for his pocket. He looked enviously at the senator, whose only acknowledgement of the heat was a coat folded carefully over a chairback.

'Henry, you get a thermostat installed last time you had surgery?'

'No. I once asked a good ol' Southern boy how he coped with the heat. He said, "It's okay if you don't move." You know Reagan and Coolidge racked up more sleep-time than all the other incumbents of the Oval Office combined?'

'And the point is?'

'When the heat's on, sit still, boy.'

The president hung up the phone.

'Laila says the Israelis are going for the low-profile option – holding the line on all fronts but everything as was. No escalation.'

The two men sighed with relief.

'Other details,' she said, scanning her notes. 'The Knesset debated state compensation for the damage to the Dome of the Rock. Right-wingers and ultra-Orthodox representatives staged a walkout and threatened to bring down the government. Latest from her own people on the ground is that three people were involved in the bomb plot – a young Palestinian, a Mameluke and Michael Flaherty.'

'What's a Mameluke when he's at home?' Henry Melly enquired.

'It's the Arabic word for slave,' Duke said. 'The Mamelukes started off as slaves of non-Arab origins, went on to become a warrior caste that dominated Egypt for about seven hundred years.'

'"And still they gazed and still the wonder grew,"' Melly said admiringly.

'"That one small head could carry all he knew,"' Duke said, smiling. 'Yeah, I know that one too – Goldsmith, Irish writer. I'm a mine of irrelevant information, Senator.'

'You undersell yourself, son.'

'If the mutual admiration society is going into recess any time soon, you two might like to hear the rest of this,' the president said. 'According to Laila, Flaherty and the young man were coerced into bringing the bomb. This Mameluke fella was the enforcer. He was shot by Israeli police before Flaherty and his companion, helped by an Israeli soldier, managed to dump the bomb in an underground stream.'

'Which saved the Dome from destruction,' Duke added.

'It still did enough damage to stir up the locals,' the president said. 'Laila's working at keeping the lid on things. She says it could go either way.'

'Where's Flaherty now?' Melly asked.

'Missing.'

'Why am I not surprised?'

'What time does our ... guest arrive?' she enquired.

'Five minutes, tops.'

'We ready?'

'We're ready,' the attorney general said quietly.

The Red Room, The White House

'The president will see you now, sir.'

Benson stopped pacing the Red Room and glared at Agent Grant.

'About time,' he snapped. 'I never liked this room. You know what Oscar Wilde said about a bedroom in France?'

'He said it was him or the wallpaper, sir, one of them had to go,' the agent said smoothly.

'What? Uh, yes, exactly, Agent,' Benson said, in a tone that managed to sound half-surprised and wholly condescending.

'Actually, it turned out to be him, sir – that went, that is,' Grant added.

Benson gave the room a last look of disgust.

'Decorated like a French bordello,' he muttered.

'Now that's something I'll have to take your word for, sir,' Agent Grant said, and opened the door.

Benson's day had started badly. He'd come awake to a muted television set broadcasting footage of the Dome of the

Rock, shots taken of an intact Dome rather than the pile of rubble he'd been expecting. Cursing Baldwin's ineptitude, he'd tugged on his clothes with one hand while punching numbers on his cellphone with the other. It buzzed and buzzed, like a wasp trapped at a window, until he'd thrown it at the drapes. Shocked into silence, it dropped to the floor and rang.

'What?' he'd snarled.

The voice at the other end informed him of the time and place and cut the connection.

The smart-ass agent at his shoulder nodded to his fellow agent, and the door to the Oval Office swung open.

The Oval Office, The White House

'Ms President,' he began, 'the Pentagon assures me it has the capability to neutralise the forces massed on Israel's borders. I urge you to authorise that action. We can cow those terrorists and have the Arabs in our pockets for a generation.'

'That's exactly what they said to me,' she said coolly. 'I listened to everything the joint chiefs had to say and disagreed with most of it.'

'You overrode the Pentagon?' he said, appalled.

'Just one of the perks of being Commander-in-Chief,' she said absently, closing a folder on her desk.

'It's not wise to alienate the forces,' he persisted. 'No president before y—'

'On the contrary, Mr Benson,' she interrupted sharply, 'the precedent is well and truly established and on the record. FDR did it because he knew isolationism would gift Europe to Hitler. There have been a number of presidents who felt the forces were becoming dangerously autonomous and clipped their collective wings. John F. Kennedy, whom you're so fond of quoting, said he was tempted to raise an army to retake the Pentagon for the sake of the republic.'

'Republic?' he stammered, his face a mask of disbelief. 'You'd settle for this piss-poor republic when we have the God-given opportunity for empire?'

She laid her palms on the desk and leaned forward.

'The empires are all gone, sir,' she said, with barely controlled anger. 'Eisenhower hammered the final nail in the British Empire's coffin when he ordered Eden out of Suez. The Soviet Empire imploded, Mr Benson, with a little help from Reagan and the Pope. The Chinese, as it happens, don't actually want a Little Red Book any more. They want freedom of expression and movement and Starbucks and McDonald's and all the things we take for granted in this piss-poor republic.'

'My advice—'

'I did not ask for it,' she said icily. 'We are not here to benefit from your wisdom. Sit down, please.'

Slowly, he eased into the chair. The president turned hers sideways.

'Mr Attorney General,' she said.

David Duke opened a file on his knees and trapped a loose leaf that had slipped its binding and tried to escape. Benson smiled at his awkwardness and settled his face into an expression of bemusement.

'In your own time, Counsellor,' he drawled.

'What? Ah, yes, eh, thank you, Mr Benson. Of specific concern to this Office, sir, is the matter of clandestine military incursions into sovereign states under the aegis of the Central Intelligence Agency.'

'Did they teach you to talk like that at Harvard, Mr Duke,' Benson asked, 'or is it a handicap you were born with?'

'I think you get the gist, Benson,' Senator Melly said quietly.

'Oh, indeed I do, Henry,' Benson said smugly. 'But old hands, like you and me, know that you can fit a pig with wings but it won't fly. These military incursions never happened,' he snapped. 'If they did, they were, as you say, clandestine. Last time I looked, that meant unauthorised. They were not authorised by me.'

'Actually, they did happen, sir,' David Duke mumbled, thumbing through his notes until he fastened on the relevant page. 'General Highlander, on, uh, mature reflection, recalls just such a sortie into Colombia. We also have the records of Michael Flaherty, forwarded from the military hospital in Virginia, which corroborate the general's testimony that such a military operation did take place and that Michael Flaherty is the only survivor of a subsequent incursion authorised by the military to stymie the first group.'

'"What is that to me or to thee?"' Benson said almost playfully. 'Surely you're not presenting this as evidence of my involvement?'

'Good quote, sir,' David Duke said admiringly. 'If I'm not mistaken, it comes from the Gospel of John, Chapter Two. Actually, you cut it a little short, Mr Benson. The full quote goes, "What is that to me or to thee? My hour has not yet come."'

Benson felt the first faint spasm of unease ripple through his contempt for the bumbling lawyer.

'It seems,' David Duke said, pushing his spectacles a little higher on his nose, 'that your time may have come, after all, Mr Benson.'

'What are you talking about?'

'I'm talking about Ms Catherine De Lancy,' the Attorney General said, and watched shock glaze the man's eyes. 'Yes, indeed,' he continued, 'a remarkable lady – such an incredible memory. Of course, that was why you retained her, Mr Benson. She was a link with fo—'

'Yeah, yeah,' Benson said dismissively, 'she was all that, but whatever she says in your little affidavit is just hearsay.'

'Pardon?'

'Hearsay,' Benson mouthed, as if explaining to a particularly dim pupil. 'Legally, it don't amount to a hill of beans.' He leaned forward solicitously towards the attorney general. 'You do understand that phrase, Mr Duke,' he said, 'you being a farm-boy from Virginia and all?'

'You're absolutely right, sir,' David Duke agreed. 'It is hearsay and inadmissible in a court of law, unless …'

Benson's eyes were riveted on the young man's face.

'Unless,' David continued, 'she took notes, sir. Now, that eventuality would elevate the hill you mentioned to something a little more impressive.'

'Don't toy with me, Mr Duke,' Benson snarled. 'You put up or shut up.'

'As you wish, Mr Benson,' David Duke said, pulling a large manilla envelope from the folder. 'It's all here, word for word.'

'You cannot be serious,' Benson sneered. 'This is your smoking gun, the ramblings of an old woman. I should have dumped her with the Remington typewriter when I took over the agency. Even then she was a has-been, someone who resisted change and now stabs her master in the back to satisfy some vengeful fantasy. These,' he said, waving his hand at the envelope, 'are the jottings of an incompetent for ever mired in middle management. This what you got, kid? This your best shot?'

'Yes.' David Dukes sighed and seemed to deflate. 'Her recollection of conversations, as you stated, is just hearsay. Her notes could very well be no more than … well, all the things you just said. The only thing neither of us disputes is that she had a phenomenal memory.'

The attorney general stood up and began to pace behind Benson's chair.

'Catherine De Lancy,' he said, 'sat in your office or in your home and listened. She listened and remembered everything – from the Colombian business to Baldwin to Jack Holland.'

Benson jerked in the chair as if he had been stung. He risked a glance at the president and flinched at her stony expression.

'Ah, come on,' he said, his lips drawn into a bloodless smile, 'it's her word against mine. Who do you think a jury will believe, Counsellor?'

'Yours,' David Duke said immediately. 'In a court of law, I have no doubt they'd believe you, Mr Benson. But let's not get too far ahead of ourselves here. We were talking about her memory, which you agreed is extraordinary. She is very precise in her affidavit. She relates how you would take her written notes at the end of each conversation, put them into your safe and lock it. She remembered everything, right down to the tiniest detail – which particular brand of whiskey you favoured, how you liked to angle your desk-lamp and the way you locked your safe.'

David Duke was standing behind Benson. He leaned forward over his shoulder and stretched out his arm before him. With his thumb and forefinger, he mimed turning the tumblers of a safe lock.

'Two left, one right, four left and straight up the middle. Open, Sesame,' he whispered.

Benson's eyes followed the finger-play like a rabbit entranced by the dance of a stoat. When the hand withdrew, he was left staring into space. 'I …' he began. 'I …' His breath failed him. For a few moments, his mouth worked soundlessly and went slack.

'You are dismissed,' the president said, in a voice too exhausted for anger. She pressed the button on her desk and spoke to the sombre agents who materialised inside the door.

'You, gentlemen, will escort the former director of the CIA from the White House and see to it that he never sets foot in this building again. Your successor has already been appointed,' she said to Benson, who was swaying on his feet. 'You are prohibited from entering your former office or any building connected with the agency. Consider yourself under house arrest until I decide what steps this government will take to bring you before a court of law.'

She nodded and the agents took him away.

Casper Benson moved like a damaged puppet between the two agents. It was only when Agent Grant bent his head to ease him into the car that a flash of his old malevolence surfaced.

'What's your name, Agent?' he growled.

'Grant, sir.'

'I'll remember you, Agent Grant,' he said menacingly.

'I wish I could repay the compliment, sir,' Agent Grant said mildly, and closed the door.

David Duke closed the folder with a snap of satisfaction.

'We have enough in here to put him away for a very long time,' he said.

The silence in the office stretched and became oppressive.

'I'd prosecute the case myself, Ms President,' he went on. 'No jury of his peers would—'

'David,' she interrupted wearily, 'we can't.'

'Can't what?'

His perplexed-little-boy look was back and she hated what she had to say.

'We can't take Benson before the courts. The trial would drag all the dirty linen of thirty years into the public forum. Think of what that would do to the morale of the country and our standing in the world.'

'But what about justice?' he asked plaintively.

'Justice is a lady who wears a blindfold when she holds the scales,' she said. 'I can't afford that luxury. The president has to take a longer view.'

'That's politics, I guess,' he said stiffly.

'Yes,' she agreed. 'Politics is the art of the possible, David, not the perfect. Prosecutors accept plea-bargains every day of the week. Criminals regularly get reduced sentences in return for giving state's evidence against bigger criminals. Presidents do it too. Ford did a deal not to prosecute Nixon. That was a decision he made for the sake of the common good. Ford was lucky,' she said, almost to herself, 'he got to spare one man for the sake of many. I got to sacrifice Jack Holland for the same reason.'

'I see,' the attorney general said slowly. 'If you'll excuse me, ma'am, I need to get back to my office. There are some things I—'

'Of course, David, and thank you.'

'I think my Santa mask just slipped,' she said sadly, when they were alone.

'Real's the deal, Ellen,' Henry Melly said. 'Think he's disillusioned enough to hand back his seal of office?'

'Hope not. David's a good kid. A wise man once said that to become disillusioned you must first have illusions.'

'That wise man wouldn't have been you, Henry?' she asked, with a small smile.

'I couldn't say, ma'am. As I recall, he was modest as well.'

The Muslim Quarter, Jerusalem

'Why do I have to take him?' Goldberg protested.

'Because I have to wait for the inspector and nobody drives like you do,' Avram said reasonably.

She couldn't be certain if it was a compliment but decided to give him the benefit of the doubt.

'Do all Israelis drive like this?' Michael Flaherty asked, as they roared through St Stephen's Gate and screamed into a right turn to parallel the wall of the Old City.

'Like what?' she said, as the Rockefeller Museum did a dizzy one-hundred-and-eighty-degree turn on their left. He was finding it hard to hold his breath and speak at the same time, so the conversation lapsed. She slotted the car between two police cruisers and a uniform peeled away from a group huddled at the gate of Baldwin's mansion.

'Goldberg?' the officer in the flak-jacket said.

'Do I know you?' she asked, flipping her ID.

'Figured it was you,' he said, looking thoughtfully at the steaming car. 'Who's this?'

'Michael Flaherty,' she said. 'Avram says it's okay for him to go in there.'

The officer ran a professional eye over the tall man.

'Want a jacket?'

'No.'

'Okay, you got thirty minutes tops before we follow. Just make sure to be flat on the floor when we do.'

Michael nodded.

'Want to go in through the gate?'

'Tradesmen's entrance is fine.'

'Okay. Wait for the distraction.'

The distraction was a grenade lobbed over the gate. Before the dust and pieces of shrubbery had settled, Michael dropped from the wall and rolled. Surprise is not an option, he thought grimly, and retraced the route he had taken last time.

❧

'Surprise,' she said softly, when his feet hit the floor.

'I'm expected,' he said, to Lady Melisande, who had lifted the gun from his waistband and now pointed it at his head. She prodded him before her into the pit and reappeared moments later to be joined by Baldwin at the rim.

'Some people never learn, Baldwin said.

'You should know,' Michael answered calmly, from the floor of the sunken chamber.

'Kill him,' Cardinal Thomas demanded.

'God knows, I've tried,' Baldwin said, pacing the edge of the pit. 'But—'

He was interrupted by the insistent beeping of a cellphone.

'Excuse me,' the female assassin Lady Melisande murmured and walked off into the shadows.

'It's over, Baldwin,' Michael said. 'Give it up.'

'I intend to,' Baldwin said. 'My ancestors, after all, were realists. When the infidel had undermined the walls and the cistern was dry, they sat and parlayed. The Mussulman was many things, Flaherty, but he wasn't a fool. Killing knights inevitably brought more knights to avenge their brothers – no profit in that. It all came down to business in the end and, in the end, that's what I do. It was all very civilised. The knights, as befitted their station, rode off under arms and with a safe passage tucked inside their breastplates. There were, however, certain guarantees of good faith left behind. Hostages to fortune, you might say. Like you, Eminence,' he said, turning back to the cardinal and laying the tip of the broadsword against his neck.

'You promised me Flaherty,' the cardinal protested.

'He's all yours, Eminence.' Baldwin bent and picked up a rope with his free hand, tossing the untethered end into the pit. 'Go and get him,' he said, angling the blade to push the cardinal to the edge.

They stood facing each other across the floor of the sunken chamber.

'A parting gift, my friends,' Baldwin called cheerily, and Michael's confiscated gun thumped on the floor between the two protagonists. 'Now, if you'll excuse me, I'm expecting visitors.'

Thomas lunged for the gun and Michael stamped on his wrist with his left foot, scything the right towards Thomas' head. Thomas ducked the kick and swept his arm to push the lighter man off-balance. He scrambled for the weapon and swept it into his right hand as Michael grasped his wrist. Their free hands clawed for and found each other's throat as the gun wavered upright between their contorted faces. For a moment, they stood locked in a straining stalemate until the strength of the younger man prevailed. Slowly, he bent the cardinal's wrist as the man's eyes widened with agony. With a grunt of despair, Thomas fell to his knees and Michael wrenched the gun from his fingers.

'Kill him,' she whispered from the shadows above. 'Kill him.'

Michael Flaherty stared down the barrel of the gun, but it was not the face of the terrified cardinal that filled his vision. He saw the drowned face of his brother Liam, flaccid from green salt water, then an old man's head tilted up from beneath a cliff edge, high over a hungry sea. He saw the quiet face of a woman with raven hair and the questioning eyes of a boy whose wind-ruffled hair rose to an exclamation mark above his forehead.

'It's over,' he shouted, straining against the pressure his finger applied to the trigger. 'It's over,' he said, more softly, as the terrible tremors in his arms eased, and he was in control again. 'There's been enough death,' he murmured, and tossed the gun aside.

He was easing himself from the rope to the stone lip of the chamber when the gunshot sounded. He shut his eyes and clung to the bare stone, then craned his neck and saw Cardinal Thomas stretched in death, the gun still clutched in his fingers. When he turned his head, she was hunkering down looking into his eyes. She held her pistol upright, leaning it, almost intimately, against her cheek.

'It seems there's been a change of management,' she said. 'I've been … retired.'

She read the question in his eyes and glanced at the body in the pit.

'He comes under loose ends,' she said. She spoke over her shoulder as she walked away: 'I hope I won't be seeing you again, Michael Flaherty,' she said, and disappeared into the shadows.

◊

'You can get up now,' the voice behind the mask said. He sat up in a circle of heavily armed and armoured police officers.

'Baldwin?' he asked.

The officer pulled off his mask and worked his jaw.

'Taking wine with Inspector Bernstein,' he said. He scratched inside his helmet with a dusty finger. 'You think you've seen everything,' he muttered.

◊

'You are the stupidest man in the world,' Goldberg said, thumping dust from Michael Flaherty's shoulders.

'I thought that was me,' Avram said, enjoying Michael's discomfort as Goldberg moved on to wipe his face with a spit-wet tissue.

'For the other three hunded and sixty-four days of the year, it is,' she muttered.

The arrival of Bernstein spared Michael any further indignities. The inspector held his hand a little longer than the time it took to shake it.

'The boy, Omar, was duped, Inspector,' Michael said. 'If it hadn't been for him …'

'I know,' Bernstein nodded, 'and, if it hadn't been for you.'

He touched Michael's cheek gently with the palm of his hand. '*Toda*,' he said. There is a car waiting to take you to the American embassy. Come back to us some time, Michael Flaherty.'

He turned to the detectives. 'You two, come and meet a real live Crusader.'

❧❧❧

Michael's driver pulled over to the side of the driveway to allow four personnel carriers with reflective windows to roar by. In the wing mirror, Michael caught a glimpse of Bernstein and the two detectives emerging from the mansion. Baldwin walked between the detectives as if he hadn't a care in the world. The driver gunned the car through the gate and Michael closed his eyes.

❧❧❧

Avram's eyes narrowed when the anonymous vehicles braked and blocked the driveway.

'The sons of Caleb,' Bernstein muttered, as the doors swung open and men in plain clothes and uniform black glasses fanned out across their path.

'Sons of bitches,' Avram growled, and pushed Baldwin behind him.

'Leave this to Papa,' Inspector Bernstein said quietly, and walked forward to meet the man who had detached himself from the group.

'We want the prisoner,' the Mossad agent said bluntly.

'You mean you want him back,' the inspector said easily. 'He was always yours.'

'I have authorisation,' the agent said, fingering a document from his shirt pocket.

'I know it comes from the director,' Bernstein said amiably, 'and you know where you can shove it.'

'The director has been retired, Inspector,' the Mossad agent mumbled, and looked away. 'You also know we can just take him,' he added, folding the piece of paper and putting it back in his pocket.

Bernstein glanced over his shoulder to where the armed officers who had stormed the mansion were now arrayed at either side of the detectives and Baldwin.

'You can try,' he said.

Slowly the man removed his dark glasses and stared at Bernstein. His eyes flicked over the inspector's shoulder and narrowed.

'Inspector,' he said, in a more conciliatory tone, 'this man can never go to trial. There are … certain people, highly placed people in Mossad and the government, who have been, let us say, overzealous in their commitment to Israel's security.'

'And what lay hidden will be revealed,' Bernstein said.

The agent had the grace to look abashed.

'This Baldwin knows names and locations, Inspector,' he said urgently. 'If we act quickly, we can mop up terrorist cells we've been hunting for years. Arms dumps, dirty money, groomers in the camps – he's got it all. We need him. Every day you drag him through the courts is a day they dig deeper. Is that what you want?'

Inspector Bernstein turned away and looked over the grounds of the mansion. He thought of the headless bodies and the attempts on the lives of his detectives. He thought of the plot that had pushed his country to the brink of war, where it still stood. His anger prodded him to make a stand, to face down the men who operated outside the law he was sworn to uphold. He knew he couldn't. The country, his country, would never survive the fallout of what some creative journalist would undoubtedly christen 'Crusadergate'. He took a deep breath and turned to the man from Mossad.

'Trade,' he said. He leaned closer to the agent and whispered in his ear.

The man's eyes narrowed. 'I'll have to run this by my superiors,' he said.

'Why don't you do just that?' Bernstein said.

When the agent returned from the personnel carrier, he nodded.

Jerusalem

The Franciscans had been in Jerusalem since 1219, when Francis of Assisi, sickened by the brutality and loose-living of the Crusaders, made a failed attempt to convert the Sultan to Christianity. When all the Christian warlords had packed their tents and retreated into obscurity or history, the Franciscans stayed. The straggly line of Franciscans making their way down the via Dolorosa excited little interest among the locals. Here and there a few tourists paused to click cameras in their direction. As they turned left into El Wad, an Israeli police officer shrilled the traffic to a halt on her shiny whistle to wave them across. They were joined on the pavement by a large contingent of monks and priests from the Eastern Orthodox community. In heavy black robes and headdress, the Patriarch took his place at the front with Tim Conway, the Father Guardian of the Franciscans. By the time they had reached the junction flanked by the Convent of the Sisters of Zion and the Church of the Flagellation, their numbers had been swollen by Armenians, Copts, Syrians and Russians.

Word of this strange procession began to trickle through the mazy lanes of the Muslim Quarter. At first spectators came singly and in small groups, then in a torrent as the procession wound itself out of the Old City through St Stephen's Gate. They were met beyond it by the Chief Rabbi of Jerusalem, who took his place with the other leaders. The Valley of Kidron dropped away to their left as they approached the Golden Gate that would have allowed them access to the Dome of the Rock.

The area before the gate was a confusion of people, police and television crews. Father Guardian noticed a ripple pass through the crowd and a kingly Ethiopian monk emerged to stand hesitantly on the pavement. The Eastern Orthodox Patriarch beckoned and the Ethiopian loped forward to join the group. A swelling rumble of voices came from the other side of the gate and an excited crowd spilled through to add their numbers and voices to those outside. Walking calmly in their midst, Tim Conway could see the Imam of the Dome of the Rock.

The Imam stood before the other religious leaders and the cacophony of voices dwindled and stilled.

'Why do you come to Haram as-Sharif?' he asked, in a voice that carried over the murmurings of anger and suspicion that seethed through the crowd.

The Eastern Orthodox Patriarch stepped forward and spoke for the group.

'The Noble Sanctuary of Jerusalem has been defiled,' he said. 'If one holy place is defiled then all are defiled.'

'Come,' the Imam said, and led them through the sullen

crowd. He guided them across the paved platform to the south entrance, which faced Mecca. They left their sandals at the door and stepped into the cool interior of the thirteen-hundred-year-old Dome.

When they were congregated beneath the marble columns that formed the first of two passageways circling the interior, the Imam spoke again.

'See,' he said, and his voice wavered with emotion on the single word.

They saw the cracked beams that linked the great columns and felt the shards of gold-enamelled wood from the ceiling beneath their bare feet. Under the great Dome itself, they craned their necks to look up at the holes gouged in the ancient columns, salvaged long before from Roman buildings, and the scarring on the seventh-century mosaics in the light that poured through shattered stained-glass windows. Mercifully, the kaleidoscope of arabesques on the inside of the great Dome itself was as flawless as the day it was completed by fourteenth-century artists, imported from India.

Their relief was short-lived. The scarred and chiselled Rock, sacred to Muslims as the place where the Prophet had left the earth to visit Heaven, lay canted sideways, tilted by the blast that had surged from below. Beside it, the reliquary, containing hairs from the Prophet's beard, was smashed to matchwood. The leaders of the various denominations and their companions stood for a long time. Then, taking their cue from the Imam, they bowed reverently and left.

Outside, the Imam led them across the platform to the standing arches that bordered the sacred precincts where chairs had been arranged for the guests. When they were all seated, the Orthodox Patriarch spoke for the others. 'Our hearts are heavy, brother,' he said, addressing the Imam. 'How can your shrine be restored?'

The Imam spread his arms in a gesture of helplessness.

'We are a poor community,' he said. 'Perhaps our Muslim brothers in Saudi or Kuwait ...'

His voice tailed off and his shoulders slumped.

'No,' Tim Conway said firmly. 'We are your brothers in Jerusalem. We will help you rebuild your shrine.'

'But how?' the astonished Imam asked.

'By giving of our plenty to our brother in his time of need,' Tim Conway answered. 'I speak for the Franciscans in Jerusalem,' he continued, 'and I make this pledge.'

'As do I,' the Orthodox Patriarch said immediately. Voices rose from the group and rang out over the foot-polished stones as the representatives of the other churches stood and pledged assistance. The relief on the Imam's face turned to euphoria when the Chief Rabbi said, 'As I do for the Jews.'

※

Tim Conway waited until the others had made their farewells. He patted the empty chair beside him and the dazed Imam sat. The Franciscan checked warily over his shoulder before leaning closer to his old friend.

'Hisham,' he said, in a low voice, 'I know it's great to have the Chief Rabbi and all the Christian big shots turn up today to show solidarity with you.'

'It's wonderful,' the Imam breathed.

'Yes, it is,' Tim Conway agreed, 'but fine talk and fancy words won't repair your shrine or stop the hotheads shouting for *intifada*.'

The Imam considered, then nodded. Tim Conway handed him an envelope.

'This is a gift from the Franciscans,' he said, 'to get you started.'

With trembling fingers, the Imam fumbled it open. His lips quivered as he grappled with the figure written on the cheque.

The Church of the Holy Sepulchre, Jerusalem
'A million dollars.'

'I think I misunderstand you, Tim. We must have a faulty connection. Can you repeat, please?'

'I said a million dollars, Father General, and you heard me fine the first time.'

'*Dios*, Tim, that will leave our Franciscan coffers very bare.'

'Well, my Jewish accountants estimate that a fairly large chunk of that figure is on tap in Werner's offshore accounts. It seems old Werner was a sort of bagman for Baldwin. I just have to pick up the phone, quote the numbers and bingo. The accountants are really impressed. They think I'm some kind of financial hotshot. Offered me a partnership if I ever took off the habit.'

'Tim!'

'And, Father General, I seem to recall that Francis had an aversion to his followers having any money at all.'

'You fight dirty, Tim.'

'I'm a Bronx kid, Father General, what can I say?'

The Jordan River Highway

Inspector Bernstein had two reasons for asking Avram to drive. He wanted the big man to have something to do with his hands until his rage had subsided and he wanted to arrive alive. Goldberg fretted in the back seat until Jerusalem disappeared behind them, then slept. Bernstein leaned back to insert a cushion between her head and the window.

'Thank you, Papa,' she murmured, without opening her eyes.

He noticed Avram watching him in the mirror.

'What?' he grunted.

'Nothing … Papa,' Avram replied, with a small smile.

They pulled off the highway at Beit Shean and Bernstein directed Avram to a fish restaurant tucked away behind the synagogue. The inspector was outvoted by the detectives on eating outside under the bougainvillaea and sighed as they sat inside with their backs to the wall, angled away from each other to cover the doors.

'Had a call from the US Secretary of State,' Bernstein said casually.

They took turns looking at him. God, they're good, he thought, too good for their own good.

'It seems Michael Flaherty has been exaggerating your abilities,' he continued.

'The papal envoy,' Goldberg quipped.

'We are the stuff of myth,' Avram offered, through a mouthful of bread.

'Or, in your case, mythsther,' she added automatically.

It felt good to hear them back on the banter-wagon and he pressed on, 'Anyway, laurels and garlands to you both and two tickets to Disneyland.'

'You made that up,' Goldberg protested. 'God, I'd love to go to Disneyland.'

'We already live there,' Avram said sourly.

'Before he left,' Bernstein said, 'Flaherty suggested we should check for a missing police officer at the mansion.'

'What?' they chorused.

'I asked the sergeant before we left. He said headcount in and out tallied. I said, "Humour an old man." They found the officer sleeping off a lump on his head behind a tapestry – fifteenth century, I think it was …'

'Inspector!'

'So, someone slipped the net,' Avram said.

'Yes, but not all the little fishes,' Bernstein said, spearing some vegetables. 'Baldwin had quite a network and something of a mania for keeping records.'

'Which Mossad now have in their grubby little paws,' Avram said bitterly.

'Yes, but he did love to talk,' Bernstein mused.

'You had wine together,' Goldberg said slowly.

'Bordeaux and bombast, you might say,' he agreed. 'Fascinating stuff – I even took notes.'

'Names?' she whispered.

'And places and all the distasteful little details of who did what to whom and for how much. They came from every denomination and from lots of government departments. There was no shortage of funds to recruit the best people money could buy.'

'Tell me there was a certain sleazy, diplomat monsignor on the list,' Goldberg said.

'You know I can't di—'

'Knew it,' she said happily. 'Can I shoot him?'

'Goldberg!'

'And Mossad gets them all,' Avram said morosely.

The inspector tasted the wine and nodded appreciatively.

'The Sons of Caleb are more interested in the guns-and-bombs brigade, Avram,' he said easily. 'They're going to be busy on that front for a very long time.'

'And the rest of the network?' Avram asked.

'Police business.'

'That's us, Avram,' Goldberg said helpfully.

'So,' Avram said doggedly, 'we arrest them, they hire lawyers, claim diplomatic immunity, get deported and laugh all the way to their Swiss banks.'

'That's one scenario.' Bernstein nodded. 'We could just step in and fill the gap.'

'You mean take over the network?' Goldberg clarified.

'We could.'

'Who exactly is this "we"?' Avram asked suspiciously.

'Thee and me,' Goldberg said patiently. 'God, thee is so slow sometimes.'

'You two and others,' Bernstein said.

'Others?' Goldberg said. 'Others are usually the ones trying to kill us, Inspector.'

'Paranoia becomes you, Goldberg,' he smiled, 'but you need more people.'

'What kind of people?' Avram asked cautiously.

'Oh, I dunno,' the inspector said, dabbing his lips with his napkin. 'Maybe people like Uri and Owl.'

'And bozo,' Goldberg said.

'Who?'

'Goliath,' she explained. 'Think of a pocket-giant with attitude.'

'Inspector,' Avram said slowly, 'you are some …'

'Piece of work, son-of-a-bitch, smooth operator,' Goldberg listed.

'All the above,' Avram said, smiling.

'Deal?' Bernstein asked.

Avram looked at Goldberg, who nodded.

'Deal,' he said.

⚜

They walked along the path in the shade of olive trees and climbed to the terrace. A woman sat there shelling peas into an Armenian pottery bowl. Goldberg watched the way her hands moved and concluded that her mind was elsewhere.

'Who is she?' Avram whispered.

'She's the former director of Mossad,' Bernstein said softly.

'The one who set Goliath on us,' Avram growled.

'She's my sister,' Bernstein said simply. 'Could you two find some coffee in the house – slow coffee?'

She didn't look up as he sat. She continued to run her thumbnail down a pod and split it between thumb and forefinger, spilling vivid green peas to gleam damply in the bowl.

'Brother,' she said, her face averted, 'and those two are Avram and Goldberg.'

'Nothing surprises you, Elena,' he said softly.

Her hands paused uncertainly in their work and she drew them to her lap for reassurance.

'What a terrible thing to say,' she said thoughtfully. 'What a terrible way to live, without surprises. I wasn't surprised when the prime minister affected outrage and dismissed me.

Had things worked out otherwise, he would have tacked to the prevailing wind. There are no guards here, brother, no contact. When I heard your car, I thought it was … I was disappointed it wasn't. Am I babbling?'

'No more than you always did.'

She smiled briefly and he imagined the sun had decided to shine, then immediately thought better of it.

'I think,' she said, 'the only conversation I had in twenty years was the one I had with you in the bunker. My husband was such a quiet man, a bookman of the old school. When he wasn't reading, he loved to hear us talk. And Sonia, such words! We two built all those word-bridges over his head and he'd look up and smile, like a little boy. After they …' Her tongue came to her teeth twice before she could unclench them and let the word through. 'After they died …' The half-sentence sent a series of aftershocks through her. She took a deep breath and blew it out slowly.

'They did die, didn't they, brother?' she asked.

'Yes, Elena, they died.'

She nodded.

'It was as if I had been struck dumb. All my bright, normal words were gone and I had only the functional ones left. Words form us, brother. They shape us. No one can say 'laughter' without putting the head back, even a little. No one can say 'love' without the face softening. I took the form of my functional words and became someone – no, something – else.'

She turned to look at him with haunted eyes.

'Do you think an old woman could learn to talk again?'

'I think I just heard her,' he said gently.

'Why did you come?' she asked.

'I came to bring you home, Elena.'

She clutched his lapels and pulled him forward so that she was staring into his eyes.

'I know everything about your children,' she said. 'I know everything there is to know from their files. Can you live with that knowledge and not hate me?'

He covered her hands with his and pressed them to his chest.

'That's just information, Elena,' he said softly. 'It's not who they are. I think you'd like to discover who they are. Please come.'

'Oh, brother,' she said, and her eyes seemed startled by their own tears, 'I'm so afraid.'

He put his hand to the back of her head and brought her forehead to rest against his own.

৪৩৫৪৩

Slow coffee, he'd insisted, and they'd complied. Goldberg felt the quiet of the stone kitchen in her stomach and breathed it in long, slow draughts. She found herself moving differently as if some slow music played in the background and she didn't want to jar the beat. Avram seemed … strange. His face had lost the wariness she'd seen pinch it on the terrace. He seemed uncoiled, softer, and they moved around the kitchen and each other like an old …

'The milk will spill,' he said, holding her hands steady with his own at either side of the tray. She turned away and climbed the stone steps to the terrace, aware of his tread echoing hers as he followed, aware, the moment she stepped onto the terrace, that she and Avram had not been slow enough.

She stood rooted in the doorway and heard every word that passed between the inspector and his sister. She wasn't aware of her tears until Avram brushed them away with a huge white handkerchief. He coughed loudly and called, 'Anyone for warm coffee?'

Bernstein tucked her tiny bag under his arm and helped his sister to her feet.

'You know,' she said to the detectives, 'I authorised your ter— your deaths, if you obstructed my plans.'

'We know,' Avram said gruffly.

'You were doing your duty, ma'am,' Goldberg added.

'You have a good heart, Goldberg,' she said approvingly. 'Be sure it has something better to nourish it than duty.'

She walked resolutely down the steps and disappeared among the olives.

'You two ready?' Bernstein asked.

'We're going to stay for a few days,' Avram said, 'and catch up on the paperwork.'

'We are?' Goldberg said. 'What paperwork?'

'Yes, what pap—' Bernstein stopped. 'Oh,' he said. He tucked the tiny bag a little higher under his arm and reached to hug Avram with the other. He kissed him tenderly on both cheeks and cleared his throat.

'Good luck,' he said huskily, 'with the, uh, paperwork.'

※※※

'Avram, what was that a—'

'Goldberg.'

'Avram, what are you doing?'

'I'm stroking your hair.'

'Why?'

'I wanted to do that the first time I met you.'

'I'd have broken your arm.'

'It would have been worth it,' he said, and kissed her.

The Camps, Bethlehem

Shepherd sat on the rickety cot, clutching the money-box to his chest. The tears had dried into stiff lines on his cheeks and salt stung the corners of his mouth. He felt numb.

The plan had been to hide in Bethlehem until the destruction of the Dome of the Rock, then distribute the guns to fuel the intifada. But the Dome had not fallen and the Arab states had not risen. Shepherd and his companions had stewed in their sweat beneath the apple-store, waiting for word. When it had come, he had shaken the messenger until the boy's teeth rattled. It hadn't changed the message. The Christian leaders and the Chief Rabbi of Jerusalem had pledged to restore the Dome and the Imam had accepted their offer. That message had run through the Muslim Quarter, speeding out of the Old City to Gaza and beyond. His companions had chewed over the implications, raising their voices as men do who seek to persuade themselves. When it had been his turn to keep watch, he'd raised the trapdoor and disappeared.

Before dawn had given definition to the shadowed houses, he'd followed a man to a basement and handed over the dollars that would take him through the tunnel to Egypt. After twenty minutes of crawling through the fetid hole in the ground, the light had disappeared suddenly, along with the guide who held it. He'd sat in the dark while the earth groaned around him, like Jonah in the belly of the whale, until terror had fuelled his flight and brought him gasping back to the hole in the basement floor.

'You lose some sheep down there, Shepherd?' the Israeli army officer had asked sarcastically in mangled Arabic.

He'd been too relieved to be above ground again to feel frightened. That would come later. They took him, wedged between their lean, hard bodies in the back of a Jeep. The blindfold tickled his face and the twists and turns of the vehicle made him nauseous. When the blindfold was removed, he was in a windowless room, strapped to a chair. He sensed the men standing behind him and smelled his own fear. A worm of terror twisted and slithered through his guts when the man entered the room. He wore a white shirt and black slacks. He had a lean face and impenetrable eyes. A man might look into those eyes for ever for some hint of emotion, he'd thought, and see nothing but the reflection of his own fear. He was Mossad, Shepherd felt certain. In a toneless voice, the agent listed a litany of names, pausing after each one to read Shepherd's face for any sign of recognition. He felt sure he had given him nothing, even when the names Baldwin and Holland had fallen from the bloodless lips. The photographs had appeared next: a gallery of young men holding weapons interspersed with photographs of their bodies after they'd exploded their lethal cargo on buses and in crowded markets. Finally, the black-and-white glossies of the bodies in the apple-store had fallen to the table, one by one. The agent shuffled the pictures and placed them in a folder, which he secured with a rubber band. Its snap had raised goosebumps on Shepherd's body.

'All this is … circumstantial,' the agent had said reasonably. 'Even this,' he'd continued, pushing a DVD into its slot and angling the small monitor on the table. Shepherd had felt his testicles shrivel and rise to find refuge between his legs as Jack

Holland crouched on the screen. He watched the drama unfold until the hooded man extended a pistol to the back of the American's head and then the picture froze. The Mossad agent pulled up a chair beside him and sat astride it so that his face was just inches from Shepherd's.

'Amazing the things that can hang a man,' he murmured, and Shepherd smelled coffee on his breath. 'Small things,' the agent continued, in a quiet, bemused voice, 'a tattoo, gold tooth, mole, scar. We have experts who spend hours on every frame of a recording like this. They each take a different subject and watch only that person, looking for something – anything – that might reveal their identity. It took just five minutes to find this,' he added, and activated a computer linked to the television monitor. A box appeared on the executioner's wrist and swelled to fill the screen. 'Yes, a Rolex.' He nodded, as if Shepherd had agreed with him. 'A real one,' he added.

He leaned forward and drew Shepherd's unresisting hand to the table.

'Like this one,' he said, pushing back the sleeve to reveal the watch. 'Circumstantial,' the agent said again, and shook his head. 'We have new leadership in Mossad,' he confided softly. 'Now everything must be done by the book. Therefore I have decided that we do not have enough evidence to detain or charge you.'

He had felt no sense of relief, no surge of exhilaration. He was already clutching the sides of the table when the agent said, 'We will return you to the camps.'

They had dragged him halfway to the door before the table had fallen from his fingers.

He knew how they operated. He had been an apt imitator

of their methods. Informers would already have woven rumours through the souk, the coffee shops and the marketplace: 'Shepherd is a double-agent'; 'Shepherd received dollars from the Israelis'; 'Your son, the martyr, was a pawn in Shepherd's game.'

Already he could hear small, furtive movements outside. Soon they would come. They would hover at the door, uncertain, until one plucked up the courage and began to search. They would find the money in his pockets and the lists of instructions from his Mossad masters, hidden in places he didn't know of. And then?

He had seen how others had died under attack from a mob. He clutched the empty money-box in his lap as if he could hold the terror at bay with his dream. He tried to remember a prayer and couldn't.

Benson's Residence, Washington DC

Benson savoured the sound the amber liquid made as it gurgled into the glass. He had a moment of annoyance when the heavy decanter dipped and struck a note from the cut-glass goblet; a note that whined through the silence until he stilled it with his finger.

'*Sic transit gloria mundi*,' he toasted himself mockingly, and spilled some down his shirt front when a voice translated, 'Thus passes the glory of the world.'

'Scylla?' he whispered.

She moved from the shadow of the drapes and slid into a chair.

'Scylla is dead,' she said, 'shot by a little black lady with a very large gun.'

'Oh, how the mighty have been brought low,' he said, smiling, and sipped his whiskey.

'That would be you, Benson,' she said coldly.

He rolled the burning liquid over his tongue, then swallowed it and licked the rim of the glass.

'And you, Francine,' he riposted, pleased at the way his use of her real name caused a ripple of anger to cross her face. 'It must be ... humbling to be bested by an amateur like Flaherty. Still, you did notch up an elderly monk and a deranged cardinal. And you escaped. But you always were a chameleon, able to blend with the available background. I'm sure your new ...,' he pursed his lips while he chose the appropriate word, '... your new keepers,' he said finally, 'will find some use for you.'

'It seems not,' she said. 'They might have done if you hadn't kept such comprehensive notes, Benson. Your department is being swept clean and those of us who survive the new broom must lie low or seek pastures new.'

His keen antennae vibrated at the hint of menace in her tone and his fingers tightened convulsively on the glass. Scylla, he mused, had always talked to his victims – talked them to death, some said. He'd had an urge to console or confess but he'd always dispatched them quickly. Francine, he knew, was more feline in her methods. She liked to play with a target until she tired of the game but, by then, they were past begging for release.

'You were always special, Francine,' he said, leaning back in his chair. 'I remember the day I drove to the Muncie Penitentiary in Pennsylvania. My talent scout was quite insistent I see for myself. "A rare specimen", I think was the phrase she used. I remember walking behind an officer down a long corridor between cells wondering what I was doing there, wading through the torrent of filth and abuse that came spitting from the deranged women caged on either side. But I was allowed access to the Holy of Holies, the abode of the ladies who had, according to a large lady in uniform, "made bad life choices". Such a power of understatement that lady possessed.'

He lowered his voice to little more than a whisper.

'There were three ladies on Death Row, Francine. The governor hadn't the stomach to execute a woman but he was willing to make an exception in your case. I read your files. You didn't look like a woman who had strangled her children, but who does?'

He saw the gun appear in her hand and went on. 'You had such a complete lack of feeling to qualify you as human, Francine. I thought you had potential – heck, even a tiger can be trained to obey a leash. I had you caged in one of our medical facilities in Virginia where they trained you to kill on command – my command. They even managed to impress on you the importance of acting human.'

She was pointing the gun at him, her face contorted into a snarl. It only needed one more push.

'So many masks, Francine, so many parts to play so that you don't ever have to be Francine. But I know you. I know your real name.'

The bullet rocked him back in the chair and the glass flew from his hand to bounce against the wall. With agonising effort, he unclenched his other hand from the hole in his chest and held it up before him as if inviting her to admire her handiwork.

'Good doggie,' he whispered.

It had the desired effect. A small hole appeared over his right eyebrow and Casper Benson III slumped forward on his desk.

Church of the Holy Sepulchre, Jerusalem

The leaders of the various Christian denominations crowded into the chamber beneath the site of the Crucifixion. Tim Conway stayed in the background, Omar at his shoulder. He watched admiringly as Brother Juniper picked up the rope that dangled from the pulley system arranged over the round stone set in the floor. With professional ease, the tall Franciscan clipped the metal clasp at the end to the rusted bar that bisected the depression in the stone. He tugged it experimentally, then went to the pulley.

'I'll need a hand here,' he said.

Immediately a burly Armenian monk and two Syrian priests moved to join him.

'Like this,' Juniper said, miming a long, slow pull on the rope. 'Don't jerk, okay? On a count of three,' he added, as they arranged themselves in a line along the rope.

The stone groaned in the groove that had held it for centuries. Tim Conway saw the metal clasp grind flakes of rust from the iron bar and didn't realise he was holding his breath until the circular stone rose slowly.

'Keep the tension,' Juniper panted.

When he was satisfied that the stone was high enough, he tied it off deftly and moved to the hole.

'Bring the torch,' he said, and a squat Copt bustled forward importantly to illuminate the shaft.

'Don't see anything much from here,' he murmured, his frown accentuated by the reflection from the light.

'Someone's got to go down.'

After a beat, a young voice spoke from the rear of the group.

'I'll go,' Omar said.

The rope crew quickly removed the stone from the clasp under Juniper's watchful eye. He strapped Omar into a light harness and attached it to the end of the rope.

'Tug once when you want us to halt,' he instructed, 'and twice to come back up.'

He handed the young man the torch and clapped him on the shoulder. Omar disappeared into the hole in the floor and the light gradually faded from around the rim as he sank deeper. Juniper squatted on the floor, letting the rope slide through his hands, testing for the tug. It didn't come and he peered into the opening like an Eskimo hunter watching a hole in the ice.

'Hold,' he shouted, as the rope twitched in his palms.

Tim Conway wondered how much time had gone by since Omar's disappearance and rubbed his hands dry on his habit.

'Up,' Juniper commanded, and his pulley crew leaned into their task. Entranced, the group watched a faint glow illumine the rim of the shaft and burgeon into a tiny rising sun as the torch held aloft in Omar's hand emerged from the bowels of the earth. Beneath the light, Omar's hair glinted with diamond droplets that almost rivalled his smile for brilliance.

'Water,' he said delightedly, and the chamber echoed to cheers and clapping. Monks and priests of all denominations rushed to help the young man stand upright.

'How much water?' the Eastern Patriarch asked, when the hubbub subsided.

'It is an aquifer,' Omar said. 'I would need instruments to

measure how much it contains. But I was swimming in it before you halted the rope and I felt … I felt like I was in a great lake.'

Again, the cheers rang out and he was pummelled so enthusiastically on the back by the Copt that droplets flew from his body.

'We should call it Omar's Aquifer,' Juniper suggested, as he freed the young man from the harness.

'Omar's Aquifer,' the others shouted.

'No,' Omar said, and silence returned. 'You Christians gave your gift to my Muslim brothers when Haram as-Sharif was damaged. This aquifer is Allah's gift to you in return. My grandfather,' he continued, 'told me that when the Prophet Jesus was dying, he had a vision of how people would divide one against another after his death and he wept with sadness. Is this so?'

'There is such a legend,' a bearded Syrian priest confirmed.

'And does the legend also say that the tears of the Prophet Jesus fell from His Cross into the earth at this place and formed the waters below?'

'Yes,' the Syrian said. 'It is so written.'

'What name did the followers of Jesus have for those waters?' Omar asked, and a hush fell over the group.

'They called them the Tears of God,' Juniper whispered.

'Then,' said the young man, 'let it be called the Tears of God.'

The Oval Office, The White House
Ellen Radford massaged her temples with her fingertips.

'Tired?' Henry Melly asked.

'A little,' she admitted, and forced herself upright in the chair. 'Laila says everything's gone back to Code Green on both sides of the Israeli border, so that's promising. The Israeli ambassador assures me that the director of Mossad has been replaced and there's to be an internal inquiry et cetera. A head or two will roll and a number of windows will be dressed.'

'We know all about that,' Henry Melly said drily.

The phone buzzed on her desk.

'Okay, send him in,' she said. 'Gentleman caller coming through,' she said, smiling.

Henry Melly winked broadly and went out of the Oval Office, leaving the door ajar.

John Hancock in a suit was like a grizzly in a tutu, she thought, and struggled to suppress a smile.

'What?'

'Oh, nothing,' she said, directing him to the armchairs ringing a low coffee table. 'You look different in a suit.'

'Like a stuffed dummy?'

'That too.'

'I ... I thought I should come by and offer my condolences,' he said awkwardly. 'I was very sorry to hear about Jack Holland. Can't say I ever saw eye to eye with him on environmental issues but ... I'm sorry.'

'Thank you. Actually, I was going to call you about funding for your new department.'

'Oh?'

'The lawyers tell me that Jack left everything to me. I'd like to pass it on to your department. It should give you a chance to show what you can do without all the strings attached.'

'Well, that's really great.'

'I had a call from the Pope earlier.'

'As one does,' he added, and they both laughed.

'You should laugh more often,' he said, and blushed.

She took refuge in the notes she'd put on the table.

'Pope said he'd heard about the new department and wants a tie-in with the Pontifical Academy of Sciences. Sounds medieval enough to have Galileo as dean of the faculty.'

'Actually, they've got some of the brightest scientific brains in the world but it's never had a high profile or enough money. Maybe the Pope's planning to give it a kick-start on both fronts.'

'The kick-start could be this hotshot Jesuit he was talking about. He's appointed him to the academy to set up a faculty in eco-theology.'

'Not McFadden?'

'Yes, as a matter of fact, it is. You know him?'

'Hell, yes. Heard him once in Fordham – sounded like the Martin Luther of Roman Catholic eco-theology.'

'Is that a good thing?'

'The best! He knows McDonagh and Hayden and all the heavy-hitters on the Church eco-scene.'

'Well, the Pope wants him to hook up with you. While I think of it, the Secretary of State tells me there's a young Palestinian guy who was involved in the Dome business. Seems he's a promising hydrologist and the Franciscans in Jerusalem are willing to give him a scholarship if you'll take him.'

'I'll take him.'

'Well,' she said, closing the folder and standing, 'is there anything else the President of the United States can do for you, Professor?'

His tie was askew and she resisted the urge to centre it.

'I … I was wondering if you ever … I mean if you ever go out for a beer. Or a coffee,' he added hurriedly.

'I have a fully stocked bar and all the coffee I can drink right here, Professor,' she replied innocently, enjoying his discomfort.

'I meant out there,' he said. 'I wondered if you'd like to … some time?'

'Yes,' she said, 'I would like that … some time. In the meantime,' she said, offering her hand, 'people sometimes drop by for no other reason of state than to have coffee or a beer with me.'

He shook her hand warmly.

'Be seeing you, Ms President,' he said, and left.

'Hope so, Professor,' she said, and returned to her desk. She pressed the button. 'I'm ready,' she said.

Michael Flaherty stood inside the door to the Oval Office. He seemed less than awed by his surroundings and she was impressed by that. In her experience, most people adopted the tone and body language of tourists in a cathedral when they stepped into this room. It felt refreshing to encounter someone who just stood there and waited. There was a stillness about him she found attractive. He seemed to have that quality people often referred to as presence, the ability to be fully present without being distracted by where he was and who was there. It 'didn't hurt', as her mother would have said coyly, that he was broad in all the right places or that the pallor shading his high cheekbones contrasted strikingly with blue-black hair. Michael Flaherty had lines at the corners of his mouth and radiating from his eyes. She didn't doubt he could be light-hearted but the darkness in his eyes suggested something of what he'd endured. Those eyes regarded her with some amusement and she realised she'd been staring.

'Can I call you Michael?'

'As opposed to what?' he countered, and smiled.

'Maybe the Scarlet Pimpernel of the Vatican?'

'The scarlet was on loan, Ms President. I sent it back.'

'Please sit,' she said, indicating the armchair recently vacated by John Hancock.

'I want to thank you for what you did in Jerusalem.'

He nodded. 'I can't say I thought it through at the time – it just seemed to be the right thing.'

So that's what heroism's like, she thought.

'Do you think the peace can hold?'

'I'm no politician, ma'am.'

'That's why I'm asking you. I've got hot and cold political opinion on tap right here in the White House, Michael. I'd appreciate a layman's take.'

'I think Tim Conway's intervention was crucial,' he said slowly. 'I don't think he gave much thought to the wider political implications, just did it because he's the man he is. As to whether or not the peace can hold, I'd have to say no. I don't think it can.'

'Why not?'

'Things don't just hold, ma'am, not for long anyway. Generally, they either move forward or reverse. Tim's action wasn't a once-off, it was part of a process he put in place by bringing the leaders of the various religious groups together on a regular basis. The response of the Christians and the Jews to the Dome crisis came from all the talking and cups of tea they'd had with the Imam in the Russian convent. I think Tim's take on peace is that it's something you prepare the ground for and then build on. I heard, before leaving Jerusalem, he's planning to open a Franciscan friary in the refugee camps. In the longer term, he'll channel funds into education, clean water and decent housing.'

'You know that the crisis was masterminded here?'

'I suspected as much, and then Jack Holland confirmed it.'

'You met him?'

'Yes, briefly, in Baldwin's mansion. I was in a sort of pit at the time and I'd just had visits from Cardinal Thomas and a lady assassin ...'

'Jack could really pick 'em,' she said, with a hint of bitterness.

'He was the only real human being I met in that place, ma'am,' he said.

He had spoken with such calm conviction that she didn't feel chided.

'Please go on,' she said.

'He'd figured out that Baldwin was going to generate a crisis in Jerusalem that would have repercussions throughout the Middle East. The cardinal was to be Rome's man on the spot, whether Rome wanted it or not ...'

'And Jack?'

'A former president in a situation like that could come into the frame as a credible voice for the West.'

'I'd never have bought that.'

'Neither did Jack. Last thing he said was he was going to bring the cavalry. He didn't make it. I'm sorry.'

'He was used, Michael,' she said sadly. 'He was set up to test me and distract us from the real plan. I couldn't bow to that pressure.'

He didn't try to console or excuse, and she was grateful for that. They sat in comfortable silence for a few moments.

'He told me he thought he'd killed his brother,' he said softly, 'when they were kids.'

'He told you that!' she exclaimed. 'He never really talked about that to anyone. Fact is, William fell through a hole in the ice and drowned.'

'I think Jack the adult knew that,' he agreed, 'but the boy inside him never accepted it. He said he thought he had to be William to make some kind of restitution to his parents, and when he'd done all the things William might have done, it still wasn't enough. By then, he'd been distanced from himself for so long he could never see himself making it back. He said you understood that.'

That simple sentence was more than she could bear. All the old rage at Jack-the-lad conspired with her grief for Jack-the-lost-boy to bring on a flood of tears. Michael Flaherty moved quietly to the sofa beside her and held her hand. She clung to it while her heart wrung itself dry and until the harsh gasps eased into silence. He took his hand back and returned to his seat across the table. She plucked some tissues from a box on the table and patted her face dry. When she spoke, her voice was steady.

'Will you go home now – to the Island, I mean?'

'Yes, but not immediately. I brought a lot of baggage back with me last time.'

'Is there anything we can do for you, Michael?'

'No, not for me,' he said. 'There may be something you can do for some friends of mine.'

She listened attentively as he outlined his request and nodded.

The O'Donnell Apartment, Bronx, New York
'Newspaper says all's quiet on the Eastern front, Hanny,' Mal gathered the loose pages strewn over the kitchen table.

'So, no riots in Newark, New Jersey.' She sniffed. 'Big deal.'

'Hanny,' he chided, 'you gotta broaden your horizons.'

'So, take me somewhere.'

'There's no such place, Hanny.'

'I know. We go there every vacation.'

'Let's go on the Circle Line,' Michael said, from the doorway.

They looked at him.

'You know,' he said, 'it's a boat that goes around Man—'

'I know what the Circle Line is,' Mal said, snapping the newspaper. 'How could I forget? Last time I took Hanny she got seasick before we left the dock.'

'That was thirty years ago, Mal.'

'Ain't no statute of limitations on that kind of memory, Hanny. Wild horses wo—'

'We'll go,' she said.

It had been like that since he'd stepped off the flight from Washington and Michael had loved every minute. They'd 'done' New York, visiting the must-see places they'd shown him when he'd first arrived from Ireland to stay with them before enlisting in the army.

He'd thought the Empire State Building looked as drab and dated as ever, smirking across Fifth Avenue at the Chrysler Building, its smaller and older sister. They had squeezed into an elevator with what Mal called 'the whole population of Honshu' and zoomed to the top to circle the viewing platform. Down below, Central Park glowed as if underlit by the first umber light of fall. Tiny trees stood in nodding groups, checking their reflections in still ponds, like gangly girls with new colours in their hair. On the other side, Manhattan stepped down to the waterfront. The gap in the skyline silenced them for a time before they moved on.

The Circle Line provided the perfect platform for watching the city glide by, and Mal provided his usual commentary. It was his cop's-eye view of New York where various landmarks were linked with busts and heists and the bridges …

'Enough already,' Hanny protested.

She'd pretended to feel queasy for old time's sake but Mal's spiel was bringing on the real deal. The Bronx Zoo put her back in good spirits. While the two men sipped coffee from paper cups and debated the ethics of caging wild animals, Hanny watched some children grimace at a gorilla and smiled wistfully. It was a toss-up between Benihana's and an Italian mom-and-pop place for lunch, and the Italians won. Mal was greeted like a long-lost relative and the number of diners who paused at their table to pay their respects confirmed Michael's suspicion that Mal's retirement from the Police Department was a fiction he maintained and Hanny tolerated.

'You like the fish, Hanny?'

'Better to eat them than sleep with them, Mal.'

The Metropolitan Museum of Art had been Michael's idea, prompted by the promise of a Van Gogh exhibition. Hanny's enthusiasm for the brooding Dutch master flagged and came to a full-stop before the *Self Portrait*. Mal offered the opinion that Van Gogh had painted himself in profile because he'd cut off the other ear. Hanny riffled noisily through the guide to the museum.

'Whatcha looking for, Hanny?'

'Maybe they have a Bobbitt here.'

'You're a Philistine, Hanny.'

'Only by marriage, Mal.'

The evenings in the apartment were the times Michael remembered best from before and savoured now. Mal sat enthroned on his La-Z-Boy, flicking through a zillion channels in his never-ending search for sports programmes. Hanny pottered from room to room, keeping up her end of the banter without ever missing a beat. They talked, mostly in non-sequiturs, about which Irish guy had sold a bar to some other Irish guy, and gradually segued back to talk of home and the circumstances that had brought them to the Bronx. Hanny's West of Ireland accent reasserted itself as the shadows lengthened outside until all her sibilants were mushed and all her 'th' had been discarded. Detective Rosa Torres, Mal's sidekick during the Remnant affair, came over to cheat at cards, talk cop-code with Mal and share despairing faces over his head with Hanny. The cardinal arrived with a bottle and left with two.

It was early Saturday morning when the call came.

Mal and Michael were washing and drying the breakfast things as Hanny scooped the receiver from the kitchen wall. Michael knew what it was from the slump of her shoulders and the way she said, 'Oh, hi, Raphael.'

He folded the tea-towel and set it on the counter-top.

'We're all done here, old man,' he said, and went to pack.

❧

The Hudson river ran companionably on their left as they drove north through White Plains and Westchester. At Carmel, they eased off the highway for coffee and doughnuts. He knew Hanny and Mal were prolonging their time with him and didn't grudge it. Their easy company and rough affection had allowed him down from the level of high alert that had been his norm for too long.

Mal parked the Taurus at the monastery gate and hefted the small bag from the trunk.

'You coming in?' Michael asked.

'No,' Mal said. 'Raphael'll give us a call.'

Michael held the door while Hanny climbed out.

'You sure you got enough socks and stuff?' she asked.

'Yeah, I'm sure.'

'You keep a sweater on,' she said. 'It gets real cold up here.'

He held her for a long time. Mal came and stood beside them, circling Hanny's shoulders with one arm and patting Michael's back with the palm of the other.

'Go on now,' he said gruffly. 'Do what you have to do.'

Vietnam Veterans' Memorial, Washington DC
Alison Fox skipped along the path bordering the reflective black stones. Her father watched her image slip from stone to stone, appearing and disappearing, like a pigtailed wraith.

'Don't get too far ahead, honey,' he called, hoisting her younger sister higher in his arms.

'I know where he is, Dad,' she called over her shoulder.

He knew she'd be rolling her eyes in exasperation. Single fathers tended to be a tad over-protective and Alison liked to push the boundaries.

'Grandpa's not really there, is he, Daddy?' his younger daughter whispered in his ear.

'No, Emma,' he said, touching his cheek to hers. 'Grandpa Fox died in Vietnam. He's buried where we used to live in New York State.'

Alison was already arranging the flowers with all the solemn reverence of an almost-eleven-year-old.

'Does he like freesias, Dad?' she asked, stepping back to admire her handiwork.

'Always did,' he said. 'Got them for Gramma on her wedding day.'

'You can put me down now, Daddy,' Emma said.

She stood before the stone, running her finger from the smooth surround into the rough, grey letters that spelled her grandfather's name.

Congressman Fox felt a tug on his sleeve.

'They've got a new one,' Alison said excitedly. 'Come and see.'

He swept Emma into his arms and followed his older daughter to where a group of workmen were bedding a stone in freshly turned earth. One of them buffed it with a rag while the others tidied their tools and left.

'New one, huh?' Fox said.

'Yup.'

'You know who they are?'

'No, sir.'

The man pushed the rag back into the pocket of his overalls.

'Don't say on the stone neither. Bossman says this stone come by direct order of the president.'

He stamped some earth flat with his boot and left.

Congressman Fox folded to set his daughter on her feet and leaned in to read the names. His mind flipped back to the documents Mal O'Donnell had forwarded. There had been a list among them of those soldiers who had gone into Colombia and never returned. He leaned closer, his lips silently forming the names as his eyes read the stone.

Bryson, Mendez, Philips, Wilder, Brown, Kowalski.

They were all there, he realised, except for the survivor, Michael Flaherty.

'Daddy.'

Alison's voice drew him from his reverie.

'D'you think Grandpa would mind sharing his flowers?'

'What? Oh, no, honey, I think he'd be really pleased to.'

'Why do we bring flowers?' Emma asked.

'To remember, sweetheart,' he said, hunkering down beside her. 'To remember Grandpa and … and Mom and …'

He buried his face in her hair and inhaled her sweet, little-girl smell.

'Does someone 'member these soldiers, Daddy?'

'Yes,' he said, 'someone does.'

The Benedictine Abbey, Carmel, upstate New York
Michael saw Raphael standing on the far side of the courtyard. He put his bag on the ground and waited.

The abbot was dressed formally in his Benedictine garb. The white robe and black tabard contrasted sharply with the vivid carpet of leaves underfoot and the slender tree that flamed behind him. The effect was spoiled somewhat by the Day-Glo bunny slippers on his feet. Michael knew the hectic footwear concealed the price the man had paid for being a Roman Catholic priest in China. His heart warmed to see the old friend who had given him sanctuary before he'd encountered the Remnant in Rome.

'Who are you?' Raphael asked.

'I'm Michael Flaherty.'

'What are you?'

'I am a person.'

'Did you kill your brother?'

'No, I did not. My brother Liam drowned.'

'Did you kill the priest who was your friend and mentor when you released his hand and he fell to his death?'

'No,' Michael answered, and the tears that had been dredged from his heart by the previous questions began to flow. 'No,' he repeated, 'I didn't kill Father Mack. I let him go.'

Raphael began to close the distance between them, keeping up the barrage of questions as he approached.

'Did you kill the priest Stefan, the leader of the Remnant in Rome?'

'Yes, I did.'

'What do you feel when you think of that?'

'I feel shame and sadness – anger also.'

Abbot Raphael stood directly before him. Through his tears, Michael saw moisture glisten on the old man's cheeks.

'Why have you come here?' Raphael asked.

When Michael answered, his voice seemed to come from the deepest part of himself. It was a place of blood and loss, and his reply to Raphael was like the groan of a man in agony.

'To find my way back … to myself.'

The Abbot nodded approvingly, and a tiny smile quirked the corners of his mouth.

'Will you sweep the leaves?' he asked.

'Sweep your own damn leaves,' Michael answered, laughing and crying at the same time.

The Abbot reached out and folded Michael in his arms.

'Welcome back, Michael Flaherty,' he whispered.

Acknowledgements

My thanks to everyone at Hachette Books Ireland for keeping faith with Michael Flaherty and me. Special thanks to Claire Rourke, who edited the manuscript and encouraged the author, and to my literary agent, Jonathan Williams.

Christy Kenneally
January 2009